March 2014

Dear Friends,

Some years back, my husband, Wayne, worked on Alaska's North Slope and returned with wondrous tales of listening to the northern lights. He spoke of midnights as bright as the noonday sun and of being in a cold so deep it hurt his lungs to breathe. What struck me most was his claim that while Alaska is isolated, it isn't a lonely place.

In fact, Wayne loved the state so much that he wanted to share it with me. Since then he and I have made two trips to Alaska. I soon discovered that my husband was right—Alaska was everything he'd claimed and more. I fell in love with it the same way Wayne had.

It wasn't long before this glorious state captured my writer's heart, and stories started to weave themselves into my imagination. You're holding two of them in your hands now. *That Wintry Feeling* and *Borrowed Dreams* were both published early in my writing career. I've refreshed the stories so they are slightly changed from the original publication.

My wish is that you'll fall in love with Alaska just as Wayne and I did. My readers are near and dear to me; I find your feedback informative and helpful. You can reach me in a number of ways. You can log on to my website at www.debbiemacomber.com and leave me a message or write me at P.O. Box 1458, Port Orchard, WA 98366. You can also find me on Facebook.

Now enjoy these two stories!

Warmest Regards,

Debbie Macomber

Praise for the novels of #1 *New York Times* bestselling author Debbie Macomber

"Macomber is known for her honest portrayals of ordinary women in small-town America, and this tale cements her position as an icon of the genre."
—*Publishers Weekly* on *16 Lighthouse Road*

"Romance readers everywhere cherish the books of Debbie Macomber."
—Susan Elizabeth Philips

"Debbie Macomber's name on a book is a guarantee of delightful, warmhearted romance."
—Jayne Ann Krentz

"Popular romance writer Macomber has a gift for evoking the emotions that are at the heart of the genre's popularity."
—*Publishers Weekly*

"With first-class author Debbie Macomber it's quite simple—she gives readers an exceptional, unforgettable story every time and her books are always, always keepers!"
—*ReaderToReader.com*

"Debbie Macomber is one of the authors who led me to appreciate romantic fiction. She can take a well-worn plot device...craft her characters carefully, having them grow and develop as the story unfolds, and leave readers with a sense of the goodness of strong values."
—*The Romance Reader*

"Debbie Macomber is one of the most reliable, versatile romance authors around."
—*Milwaukee Journal Sentinel*

"Macomber is a skilled storyteller."
—*Publishers Weekly*

DEBBIE MACOMBER

North to ALASKA

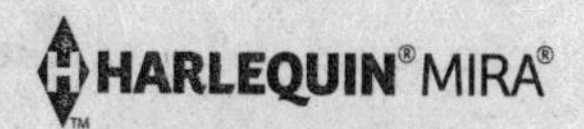

ISBN-13: 978-0-7783-1598-8

NORTH TO ALASKA

For questions and comments about the quality of this book, please contact us at CustomerService@Harlequin.com.

Printed in U.S.A.

To Jazmine, Bailey and Maddy
My precious granddaughters

Also by Debbie Macomber

Blossom Street Books
The Shop on Blossom Street
A Good Yarn
Susannah's Garden
Back on Blossom Street
Twenty Wishes
Summer on Blossom Street
Hannah's List
The Knitting Diaries
"The Twenty-First Wish"
A Turn in the Road

Cedar Cove Books
16 Lighthouse Road
204 Rosewood Lane
311 Pelican Court
44 Cranberry Point
50 Harbor Street
6 Rainier Drive
74 Seaside Avenue
8 Sandpiper Way
92 Pacific Boulevard
1022 Evergreen Place
Christmas in Cedar Cove
(*5-B Poppy Lane* and
A Cedar Cove Christmas)
1105 Yakima Street
1225 Christmas Tree Lane

Dakota Series
Dakota Born
Dakota Home
Always Dakota

The Manning Family
The Manning Sisters
The Manning Brides
The Manning Grooms

Christmas Books
A Gift to Last
On a Snowy Night
Home for the Holidays
Glad Tidings
Christmas Wishes
Small Town Christmas
When Christmas Comes
(now retitled *Trading Christmas*)
There's Something About Christmas
Christmas Letters
Where Angels Go
The Perfect Christmas
Angels at Christmas
(*Those Christmas Angels* and *Where Angels Go*)
Call Me Mrs. Miracle

Heart of Texas Series
VOLUME 1
(*Lonesome Cowboy* and
Texas Two-Step)
VOLUME 2
(*Caroline's Child* and *Dr. Texas*)
VOLUME 3
(*Nell's Cowboy* and *Lone Star Baby*)
Promise, Texas
Return to Promise

Midnight Sons
VOLUME 1
(*Brides for Brothers* and *The Marriage Risk*)
VOLUME 2
(*Daddy's Little Helper* and *Because of the Baby*)
VOLUME 3
(*Falling for Him, Ending in Marriage* and
Midnight Sons and Daughters)

This Matter of Marriage
Montana
Thursdays at Eight
Between Friends
Changing Habits
Married in Seattle
(*First Comes Marriage* and *Wanted: Perfect Partner*)
Right Next Door
(*Father's Day* and *The Courtship of Carol Sommars*)
Wyoming Brides
(*Denim and Diamonds* and *The Wyoming Kid*)
Fairy Tale Weddings
(*Cindy and the Prince* and *Some Kind of Wonderful*)
The Man You'll Marry
(*The First Man You Meet* and *The Man You'll Marry*)
Orchard Valley Grooms
(*Valerie* and *Stephanie*)
Orchard Valley Brides
(*Norah* and *Lone Star Lovin'*)
The Sooner the Better
An Engagement in Seattle
(*Groom Wanted* and *Bride Wanted*)
Out of the Rain
(*Marriage Wanted* and *Laughter in the Rain*)
Learning to Love
(*Sugar and Spice* and *Love by Degree*)
You...Again
(*Baby Blessed* and *Yesterday Once More*)
Three Brides, No Groom
The Unexpected Husband
(*Jury of his Peers* and *Any Sunday*)
Love in Plain Sight
(*Love 'n' Marriage* and *Almost an Angel*)
I Left My Heart
(*A Friend or Two* and *No Competition*)
Marriage Between Friends
(*White Lace and Promises* and
Friends...And Then Some)
A Man's Heart
(*The Way to a Man's Heart* and *Hasty Wedding*)

Debbie Macomber's Cedar Cove Cookbook
Debbie Macomber's Christmas Cookbook

CONTENTS

THAT WINTRY FEELING

One

Cathy Thompson's long nails beat an impatient tempo against the formica counter top as she waited.

"Yes, I'll hold," she said and breathed heavily into the telephone receiver. Her deep gray eyes clashed with Linda Ericson's, who sat at the desk, a large newspaper spread over the top.

"Any luck?" Linda whispered.

A voice at the other end of the line interrupted Cathy's response and she straightened, her fingers tightening around the phone. "This is Cathy Thompson again." The inflection of her voice conveyed the irritation. "Would it be possible to speak to Grady Jones?"

"Grady's in the air," a gruff male voice informed her. "Be with you in a minute, Harry." He spoke to someone who was obviously waiting in the office.

"When do you expect him back?" Cathy asked in her most businesslike voice.

A lengthy pause followed, and Cathy could hear the rustle of paper in the background. "Thursday afternoon. Will you hold the line a minute?"

Cathy's sigh was full of exasperation. Cradling the

telephone receiver against her shoulder with the side of her head, she pulled out a piece of paper and a pencil. As she looked up she happened to catch a glimpse of the school play yard. The sights and sounds of the last recess of the day drifted in through the open window. Her gray eyes softened as she unconsciously sought Angela Jones. A frown creased her narrow forehead as she discovered the pigtailed first grader leaning against the play shed watching the other girls jump rope. Angela always seemed to be on the outside looking in.

"Do you want to leave a message?" The harried male voice came back on the phone.

"I've already left four," Cathy snapped.

"Listen, all I do is take the message. If Grady doesn't return your call it's not my fault." He hesitated. "Are you the gal from the school again?"

"Yes, I'm the gal from the school again." She echoed his words doing her best to disguise herfrustration.

"All I can tell you is that Grady is flying on assignment. I'll tell him you phoned."

The man wasn't to blame if Grady Jones didn't wish to speak to her, and Cathy's reply was less agitated. "Please do that." Gently she replaced the receiver in its cradle.

"Well?" Linda looked up expectantly.

"No luck. It's the same as before. They'll take a message, but he won't be back until Thursday afternoon."

"What are you going to do?" Linda asked, concern knitting her brow.

Cathy shrugged. "Maybe it's time I personally introduced myself to the elusive Grady Jones. He'll have a hard time not talking to me if I show up at the airfield." Cathy had done her research well. The school information card had been sketchy. The father's occupation listed him as a pilot, employed by Alaska Cargo Company. No business phone number had been given, and when Cathy looked it up in the yellow pages she found a large commercial ad. The fine print at the bottom of the advertisement stated that Grady Jones was the company owner. The information card had stated that Angela had no mother. Cathy had found the comment an interesting one. How could any child not have a mother? It could be that Angela's parents were divorced. What Cathy couldn't understand was how someone as unconcerned and uncaring as Grady Jones could have been awarded custody of the child. Cathy had tried on several occasions to contact him at home, but the only adult she had ever reached was a housekeeper, who promised to give him a message. Cathy had stopped counting the times she'd left messages for him.

"After all the trouble you've gone through, I'd say that's about the only way you're going to get his attention."

"Believe me, I won't have any problem getting his attention. His ears will burn for a week."

"Cathy..." Linda warned, her large brown eyes worried. "Alienated, Angela's father won't help her."

"I know, but I can't help dislike the man."

The bell rang indicating the end of recess. Emitting a soft groan Cathy turned around. "Back to the salt mine." It had been another break wasted trying to contact a parent. Next time she'd pour herself a cup of coffee before making a phone call.

"Don't go yet," Linda called. "I want to read you this personal."

"Linda," Cathy said with a sigh but she knew better

than to argue. Her friend would insist she listen anyway. "All right, but be quick about it."

Rustling the paper, Linda sat upright and read. "Sincere gentleman seeking sincere lady for sincere relationship—"

"Only sincere women need apply," Cathy interrupted. "Dull, Linda, dull. If you insist on playing matchmaker, the least you can do is find someone with a little personality."

"Okay, here's another." She glanced up. "Man with large house, large cat, six kids. Cat not enough."

"Six kids." Cathy choked.

"That says a lot," Linda defended. "At least he's honest and forthright. He must like animals."

"That would make Peterkins happy, but unfortunately I'm the one that has to be satisfied. Six kids are out."

The shuffle of feet could be heard above the laughter as the children filed into the school building. The afternoon could no longer be delayed.

Two hours later, Cathy unlocked the door to her rental house on Lacey Street. She had rented a home so that Peterkins, her black cocker spaniel, would have a yard to roam. Steve had given her Peterkins, and he was probably the only good thing she had left of their relationship. In the beginning she had resented the fact Peterkins had been a gift from Steve. Every time she looked at her floppy-eared friend she was reminded of a soured relationship. But Peterkins wasn't to be blamed, and there was far more than a dog to remind her of Steve. It was funny how many of her thoughts he continued to dominate. Yet it was totally, completely over. Steve was a married man. A knot twisted the sensitive muscles of her stomach. He'd been married for five months and six days. Not that she was counting. Bravely she had attended the wedding, had been a member of the wedding party. The maid of honor. Her sister wouldn't hear of anything else.

Exhaling a quivering breath, Cathy turned the key in the lock and pushed open the door. Immediately Peterkins was there, excitedly jumping up and down. When she crouched down to pet him, he fervently lapped her hand with his moist tongue.

"Let me relax a minute, and we'll go for our walk," Cathy told him. Peterkins knew her moods better than anyone, Cathy mused while she changed clothes and sorted through the mail. Peeling an orange, she sat at the small circular table in her kitchen and leaned against the back of the chair.

Memories of Steve again ruled her thoughts. They'd quarreled. It wasn't any major disagreement; she couldn't even recall what it was that had sparked the argument. But something was different this time. Cathy had decided she was tired of always being the one to give in, apologize, change. They had talked about getting married on several occasions. If their relationship was to be a lasting one, Cathy had decided, then Steve must learn to do his share of giving. It would be a good lesson for him to admit he was wrong for once.

She pulled each of the orange segments apart and set them on the napkin, fingering each one. Her appetite was gone, and she scooted the afternoon snack away.

The whole idea of teaching Steve a lesson had been immature and foolish. Cathy realized that now. She gave a short laugh. What a wonderful thing hindsight was.

When Steve began dating her sister, MaryAnne,

Cathy had been amused. He wasn't fooling her, she knew exactly what he was doing. She had taken great pride in meeting him at the door when he came to pick up MaryAnne for a date. With a gay smile she had proven she wasn't in the least bit jealous. He could date whom he liked. Twice she had arranged dates at the same time MaryAnne and Steve would be going out so that they would all meet at the apartment she shared with her sister.

The only one who had shown any concern over such foolishness had been their mother.

"Mom." Cathy had strived to brush off Paula Thompson's concern. "MaryAnne and I cut the apron strings when we moved out and got an apartment of our own. From now on you're only supposed to give advice when we ask. Remember?" Her words were a teasing reminder of what their mother had told them when they decided to move in together. Although her mother never mentioned a word again about MaryAnne and Steve, the question was in her eyes.

Six weeks had passed, and still Steve continued to play his game in an attempt to make her jealous. If she hadn't been so stubborn she would have seen what was happening. Twice MaryAnne had come to her.

"You don't mind do you?" The gray eyes so like her own had pleaded. "I'd stop seeing him in a minute if our relationship was hurting you in any way."

Cathy had laughed lightly. "It's over," she said with a flippant air. "It was over a long time ago. There's no need to concern yourself."

Then one night MaryAnne had burst into the apartment and proudly displayed the beautiful diamond engagement ring. Cathy had been shocked. This was carrying things to an extreme. Steve had gone too far. She wasn't going to allow him to use her little sister like this another minute.

The argument when she'd confronted Steve had been loud and bitter. They'd hurled accusations at one another faster and sharper than a machine gun.

All through the preparations for the wedding Cathy had expected Steve to put a halt to things. It was unbelievable that a minor disagreement three months before had been allowed to go this far.

Throughout the time they had prepared for the wedding, MaryAnne had been radiantly happy. A hundred times Cathy had to bite her tongue to keep from saying. "Listen, sis, I'm not completely sure Steve loves you. He loves me, I know he does." Maybe she should have said it. The message was in her eyes, her mother read it the morning of the wedding. Steve saw it as she marched up the aisle preceding her sister. It was there when the minister pronounced Steve and MaryAnne man and wife.

The memory of those words seemed to echo assaulting her from all sides. Urgently, Cathy stood and pushed her chair to the table. She needed to get out, away from the memories, the hurt.

"Bring me the leash, Peterkins," she said to her dog, who promptly stepped into the bedroom and pulled the rhinestone-studded strap off the chair. Cathy paused, fingering the red leather. The leash had been another gift from Steve. Would he continue to haunt her the rest of her life? Would it always be like this?

For two months after the wedding Cathy had walked around in a haze of pain and disillusionment. This couldn't be happening to her. This wasn't real. It became almost impossible to hide her emotions from her family. She had to get away, to the ends of the earth. Alaska. The opportunity to work as a basic skills instructor had come as a surprise. Her application had been submitted months before. She had never intended to accept the job even if it was offered to her. She had done it to tease Steve, telling him if he didn't proclaim his undying love she'd abandon him for parts unknown. Willingly, Steve had obliged. When she hadn't heard from the school district, Cathy was relieved. It had been a fluke, a joke. Now it was her salvation, a lifeline to sanity.

No one had understood her reasons for going—except her mother, and perhaps Steve. With a sense of urgency she had gone about building a new life for herself. Forming friendships, reaching out. It was only in the area of men that she withdrew, held back. Eventually that reserve would abate. A soft smile curved up the edges of her lips. Linda and those crazy personal ads she was always reading to her. If her friend had anything to do with it, Cathy would be married by Christmas.

She dressed carefully Thursday morning, the meeting with Grady Jones weighing her decision as she chose a dark blue gabardine business suit. The line of the suit accentuated the slender curves of her lithe form. Cathy was nearly five eleven in her heels and secretly hoped to meet the man at eye level. She did with most men. Not once had she regretted the fact she was tall. In most cases height was an advantage. Steve was tall. Her hands knotted at her side as her resolve tightened. It was ridiculous the way her mind would bring him to the forefront of her consciousness. It had to stop, and it had to stop immediately. She needed to start dating again, meet other men. She'd do it. The troubled thoughts that had continually plagued her were all the convincing she needed. She'd answer one of those crazy ads Linda was always telling her about.

"Be a good dog, Peterkins." She ruffled his ears playfully. "You do like cats, don't you? What about six kids?" The large brown eyes looked up at her quizzically, and Cathy laughed. "Never mind."

Dawn was breaking as she parked her Honda in the school parking lot. Gracefully she slid across the upholstered seat and climbed out the passenger side. As soon as she was paid she was going to get that other door fixed. She paused to watch the sun's golden orb break out across the pink horizon. There was a magical quality to an Alaskan sky that stirred something within her. The sky was bluer than blue, the air fresher, cleaner. Even the landscape that appeared dingy and barren held a fascination for Cathy. She hadn't expected to like Alaska but found herself mesmerized with its openness, enthralled with its beauty.

"Whew-yee." Linda whistled as she walked into the teachers' lounge. "You look fit to kill."

"I may have to," Cathy replied flippantly as she poured herself a mug of coffee. "But that man's going to listen to me if I have to hogtie him."

"Hogtie him?" Linda repeated with a laugh. "Is that a little Kansas humor?"

Pulling out a chair, Cathy sat beside her friend. "It could be, but by the time I finish with Grady Jones he won't be laughing."

"With that look in your eye, I almost pity the poor man."

Her long, tapered fingers cupped the coffee mug as she glanced at the paper Linda had placed beside her purse. "Without meaning to change the subject, but are there any new ads today?"

"New ads. You actually want to look at the personals? As I live and breathe..."

The rest of what she was going to say faded away as she took the paper and opened it on top of the table so they could both read through the columns. Several of the listings were almost identical with lengthy descriptions of their likes and wants. It was a small ad at the bottom of the page that captured Cathy's attention. It read "Red Baron seeks lady to soar to heights unknown." It gave a post office box number for the response.

"This one looks interesting." Cathy pointed it out to Linda.

Her friend twisted the newspaper around so she could read the ad. She didn't comment on the contents. "Go ahead and write something, I'll put it in today's mail."

"Linda...I don't know what to say. Let me think about it a while then I'll—"

"No," Linda interrupted, her voice emphatic. "If you think about it you won't do it. There's paper here, and I've got an envelope and stamp in the office. Go for it."

Cathy's hand hovered over the paper while Linda left for her office. She chewed on the end of the pen and shifted her chin from the palm of one hand to the palm of the other. Finally she scribbled, *Interested in soaring. Heights negotiable.* She signed it *Snoopy* and gave the post office box where she collected her mail. She'd read the six-word message ten times and was ready to throw it away when Linda returned, snapped it from her hand, and placed it inside the envelope.

"I can't believe I'm doing this," Cathy mumbled. "There must be something basically wrong with me."

"There is," Linda confirmed. "You're lonely."

Cathy's responding smile was weak. It was a lot more than lonely, but she didn't explain.

Having made arrangements with the teachers earlier in the week, Cathy was able to leave the school before twelve. She was determined to speak to Grady Jones one way or another. Following the directions Linda had given her, Cathy arrived at the airfield promptly at noon.

Her car door slammed with the force of the September wind, shutting it for her. Another gust whipped her hair about her face and stimulated her cheeks until they were a rosy hue. She stopped to examine the buildings. A large hangar took up one side of the open field to the right of the runway. Directly beside the hangar was a smaller building she assumed must be the office. A large overhead sign read Alaska Cargo Company.

Checking her wristwatch, Cathy noted it was thirteen minutes after noon. Right on time. Her watch naturally ran thirteen minutes fast, which suited her since she hated being late. If Grady Jones hadn't arrived she was prepared to wait. With her black leather purse tucked under her arm, she approached the smaller structure. As she neared the office a man dressed in grease-smeared overalls and a matching cap emerged from one of the hangars.

"Can I help you?" he questioned, his eyes surveying her with interest.

"I'm here to see Mr. Jones," she replied in a crisp, business tone.

Something indecipherable flickered across the weathered face, but Cathy coundn't read him. She wondered if this was the man who'd answered her persistent calls. Had he recognized her voice?

"Grady's inside," the man replied and wiped his hands on a rag which hung from his hip pocket. "I'll take you to his office. Follow me." He led the way, yanking open the office door. He was halfway through the entrance when he stopped as if suddenly remembering his manners and hurriedly stepped aside, allowing Cathy to enter ahead of him.

It took a moment for her eyes to adjust to the dim interior.

"Make yourself comfortable," he said and indicated two worn chairs just inside the door. He disappeared behind another door around the counter. The office appeared to be divided into two areas. The outer room contained a long counter that was littered with papers, graphs, and charts. Behind it the walls were obliterated by several maps. The two chairs were covered with old newspapers and dog-eared magazines. Cathy decided to stand.

When the mechanic returned, his eyes glanced over her appreciatively. "Grady will see you now." He held the door open as Cathy moved behind the counter.

Her heels clicked against the faded linoleum floor, and the sound seemed to echo all around her. Unconsciously she held her breath and clenched her purse, as if to steel herself for the encounter.

Grady Jones was standing when she entered the room, and her eyes were instantly drawn to the lean, dark features of the strikingly handsome man. Naturally curly chestnut-colored hair grew with rakish disregard across his wide forehead. His eyes were surprisingly blue, the same color as an Arctic blue fox's. They glinted round and intelligent. His full, almost bushy eyebrows were quirked expectantly, and Cathy realized she was staring. Nervously she cleared her throat.

"Grady Jones?" she questioned briskly, disguising her shattered composure.

"Yes." His mouth twitched with humor.

This man was well aware of the power of his attraction, Cathy mused, disliking him all the more. If he thought he could disarm her with one devastating smile, then he was wrong. Leaning forward slightly, Cathy extended her hand over the cluttered desk.

"I'm pleased to meet you, at last, Mr. Jones," she said with a trace of contempt. "I'm Cathy Thompson, Angela's basic skills instructor."

Grady accepted her hand, capturing it between two massive ones and holding it longer than she liked. Their eyes dueled, hers cool and distrusting, his deepening as they narrowed.

He dropped her hand, and it fell limply at her side. "Yes, I've heard quite a lot about you, Miss Thompson."

"You've heard quite a lot *from* me, too," she emphasized. "However, you've chosen to ignore my messages and phone calls."

"Listen, Miss Thompson, I'm a busy man. I've got a business to run. I can't—"

"Let me assure you, I'm just as busy," she interrupted curtly. "But I believe Angela is important enough for us both to spare a few minutes."

"All right, I'll admit Angela's got problems."

Cathy had to restrain herself from saying that she thought most of the girl's difficulties stemmed from an uncaring father. "Angela's a sweet, sensitive, six-year-old child with social and academic deficiencies," Cathy began. "But it's my guess that most of her academic difficulties are a result of dyslexia. I'd like your permission to have her tested."

"Dyslexia?" Concern furrowed the tanned brow.

"It's not as bad as it sounds," Cathy was quick to assure him. "It's a neurological disorder that affects one's ability to read, spell, and sometimes speak correctly. It's not uncommon for a girl to be dyslexic, but almost three times as many boys are as girls."

"Dyslexic." He repeated the word and slumped into a large rollback chair.

"Angela's in the second grade and has problems reading at the first-grade level, or printing her letters correctly."

"She's a lot like I was at her age," Grady murmured. "Only back then they called it word blindness."

"They have a name for it now," she said softly.

Grady looked up and for the first time seemed to notice that he was sitting, while she was standing. "Sit down, Miss Thompson, please."

Cathy obliged. "Dyslexia affects three areas of learning. Audio, visual, and kinetic, which is the sense of touch or feel. Angela is affected in each area, but to what extent won't be known until she's been tested."

He drew in a deep breath. "You say there's a name for it now. Is there a cure?"

"No," she explained bluntly. "But there is help. Once my suspicions have been confirmed, Angela is going to need a tutor."

"It's done. Send me a bill."

Anger gripped Cathy. This man seemed to think everything could be solved with a signature at the bottom of a check.

"It's not quite that simple, Mr. Jones," she said keeping a tight rein on her feelings. "It's not my responsibility to find a tutor for your daughter. I'll be happy to give you a list of those recommended by the school district. But finding the one who would work best with Angela is up to you." She spoke in a stiff, professional manner. "I'm also of the opinion that your lack of interest may be the cause of the emotional problems Angela has..." She stopped, clenching her hands tightly. Stating her feelings on the way Grady Jones chose to raise his daughter wasn't part of her job.

"That may be." The blue eyes became chips of glacial ice. "But I'm only interested in your academic impressions. I could care less if you think I rate a Father's Day card or not."

"I'm sure." Abruptly she rose to her feet. "I won't take up any more of your time." She couldn't prevent the waspish tone. "After all, time is money."

"That's right, and you've taken up fifteen minutes already."

Fists balled at her side with building outrage, she stalked from the office. He followed her out, opening the front door as if he couldn't be rid of her fast enough.

"I'll mail you the list of tutors," she said in a way that conveyed the message she would rather have communicated with him by means of the post office.

"You do that," he shot back.

His eyes seemed to bore into her back as she moved across the parking lot. Hating that he was watching her, she opened the passenger side of her car and climbed inside, scooting across the narrow enclosure. She couldn't leave the airfield fast enough, her tires spinning as she rounded the corner and merged with the street traffic. .

Her fingers were trembling by the time she pulled into the parking lot at the school. If the meeting had gone poorly, it was her fault. She should have left her opinions out of it. Everything had been fine until she'd impulsively overstepped the boundary.

Looking at Grady Jones was like looking at her father. Not that there was any striking physical resemblance. Her father had died when Cathy was sixteen, yet she hardly remembered his physical features. It was a vague image of a tall, lanky man who drifted in and out of her life at inconvenient intervals. Donald Thompson had been a workaholic. Her mother had recognized and accepted the fact long before his death. And in reality little had changed in their lives after he was gone. He was so seldom home for any lengthy period of time that life went as it had in the past.

Grady Jones showed all the symptoms. He was never home when she phoned, no matter how late. He worked himself hard and probably expected as much from those he employed. The lines of fatigue had fanned out from his eyes as if it had been a long time since he'd seen a bed. If he continued as he was, he'd probably end up like her father. Dead at fifty-five. Why the fact should bother her, Cathy wasn't sure. Personally she didn't care for the man. Striking good looks didn't disguise the fact he was ambitious, selfish, and hard nosed. She preferred a man who was kind, sincere, gentle. A man like— Her mind stopped before the name could form.

"You're back already?" Linda greeted her as she stepped into the school. "That didn't take long."

"I didn't imagine it would," Cathy said, the inflection in her voice her sentiment. "Grady Jones is a busy man."

Linda nodded knowingly. "Relax a minute. There's no need to hurry back, Tom's taking over for you. I bet you didn't eat lunch."

"No," Cathy admitted, "I haven't."

"I could use a break myself. I'll come with you." A smile formed in Linda's large brown eyes. The two women had been instant friends. Although they'd only met two months before, it was as if they had known each for years. The contrast between them was impressive. Linda was barely five feet, a cute, brown-eyed pixie. Her laughter was easy, her nature gentle. Linda had met her husband, Bob, through the personal column, naturally, and they had been happily married for seven years. The only gray cloud that hung over her friend's head was that Linda desperately wanted children. The doctors had repeatedly assured them there was nothing wrong and that eventually Linda would become pregnant. Once Cathy had overheard someone ask Linda how many children she had. Without so much as blinking Linda had looked up and replied three hundred. By all accounts she wasn't wrong. As the school secretary, Linda did more mothering in one day than some mothers did all year.

"Do you want to talk about it?" Linda asked as she sat at the table they had occupied that morning.

Cathy took the sandwich from the bag she'd brought with her that morning, examining its contents as if she had forgotten it was bologna and cheese. She knew that one look at her face and Linda knew everything had not gone as she'd wanted. "I blew it, plain and simple."

"He agreed to the tests, didn't he?"

Miserably she nodded, shoving the bread back inside the brown paper sack. “He agreed to the tests more or less, but I may have alienated him forever. I think it would be best if any future communication with Grady Jones were handled by mail.”

“Don’t be so hard on yourself. If he agreed to having Angela tested, you succeeded.” The persistent ring of the office telephone jerked Linda’s attention. “I better get that. Oh, by the way I mailed your envelope.”

“Great.” Cathy’s reply lacked enthusiasm. What kind of man did she ever expect to find through the personals?

Cathy spent Monday afternoon with Angela Jones. The child invoked a protective response in her. She was small for her age, her blue eyes as large and trusting as a baby seal’s. She followed the directions carefully, doing everything that was asked of her.

“You were very good, Angela.” Cathy playfully tugged a long brown pigtail.

“Daddy said I should be,” she replied shyly, her eyes not meeting Cathy’s. “You’ll tell him I was, won’t you?”

Cathy didn’t have the heart to tell the little girl that she doubted she’d ever see her father again. “When I see your father, I’ll tell him you were one of the very best.”

Angela smiled, revealing that her two front teeth were missing. Cathy couldn’t remember ever having seen the child smile. It was the memory of that toothless grin that buoyed her spirits as Cathy stopped in at the grocery store for a few items Monday after school. The store was directly beside the post office, which made it convenient if she needed anything. She was sorting through her bills when the boldfaced handwriting stared up at her. She nearly missed a step as she stopped cold. The envelope was addressed to *Snoopy.*

Two

Cathy glanced at her watch as she slid across the red upholstered booth in the restaurant. Eight-fifteen. Because her watch was thirteen minutes fast she realized she was almost a half hour early. The letter had said eight-thirty.

A waitress came with a glass of water and a menu. "I'm waiting for someone," Cathy told her hesitantly. "I'll just have coffee until my…my friend arrives."

"Sure," the woman said with a distracted smile.

Cathy had chosen to sit in the booth that was positioned so she could watch whoever entered the restaurant. At least that way she would recognize him the minute he walked in the door. His letter said he'd be wearing a red scarf. With unsteady fingers she opened the clasp of her purse and removed the letter. She must have read it thirty times, not sure what she expected to find. There didn't seem to be any unspoken messages or sexual overtones. The whole idea of meeting a total stranger was absurd. At least he'd suggested a public place. If he hadn't she wouldn't have done it. She wasn't quite sure what had prompted her coming as it was. It was more than curiosity.

Cathy had dated a couple of times the first month she was in Fairbanks. It hadn't worked out either time. She hadn't been ready to deal with a new relationship. She wasn't convinced now was the time either, but she realized she had to try. Living the way she had been, with thoughts of Steve taunting her day and night, was intolerable.

Extracting the letter from the envelope, Cathy decided for the tenth time she liked the handwriting. It was large and bold, as if the man knew what he wanted and wouldn't hesitate to go after it. The message was direct without superfluous words to flower the letter. It read "*Snoopy: negotiations open. Meet me Friday 8:30 P.M., Captain Bartlett's. I'll wear red neck scarf.*" He hadn't asked her to identify herself. Cathy appreciated that. If he walked in the restaurant and she didn't like what she saw she could leave. Somehow, she decided, it didn't matter what he looked like. In an unexplainable way she liked him already. Certainly she wasn't expecting a handsome prince on a white stallion. Any man who would place an ad in the personals was probably unattractive, shy and…

Her thoughts did a crazy tailspin as the restaurant door opened. Cathy saw the red scarf before she recognized the face. She swallowed in an attempt to ease the paralysis that gripped her throat. It was Grady Jones, Angela's father.

Grady's unnerving blue eyes met hers across the distance. He knew. A smile of recognition flickered over his mouth as he came toward her. Cathy felt trapped, her eyes unable to leave the muscular frame. Darn it, he was good-looking. He wore a dark wool jacket over a blue turtleneck sweater. The sweater intensified the color of his eyes, making them almost indigo.

"Snoopy?" he queried evenly, resting the palms of his hands on the edge of the table.

Cathy gestured weakly, instantly conveying how unsettling this whole experience was to her. "Yes." The one word sounded torn and ragged.

"Do you mind if I sit down?" he asked, clearly struggling not to laugh.

She was glad he found the situation amusing. There didn't seem to be any other way to look at it. "All right," Cathy agreed, her voice somewhat steadier.

He slid into the booth sitting across from her. The waitress came and he turned over his coffee cup so she could fill it.

"Would you like a menu?"

"No," Cathy answered quickly.

"Yes, we would," Grady contradicted.

The waitress glanced from one to the other, unsure. "I'll leave two. Let me know when you're ready to order, but I have a feeling it's going to be a while."

Grady looked at her. "Well, Miss Thompson, we meet again. I'll admit I'm surprised. You don't look like the type of woman who plays the personals."

"I don't…normally," she qualified, feeling defensive.

"What made you this time?"

"I have this friend…" she began and paused. She couldn't blame Linda. She'd made the decision to go ahead with this idea herself. "I liked your ad," she told him honestly.

The bushy eyebrows quirked upward. "I liked your response."

"Did you get many?"

"A few."

Silence.

"You don't like me do you?" There wasn't any derision in his voice. It was a statement of fact more than a question.

"I don't think I do. You're a rotten father, and you work too hard."

Grady shrugged. "I'm not sure I like you either."

Cathy's short laugh was genuine. "I can imagine."

"You're opinionated, judgmental, and stubborn."

"Impulsive and quick-tempered," she finished for him.

"Not bad-looking though."

She flashed him a wide smile. "And my teeth are my own."

Laughter crinkled lines about his eyes. "Would you like to order something?"

Cathy's gaze met his, and she shrugged. "Why not?" She hadn't eaten much dinner, her stomach uneasy over the coming meeting.

Grady signaled the waitress, who pulled a pad from her apron pocket as she approached. "Are you ready?"

"I think so," Grady looked at Cathy, indicating she should order first.

"I'd like a piece of apple pie and a Diet Coke."

"I'll have the pie and a cup of coffee." As soon as the woman moved away from the table, Grady asked, "Do you normally order a diet drink with pie?"

Her eyes laughing, Cathy nodded. "It soothes the conscience somehow. I know I probably shouldn't be eating desserts."

"Why not?" Grady questioned. "It looks like you can afford to put on a few pounds."

It was the truth. She had lost weight before and after Steve and MaryAnne's wedding. Thoughts of them together caused her to look away.

When their order arrived, Cathy noted that he was studying her. They talked for a while about things in general, Alaska, and the coming winter. She told him about Peterkins and a little of her life in Kansas. She noticed he didn't mention Angela or talk about his job. In an hour there wasn't anything more to say.

"Well, I suppose I should think about heading home," Cathy said. "I hate to worry my dog."

"It's been—" he paused as though searching for the right word "—interesting," he concluded.

Cathy quickly noted that he hadn't admitted that their time together had been pleasant. At least he was honest. If she had to find a one word summary of their date, *interesting* said it well. She was glad he didn't suggest they meet again because she wasn't sure how she'd respond. Probably with a no.

He walked to the car with her. "Thank you, Grady. As you say, it's been interesting." As she withdrew the keys from her purse, Grady opened the car door for her. When Cathy glanced up, her mouth opened then closed. "How'd you do that?" she burst out.

"Do what?" He looked puzzled.

"Open that door," she demanded, her voice high and unreasonable. "It's broken. It's been broken for two weeks. I was waiting until payday because I couldn't afford to have it fixed."

Grady was laughing at her again, a lazy smile curved

his mouth. "Sorry, I didn't know. If I had I would have left it alone."

Her own mouth thinned as she scooted inside the car. "Curse you, Red Baron," she murmured and slammed the door shut. Cathy could feel his eyes following her as she drove out of the parking lot. By the time she pulled into her driveway, she found herself smiling. But the amusement died when she attempted to open the door. It wouldn't budge. Ramming her shoulder against it as hard as she could, still it wouldn't give. Sighing, she shook her head in disgust and climbed out the passenger side.

Linda phoned at ten Saturday morning. "Well?" she demanded. "How was he?"

"Okay," Cathy admitted noncommittally. She felt strangely reluctant to explain that the man she had met was Grady Jones.

"That's all?" Disappointment coated Linda's naturally soft voice. "Will you be seeing him again?"

"I don't think so."

"Are you disappointed?"

Somehow it seemed important to Linda that Cathy have a good time. "No, I'm not disappointed in the least. It was an interesting experience." There was that word again.

"Want me to look through the personals for you?"

"I doubt if you'll wait for my approval," Cathy said in slight reprimand. "But next time I think I'll revert to the more conventional means of meeting a man."

"Don't give up after one try," Linda pleaded. "I kissed a lot of frogs before I found my prince."

"I have no intentions of kissing anyone." She hadn't

either. Not since Steve, almost a year. She was a healthy, reasonably attractive female. There had to be something wrong with her not to have been kissed in a year. She didn't even want to be kissed unless it was Steve.

"I've got to go, Linda. I'll talk to you Monday." Cathy didn't mean to sound abrupt, although she realized she did. Replacing the receiver, she exhaled. Why did everything come back to Steve? Why couldn't she sever him from her thoughts as sharply and effectively as she'd cut herself away from her family and Kansas?

School went well the next week. Routine filled her days. She wasn't a regular teacher in a classroom. Her job involved working with the students who had problems with basic skills such as phonics, reading, and fundamental math. In all she worked with sixty students during the week for short periods of time in small groups. A great deal of satisfaction came as a result of seeing a child make strides in a particular problem area.

Linda continued to read her the personal ads every morning, but Cathy was successful in warding off any attempts to contact another potential relationship. The last week of September merged with October and the hint of the first blast of a frigid winter. Already the days had begun to grow short.

The letter caught her off guard. Although it was addressed to Cathy Thompson, Cathy recognized the handwriting immediately. Her heartbeat raced as she stared at the blunt lettering on the business-size envelope. The minute she was in the car she tore it open. Normally she waited until she was home and had relaxed a bit before sorting through her mail. Her bottom lip was quivering as she read the message. "Interested in renegotiating heights. Captain Bartlett's Friday, 6:30 p.m. Grady."

Cathy wasn't sure why she was so pleased. She didn't really like Grady Jones. He was everything she had accused him of being and more.

"I'm not going," she told Peterkins Friday after school. "It would be a waste of time for us both. We're not alike at all. I can't see furthering a relationship that won't go anywhere."

Peterkins raised his head from its resting position on her thigh, then lowered it again. Immersed in her thoughts, Cathy continued to run her hand down the dog's black coat.

"Maybe I should. I hate to keep him sitting there alone. It wouldn't hurt anything, would it?" Again Peterkins looked up at her, cocking his head at an angle. "All right, I'll go. But I'm going to make it clear this is the last time."

She changed clothes twice. First she chose a pale blue wool dress. One glance in the mirror and she realized she looked far too formal for Alaska. She didn't want Grady to think she'd gone to any trouble, or that this meeting was important to her. Designer jeans and a thick red cable-knit sweater seemed to satisfy her need to appear casual along with her thick coat, knitted scarf and matching gloves.

Peterkins laid at the foot of the bed, watching her movements in and out of the closet.

"Don't look at me like that," she mumbled irritably. "I know I'm being ridiculous."

Grady was already at the restaurant by the time she arrived, sitting in the same booth they'd occupied on their first meeting.

He didn't smile when she entered the restaurant, and Cathy had the impression he wasn't sure what he was doing there either. Their eyes met and held for a moment as she paused before walking across the room.

"Hi." She felt awkward and slightly gauche as she slid into the seat opposite him. "You're early."

"No, I'm not," he immediately contradicted her.

She made a production of examining her wristwatch. "It's precisely 6:08," she said, showing him the digital face. "Your letter said six, which means you're five minutes early."

Grady looked taken aback for a moment. "I don't think I want you to explain that."

"Fine. Just believe me, you're early." Without further comment she picked up the menu, feeling the color invade her cheeks. What an absurd way to start an evening, arguing over the time.

"I hope you didn't have dinner."

"No, I was too busy deciding if I was going to show up tonight or not." She hadn't meant to be quite that honest.

Their eyes clashed above the top of the menu. He released her gaze by focusing his attention on the softly parted lips. "I was sure you would," Grady said with complete confidence.

Deliberately Cathy laid her menu aside. "I think you should know that the only reason I came is because my car door's broken again. I just wanted to see if you could open it a second time."

A smile twitched at the corners of his mouth.

Cathy couldn't keep from smiling herself. Every time she was with Grady she couldn't help marvel what a handsome devil he was. Tonight he wore a smoke-colored sweater and charcoal-gray slacks. He was provocative, stimulating, and all male. If it weren't for Steve she could see herself easily being attracted to him. When she realized she was staring, Cathy quickly averted her attention by seizing the menu.

"What do you recommend?"

"The crab's excellent."

"No." She shook her head, ruffling the short brown curls. "I don't eat anything that walks sideways."

Studying the menu, Cathy was surprised to note that it catered to a full range of appetites. "I think I'll try the shrimp scampi."

Grady gave the order for two of the same to the waitress, who glanced from one to the other, obviously remembering them from the last time. "Glad to see you two agree," she murmured.

Cathy's fingers nervously toyed with the water glass. "I was surprised to get your message."

"I hadn't planned to see you again," Grady admitted. "I was flying into Deadhorse for one of the oil companies and—" He stopped. "You have a beautiful smile, Cathy."

She gave him one of her brightest. "A lot of men are impressed with my teeth." It hadn't taken her long to realize the only way she was going to be comfortable with Grady was if she could joke.

Their meal arrived. Cathy was surprised when Grady began talking about himself. He explained how he had started out with one airplane and had built the company to its present holdings. The facts were stated without bragging or boasting. He didn't need to mention how much of his life Alaska Cargo Company had required. It had cost him a marriage already. If Grady was anything like her father, there were a lot more sacrifices to come.

"Alaska Cargo is important to me," Grady said after pushing his empty plate aside. "But so is Angela. I realize I'm gone too much and too involved to be a decent father."

Cathy was surprised that he would openly admit to as much. "What about her mother? Perhaps it would be better if she lived with her."

"Pam's dead." The words were blunt and clipped.

Cathy lowered her gaze. "I apologize, Grady, I didn't know. I assumed you were divorced."

Without looking up, he said, "We were headed that way."

"Who cares for Angela while you're away?"

"Louise. She's the housekeeper, but she's retiring and moving to Seattle to be closer to her children."

"Who will care for Angela once the housekeeper moves to Seattle?"

He shrugged. "I don't know yet." He frowned. "Come on, let's go." He paid for their dinner and walked Cathy to her Honda.

Her car keys in her hand, Cathy stood beside the driver's side of the vehicle. "Well," she insisted, "go ahead. I'm waiting."

"Waiting?" A perplexed look widened his eyes.

"I want to see you open the door," she insisted.

He gave her a half-smile With little difficulty and one fierce jerk the door opened.

"I don't believe this," Cathy mumbled with an exasperated sigh.

"I'll admit it was a little tight," Grady said.

"A little tight?" she repeated loudly. "I've seen bank vaults with easier access."

"Come around tomorrow and I'll have Ray fix it for you."

"Ray?"

"My A & P mechanic, secretary, and all around fix-it man," Grady explained.

The memory of the gruff-voiced man who had answered her repeated calls to Grady and the picture of the older man who had escorted her into his office came to mind. "Yes, I believe we've met."

"Can you be there about eleven?"

Tomorrow was Saturday, and she didn't have anything planned. "Sure." She hesitated, her fingers clenching the strap of her white purse. "Thanks for the dinner."

"The pleasure was mine." He took a step closer, and Cathy's heart skipped a beat. He was going to kiss her. A feeling of panic rose within her, and she moved to climb into the open car. A hand at her shoulder stopped her.

"Don't look so frightened." He sounded as though he was silently laughing at her. "My kisses rarely inflict pain. A few women have been known to like 'em."

Forced to meet his eyes, Cathy felt an embarrassed rush of hot color sweep over her features.

His index finger tilted her chin upward. As he lowered his mouth to hers, Cathy slowly closed her eyes. The lips that fit over hers were gentle, sweet. Gradually the kiss deepened, and she slid her arms around his neck. The sky didn't burst into a thousand shooting stars; she didn't hear sky rockets, not even tinkling bells. The kiss was nothing more than pleasant.

When he lifted his head, his gaze searched hers. "You'll be there tomorrow?"

Cathy nodded.

"I don't know how else to describe it," she told Peterkins some time later. "The kiss was—" she paused and laughed "—interesting."

She lay awake for a long time afterward, staring at the ceiling. When she kissed Steve, her body's response to him had been immediate. But she loved Steve, she was supposed to react like that. Try as she might she couldn't recall what it had been like when she had been kissed by men she'd known before him. He had filled her life for so long it was hard to remember. Not that it mattered now, she reminded herself.

Sleep came several hours later, her mind battling her will, forcing out the memories. It was six months since the wedding now. How much longer? her heart asked. How much longer would it continue to hurt?

At precisely eleven-thirteen, Cathy pulled off Airport Way and drove toward the sign high above the building that read Alaska Cargo Company.

Wiping his hands on a rag, Ray sauntered out from one of the hangars toward Cathy. "Hello again."

"Hello, Ray." She'd washed her hair, curling it carefully. Grady hadn't said anything about seeing her this morning. Even if he had agreed to meet her, she wouldn't want him to think she'd done herself up for him. As if to prove something to herself, she wore her most faded jeans and an old sweat shirt.

"Grady said you'd be coming. He's waiting for you in his office."

"He is?" She hoped some of the astonishment she felt couldn't be detected in her voice.

"While you're with him I'll see to your car door."

Her attention swiveled from the office building back to the mechanic. "Ray," she asked a little shyly, "would you mind opening the car door on the driver's side for me?"

There was a mocking light to the faded blue eyes, but he did as she asked and moved to her car. He pulled, jerked, and heaved. His fists hammered at the lock, and still the door wouldn't budge. "I'm afraid it's shut solid, miss," he pronounced gravely.

"Just checking." Her eyes shined with a happy light. "Thank you, Ray, thank you very much."

Ray paused and removed his cap to scratch his head, a puzzled look furrowing his brow as Cathy walked toward Grady's office.

Grady was on the phone, his voice low and lazy, when Cathy entered the building. The outer room looked exactly as it had the day of her visit. Newspapers and magazines littered the chairs, the ashtray looked even fuller, the butts balanced carelessly in a large heap. Cathy was standing at the counter trying to make sense out of one of the charts when Grady stepped out of his office and came to stand beside her.

His voice was filled with laughter when he took the chart and turned it around. "You're looking at that upside down."

"I knew that," she lied with the ease of a beguiling child.

"I'm glad you're here. I've been waiting for you," he said as he took a thick winter coat off a rack.

"I'm not late, am I?" She examined her watch. "It's eleven-fifteen. Two minutes, if that."

Grady's arm was in one sleeve when he hesitated. He looked as if he was going to question her but lightly shook his head. "Never mind." His smile was full.

His charm might have phased at lot of women, Cathy decided. Fortunately she wasn't one of them. "You've been waiting for me? What for?" He hadn't mentioned anything last night.

"I thought you might like to take a short run with me. It's clear enough to get a fantastic view of Mount McKinley."

"A short run?" she questioned. "You don't mean fly, do you?"

He was laughing at her again. "Yes, my sweet school-marm, I mean fly. You don't get air sick do you?"

"How would I know?" she shot back, losing her patience. "I've never flown before. Not ever."

"Never?" he asked and sounded incredulous.

"Never."

"Then how'd you get to Fairbanks from Kansas."

She would have thought the answer was obvious. "I drove."

"From Kansas?"

"Yes." He made it sound like an impossible feat. The truth was she'd enjoyed the trip and considered it an adventure.

"There's always a first time. Are you afraid?"

"Darn it, how am I supposed to know? I've never been in a plane. Did you hear what I said?" she asked him, doing her best to disguise the panic in her voice. She rammed both fists inside the thick jacket.

His hand was already on the doorknob. "Do you want to go or don't you?"

Was she afraid? It wasn't that she'd avoided flying, there had never been much opportunity. She'd lived and vacationed in Kansas all her life. But there hadn't been many vacations when she was a child. Her father wouldn't allow the time away from his work. When she'd gotten the job in Alaska it would have been the perfect time to fly, but she'd decided she'd rather drive up, using the excuse it was too expensive to ship her things. In her heart she knew the real reason. If she drove to Fairbanks she could leave home sooner, get away as quickly as possible without raising suspicion.

"Well?" Grady questioned her again.

Grady Jones may have his faults, but Cathy knew he'd be a darn good pilot. When it came down to it, she trusted him. The thought caught her by surprise. She did trust Grady. "All right," she mumbled.

"You don't sound any too sure."

"I'm not," she snapped.

"Here." Grady removed a long red scarf from the coatrack and wrapped it around her neck. "This is my good luck charm. It'll protect you from harm."

"Wonderful," she murmured sarcastically. "What's going to protect you? You're the pilot." She removed the scarf and handed it back to him. "If it's all the same to you, I think I'd prefer it if you wore the good luck piece."

Fifteen minutes later they were taxiing onto the runway. Belted into the seat of the Cessna 150 beside Grady, Cathy faced a panel full of gauges and equipment that looked complicated and foreign. Communicating with the air traffic controller, he gave her a reassuring smile and winked as the plane gathered speed. The roar was deafening, but Cathy realized it wasn't the plane's engine making the noise but the sound of her heart hammering in her ear. Her stomach lurched wildly as the wheels left the runway and the aircraft began its assent into the blue sky.

A hand squeezed her clenched fist. "That wasn't so bad was it?"

"Not at all," she lied. The world below became smaller and smaller. Houses and buildings took on an unreal quality that enthralled Cathy. She was silently congratulating herself because she hadn't given way to her fears. Flying wasn't a frightening experience at all, but wonderful and exciting. "This is great," she shouted to be heard above the noise.

It seemed they were only in the air a few minutes when Grady pointed to Mount McKinley.

Its massive beauty mesmerized her, and Cathy was speechless. The mountain was unlike any other she had seen. She could understand why the native Alaskans had named it Denali, "The Great One." If an artist had painted a picture contrasting the stark white peaks against the blue blue sky, the painting would have taken on an unreal quality. "It's so big," she said after a while.

"At 20,320 feet, it's the largest mountain in North America. McKinley is three thousand feet higher than its nearest neighbor, extending a distance of one hundred and fifty miles from Rainey Pass to the valley of the Nenana River. Denali National Park, which we're flying over now, has three thousand square miles of subarctic wilderness."

"You sound like a tour guide," Cathy told him, laughing.

His mouth twisted, a fleeting smile touching the sensuous corners. "I've done my share."

"Say, where are we headed? You never did say."

"I didn't?" he teased.

"Come on, fellow, this is no time to announce you're kidnapping me."

"I'll admit it's a tempting thought."

"Grady!" She shifted so she could give him her chilling glare. It never failed to get results with her students. She should have known better than to try it on Grady.

"Don't move," he shouted in warning. "You'll rock the plane."

With a startled gasp, Cathy gripped the seat, her fingers digging into the thick cushion. The blood drained from her face before she noticed the mischievous light glimmering in the deep blue eyes. "You're going to pay for that, you rat."

The humor fled as his eyes grew serious. "That's something I'll look forward to."

The way he was looking at her brought an uncomfortable sensation to the pit of her stomach. She had seen the look in Steve's eyes, the primitive hunger. It was as if he were making love to her in his mind.

"Don't, Grady," she told him, shocked at how incredibly weak she sounded, how affected she was by the look.

His gaze narrowed on her mouth, and Cathy had to fight the temptation to moisten her lips. In an agitated movement she turned her head, pretending to look out the far edge of the window.

The remainder of the flight to Anchorage was accomplished without incident. Grady pointed to interesting sights, but the conversation was stilted and unnatural. He explained that he was picking up a part for a gold-dredging operation that wouldn't be in Anchorage until two-fifteen. They were only going to touch down, get the part, and take off again.

They were back in the air within forty minutes of landing. The sexual tension between them lessened as the kidding resumed on the return flight.

By the time they touched down in Fairbanks, Cathy felt like a seasoned traveler. After Grady had tied down the Cessna, he walked her to her car, which was parked outside his office. A note in the windshield told Cathy the keys were in Grady's office.

A hand resting on her shoulder seemed to burn all the way through her thick coat and sweat shirt. Grady removed it to unlock his office door, and Cathy released an unconscious sigh of relief. She didn't want to feel these things. Not for Grady. Her appreciation for him was growing with every meeting, but she didn't want to become involved with him. Maybe it would be better if she didn't see him again.

"Here are your keys." He handed them to her.

"Thanks, Grady," she answered absently. "I enjoyed the trip. I'm glad I went along."

"I enjoyed the company. We'll do it again sometime."

"Yes, sometime," she responded vaguely. "Good night." She was halfway out the inner office door when a hand at her shoulder turned her around.

His gaze roamed her face, and his smile was gentle but fleeting. His long, masculine fingers curved around the back of her neck, exerting a slight pressure, bringing her toward him. The other hand cupped the side of her face, his thumb ran leisurely over the fullness of her lips before his warm mouth covered hers. As before the kiss began without passion, a tender meeting of lips. As before it was pleasant, not an earth-shattering experience. Would she ever feel that again with any man, she wondered. Without conscious thought Cathy decided she had to know.

Her hands spread over the lean ribs under his coat as she molded herself against him, arching closer as she parted her lips.

Grady moaned, crushing her closer, his mouth slanting over hers, demanding, taking, bruising her lips. He lifted his face from hers and buried it in the side of her neck, his voice muffled as he spoke.

"How was the comparison?"

Three

Cathy could feel Angela Jones's eyes following her as she moved away from the blackboard. The other four children in the basic skills class were busy carefully lettering the sentence Cathy had written on the blackboard. Their small hands tightly clenched their pencils. Timmy Brookes's tongue worked at the side of his mouth as furiously as his fingers worked the lead.

Cathy read over the short paragraph and stepped to Angela's desk. "Is there something wrong?" she whispered, squatting down to watch Angela's expression.

Immediately the small child lowered her eyes, hiding her gaze. Cathy noted the red color that flowered Angela's cheek.

"No, Miss Thompson."

"Are you sure?" Cathy asked and placed a reassuring hand across the child's back.

Angela quickly denied the question with an ardent shake of her head, the long pigtails danced with the action.

Cathy gave her back a gentle pat before standing. Angela was so shy and withdrawn that it was seldom she said anything more than was required. According to the latest report given her, Cathy knew that Grady's daughter was now being tutored three nights a week after school. The improvement in her work was slow, but nonetheless the child was getting the help she needed.

"Miss Thompson." Cathy heard her name softly whispered. The call cut into her thoughts.

"Yes, Angela." Again she lowered herself so she could bring her attention back to the child.

"Daddy's right. You are real pretty."

The compliment was so unexpected that Cathy could feel her own cheeks fill with color. "Tell your daddy that I think he's real pretty too."

Angela giggled and placed a cupped hand over her mouth.

Cathy stood and pointed to the blank sheet of paper on the desk. "Now, I think that you should get busy and do your work."

Eagerly, Angela nodded.

Cathy thought about the incident with Angela all day. It was apparent Grady was talking about her in front of the child. Cathy wished he wouldn't. As far as she was concerned it would be better if she never had anything to do with Grady Jones again. After the kiss at the airfield, Cathy had driven home feeling almost numb. How had he known she was comparing his kisses to another man's? And not just any man, but Steve, the man she had loved more than life. It shocked her that she'd been so readable. Having revealed a part of herself, Cathy wasn't eager to make a repeat performance.

When she arrived home from school that afternoon and sorted through the mail, she discovered a letter from MaryAnne. Her hand was shaking as she examined the envelope.

"It's from MaryAnne," she told Peterkins as she set the letter on the kitchen table. "But you come first." Her tea was already poured as she sat at the table and patted her lap, indicating to her black-haired friend that she was ready for him.

With one leap the dog reached her lap, laying his head on her knees and snuggling the small body into the position he had known since he was a puppy.

Absently Cathy's fingers ran the length of Peterkins's body, stopping occasionally to scratch his ears. A warmth began to seep into her fingers, and she realized that she was cold, but the chill had nothing to do with the room temperature. It was the same feeling she had every time a letter arrived from home, especially when it was from her sister.

After several minutes, Cathy forced herself to open the envelope. It was a newsy letter, filled with little tidbits of information about old friends, their mother, and Kansas's infamous weather. Casually at the bottom of the letter, almost as if she'd forgotten to include the information, MaryAnne mentioned that Steve had quit his job.

Cathy felt a wintry feeling wash over her. Steve quit his job? Impossible! He loved his work as a supermarket manager. He had worked at the same store for the same chain from the time he was sixteen. He had been extremely proud of the fact he had worked his way up through the ranks. His goal had been to move from managing the store to working the corporate offices.

Biting into her trembling bottom lip, Cathy had the

desperate feeling that Steve was restless and unhappy. It's too late! her mind screamed. Far too late.

She stuck the letter in a drawer, delaying the time she would be faced with answering it.

The week passed with surprising quickness. Cathy was looking forward to sleeping in late Saturday morning. Friday she stayed up half the night reading. Unwillingly she discovered her thoughts drifting to Grady. All week she'd been practicing what she was going to say if he contacted her again. Now it looked as if she needn't have worried. He must have experienced the same doubts she was having. And if she was going to be honest with herself, it was probably best if they didn't continue to see one another. It was too soon, the pain of losing Steve remained too fresh. The day would come when she was ready to meet another man, perhaps even get serious, but not yet. And probably not for a long time.

Peterkins's bark woke her early Saturday morning. "Come on, fella," she groaned and pounded her pillow. "Give a girl a break. It's Saturday. I don't have to wake up early."

Ignoring her, Peterkins continued to scratch with both paws at the bedroom door.

"All right, all right." She tossed back the thick blankets, grabbed her housecoat from the end of the bed, and paused to stretch, lifting both hands high above her head. She had just finished a giant yawn when the doorbell chimed.

"Someone's at the door? Is that what you're trying to tell me?" Pushing her long reddish-brown hair away from her face, Cathy walked into the living room and tightened the sash to her pink velour housecoat.

Unsuccessfully she tried to stifle a groan when she glanced through the peephole in the front door. It was Grady. *Go away!* her mind shouted. *Leave me alone, I don't want to see you!* Was she crazy to hope that some form of mental telepathy would transmit her thoughts and make him go?

The doorbell rang again, this time more persistently.

"Come on, Cathy," he called, his tone insistent. "I know you're in there."

So much for sensory communication, Cathy mused angrily.

The security chain intact, she opened the door just enough to make the sound of her voice carry. A rush of cold air scattered gooseflesh up her forearms.

"I'm not dressed yet. Come back later."

At the sensuous sound of his chuckle, Cathy's eyes flashed a stormy gray. "This is a rotten trick to pull early Saturday morning." The sound of her indignation was drowned out by Peterkins's bark. One black paw flew out the crack in the door in a frantic effort to reach the intruder.

"Daddy, look! Miss Thompson has a doggie."

Cathy was pulling Peterkins back from the door by his collar when she heard Angela's excited voice. Grady had brought his daughter with him?

"Are you going to let me in or not?" Grady insisted, his male voice bringing with it the image of the tall muscular man she could like and distrust within a minute's space.

"Oh, all right," she conceded ungraciously and closed

the door completely to unlatch the chain. Standing far out of view, Cathy pulled open the large front door.

Traitor that he was, Peterkins's short bobbing tail began shaking wildly in greeting.

"She does have a doggie." Angela squealed with delight and fell to her knees the minute she was in the door. Eagerly petting the dog the child accepted Peterkins's wet tongue as he licked her face and hands. "Oh, Daddy, look, she likes me."

"He," Cathy corrected, crossing her arms ominously in front of her as she cast a frosty glare at Grady.

"What's his name?" Angela wanted to know.

"Peterkins." Cathy's smile was stiff.

"Peterkins?" Grady repeated, making the name a question. His mouth quivered with the effort to suppress a smile, which did little to calm Cathy's indignation.

"What are you dong here at this unearthly hour?" she demanded in a hissing breath. She hated to display her anger openly in front of Angela. The child was shy, and the least amount of shouting was likely to intimidate her. Grady knew that and was using it against Cathy, which angered her all the more.

"Are you usually this surly in the morning?" His blue gaze lingered briefly on her lips, then lifted.

"Only when I've been rudely awakened. What time is it anyway?"

"Eight." The lone word came smooth and low.

Charged electric currents vibrated in the air between them. Cathy was uncomfortable enough without adding sexual tension.

"You don't expect to sleep your whole weekend away do you?" he asked, his eyes doing a lazy inspection of her.

Uncomfortably aware of her housecoat and tousled

hair, Cathy lowered her gaze. "Excuse me a minute while I change." No need to add ammunition to the already powerful effect he seemed to have on her.

Cathy leaned against the closed bedroom door, her composure shattered. Her knees were shaking, and she moved to sit on the edge of the bed. What kind of game was Grady playing? It was almost as if he couldn't decide if he wanted to continue to see her or not. A week had lapsed since the flight to Anchorage. She hadn't heard a word from him. She'd thought she was grateful for that, but was she? Everything was so confused in her mind, she didn't know what she wanted.

Jeans, a pullover sweater, and ankle boots were her normal Saturday attire, and she couldn't see any reason to dress otherwise on Grady's account. A pink ribbon tied back the unruly mass of long hair. After brushing her teeth she applied a light coat of lip gloss and heaved a giant breath before making her entry.

Peterkins was reveling in Angela's attention. The spaniel had climbed into the little girl's lap while she sat on the living room sofa, as he so often did with Cathy. A bright smile lit up Angela's face as she beamed happily at Cathy.

"It looks like you've made yourself a friend," she told her dog, pausing to scratch his ears.

Peterkins lifted his face but, seeing she didn't expect him to move, was content to stay where he was.

She followed the smell of perking coffee into the kitchen. An open can of ground coffee sat on the counter top while Grady examined the contents of her cupboards.

"Not much into food, are you?"

"You're a fine one to talk," she bit back defensively. "When was the last time you ate a sit-down meal?"

Grady chuckled, infuriating her further. "You are testy in the mornings, aren't you. Here, try this." He handed her a cup of freshly brewed coffee. "This should take the sting out of your tongue."

With ill grace, Cathy accepted the mug, pulled out a kitchen chair, and sat down. Grady joined her, turning the chair around and straddling it. He crossed his forearms over the back of the chair.

"Now tell me what was so all-fired important that you had to ruin the only day of the week that I can sleep in?" she questioned in one long breath.

"What about tomorrow? You can sleep in Sunday." He asked another question instead of answering hers.

"Church," she informed him politely.

Grady shook his head mockingly. "You are a good girl, aren't you?"

"Will you cut it out?" The hands cupping her mug tightened until the heat of the coffee burned her palms. Slowly she slacked her grip, focusing her attention on the black liquid. "Why are you here? What do you want?"

The hesitation was long enough to cause Cathy to raise her eyes and find him studying her long and hard. The laughter lines had disappeared, and his blue gaze had darkened with purpose. A hand lifted to gently caress her cheek. The rough, calloused fingers felt strangely smooth against her face. It was so gentle, so sweet, that Cathy succumbed to the swelling tide of warmth building within her and lowered her lashes. When his mouth touched hers, she breathed in slowly and parted her mouth in welcome.

Peterkins's sharp bark shattered the moment, and Cathy jerked back in surprise. Grady looked no less unsettled as the dog scampered into the kitchen, slipping on the slick linoleum floor and crashing against Grady's leg. Quickly regaining his form, Peterkins's bark was repeated again and again, piercing the quiet.

"Peterkins!" Cathy shouted. "Stop it! Stop it immediately!"

He did as she bid with a defiant air, quickly lowering his rump to the floor, and positioned himself at her feet.

"I didn't know you had a protector." Amusement coated Grady's words.

Cathy couldn't prevent a disbelieving stare that darted from her dog back to Grady. "I didn't either. I'm as shocked as you." It stood to reason. Steve had been the only man Peterkins had ever seen kissing her. The dog in his own way was laying claim to what he considered to be his other master's property. The realization knotted a hard lump in Cathy's stomach.

"What's wrong?" Angela's small voice broke into her thoughts.

"Peterkins didn't like me kissing Cathy," Grady supplied the answer, a laughing glint to his eyes.

"I didn't know teachers kissed." Angela's attention quickly turned from the black-haired spaniel.

"Thanks," Cathy mumbled under her breath to Grady. "I can hear it all over the school grounds Monday."

"Some teachers are so special you can't help kissing them," Grady said, playfully tugging one long pigtail. "Now why don't you tell Cathy what we have planned for today." He looped one arm over the thin shoulders, bringing his daughter close to his side.

"Oh, Miss Thompson, it's so special. Daddy said he'd take us for a long drive through Denali National Park. He said we might see bear and moose and deer and rabbits and maybe a wolf. Won't you please, please come? Daddy and I have already packed a picnic. Can Peterkins come too?" A pleading note entered the young voice. Cathy couldn't remember hearing Angela say so much all at once.

Indecision swelled within her. The trip sounded wonderful. Ever since moving to Fairbanks she had wanted an opportunity to visit the park. To refuse now would burst Angela's happy bubble. But to accept would be giving encouragement to an uncertain relationship.

"Please," Angela repeated.

Cathy nodded and laughed, the sound unnatural, almost forced. "All right."

"And Peterkins?"

Cathy caught the humorous sparkle in Grady's eyes. "Oh, definitely Peterkins."

"You feel the need for protection, do you?" he whispered tauntingly. A hand reached out and captured hers, carrying her fingers to his mouth. Immediately alert, Peterkins growled, baring his white teeth.

Unaccustomed to such behavior from her friendly mutt, Cathy again issued a stern warning.

After a quick breakfast of orange juice and toast, Cathy gathered her coat and the leash for Peterkins. Accepting Angela's hand, Cathy was led to the waiting car. The air was crisp and clear, the vast, cloudless, blue sky beckoning. Cathy didn't think there could be a more perfect day for the outing.

Dog and child were relegated to the backseat, leaning as far forward into the front as possible until Grady instructed everyone to secure their seat belts.

Happy for the excuse to do something with her hands, Cathy snapped one section of the cold metal clasp into the other, then primly folded her hands on her lap.

Grady's roguish glance flickered over her, and he smiled. That was the problem with Grady, Cathy decided. He was too darn handsome for his own good. He expected a woman to be so taken with his male charm that she would fall into his scheme of events. Well, not with her.

"I've got a penny."

"For what?" she said quickly, turning her attention to the road.

"Your thoughts?"

She laughed lightly, almost disliking him for the way he could read her so easily. "They're worth a lot more than that."

"I'm sure they are." Lines crinkled at the corners of his eyes.

"I can't figure you out, Grady Jones."

He looked puzzled. "What's there to figure?"

"Plenty," she murmured and paused to expel a deep breath, trying not to show how easily he could irritate her. She shifted her position. "I was just beginning to believe that I wouldn't hear from you again."

"I've been busy." The response was clipped, and the muscles of his jaw worked convulsively.

Cathy arched both brows upward in surprise. Grady didn't like to account for his time to anyone. It was probably one of the reasons he owned his own business. Probably one of the reasons he claimed his marriage was in trouble before his wife died.

"Don't get shook," she challenged. "I wasn't exactly sure I *wanted* to see you again."

His laugh was as rich and full as it was unexpected. "There was never any doubt in my mind," he concluded. "You'll be seeing a lot more of me before this winter is over, so you might as well get accustomed to it now."

"Is that so?" A cold chill ran down her spine. What was it Grady wanted from her? He wasn't the type of man to idly waste his time on anyone or anything. When he wanted something, he went after it. But what did she have to offer him? Cathy supposed she should feel complimented that Grady was interested in her. Instead, his acknowledgment filled her with a sense of quiet desperation.

"Have you taken pictures of the pipeline yet?" The question came out of nowhere, slicing into Cathy's thoughts.

"No, as a matter of fact, I haven't."

"Good, I brought my camera along. We'll stop and I'll take a few photographs. You can mail some back to Kansas if you like. I imagine your family has never seen anything like this."

Several times Cathy had paused to view the huge twisting, curving cylinder that passed a few miles outside of Fairbanks. It was tall and so much larger than what she had expected.

Grady pulled onto a dirt road that ran alongside the pipeline.

"Wow!" Cathy shook her head in amazement. Standing on the tips of her toes, she was just able to touch the bottom of its round belly. "I've seen it from a distance before but never this close. I didn't realize it was this huge."

"Huge and expensive," Grady told her as he lifted Angela above his shoulders so she could touch the silver belly. "Eight billion dollars for the seven hundred and ninety-nine miles that stretch from Prudhoe Bay in the Arctic Ocean to Valdez in the Gulf of Alaska. I believe it works out to something like ten million dollars a mile."

"Ten million dollars?" Cathy repeated with a sense of astonished disbelief. "That can't be right."

"But it is," Grady insisted. "Of course, a lot went into protecting the environment. Those heat exchangers on top of the pillars supporting the pipe serve a dual purpose. First they protect the permafrost. The heat the oil flowing through the line generates would ruin the permafrost below. If the ground thawed, then the pylons supporting the cylinder would sink and ruin the pipeline."

The wind whipped color into her cheeks, and Cathy couldn't prevent the shiver that raced over her body.

"Need your coat?" Grady questioned.

"No. I think I've seen about everything I want to see." One last time, she stood on her toes in an attempt to touch the underbelly.

"Want me to lift you too?" Grady's whispered question was meant for her ears alone.

"Hardly."

His gaze ran over her blue and glinting. Cathy chose to ignore him, primly turning her back and returning to the car.

"Wait a minute," Grady stopped her. "I want to take your picture."

The wind whipped her hair about her face, and while one hand was lifted to her face to pull back the errant strand, Grady snapped the picture.

"Where are we going now?" Angela questioned from the backseat.

"Denali," Grady answered.

"Goodie." Happiness sounded in the young voice. "When do we get to see the lions and tigers and bears?"

"Keep your eyes peeled because there might be some around here." The words were whispered in such a way as to make her believe something unknown might lurk behind a supporting pylon.

Cathy turned around and smiled softly when she saw Peterkins was resting contentedly on the seat beside Angela. One paw and his chin were propped across her leg, as if to state she shouldn't dare move because he was comfortable.

"I don't think we need fear lions and tigers and bears as much as one wolf." Heavy emphasis was placed on the word *wolf* so that Grady couldn't doubt that she was referring to him.

"A wolf?" Grady repeated the word as if it was distasteful. "I'm sure you must mean fox." He paused and leaned closer to Cathy. "I've often been called a fox."

"Not by me." It was important that she set the record straight.

"Give my obvious charm a while. I'm sure you'll change your mind."

Cathy lifted her chin, doing her best to keep from laughing. "Have you got a year?" she teased.

"Oh, I've got time. As far as you're concerned, there's all the time in the world."

Cathy felt the color flow out of her face as an uncomfortable sensation assaulted her. Grady was doing it again. For a crazy second she wanted to scream at him to stop, leave her alone, give her time to heal after Steve. He was going too fast for her, far too fast.

A bounty of fall colors was in vast display as they traveled into the park.

"Are we there, Daddy?" Angela questioned from the backseat.

"Start looking now," Grady said. "Any minute you're likely to see some wildlife."

Cathy turned to see the child peering out the side window, the brow, so like her father's, was narrowed in concentration. Peterkins, two paws against the front seat cushion, was looking out just as intently.

"During the summer months we wouldn't be able to make this drive," Grady said and motioned to the far left-hand side of the road. "Look," he said, "there's a moose."

"Where?" Cathy asked excitedly, her eyes frantically searching for the huge mammal.

"I see it!" Angela cried. "I see it!"

Peterkins barked with the excitement as Angela bounced around in the backseat.

"Where?" Cathy repeated.

Grady slipped one arm over her, letting it settle on her shoulder as he drew her close. The other hand was used to direct her gaze in the proper direction. Within seconds Cathy caught sight of the moose, his huge antler and body blending in beautifully with his surroundings. But it wasn't the sight of the magnificent beast that had Cathy's blood pounding in her veins. Being this close to Grady was physically and emotionally exhausting.

The temptation was so strong to nestle her face in the curve of his neck that for a moment she closed her eyes.

"Beautiful, aren't they?" Grady said, his mouth moving against her hair.

Cathy nodded because speaking had suddenly become impossible. A soothing warmth began to spread its way down her arm, and she gently pulled herself from his embrace.

"Yes…yes, they are." The words sounded weak even to herself. "What was it you were saying about not being able to do this during the summer?"

"That's right."

Uncertain, Cathy glanced at Grady. His voice sounded unnatural, as if his mind wasn't on her question. "Visitors are bussed through the park during the summer months."

"Why?"

Grady's attention was diverted to the road. "As you've probably noticed, this isn't exactly the best road in Alaska. It's narrow and difficult to maneuver. In several places turning a camper or car around would be almost impossible. It's simpler to drive tourists through instead of allowing thousands of vehicles in."

"Sounds that way," she said, more for something to say than any sign of agreement.

A couple of hours later Angela spotted a brown bear. "Miss Thompson, look," she exclaimed pointing wildly out the window. "It's Yogi Bear."

"Or a reasonable facsimile," Grady added with a chuckle

"I thought bears would be hibernating by this time. It's mid-October," Cathy whispered, as if she were afraid the sound of her voice would frighten the creature away. "And speaking of bears, you don't expect me to share my lunch with that fellow do you?"

Grady's responding laugh was filled with humor. "One question at a time, sweet Dorothy from Kansas."

"The name's Cathy," she reminded him in a chilly tone. The last thing she wanted to be thought of was a sweet sixteen year old desperately seeking a way back home. Her home was Alaska now. The sooner she and everyone around her accepted the fact, the easier it would be.

"Okay, Cathy." Her name was issued softly. "Bears hibernate in the winter, not autumn. The one we saw today is fattening herself up for the months ahead. Secondly, we don't picnic outside. That would be inviting the attention of our fur-covered friends, and I for one am opposed to sharing my lunch."

"I for two," Angela added.

"Fine, but if we don't eat out of doors, just where do we picnic?"

"In the car," Angela said as if it was the most natural thing in the world.

Unable to resist, Cathy smiled. "Of course."

As promised, Grady provided the lunch an hour later. The fried chicken, biscuits, small dish of coleslaw, and ice-cold pop couldn't have tasted better. It was all so simple that Cathy marveled that her family hadn't done something like this themselves. Picnics were always a formal affair for which her mother spent whole days preparing.

Wiping their fingers with the premoistened towelettes enclosed with the chicken, Cathy paused feeling Grady's gaze, her fingers clenching and unclenching as her eggshell composure began to feel the strain of his appraisal.

"You like Alaska, don't you?"

"Surprisingly, yes. I wasn't prepared for the beauty or vastness. I don't know that anyone really is. From Kansas it sounded like the ends of the earth, which it is in a manner of speaking."

"Why'd you come?"

She'd been expecting the question for some time. Giving the impression it was of no importance, she shrugged her shoulders. "It's a job. If you hadn't noticed, there aren't many of those around these days."

"I have." Grady's tone was faintly dry.

"Anyway the position was offered, and I jumped at the chance."

"We'll see how much you love it after the first winter."

"I'll make it."

"I'm sure you will." One dark eyebrow flicked upward. "You, my sweet Cathy, are a survivor."

"That I am," she murmured stiffly, suddenly uneasy with the way the conversation was headed. "And what about you? Are you an implant like me?"

"Nope, born and raised here all my life. Tried going to school in the lower forty-eight, but I hated it and came back to where the air is clean and land unspoiled."

"I was born in Fairbanks," Angela added, apparently feeling left out of the conversation.

"At midnight on the coldest night of the year," Grady added. The creases along the side of his mouth deepened into a familiar smile. "I darn near brought that girl into the world myself."

"I don't suppose her mother should be given any credit?" The words were issued in a teasing undertone.

"As a matter of fact," Grady said low and cynically for her alone, "Pam handled her part as best she could." He straightened and turned the ignition key. The engine purred to life as he checked the rearview mirror. "I think it's time for us to head back if we're going to arrive before dark. Anyone for singing?"

Pulling onto the road, they only advanced a few feet when Cathy heard a bang and hissing sound. "What was that?" She witnessed Grady's eyes close in frustration before he turned toward her, presenting a calm facade. "That, my two helpless females, is a flat tire."

Four

"Would you care to give me a hand?" Grady asked as he released the jack lowering the car to the ground.

"Sure, anything," Cathy said and breathed in relief. "What do you need me to do?"

Wiping his greasy hands with his white handkerchief, Grady glanced upward, a roguish glint to the deep blue eyes. "I was hoping you'd applaud."

Both Cathy and Angela were clapping wildly and laughing when the creases around his mouth suddenly hardened and a wary light was reflected in his gaze.

"Get inside the car." The order was given with a frightening undertone.

Without question, Cathy helped Angela into the backseat and securely shut the door before jerking open her own. A second later Grady joined her in the front seat.

"What's the matter?" Cathy whispered, her heart hammering at the coiled alertness she felt coming from Grady.

"There's a brown bear about thirty yards ahead moving toward us. I think the time has come for us to make our exit."

"Peterkins!" Cathy looked around her frantically. Her hand flew to the door handle. "We can't leave without Peterkins." Her voice was high pitched and filled with anxiety.

Grady stopped her before she could open the door. "It would be crazy to go out there now. You'd only be attracting trouble."

"I don't care," she insisted, jerking herself free.

The harsh grip of his hand bit into her shoulder. "No," he said and shoved her against the seat. "If anyone gets him, it'll be me."

Angela began whimpering, the sound of her cries muffled as she covered her face with both hands. "I don't want a bear to eat Peterkins," she wailed.

"Grady, please," Cathy pleaded, lifting her gaze to his. "He won't come to you. It's got to be me."

Indecision flickered over the hard face. "Okay." He gradually released his hold on her. "I'll distract the bear, and you get that damn dog of yours into the car. And for heaven's sake be quick about it."

Grady climbed out first after instructing Angela not to leave the car for any reason. Cathy took in several deep breaths in an effort to calm herself. The wild beast would sense her fear, and she struggled to breathe evenly and appear calm.

The bear was advancing toward the vehicle, standing on its hind legs looming twelve or fourteen feet above them. Nothing had ever looked so large or so terrifying.

To her horror Cathy saw that Peterkins was running toward the animal, barking for all his worth.

Grady moved around to the front of the car, hands dangling at his side. It took Cathy several moments to realize he was speaking in soothing, low tones, moving slowly toward the huge mammal.

Her heart in her throat, Cathy cupped her mouth with both hands and called her dog.

Peterkins hesitated, stopping to turn around, and glanced at her.

The bear was so close Cathy thought she could smell him, then realized it was the taste of fear that was magnifying her senses. Grady was far closer to the bear than she was. Her own fear was quickly forgotten as she realized the danger Grady was placing himself in for the sake of her dog. She wanted to cry out for Grady to move back. Instead, she concentrated on gaining Peterkins's attention.

Frantically she called the spaniel, her voice sharp and demanding. This time Peterkins didn't pause, turning around abruptly and running as fast as his short legs would carry him. She squatted down so that he could leap into her arms. Moving as quickly as possible, she hurried back to the relative safety of the car.

Cathy was inside and breathing so hard she was panting. Still Grady remained outside, slowly retreating until he backed into the front bumper of the car. As if he was in no more danger than he would be attending a Sunday school picnic, he turned and climbed into the front seat, starting the engine and pulling onto the road.

Cathy looked back to note that the bear had turned and reentered the woods. It had probably been the smell of their picnic that had attracted his attention.

Relief washed over her, and for a moment Cathy had to struggle to hold back the tears. "Bad dog," she enunciated each word, her manner and voice stern. "How can you have been so naughty?"

Apparently Peterkins knew he had done wrong. Dejectedly he hung his head, and the long ears drooped forward.

"You okay?" Grady asked as an aloof mask came over him.

"I'm fine." She studied him for a minute. The dark bushy brows, the unrelenting set of jaw; his profile appeared almost hawklike. The eyes were a clear shade of deep blue, but sharp and intelligent. The dark hair, although trimmed short, was curly and framed his forehead.

"You sure? You look awfully pale for someone safe and secure." His look flickered over her.

The responding smile was weak. "I'm sure." She lowered her gaze. She liked Grady. That was the problem. If anything had happened to him she would have felt more than guilt or remorse. The realization was so new she hadn't time to properly analyze exactly what she was feeling.

"How could you act so calm?" she queried. "Anything could have happened."

"Calm?" he snorted. "Listen, I've been ten thousand feet in the air, lost both engines, and felt less nervous than facing that bear."

Laughter sighed through her as she tipped her head back to rest against the seat. "I don't think I've been more frightened in my life," she admitted.

"Can Peterkins come and sit with me now?" Angela asked, the small voice barely audible.

"Sure." Cathy helped move the dog from the front to the back, then scooted across the cushioned seat to sit closer to Grady. She stopped when their shoulders touched.

His glance was filled with surprise. "To what do I owe this honor?"

Cathy couldn't answer him. She didn't know why she felt the need to be near him. It had been an unconscious movement made without reason. "I'm cold." The excuse was a feeble one, but Grady seemed to accept it, lopping an arm over her shoulder and bringing her within the comfort of his embrace.

"Warmer?" he asked a few minutes later.

Cathy nodded.

"Daddy, can I be a Girl Scout?" Angela's head appeared between Grady's and Cathy's.

"Why the sudden interest in Girl Scouts?" Grady questioned, his gaze not leaving the road.

"Melissa Sue's gonna be one, and I thought I should do it too."

"I think she means Brownie," Cathy inserted. "The school handed out information sheets last week."

"I want to roast marshmallows and eat somemores and sing songs around a fire."

"That's the picture on the front of the information sheet," Cathy explained.

"There were some marshmallows in your cupboard weren't there, Cathy?"

Grady's gaze had scanned the contents of her kitchen that morning while she was dressing. "Yes, I think there are."

"Fine. When we get back, Cathy can invite us inside, and while I build a fire in her fireplace, you two ladies can cook some hot cocoa and find something to roast marshmallows."

"Goodie." Angela bounded against the backseat, and

Cathy could hear her telling Peterkins all about the wonderful time they were going to have.

"Now that was sneaky," Cathy murmured, resting her head against the curve of his shoulder.

"No, just quick thinking," he murmured. His eyes glanced toward her mouth, the look was so suggestive that Cathy had the desire to blush and look away. The last streaks of light were fading from the darkening sky when they rolled past the Fairbanks city limits.

"I'll drop you two off at the house."

"Three," Angela corrected. "Don't forget Peterkins."

Grady chuckled. "After this afternoon, it's not likely."

"Where are you going?" Cathy asked.

"I've got some paperwork to catch up with. It'll only be an hour or so. You don't mind do you?"

For a second she wanted to complain and tell him that yes, she did mind. This was the way it had always been with her own father. Not a single day of his life was he able to sever himself from job related obligations. Memories of Christmas Day were filled with presents and laughter and arranging the big meal around the time her father would return from the office. Cathy should have realized that a whole day was more than Grady could give her, Angela, or anyone else in his life.

"No, I don't mind," she lied. "It'll give Angela and me time to unwind." Barely concealed resentment caused her voice to tremble slightly.

Grady gave her a puzzled look. "If it's going to bother you, say so and I won't go."

The temptation was to take him up on the offer and see just how long he would be able to endure the torture of staying away from his business. Mentally Cathy gave herself a shake. She was being unreasonable, allowing the childhood memories of an overly work obsessed father to cloud her perception now.

"No it's fine, really. Angela and I will have a good time, won't we?" She directed her question to the little girl.

"If I take a bath at your house, can Peterkins come in the tub with me?"

"No."

"Yes," Grady insisted.

Playfully digging the point of her elbow into his stomach, Cathy laughed. "You're a great help, fella. Any more suggestions, and Angela and I will come to the office to help you with the paperwork."

Grady parked the car in front of Cathy's house. She half expected him to drop them off and drive away. But he came inside and brought in firewood, stacking it by the fireplace. As he was working, Cathy brewed coffee.

Grady accepted a cup, blowing into the steaming liquid before taking the first sip. His legs were crossed as he leaned against the kitchen counter.

Physically she was growing more aware of his presence every minute. Something was definitely the matter with her. Only last week she had rated his kiss as interesting. Now she longed for the taste of his mouth over hers. Not because she was falling in love with him, but to compare her reaction one week from the next.

Finishing her coffee, Cathy placed the mug in the kitchen sink. As she moved away from the counter, he placed his hand along the slope of her neck, stopping her. Cathy quit breathing. When his mouth settled over her parted lips, she slipped her arms around his neck. His hand at the small of her back arched her closer.

Passively she accepted the kiss, neither giving nor

taking. If she had stopped to analyze her feelings she would have realized Grady's kiss had gone from interesting to pleasant. Decidedly pleasant. But it lacked the spark, the urgency, the emotion she'd once shared with Steve.

Grady broke the contact, dragging his mouth from hers. He seemed to know what she was thinking. Cathy could sense it, could feel his hesitation or was that disappointment? She couldn't tell. Slowly he took control of himself.

His hands cupped her shoulders as he lifted his face, his eyes dark, unreadable.

"Grady," she whispered feeling confused, wanting to explain, knowing she couldn't. Lowering her eyes, she released a long sigh. "I'm—"

"Don't," he interrupted and raked a vicious hand through his curly hair. "Don't apologize, understand?"

"Okay."

Without a backward glance, without another word, he left the kitchen. Cathy winced when she heard the front door close.

Now she was upset, not with Grady but with herself. She couldn't help wonder how long it would take for her broken heart to heal. Another question was exactly how long Steve would continue to dominate her life? Would she ever be able to love, truly love anyone else?

Sometime later she fixed Angela a sandwich and poured the little girl a glass of milk. Nothing sounded appetizing, and she chose not to eat. Skipping meals was becoming a repeated pattern and one that must stop.

Grady returned a couple of hours later, carrying a brown paper sack and two wine goblets turned upside down between two fingers.

Smiling to herself, Cathy hung up his coat. "Wine and marshmallows. Sounds wonderful," she teased.

His lips brushed her cheek. "The wine is for later," he murmured for her ears only.

Immediately Peterkins growled, again taking exception to having another man kiss her.

Cathy cast the spaniel a warning glance. "Where were you when I needed you?" she questioned him. After Grady had left the house, Cathy had discovered Angela playing house with the dog, placing him in the bed and pulling the covers over his head. If he'd been free, the scene in the kitchen would have never been allowed to go as far as it did.

A look of impatience flickered over Grady's expression. "I refuse to be deterred by a mutt," he declared, taking out a huge bone from the bottom of the sack. "If you want to play protector, do it with this." He held up the bone, and Peterkins leaped into the air in a futile attempt to reach the goodie. Grady stooped down to pet the dog. "Later, buddy, later."

Flickering flames leaped out between pieces of wood as Grady, Angela, and Cathy sat on the carpet, their backs supported by the front of the sofa. Shadows danced across the room, forming mime figures on the opposite wall. An empty bag of marshmallows was carelessly tossed onto the coffee table while the last song softly faded from the iPad.

Angela yawned and crawled onto the couch, tucking her hands and knees into a tight ball. "I'm sleepy, Daddy and Cathy," she said on another long drawn-out yawn. "This is almost like being a real family, isn't it?"

Grady's arm rested across Cathy's shoulder. "Yes, it is," he whispered.

Together they sat before the fire. There didn't seem to be a need for words. Her neck rested against his arm, and for the first time in recent memory, Cathy felt utterly content.

In a series of agile movements, Grady placed another log on the fire, moved into the kitchen, and returned with an open bottle of wine and the wineglasses. Peterkins was nowhere to be seen. "Maybe Angela would rest better in a bed. Mind if I put her in your room?" he asked softly, as if afraid he would wake the sleeping child.

"Sure, go ahead," she agreed lazily.

He left her momentarily and smiled when he returned. He lowered himself onto the carpeting beside her. Filling the wineglass he handed it to Cathy. When his own glass was ready, he paused, holding it up. "To what shall we drink?"

Laying her head against the sofa cushion, Cathy closed her eyes. "To the personals?"

Grady chuckled and gently tapped her glass with his. "To the personals."

They both sipped the wine. "To the Red Baron," she offered next.

"And Snoopy." Grady touched the rim of the glasses again before taking a sip.

The Savignon-Blanc wine was marvelous, light, and refreshing.

"This is good," Cathy murmured after her second glass. "Very good."

"So is this." He took the stemmed glass out of her hand and placed it on the coffee table.

I should stop him, Cathy thought, lifting a strand of hair away from her face. *It's going to happen all over again. Grady's going to kiss me and I won't be able to respond.* The reasoning was there, but the desire to put a halt to his intentions wasn't.

Grady stared at her for a long minute, his eyes darkened to an intense blue as his hands framed her face. Slowly, as if waiting for her to stop him, he lowered his mouth to hers.

Cathy parted her lips, but whether in protest or welcome she didn't know. Her arms circled his neck as the pressure of his mouth hardened over hers. Where once there had been a feeling of dread, a warmth, an acceptance began to flow, spreading throughout her until she moaned softly.

Grady broke the contact, his mouth hovering inches above hers until their breaths merged. Gently, lovingly, his hands caressed the side of her neck, slowly descending over her shoulders while he spread tender kisses on her temple and face.

The gentle quality of his touch brought the first trace of tears to her eyes. It's the wine, she told herself. Crying was a ridiculous response to being kissed. This was beautiful, lovely. She should never have drunk the wine.

One tear slid down her flushed cheek. When Grady's lips encountered the wetness, he paused and kissed it away. His mouth met each tear as it escaped, and soon his lips were investigating every inch of her face. Her cheek, her forehead, her chin. When he moved to explore her parted lips, Cathy could taste the saltiness of her own tears in the kiss.

Grady lifted his head and pulled her into his arms. "Are you okay?" The question was breathed against her hair.

For a moment answering him was impossible. "Just hold me, okay?"

She was pressed so close against his chest that her breasts were flattened, but she didn't care. For the first time in months she was beginning to feel. A healing balm, a warmth began to spread its way through her. Cathy didn't know how long Grady held her. Time had lost importance. The only sensation that registered was the soothing, gentle stroke of his hand.

The pressure of his body edged her backward. The carpet felt smooth and comforting against her back. Positioned above her, Grady again studied her, lowering his mouth to kiss her nose and smiling gently into her wary, unsure eyes. The tender touch of his lips produced a languor, a state of dreaminess.

Her fingers spread over his back, but the desire to feel the rippling hard muscles of his shoulders was so very tempting. Her hands slid under his sweater, reveling in the feel of his bare skin.

Grady's kiss devoured her lips until she was breathless and panting. His touch felt right and good. Putting an end to the delicious feeling was what would be wrong, not the intimate caress.

When he moaned and dragged his mouth from hers, burying it in the curve of her neck, Cathy rolled her head to the side to encourage the exploration.

His tongue found the sensitive lobe of her ear, and dancing shivers skidded over her skin. A soft, muted moan trembled from her. Cathy could feel his mouth form a smile against her hair. Gradually his hold loosened, and he eased himself into a sitting position, helping her up.

"More wine?" His voice was slightly husky and disturbed.

Disoriented, Cathy resumed her former position and nodded. *Don't stop!* she wanted to scream. *The pain is almost gone when you hold me.* Her heart had been more than bruised, it'd been shattered. For so long she'd believed it would take more than one miracle to repair the damage, if at all.

When she didn't answer, Grady handed her a replenished glass. Her fingers were shaking as she accepted the wine. Gently he kissed her temple and placed an arm across her shoulder, pulling her close to his side.

"Who did this to you?" He whispered the question. "Who hurt you so badly?"

A chill ran down her spine. Cathy began to shake, faint tremors shaking her shoulders. Heat invaded her body, creeping up from her neck, spreading its crimson color to her ears and face.

"No one." She straightened, crossing her legs. "It's hot in here, isn't it. Should I turn down the heat?"

Grady didn't comment, but he leaned forward and brushed his mouth over her temple. "You're running away again."

"I'm not running from anything." She bounded to her feet. "Have you had dinner? I didn't and suddenly I'm starved. Do you want anything?" A quick step carried her into the kitchen. Peterkins was scratching at the bedroom door where he'd cuddled up with Angela. A gnawed bone was in front of the door, his interest having waned.

"Come in, boy," she said, welcoming him inside.

"Do you feel the need for your protector?" Grady moved behind her, placing one hand on her shoulder.

"Will you stop," she said, shrugging off his touch and forcing herself to sound carefree. "I don't need a protector. I'm perfectly capable of taking care of myself." She raised her hands in karate fashion. "I'll have you know these hands are registered weapons with the FBI." Afraid her eyes would tell him more than she was willing to reveal, she opened the refrigerator and took out a carton of eggs.

Leaning lazily against the counter, Grady's hands gripped the edge of the tile, his look was deceptively aloof, but he couldn't disguise his interest. "If that's the case, do you always cry when a man kisses you?"

"Of course not," she snapped. "It was all that wine you forced me to drink. Now do you want an omelette or not?"

"If you don't want to talk about it, just say so." A smile crinkled the lines about his eyes, and for a moment Cathy could almost hate him. She couldn't help being curious about what he found that was so amusing.

Hands positioned challengingly on her hips, she spun around. "All right, I don't want to talk about it. Are you happy?"

"Pleased. I appreciate the honestly."

"Wonderful," she murmured. Taking a mixing bowl from the cupboard, she cracked the eggs against the edge with brutal force, emptying them into the bowl. She didn't know how she was going to force herself to eat. The thought of food was enough to make her sick. "I don't ask you personal questions. I…I wouldn't dream of inquiring about your marriage or your relationship with your wife." She waved her hands in the air dramatically, then gripped the fork and furiously whipped the eggs.

Grady watched her movements for a minute. "Those eggs are going to turn into cream if you don't stop whipping them to death."

"It's clear you don't know a thing about cooking, otherwise you'd realize you're supposed to whip the eggs." She took a deep breath. "Besides, how would you feel if I started prying into your life?"

Grady shrugged and then gestured with the open palm of his hand. "My life's an open book."

"Fine," she snapped. "How's your love life? How many times a week did you and your wife make love?" She threw the questions at him in rapid succession, not pausing to breathe between.

"Rotten," he shot right back at her. "And in the end Pam and I didn't."

"Aha!" She pointed an accusing finger at him. "The truth comes out. And just why weren't you and Pam acting like husband and wife?" There was a sense of satisfaction in the way his mouth tensed and the way his jaw worked. His eyes narrowed into deep, dark sapphires that were as cold as Arctic ice.

Wiping her fingers with a hand towel, she smiled at him sweetly. "As the saying goes, if it's too hot in the kitchen…"

"Pam and I didn't make love because she was no longer interested in lovemaking or me for that matter."

Cathy flinched. She hadn't expected him to reveal so much of his life. In all actuality she and Grady were two of a kind. "Is that when you began running?" The minute the words were out Cathy knew she had made another mistake.

"Listen, Cathey." Grady rammed his fists into his

pockets. "I don't know where you come off. I've never run from anything or anyone."

"Then why do you work twenty-hour days, and spend so little time at home your daughter hardly knows you?" Now that she'd started Cathy couldn't make herself stop. Why wouldn't she quit? She couldn't imagine what made her delve into the intimate details of his life as if it was her right to know. She found herself digging at him unmercifully. She had no right to throw stones at him when she was just as vulnerable.

"All right. You want answers, I'll give you answers." His breath came out roughly.

"Grady, no." The words were ripped from her throat. "I'm sorry, I have no right. Can't we agree to leave the past buried? It's obvious we've both been hurt. It won't do either of us any good to dredge up all that pain."

He sighed heavily.

Cathy walked across the kitchen, slipped her arms around his middle and gently laid her head on his chest. His arms circled her and held her close and tight, pressing her to him while he buried his face in her hair. They stood arms around one another in the middle of the kitchen floor until Cathy felt a faint shudder rake through him.

"Did you say something about dinner?" he asked, then firmly kissed the top of her head, breaking the embrace.

Cathy smiled gently to herself. "I did," she said. Not that she really was interested in cooking or eating for that matter. But she put her culinary efforts into creating one of her specialties, a cheese and mushroom omelette.

When everything was ready she carried the two

plates to the table. Grady had surprised her by getting the silverware and folding paper napkins.

Cathy was still eating when he pushed the empty plate aside. "You're a good cook."

"Thank you."

"Pam was a good cook."

Cathy lowered her fork to her plate. She wanted to tell him to stop, she didn't want to be compared to another woman.

"In some ways the two of you are alike."

Cathy shifted uneasily. "Don't."

Grady looked up surprised. "Don't? Don't what?"

"Compare me with someone else."

He leaned back, lifting the front two chair legs off the ground. "I'm doing a poor job of this." His gaze was full of impatience, but she sensed it was directed more at himself than her. "What I'm trying to say is that my marriage was over a long time before Pam died. She hated Alaska Cargo. There wasn't a time I flew out on assignment that she didn't believe I was flying to meet another woman."

"Was she always so insecure?"

"No." He shook his head. "It was only after I started the company. In the beginning she was pleased to be a part of it, but after Angela was born she became depressed, lonely, and unhappy."

"Undoubtedly having her husband around more often would have helped." Her sympathy lay with Grady's wife. She'd grown up witnessing her mother's loneliness. For all the time her own father spent with her during her growing up years Cathy may as well have been fatherless.

Grady chose to ignore the comment. "It was more

than insecurity. Several times I recommended she see a professional who could help her deal with these emotions, but she never would." The front chair legs hit the linoleum with a thud.

"Some women are like that." She attempted to sound sympathetic. Her mother was the Rock of Gibraltar, but there were memories of lying in bed pretending to be asleep while listening to her mother cry. Her father had offered so many promises, ones he never had any intention of keeping.

"Pam would regularly pack her bags and threaten to leave me. She seemed to think that would bring me to my senses."

"Did you stop her?"

"No. Why should I?"

"Why should you?" Cathy flared. "We're talking about your wife, the mother of your child. Pam didn't want to leave. What she wanted was for you to tell her you loved her, you needed her. Clearly the poor woman was desperate for some form of affirmation."

Anger shot into Grady's eyes, and he crossed his arms in front of his chest. "Leaving me, or rather threatening to was all part of Pam's games, of which you know nothing."

"Oh, brother." Cathy stood abruptly and stalked to the other side of the room. "Here it comes, the I-don't-play-games game."

Grady rose and leaned both hands on the table as he glared at her. "You don't know the facts."

"You're right, I don't," she countered. "By your own admission you let your wife pack her suitcase and were so darn proud you couldn't tell her you loved her." She lifted her hand to her face and just as quickly let it drop to her side. "It isn't any wonder Angela is a lost, lonely child."

"Leave my daughter out of this."

"How can you expect a child to feel loved and wanted when her father can't—"

Grady slammed his fist on the table, causing the plates to jump and clatter on the top. "I've had enough of this conversation."

Lifting a hand to remove a strand of hair from her face, Cathy noted that her fingers were shaking and quickly clenched them at her side. "So have I." The words were breathless. Even now she wasn't sure why she'd let this conversation esculate to this point. Grady was right. What went on between him and his wife was none of her affair.

Without another word, Grady left the kitchen, stalked into her bedroom, and returned with a sleeping Angela cradled in his arms.

"I'd like to say the evening has been a pleasant one, but it hasn't," he said, his voice tight and terse. Without so much as glancing backward, he carried the sleeping child with him out of the door.

Her sense of righteousness was quick to dissipate. Cathy bit into her bottom lip regretting her thoughtless words. Lashing out at Grady had ruined a promising relationship. She would never see him again.

Five

Linda Ericson sauntered into the teachers' lounge and sat beside Cathy. "Morning." The greeting was cheerful, followed by a wide smile.

"It's Monday, the first day for parent-teacher conferences. You're not supposed to be so bright and chipper. The least you can do is have a sour look like everyone else," Cathy chastised with a sigh.

Her friend's eager hand covered Cathy's. "I'm too excited to worry about what day of the week it is, or conferences for that matter."

The sparkle in her friend's eye captured Cathy's attention immediately.

"I'm late," Linda whispered.

Cathy didn't move. The dark, gray eyes studied Linda's, afraid she was reading more in the words than her friend intended. "You think you might be pregnant?"

Linda laughed, the sound of her happiness filling the room. "That's what it usually means, doesn't it? Dan says we shouldn't get our hopes up until I see the doctor. I've got an appointment this morning; I wanted to take one of those pregnancy tests. I know they're generally reliable but I prefer to have a doctor to confirm my condition before I say anything to family."

Linda wanted children so badly that Cathy couldn't help but share in her happiness. "Linda, this is great news. You'll be a wonderful mother."

"The doctor appointment's at ten. I'll be back in the office about eleven. All you need to do is stick your head in the door. The expression on my face should be enough to tell you."

Cathy carried her coffee cup into the classroom with her a few minutes later. Linda's hopeful news had boosted her spirits. Since her last meeting with Grady two weeks ago, her disposition had been badly in need of an uplift. Darn Grady Jones anyway, she thought spitefully, placing the mug on her desk. The coffee sloshed over the rim, and with an impatient sigh she took a tissue and mopped up the liquid. What was it about that man that continued to haunt her? For the last two weeks she'd gone about with a feeling of expectancy. Deep down she hoped he would contact her again. He hadn't and she didn't blame him besides she was the one who owned him an apology for delving into his personal affairs. Besides if Grady's pride had prevented him from giving his wife the security she needed, he wasn't likely to reach out to her.

Surprisingly, Cathy discovered she missed him. In their short time they'd been seeing one another she had come to like Grady. Realistically, the break was probably inevitable, and the sooner it came in the budding relationship the better. They were far too different. Her only regret was that they didn't part as friends.

Angela had come up to Cathy's desk the Monday following their argument.

"Yes, Angela." Cathy had smiled gently at the young girl.

Angela's eyes were sad and for a moment Cathy was tempted to pull her into her arms and hug her.

Angela glanced away shyly. "Daddy says I should call you Miss Thompson from now on."

"I think that would be best in the classroom," Cathy agreed. "But outside of school you can call me Cathy if you like."

The child brightened for a moment, then regretfully shook her head. "I don't think I better," she said and returned to her desk, her gaze downcast.

Although Angela had always called Cathy by her formal name, the child began coming into the basic skills classroom for a few minutes after school. Together they would go over her papers. Angela was such a precious child, and it was easy for Cathy to give her the attention and affection the child craved. That shy, toothless grin was enough to endear her to anyone. But even in those few minutes they shared alone, Cathy had always called her Miss Thompson.

Between classes that morning, Cathy hurried to the school office and stuck her head in the door. Linda had her back to her.

"Well?" she questioned expectantly.

Linda turned, her mouth pinched with bitter disappointment. Tears filled the round eyes, and she hurriedly tilted her head upward. "The doctor ran another test… I'm not pregnant," she whispered and held an index finger under each eye, "and this crying has got to stop." She laughed weakly.

"Oh, Linda, I'm so sorry."

"I know." She sniffled. "The doctor explained that because I want a baby so much my mind is working to convince my body that it's pregnant. Sounds crazy doesn't it?"

"Not at all." Cathy yearned for the words that would ease her friend's disappointment but could find none.

"Don't you have a class?" Linda asked smoothly.

"Yes." Her head made a jerking action, reinforcing the fact. "Are you going to be all right?"

Linda nibbled briefly at her bottom lip. "I'll be fine. After all these years I should know better than to hope. It's my own stupid fault. Both Dan and I have reached the place where we're forced to accept that we'll probably never have children. That was Plan A. The time has come to consider Plan B."

"Adoption?"

Linda nodded. "Now scoot before I have seven first and second graders in here looking for their teacher."

Crisp, purpose-filled steps carried Cathy to her classroom.

School was dismissed two hours early the week of parent-teacher conferences. Cathy's part in these meetings was limited. As a basic skills teacher, she usually forwarded the papers and information to the child's regular teacher unless there was a specific problem she needed to discuss with the parent.

Before school that morning she had delivered the information to each of the teachers who had a conference scheduled with one of her students. She noted that Angela Jones's conference had been assigned that afternoon. After all the times she had failed to get Grady to come to the school to discuss Angela and her learning difficulties, Cathy doubted another teacher's success.

She decided to spend the free time changing bulletin boards. Busy pinning the Thanksgiving figures into the cork material, Cathy didn't hear Grady walk into the room.

"Am I interrupting something?" His low-pitched voice seemed to reach out and grab her.

Cathy gasped audibly and stuck her finger with a sharp tack. "Darn." She jumped off the chair and placed her index finger in her mouth, sucking at the blood.

"Sorry, I didn't mean to frighten you." Contrary to what he said he didn't sound the least bit contrite.

"Grady Jones." She breathed his name in surprise.

"I'd like to discuss Angela's progress." His smoldering dark eyes rested on her mouth.

Her heart continued to beat like a jungle drum. "You'll need to see Angela's teacher. I've given my portion of the report to her."

He shook his head. "Mrs. Bondi sent me to you." He stepped into the room and handed her Angela's papers.

"All right." She pulled the chair to her desk and sat down. Grady brought another from across the room and set the chair disturbingly close to her own. "What do you want to know?" she questioned.

"Is the tutor helping?"

Cathy had to bite her tongue to keep from saying Angela's regular teacher could have answered the question just as well. "Yes, she's doing great."

"Not according to these papers." He flipped page after page revealing backward letters and improper figures and consistently bad grades.

Cathy sighed, her gaze connected with Grady's. "You must accept that Angela's improvement will be slow. This work is extremely difficult for her. But she tries very hard, and I can't help but believe that, given time, there will be a vast difference in the quality of her work." The urge to fight for Angela was almost overpowering. "You will continue having her work with the tutor, won't you?"

The mask he wore faded. "If you believe this extra help will help her."

"I do, Grady." She hadn't meant to use his name. To continue in an impersonal discussion would be impossible if she removed the barriers.

"Angela likes you. I've never seen her take to anyone the way she has to you." His voice was low, almost reluctant.

Cathy looked away fearing what her eyes would tell him. "I like Angela very much, too."

"And her father?"

"Angela's father is one of the most interesting men I've ever known." She kept her gaze lowered.

"Interesting." He spat the word out contemptuously. "What about handsome, suave and several other fitting adjectives that freely come to mind?"

An involuntary smile cracked her lips. "I was thinking more along the lines of arrogant, conceited, and high-handed."

"But he's a good kisser," Grady insisted.

Cathy couldn't deny the tenderness she had experienced in his arms the evening they'd returned from Denali. "Yes," she sighed, "he's all that and more."

Grady exhaled as though relieved. "How's Peterkins?" Before she could answer he stood, placing his hands in his pockets, and walked to the window, seemingly interested in the darkening afternoon sky.

"Fine. He's still gnawing on the bone you gave him."

Grady turned around, capturing her gaze. He looked at her hard and long. He was waiting it seemed, waiting for her to bridge the differences between them. His eyes told her, he'd made the effort, done his part and now it was her turn.

"You want me to apologize for the other night, don't you?" she whispered, and by all that was right, she should. She owed him an apology.

"Not really."

She didn't understand her reluctance. She had no right to speak to him the way she had. Standing, Cathy returned to the desk that contained the colored paper letters she'd been pinning on the bulletin board.

"A plain 'I've missed you' would do nicely."

She lifted an orange letter. "All right, I've missed you." That was an understatement. She whirled, tacked the letter into the bulletin board.

"Come flying with me."

The blood drummed through her veins with a long list of excuses why she should refuse. Instead she asked, "When?" She remained facing the wall, unwilling to turn around.

"Now. I've got a short run to do this afternoon, two hours' air time. I'll take you to dinner afterward."

Cathy squeezed her eyes closedd. She'd be crazy to go, she told herself.

"Well?" he questioned smoothly as if he were sure of her response, as if he realized how exhilarating the first flight had been for her.

Her heart was beating with a wild tempo against her rib cage. "I'd like to," she said and turned.

A look of satisfaction showed in Grady's eyes. "Grab your coat," he instructed briskly. "I'm already fifteen minutes late for takeoff."

"But I have to finish—" She stopped midsentence,

letting the rest of what she intended to say fade as Grady grabbed her hand and nearly pulled her off balance.

Laughing, Cathy was able to restrain him long enough for her to retrieve her coat and purse. Together they ran down the school hallway. Linda met her coming outside the office, a shocked look drawing open her mouth.

"What in the world?"

"I'll explain later." Cathy waved, and Grady placed an arm around her waist, helping her steps to meet his faster paced ones.

Before Cathy had a chance to catch her breath normally again she was strapped in the passenger side of the cockpit as Grady reviewed the preflight checklist.

Soon they were taxiing on the runway, waiting for confirmation from the air traffic controller. The okay came in a muffled voice Cathy couldn't hope to understand.

In response, Grady moved the throttle forward. Cathy closed her eyes at the sudden surge of power. The engines whirled, and within minutes the airplane was ascending into the dark, cloud-filled sky.

Her hand clutched the cushion while gusts of wind buffeted the small aircraft.

Grady's hand touched her forearm. "You can open your eyes now."

She released a long breath and relaxed. They were climbing rapidly through a layer of thick clouds. Below the world was obliterated by what looked like a mass of marshmallow topping and above a thin layer of gray clouds.

"How are you supposed to see to fly this thing?"

"I don't," Grady said with a mischievous grin.

"This isn't the time to tease, Grady Jones. If you wish to see a perfectly sane woman panic at ten thousand feet, just continue."

"Seventeen thousand," he corrected.

Her fingers gripped both sides of the safety strap, but she decided not to give him the satisfaction of unsettling her. "It looks like it might snow." She changed the subject deliberately, looking at the sky around her.

"Say a prayer it doesn't."

"Grady." She hissed his name. "If you don't stop, I'll never fly with you again."

His roguish smile was directed at her. Cathy was powerless to resist his charm or appeal and when his hand moved to cover hers, she turned and smiled back at him.

"Your eyes are about the same color as these clouds." He lifted her fingers to his mouth and lightly brushed his lips over her knuckles. "And when you're angry. Watch out! I swear they harden into the color of burnished silver."

No one had ever spoken to her like that, and Cathy found herself struggling for a witty comeback. "Oh."

"For two weeks I've been flying in a sky that seemed to be filled with you watching me from all sides."

"Oh." She looked away, unsure how best to respond.

"Is that all you can say?"

"Well, for heaven's sake, what do you want me to say?"

He sighed. "Well for starters you can admit you've dreamed of me every night too."

"I did," she inserted. "But they were nightmares."

Unexpectedly the plane took a sudden plunge downward. Grady gripped the control, and Cathy's heart leapt wildly to her throat.

"I lied," she whispered through the fear. "They were wonderful dreams, just don't do that again."

Grady's laughter was rich and full. "I didn't do anything. We hit an air pocket, that's all."

"Oh."

"Are we back to those again?"

Two and a half hours later they landed at Fairbanks Airport. Ray was in the hangar waiting for them. Rubbing her bare hands together to keep her fingers from stiffening with the cold, Cathy hurried into Grady's office. Ray followed her in and handed her a cup of coffee.

Cathy nearly choked on the bitter-tasting fluid.

Watching her expression, Grady looped an arm across her shoulder. "One of these days, you're going to kill someone with that stuff you pass off as coffee."

Ray mumbled something unintelligible under his breath. "There are a couple of phone messages on your desk."

"Thanks, Ray." Cathy smiled and caught his returning wink.

Grady's hand was linked with Cathy's. He pulled her into his office and sharply closed the door with his foot. The minute the door shut, he backed her against the wooden frame.

"I've been waiting two weeks for this." The whisper was a husky caress as his hands framed her face. Slowly, almost as if he was waiting for her to protest, he lowered his mouth to hers. When their lips finally met, the kiss was devastating. It felt as if his kiss was a wildfire shooting through her blood, and her bones seemed to liquify. She eased her arms around his neck, molding herself against him.

Grady dragged his mouth from hers, burying it in her neck, spreading tiny kisses at the delicate hollow of her throat. The door was pressing into her back, offering reality to a world that suddenly seemed to have taken a tailspin. Unexpectedly Cathy felt the tears well in her eyes and the need to cry again. This kiss was completely unlike that of the night in front of her fireplace. The wine and his gentleness had produced those tears. Now it was the realization that Grady could make her body respond to him, but not her heart.

Grady seemed to sense her withdrawal. He raised his head, his gaze holding hers. A thumb wiped a lone tear from her cheek. Tenderly he kissed the spot where the moisture had appeared.

"Someday," he whispered, "I'll be able to kiss you and you won't need to cry." His mouth lowered to hers again, his lips, his hands arousing her and playing havoc with her senses.

After dinner, Grady drove her to the school to pick up her car, then followed her to the house. Parking her vehicle inside the garage, Cathy lowered the door, closing it from the outside. Grady had parked at the curb. She sauntered over to his car and opened the passenger door.

"Do you want to come in for coffee?"

Grady looked over to her and smiled, his look absent, preoccupied. "All right."

"Remember, Peterkins is my protector," she said in a teasing tone.

It didn't take long to brew two cups of coffee. Grady

sat at the kitchen table, his eyes following her movements around the compact kitchen. After barking and racing around the house at the sight of his mistress, Peterkins was sleeping on the throw rug in front of the refrigerator.

"I still find it unbelievable that you put an ad in the personal column," she commented as she set the steaming cups on the table. If a woman could have guessed that someone as good-looking and compelling as Grady would place an ad in the paper, every woman in Fairbanks would be answering the personals.

"It seemed the quickest way," Grady said and blew into the black liquid before taking the first sip.

"The quickest way to do what?" she asked curiously.

"To find a wife."

Her cup made a sharp clang against the saucer. "A what?" she gasped.

"A wife for me, a mother for Angela," he replied calmly. "I just don't have the time for the singles scene. An ad in the paper seemed the most direct route."

"Oh." She gulped on a swallow.

"We're back to those, are we?" Laughter fanned out lines about his eyes. "Don't look so shocked. Why else does someone advertise in the personals?"

Cathy waved her hand, slicing the air. "Companionship, seeking new friends, adventure. I don't know."

"Now that it's out, will you?"

"Will I what?"

"Marry me?"

"Grady!" She was so shocked she could barely breathe. "I hardly know you."

"Go ahead, ask me anything you want to know."

"What size shoe do you wear?"

"Ten and a half."

Standing, she walked across the room. "I can't believe we're having this conversation."

"I also eat cornflakes every night about midnight and leave my dirty clothes lying on the bathroom floor."

"Stop!" The whole thing was so ludicrous she couldn't help giggling. "You're crazy."

"I'm serious."

"Grady, please, be reasonable."

"I am. My housekeeper is retiring, Angela is in desperate need of a mother's influence. I've had three housekeepers in three years. The kid needs someone who isn't going to move in and out of her life every few months."

"What about love? I don't love you, and you certainly don't love me."

Grady exhaled a heavy breath and pushed the hair off his forehead. "I knew this was going to come up sooner or later. You're looking for the magic words?"

"No," she answered honestly. "I'd be shocked if I heard them. It just seems that a marriage between a man and a woman should be built on something stronger than a little girl's need for a mother."

"I find you desirable, Cathy. We'd have a good life."

"A marriage needs more than mutual attraction," she said and breathed in deeply.

"I agree. I'm attracted to you and from your response to my kisses, I'd say the attration is mutual."

Unable to claim otherwise she flattened a hand against her breast. "Why me?" Grady was handsome enough to attract any woman.

"Several reasons." His voice suggested that his reasoning was purely academic, that feelings, emotions didn't really play a part in his decision. "The first and most important one is that Angela thinks you're wonderful."

"Don't forget Peterkins. She's pretty crazy about him, too."

"Oh, yes, let's not forget the dog. But more than that, you're a sensible woman. Neither one of us is a teenager lost in throes of hormones and passion. You've been hurt, I've been hurt and we're both looking to build a new life. I like you. In fact I like you very much."

"I like you too. But marriage?" She shook her head, rejecting the idea.

"I don't expect an answer tonight."

"That's encouraging," she said on a dry note.

"Think it over and give me a call next week sometime. You have my number don't you?"

Arms cradling her waist, Cathy nodded. She watched as Grady emptied his mug. He looked tired. Lines of fatigue were penciled about his mouth and his eyes. He stood and placed the mug in the sink. Peterkins raised his head, watching Grady's movements.

"You're exhausted."

"I must be." He ran a weary hand over his face. "I decided I'd rather do without a kiss than fight that mutt."

Cathy smiled. "Peterkins is no mutt." Lifting her fingertip to her mouth she blew him a kiss. "That'll have to hold you."

He lifted his gaze, his eyes seeking hers. "I'll be waiting."

She let him out, locking the door and leaning against it for support after he'd left. "The man's crazy," she told Peterkins. "And I'd be even crazier to consider marrying him."

The dog followed her into the bedroom, jumping on the bed and snuggling into a tight ball at the foot of the mattress while she undressed, removed her makeup and brushed her hair. "It's a stupid idea for everyone concerned."

Peterkins lifted his head, cocking it at an inquiring angle. Cathy stretched out an arm, pointing a finger toward the front door. "You wouldn't believe what he just suggested." Slipping the long flannel gown over her head, she threw back the covers and climbed between the sheets. After reading for a while, she turned out the light. But it was a long time before she went to sleep.

Linda was waiting for Cathy at school the next morning. "When did you start seeing Grady Jones again?" she asked the minute Cathy sat down in the teachers' lounge.

"A while ago," she answered cryptically. "How'd you know I was with Grady?"

"Someone told me he was the best-looking man in Fairbanks. One peek yesterday and I knew it had to be him. You've been holding out on me, Cathy Thompson."

"No, I'm not," she denied. "And don't you dare tell him he's good-looking, his head's too big as it is." Cathy pushed the coffee aside, its taste bitter and unsatisfying. She hadn't slept well and she didn't need until next week to make her decision. It was already made. It would be crazy to marry Grady, particularly for the reasons he gave. The proposal had to be the most unromantic offer she'd ever heard. It bordered on insulting.

"How can you go out with someone that handsome and keep from drooling?" Linda questioned.

Rising impatiently to her feet, Cathy rubbed her arms

as a sudden chill came over her. “In Grady’s case, it’s easy.”

Linda’s hand stopped her. “Before you go to class I want to tell you something.” She lowered her gaze. “Dan and I are contacting an adoption agency this week. After yesterday’s disappointment we’ve decided we can’t go on like this.”

Cathy witnessed a renewed glow of happy anticipation sparkle in her friend’s eyes. “Is this what you want?”

“Oh, yes,” Linda breathed. “I’ve wanted to do this all year. It’s been Dan who’s been dragging his feet.”

Squeezing Linda’s hand, Cathy offered an encouraging smile. “Put me down as a reference if it’ll help.”

During her lunch hour Cathy tried to phone Grady. No need to keep him waiting since she’d made up her mind. As her finger punched out the number she couldn’t help smiling. There wasn’t anyone more arrogant in the world than Grady Jones to believe a woman would accept a marriage proposal on his terms.

“Alaska Cargo.” A gruff, impatient voice came over the line.

“Good afternoon, Ray. This is Cathy Thompson. Can I talk to Grady?”

The gruff voice softened perceptibly. “He’s in the air, miss, flying some hunters to camp. He’ll be back this evening. Want me to tell him you called?”

“Please.” Disconnecting the call, she released a slow breath. The sooner this whole business was over, the better she’d feel. Unfortunately Grady would be out of her life forever. At least she wasn’t naive enough to believe he would waste time dating her. Once he’d received her answer, he'd move on to the next most likely candidate. Poor girl, whoever she might be.

Because she hadn't gotten her mail the day before, Cathy swung by the post office on her way home from school. An accumulation of bills greeted her, and she threw them on the seat next to her as she drove home. Not until she was inside the house did she notice the letter.

One look at the handwriting told her the letter was from Steve. For a moment it was as if someone had slammed a fist into her stomach. She couldn't breathe, she couldn't swallow, even standing became impossible. A hand reached out and gripped the back of the kitchen chair as the letter fell from her hand onto the table top.

Peterkins barked expectantly, demanding attention, and still Cathy couldn't move.

"It's from Steve," she said, her voice soft, almost choking. "You remember Steve, don't you, Peterkins?"

The spaniel gave her a funny look, jumping up on his hind paws, seeking the affection she usually offered when she walked in the door.

Acting out of habit, she leaned down and ruffled the long black ears. Straightening, she blindly hung her coat in the bedroom and slipped off her shoes, replacing them with fuzzy slippers.

The letter seemed to radiate heat, drawing her back into the kitchen. Like a moth drawn irresistibly to a flame, she was attracted to the letter. Ten months had passed since their argument, seven since the wedding. What could he possibly have to say to her now? He had to know that she was just beginning to build a new life for herself. Surely he knew she was beginning to feel again.

The phone rang, jolting her into reality. Her attention swiveled to the kitchen wall, and she mentally shook herself before lifting the receiver.

"Hello."

"Cathy, is that you? This is MaryAnne."

"MaryAnne," she repeated, stunned. "Is everything all right?"

Her sister's laugh echoed over a line that linked several thousand miles. "Everything's wonderful. I've got some fantastic news," she said and took a deep breath. "News so good, I couldn't wait for a letter. Mom and I decided to phone. Guess what. No—" she laughed again "—don't guess. You're going to be an aunt. Steve and I are going to have a baby."

"A baby." All these months Cathy had dreaded the thought her sister would become pregnant. Steve and her sister would be having a child together. The pain was suddenly so sharp she could barely breathe.

"I haven't even told Steve yet. Mom went to the doctor with me this morning, and we decided to phone you. I'm at Mom's now."

"Congratulations." Somehow the word made it past the lump in her throat.

A short silence followed. "Are you all right, sis? You don't sound right."

"I have a cold," she lied. "A rotten cold. Let me talk to Mom."

By some miracle she made it through the remainder of the conversation. Her mother was ecstatic with the news of her first grandchild, but her voice carried a note of warning. If Cathy hadn't been so upset she might have been able to decipher the unspoken message.

Frozen by the impact of the phone call, Cathy stood

for several minutes unable to turn around and face the letter waiting for her on the table.

Peterkins jumped into her lap when she sat at the table. Long minutes passed before she lifted the letter and gently tore open the envelope.

At the salutation, Cathy squeezed her eyes shut. The letter began, "My Darling."

A huge sob broke from her and she covered her mouth to stiffle it. How could she be *his* darling when he was married to her sister? Cathy forced herself to continue reading. Ten months, almost a year. It had taken him that long to admit he had been wrong. As she continued to read he said everything Cathy had longed to hear…before he married her sister. Steve admitted he'd married MaryAnne out of spite. Like Cathy he had been caught in the whirlpool of stubborn pride, unable to free himself. A thousand times before the wedding he had thought she would put a stop to everything. When she didn't, he believed she must not truly love him. Now he knew differently. She had to love him because he loved her so desperately.

Cathy could barely see to read further. Tears blurred her vision, streaming down her face as she continued to cup her mouth as a sense of unreality settled over her.

It wasn't too late, he went on to say. He couldn't continue to live with MaryAnne when he loved Cathy. If she wouldn't come to him, he would fly to Alaska and get her. Somehow he'd make things right with MaryAnne.

A bitter anger welled deep within her. How could she possibly feel anything but contempt for a man like Steve? How could she have been so blind? She took the letter, crumpled it in a tight ball, and hurled it across the room. The force of the action seemed to drain her of energy, and she slumped her shoulders forward and wept. She should hate Steve, he was contemptible. Yet without question, she realized she didn't.

The phone rang a second time, and Cathy blew her nose before answering.

"Hello."

"It's Grady." He sounded stiff, almost formal. "I take it you've made a decision."

"Yes." The one word trembled from her and she hardly recognized her own voice. Her decision had been made. But in the course of a few minutes everything had changed. Nothing was as it had been. Inhaling sharply, she squared her shoulders, straightened and whispered, "I've decided to accept your proposal."

Six

What had she done? Cathy stared at the phone in a dreamlike trance. This couldn't be happening to her. This horrible, stomach-wrenching knot was the same feeling she'd experienced during Steve and MaryAnne's wedding. Now she had agreed to marry Grady. A man married to his company. A man who openly admitted he didn't love her but needed a mother for his child.

The choice had been made for her. No matter how much Steve wanted her back. It was too late. What was done was done. Yet despite it all, she couldn't stop loving him. If he were to come to Alaska as he claimed, she wouldn't be able to resist him. Not when her whole being was crying out to be his. In taking him back, she would destroy her sister, and her relationship with her family. It was too late for her and Steve. And now there was a baby in the mix. The situation was impossible.

She closed her eyes to block the pain. The enormity of her decision was only beginning to hit her. With a sense of urgency she took a long bath, scrubbing her skin with unnecessary harshness as if to remove every trace of Steve from her life.

Later she took his letter and placed it in the fireplace, setting it aflame with a match, desperately hoping the action would forever burn him from her life.

Grady came to her house late that night. He had showered, shaved, and changed clothes. From beneath his heavy overcoat he produced a bottle of champagne.

Cathy greeted him with a weak smile, but her mouth trembled with the effort. If Grady noticed the puffy, red eyes or the deathlike expression, he said nothing.

"First things first." He set the bottle aside, pulled her into his arms, and kissed her soundly.

Cathy felt like a rag doll with no will, with no desire to accept or refuse Grady's advance. Her arms hung lifelessly at her side.

When Peterkins growled and nipped at Grady's pant leg, Cathy felt Grady pull away and bury his face in her neck. Simultaneously he nudged the dog away with his foot.

Raising his head, Grady drew in a ragged breath. Cathy could feel his lips move against the top of her head as he issued a half-smothered oath. "We're going to have to do something with this mutt. Sooner or later he's going to have to accept that I'm going to touch you, and as often as I like."

Cathy nodded and broke the embrace. A hand on the spaniel's collar, she placed him in her bedroom and closed the door.

"I'm not sure that was the wisest place to put him," Grady said with a chuckle. "Now if you want to make yourself useful, bring out two glasses. I'll light a fire and we can enjoy the champagne in here."

Cathy hesitated. She could see no reason to celebrate, not when her life, her hope of ever finding happiness, felt as it was gone forever. The corners of her mouth drooped as she struggled within herself. Grady deserved better. At least he had been honest with her. Entering the kitchen, she took down two wineglasses and brought them in to Grady.

Forcing herself to smile, she settled beside him on the carpet. Peterkins was scratching against the bedroom door, wanting out, but Cathy ignored his repeated pleas.

With their backs supported by the sofa, knees raised, Grady opened the champagne. The plastic top made an exploding noise as the foaming liquid escaped from the spout of the long green bottle. Laughing, Grady poured the sparkling drink into the glasses, handing Cathy the first one.

The laughter drained from his eyes as his look met hers. He held up his glass to propose a toast. "To many happy years." His voice was low and serious.

Cathy touched her glass to his. "To many years." Purposely she deleted one word. At the moment it seemed impossible that she would ever be happy again.

Together they took the first sip. The liquid felt cool and soothing against a parched, raw throat, and Cathy eagerly returned the glass to her lips.

Grady removed the champagne from her hand, setting it aside. An instant later his mouth covered hers. Cathy was better able to respond, placing both hands against his chest. Grady's heartbeat felt strong and loud against her palms.

The moment was broken when the fire crackled. She jerked at the unexpected interruption. His hands tangled her hair, pressing her face into his sweater. The warmth, the comfort of his embrace was so potent that she slowly lowered her eyelids. Grady would never replace Steve, but he was gentle. She could count on him being tender. And never had there been a time when she needed it more.

After a second glass of champagne, Cathy's smile was less stiff, her response more relaxed. Grady's kisses were sweet and tender, but he seemed to be restraining himself from deepening his desire.

"Shall we set the date?" he asked her, his arm cocked beneath his head as he stretched out on the carpet.

"Any time you say." She took another large gulp of her drink, needing the fortification.

"Thanksgiving weekend?"

So soon! her mind screamed in alarm. "Sure." She threw her head back, ruffling the mass of long brown curls. "Why not?" Immediately her mind tossed out several logical reasons why not. Cathy chose to ignore them.

Grady looked pleased. "The wedding will have to be small. You don't mind do you?"

"No." She preferred a minimal amount of fuss. "Linda can be my witness, and Angela the flower girl."

Grady shifted his position, sitting upright. "I don't know that I'll be able to take the time for a honeymoon." His eyes seemed to bore into hers.

"I have to go back to school on Monday anyway." Shrugging her shoulders she looked away. *Get used to it now,* she told herself. Every important family function, Christmas, Angela's birthday, their anniversary would all come second behind Alaska Cargo. In the long run, it might even work out better that way.

They emptied the bottle, and Cathy suddenly giggled. "Did I tell you the good news?" Not waiting for his answer, she let the words rush out on a hiccupping sob.

"I'm going to be an aunt. My sister… My little sister, is going to have a baby." The whole living room began to sway, and she reached out to brace herself.

Kissing the tip of her nose, Grady placed a hand on each of her soft shoulders. "You're drunk, Cathy Thompson."

"I'm not…no way," she denied. "But I will be soon."

Her head was throbbing when she woke the next morning. Sitting up, she glanced around and pressed massaging fingers to her temples. The events of the past night were cloudy and unclear.

School. She was supposed to be at school. In an attempt to untangle herself from the sheet and blankets, her head pounded all the harder. Finally she gave up the effort and fell back against the pillows.

What had happened last night? She couldn't remember undressing. When had Grady left? Dear heaven, he hadn't spent the night, had he? Fearfully she bolted up again, her eyes flew around her searching for evidence. Thank goodness, no.

Without making excuses, she phoned the school and reported that she wouldn't be coming in. Later Linda called to check on her and see if there was anything she could do. Cathy assured her there was nothing. There was nothing anyone could do anymore. Her fate had been cast.

Aspirin dulled the throbbing pain in her head, yet she remained in her housecoat, sitting with Peterkins on her lap in a cold living room. There were no paths her thoughts could travel that hadn't been maneuvered a dozen times or more. She felt numb, lifeless.

The doorbell chimed before noon.

"Who is it?" she asked, surprised at how weak her voice sounded. She didn't open the door.

"Grady," the male voice boomed, and Cathy pressed her fingers to her temples at the rush of pain.

"Let me in."

Releasing a long sigh, Cathy turned the lock and pulled open the door.

"You okay?" His brow was furrowed with concern as he came into the house. He was dressed in his work clothes. "You look terrible. I called the school and they said you phoned in sick today. I knew I shouldn't have left you last night."

"I'm fine." She ran her fingers through limp, uncombed hair.

"Am I suppose to ignore the large birds circling your house?" he demanded.

Cathy winced at the sound of his raised voice. "The what?"

Impatiently, Grady shook his head. "Never mind. You should be in bed." His rough, male hand cupped her elbow, directing her toward the bedroom.

"Grady," she hissed. "Let go of me. I'm fine. No thanks to you and several rather large glasses of champagne. I've got a hangover, is all." Placing the blame on him sounded so logical at that moment.

For a second he looked stunned. "My fault! You're the one who emptied her glass and mine and then insisted we open another bottle. I knew this was going to happen. I should have put an end to it long before I did."

Embarrassed, she looked away. "And…and just how did it end?"

Grady's laugh was filled with genuine amusement

as he brought her into his embrace. "Wouldn't you like to know."

Bracing her hands against his shoulders she struggled for release. "You're impossible."

"And you're very beautiful, especially with your clothes off."

Immediately her cheeks flamed crimson. "You're no gentleman, Grady Jones."

"I'm more of a gentleman than you realize," he laughed. "Now get dressed. If you aren't feeling all that bad let's go get the blood tests and wedding license taken care of."

"How can you act so calm?" Linda questioned.

Cathy looked across the dining room table complete with Thanksgiving turkey and all the trimmings. "What do you mean?" she answered with a question of her own.

Linda pushed herself away from the table. "The wedding's in two days, your mother's flying in tomorrow night, and you're as cool as a cucumber."

"It'll probably hit her all at once," Grady said, briefly flickering a look to Linda.

"More than likely at the altar," Cathy added, noting not for the first time the way Linda studied her.

The subject came up again while they were doing the dishes. "I may be an old married lady," Linda began, "but it seems you and Grady are both acting extraordinarily calm. You both appear to look upon this wedding more like a dinner party than a lifetime commitment."

"Oh, honestly, Linda," she said and rubbed the pan she was drying with more energy than necessary. "Both of us are beyond the age when we stare breathlessly into one another's eyes and sigh with deep longing." She placed a hand over her heart and breathed in a giant mocking breath.

Rubbing off the sudsy water, Linda's hand sliced the air with the cutting motion. "It's not only that. No one buys a wedding dress the way you did."

Again Cathy negated her friend's concern with a shake of her head. "I just happen to know what I like, that's all," she replied somewhat defensively.

"I shopped for weeks for my wedding dress. You walked into one store, picked a dress off the rack, tried it on, and bought it."

"As I said, I know what I like."

Linda tilted her head at a disbelieving angle. "Whatever you say." She paused, and took in a breath before changing the subject. "I'm pleased that Dan and Grady get along so well."

Linda's gaze followed hers into the family room, where Grady and Dan were both intent over a game of chess. Angela was sitting on the carpet in front of the television watching a Thanksgiving cartoon special. She noticed the way Linda's gaze studied the child.

"Have you heard anything from the adoption agency?" Cathy asked.

Immediately a warmth glowed in her friend's expression. "Yes. Both Dan and I are surprised at how fast everything is progressing. We went into the idea of adopting thinking we'd spend several years on a waiting list."

"Won't you?" Everything Cathy had heard about adopting indicated as much.

"Only if we're interested in a Caucasian newborn. The agency has plenty of children needing a family now.

Dan and I decided we were willing to make a home for any child. There's even a possibility of our having a preschooler after the first of the year."

"Oh, Linda, that's wonderful news." Again Cathy's gaze drifted to Angela. She almost had to bite her tongue from telling her friend that she was marrying Grady for almost the identical reason. To give Angela a real home. Her eyes became tender as she studied the little girl. Angela was well named, her look trusting, almost angelic. More and more she was opening up around Cathy, bouncing into her classroom after school, beaming her a smile as she slipped her hand in Cathy's.

Linda asked her something, and Cathy turned. As she did, her gaze skidded across the diamond engagement ring Grady had given her. Cathy had gasped when he unceremoniously slipped it on her finger. It was a magnificent piece of jewelry interweaving gold and diamonds. At first it had weighted her hand, but now she was accustomed to the feel of it, often toying with it, especially when she was nervous. Like the first time they visited the minister who'd insisted on a counseling session before the wedding. Cathy could have sworn the man of God knew this was no love match. Both she and Grady had answered his questions as honestly as humanly possible. For a moment she had been half afraid Pastor Wilkens would refuse to marry them.

"Did you want pumpkin or pecan?" Linda repeated the question, gently touching Cathy's sleeve.

"Oh, sorry." She looked up, startled. "Pumpkin, I guess. Want me to check with the guys?"

"Go ahead. We've finished these dishes. It's time to dirty more."

Grady's face was knit in concentration as he studied

the chessboard. Cathy sat on the arm of the chair, placing a hand across his back, waiting until he had made his move before speaking.

"Do you want pie?"

He looked up to her, his features softening as their eyes met. "No," he said and glanced abruptly at his watch. "In fact I think it's about time we left."

A protest rose automatically, but Cathy agreed. She was lucky to have spent this much of the holiday with Grady. She knew there were any number of things that needed to be done before the wedding.

They made their farewells. Cathy promised to have Dan and Linda over for a meal right after she and Grady were married. The minute the words were out, she realized she'd said the wrong thing. Newlyweds were supposed to want privacy.

Angela fell asleep in the car on the way home.

"Grady." Cathy braved the unpleasant subject a few minutes later. "I know this is difficult, but we're going to have to look like we're more in love."

"What?" Grady choked, his eyes momentarily leaving the road.

Flustered, Cathy looked away. "Well, we're going to be married in a couple of days. My mother is going to take one look at us and—"

"And what?" Grady demanded.

Crossing her arms, Cathy exhaled. "You're not making this any easier."

"I'll behave." His hand squeezed hers, and their fingers locked.

Cathy smiled. She did enjoy Grady's company. He could be warm and teasing and a lot of fun. "I don't want my mother to worry about me once she returns to Wichita."

"I'll fawn on your every word," Grady promised, his lips brushing her gloves as he chuckled.

Cathy couldn't prevent a smile. She couldn't imagine Grady being any different from what he was. Sometimes she was curious about his relationship with his first wife, but the questions remained unasked. The curiosity centered more around what Grady would be like when he deeply cared for something other than Alaska Cargo. "Be natural about it for heaven's sake," she pleaded.

"I will, don't worry."

Grady couldn't seem to relax, Cathy noticed.

"Relax, will you?" Her hand reached for his. The airport was bustling with activity. The Thanksgiving rush of travelers filled the small airport.

Grady's mouth twitched in a series of undecipherable expressions. "What are you doing?" she asked with an exaggerated breath.

"I'm practicing looking like I'm in love."

Cathy burst out laughing. "You're hopeless, you know that?"

His eyes smiled into hers. "This isn't easy, meeting your mother and all. Mothers-in-law and I don't have a fantastic track record."

It was the first time Grady had mentioned Pam's mother. "You don't need to worry," she assured him, "you'll like my mother. We're a lot alike." More than Grady knew. They both had chosen the same kind of men to marry.

Seeing a plane approach from the runway below,

Cathy stood. "That's Mom's flight now, and she's right on time." Her heart beat excitedly as she placed her hand in the crook of Grady's arm.

Grady straightened, brushing imaginary lint from his jacket. "How do I look?"

"A little rough around the edges, but you'll do."

"I better," he murmured in a low growl.

Seeing her mother enter the baggage claim area, Cathy had to fight the urge to wave. Her mother was unlikely to see her standing where she was, so she stood on tiptoes raising her hand in greeting.

Her mother paused, and looked over her shoulder. Cathy felt the blood rush out of her face, and for a crazy moment she thought she might faint. Following Paula Thompson into the baggage claim area were Steve and MaryAnne.

Seven

"Cathy." Paula Thompson hugged her daughter tightly, patting her back. "You look marvelous."

MaryAnne's arms circled her sister next, holding her as if it had been years instead of months since Cathy had moved to Alaska. Patting her flat stomach, she asked with a good-natured laugh, "Can you tell I'm pregnant?"

"Of course." By some miracle Cathy managed to keep her voice level.

Steve moved forward, expecting the same greeting she had given her mother and sister. Removing herself from his reach, she turned and looped an arm into Grady's. "Mom, MaryAnne, Steve, this is Grady Jones, my soon-to-be husband." She managed to avoid eye contact with Steve, but a feeling of cold dread instantly filled her. She couldn't imagine what Steve would want to attend the wedding. What did he hope to accomplish?

Formal greetings were exchanged between her family and Grady. Although her mother's expression was friendly, Cathy was quick to note the worry in the slightly narrowed blue eyes. Her mother knew her best of all, and it would take more than reassuring words to fool this woman.

"I understand you own your own business?" her mother asked Grady.

Undoubtedly her mother had been mulling over the question ever since Cathy had phoned and told her about the wedding. Cathy understood her mother's concern. Paula didn't want her daughter to repeat the mistakes she had made.

"Listen," Cathy interrupted, "let's go to the house and have coffee. I know Angela is anxious to meet everyone." The remainder of her things had been moved into Grady's house earlier in the day. With the wedding scheduled for noon, it made more sense to spend the night in a hotel with her mother than to pay rent on an empty house.

"You should have brought Angela with you," her mother admonished gently. "I think I'm fortunate to receive a built-in granddaughter," she added.

"She's a bit shy," Cathy explained, looking to Grady. "We both felt she'd be more comfortable meeting you in familiar surroundings."

Cathy gave her mother's waist a tiny squeeze, silently expressing her appreciation for her easy acceptance of the little girl.

As they retrieved their luggage, Grady leaned over and whispered, "You can let go of my arm now. I think the circulation's been cut off."

"Oh, sorry," she murmured and relaxed her hold.

"Is everything okay?" he questioned, his voice laced with concern. "You look pale all of a sudden. You're not getting those prewedding jitters are you?"

"Of course." She tried to laugh it off. "Every woman does."

She felt Grady's piercing gaze study her but had no words of reassurance to offer him.

The minute Steve walked in the door Peterkins went wild. Barking excitedly, he raced around the room in several wide loops, leaping from the couch to the chair and back down to the carpet before vaulting into Steve's waiting arms.

Crouched to the floor, Steve gave the spaniel his full attention. "You remember me, do you, boy?" Ruffling the long, black ears, he accepted as his due Peterkins's adoration.

Uncomfortably aware of Grady's eyes following her, Cathy ignored the unspoken questions he seemed to be hurling at her.

"I get quite a different reception from Cathy's dog," Grady commented after Peterkins had calmed down. Cathy wasn't fooled by the veiled interest.

"Peterkins and I go way back, don't we, boy?" Steve directed his attention to the dog before he turned and smiled boldly at Cathy.

Her legs turned to mush, and she sat with her mother, Angela positioned between them. She wanted to shout at Steve to leave her alone. Surely he understood how difficult this was for her. She couldn't help wonder if he'd always been so selfish and uncaring. All along she'd feared how she'd feel when she saw Steve again. Now that he was here, in the same room, and they were separated by only a few feet, she felt embarrassed, and terribly uneasy.

Her peripheral vision caught a glimpse of a muscle

which jerked in Grady's jaw as he stood and sauntered to the fireplace. He placed another log on the already roaring fire.

"I gave Cathy the dog," Steve explained.

"That was a long time ago," she qualified, wanting to reassure her husband-to-be.

"Not that long ago," Steve contradicted. He was toying with her, in a cat and mouse game. She wanted to scream at him to stop. It was almost as if Steve wanted to make her as uncomfortable as possible, punish her for marrying Grady, hurt her further.

Her mother was busy making friends with Angela. She sat beside the little girl, an arm draped over the thin shoulders, and told her bits and pieces of information about Kansas. MaryAnne, feeling tired, had gone to rest in the spare bedroom for a few minutes.

Apart from a few whispers coming from Angela and Paula Thompson, the room seemed to crackle with a tension.

Grady came to stand behind Cathy, and he placed his hands on her shoulders, staking claim to his ownership. Cathy bit into her quivering lip, praying Steve would accept the unspoken message.

In that instant he caught her eyes. A lazy, knowing grin deepened the lines at the side of his mouth. Steve knew. He knew how confused she was and planned to use her own feelings against her.

Cathy closed her eyes to the rush of bitterness and sucked in a stabbing breath. With a determined effort she forced herself to lift her hand and place it on top of Grady's. Her eyes were imploring Steve to accept her decision. But one glance at the anger coming from him made Cathy realize he would ignore her silent plea.

The same way he had the day of his and MaryAnne's wedding.

Making an excuse to check on her sister, Cathy stood and moved slowly down the hallway to the bedroom. As quietly as possible she cracked the door, not wanting to disturb her sister unnecessarily.

"Is that you, Steve?" The weak voice came from across the room.

"No, it's Cathy. I didn't mean to wake you. Go ahead and rest." Just as quietly she moved to close the door.

"Don't go." MaryAnne sat up in bed and motioned for Cathy to join her. Raising her arms high above her head she stretched and released a wide yawn. "It's crazy how tired I get." She placed a protective hand on her abdomen, gently patting at the slight roundness there. "This little one seems to think I should spend my life sleeping. Mom said it was the same with her each time she was pregnant."

Cathy sat on the end of the bed. "You're happy about this baby, aren't you?"

"Oh, yes," she said and breathed in fervently. Tears shimmered in the deep gray eyes, and a delicate finger wiped them away. "Look at me," she said with a shaky laugh. "I cry so easy. Just wait until you're pregnant, Cath. I'm so emotional lately. I don't know how Steve puts up with me."

"Has he been understanding?"

MaryAnne nodded eagerly. "I can't tell you how great he's been about everything. Are you and Grady planning on a family?"

The question took Cathy by surprise. She didn't know; they'd never discussed having a child. "Not right away." Her fingers nervously traced the flower pattern of the bedspread. "We'll wait a while."

"Don't wait too long," MaryAnne advised solemnly. "I don't think a man can love you any more than when you're carrying his child."

Was it possible that Steve genuinely loved her sister? Truly love her? Perhaps his feelings had changed once he realized MaryAnne was pregnant. He hadn't known about the baby when he wrote the letter. The letter. A hundred times she'd regretted burning it. She would never have let Steve back into her life, but she could have had the confirmation of his love for her. In her agony she had destroyed that.

Silently he entered the room behind her, and for a second Cathy thought her mind had conjured up his image. Gently she shook her head to force herself back in to reality. Desperately she wanted to hate him as he walked to his wife's side. Despite everything she couldn't make herself stop loving him. Before she betrayed herself, Cathy made an excuse and left.

Her mother met her outside the bedroom door. "I'm going to freshen up a bit. Grady said something about all of us having dinner, and I want to redo my makeup."

"I'll see if Angela needs anything," Cathy said, avoiding looking directly at her mother.

"Cathy." A hand on her sleeve stopped her. "I like Grady, but I don't mind telling you I've been worried about you."

Her pulse rate soared to double time. Had her mother guessed her true feelings for Grady. "Why?" She strived to sound incredulous as she walked into the bathroom with her mother and sat on the toilet seat while her mother washed her face.

"You've been in Alaska such a short time. Are you sure of your feelings for Grady?"

"Honestly, Mom." She laughed lightly, handing her a fresh towel. "Of course I am." The words slipped out without thought. Naturally she knew how she felt about Grady. But it wasn't love.

"Stepping into a ready-made family has me concerned."

"But I love Angela."

"I can understand why. She's a precious child."

Cathy smiled. Her mother was like this. Even as a teenager their most serious discussions were often done in the most unlikely places or under the silliest conditions. Once they had a terrible argument in the aisle of a grocery store about a boy Cathy was dating. Cathy guessed that her mother was uneasy bringing up the discussion and tried to do so in the most natural way possible.

"Probably the one thing that worries me the most is Grady's business. I don't want you married to a man like your father." She didn't need to elaborate.

Now it wasn't easy to disguise her feelings. "Just because a man owns his own company doesn't make him a workaholic." Cathy stiffened and stood easing her way around her mother in the small bathroom. "I know the signs."

"Don't make the mistakes I did." Her mother warned.

"I won't." Cathy prayed she sounded convincing as she left the room, silently closing the door.

Grady's look sliced her as she entered the living room. She wasn't fooled by the easygoing facade he had assumed in front of her family. He was upset. Cathy knew him well enough to recognize what the hard set of his mouth meant.

"You're the one who looks pale all of a sudden." The gaiety sounded forced. "Don't tell me you're getting prewedding jitters." She tossed his own words back at him.

"No." The word was clipped, impatient. The slant of his mouth didn't suggest humor or a smile.

"Is something the matter?" A frown flickered across her face, drawing her delicate brows together.

"You tell me."

Cathy hesitated, fighting the growing panic. Grady knew. With all the innuendos Steve had been hurling at him, it would be a miracle if he hadn't figured it out. Dear heaven, how was she ever going to make it through the wedding? "I'm not up to playing guessing games with you. If you want to clear the air, that's up to you," she said in wary anger.

Grady rammed a hand through the thick, naturally curly hair and walked to the fireplace, bracing a foot against the hearth. He turned, his eyes bright but unreadable until the light slowly faded and he looked away.

Hands clenched in front of her, Cathy watched the transformation in Grady's features and followed his gaze.

"Can I give Cathy the present now, Daddy?" Angela requested softly. "Remember you said I could be the one to give it to her."

He answered his daughter with a curt nod.

Angela skipped down the hall and returned a minute later with a brightly wrapped box. "Daddy said that it's trad..." She stumbled over the word.

"Tradition." Grady helped her out.

Angela shook her head, the soft curls bobbing with the action. "Daddy said it was tradition for the bribe to get a wedding gift from the groom."

"Bride," Grady corrected.

"This is yours. Daddy and I bought it together." Proudly she handed Cathy the small package.

Cathy's eyes met his across the room. She hadn't gotten him a gift. She wanted to apologize, make an excuse, but nothing seemed to make it past the lump of surprise growing in her throat.

"Go ahead, open it," Angela encouraged. "I wanted to buy you a real pretty tea set, but Daddy said you needed this more."

Slowly Cathy lowered herself to the sitting position, and almost immediately Angela joined her. It was obvious the child had wrapped the gift. It looked as if a whole role of cellophane tape had been used. The bow was glued on top and the paper twice the size needed.

"Do you want me to help you?" Angela volunteered, eagerly ripping away the pink bow.

The paper revealed a jeweler's box. Cathy paused, glancing up to Grady.

"Go ahead open it," Angela urged. "Daddy said you needed one of these real bad."

Returning her attention to the oblong velvet case, she gently lifted the lid. An expensive gold watch and intricate watchband stared back at her. A rush of pleasure and surprise caused her to look at Grady. "It's beautiful." She hardly knew what to say until she finally blurted out, "Thank you."

"Daddy said you'd like it." Angela sounded pleased and proud. Cathy reached for her, hugging her close. So many times over the past weeks Grady had teased her about her watch and her timekeeping methods. No gift could have been more perfect. No gift could have touched her more.

Suddenly Grady was there, kneeling at her side. He took the case from her hand. "Let me help you put it on."

Placing a hand on either side of his face she turned his head toward her. Only a few inches of space separated them, but from the hard look in his eyes it could have been several miles.

"Thank you," she repeated softly, overwhelmed by his thoughtfulness.

Grady emitted a low groan as he tilted his head slightly and unerringly located her mouth. The kiss was deep and long. Cathy remained passive under the brutal possession. There was pleasure with the pain, almost as if the pain were necessary for her to experience the pleasure.

"Do you still want to thank me?" he breathed the question against her throat.

"Yes." Her response was so low Cathy barely heard herself speak.

"Is that the way people kiss all the time?" Angela queried.

Cathy had forgotten the little girl's presence, as she was sure Grady had too.

"Not always," Grady murmured, his voice faintly husky. He broke the contact, and Cathy marveled at his control. Outwardly he appeared unmoved by their exchange, while she was left breathless and uncertain. He paused and unemotionally removed the watch from the black velvet case and placed it on her wrist.

"Throw the other one out," he said and, standing, walked to the other side of the room.

Cathy understood what he was asking. He was referring to far more than her old watch. He wanted her to throw away the past, to begin again.

On shaking legs she stood, and joined him at the fireplace, opened the screen, and carelessly tossed her old watch inside.

Grady's arm circled her waist, bringing her close to his side. Cathy felt him breathe hard against her hair.

Paula Thompson left the hotel room, kissed Cathy on the cheek and promised to meet her at the church. A tear sparkled in her mother's eyes as the door closed with a soft clinking sound.

Dressed and ready, Cathy wore a close-fitting white wool suit. She had purchased it just as Linda suggested without thought or concern, but now she realized that the outfit couldn't have been more perfect.

Hauntingly beautiful was the term her mother had used. Haunting was the word Cathy would agree upon. Beautiful she wasn't sure. She didn't feel beautiful. Scared, tense, nervous, wanting to get this whole thing over as quickly as possible were the emotions that were easier to identify. This should be the happiest day of her life, and she felt much as she had at her father's funeral. Instead of joy to be linking her life with a man she deeply loved, she dealt with a sense of fear of what the future would hold.

Someone knocked at the hotel room door. Cathy glanced at the new gold watch thinking Linda and Dan were early. Not that it mattered. She was ready. Arrangements had been made for them to take her to the church.

Only it wasn't Linda and Dan.

It was Steve.

"Steve." She breathed his name with a sense of unreality.

His look was haggard as he pushed his way past her and into the hotel room.

Her hand still on the doorknob, Cathy closed her eyes. Looking at him, seeing the torment in his eyes, knowing her own doubts were there for him to see was almost more than she could bear. "Where's Mary-Anne?" Desperately she hoped her sister's name would be enough to bring him to his senses.

With a hand on each of her shoulders, he pinned her against the door. The weight of his body slammed it shut. Before she could protest, he lowered his mouth to hers, greedily kissing her.

Cathy fought him as long as she could. Frantically she withered her head from side to side in a fruitless effort to free herself from his clenches. But he was far too strong. Palms pushing against his chest, she tore her mouth from his.

From the moment Steve had walked off the plane she had worried something like this would happen. Desperately she was afraid that once he touched her she wouldn't have the will to resist him. She was wrong. His kiss didn't ignite any spark of desire. She felt nothing. Nothing.

"Don't," she pleaded. "Don't."

Steve reached for her again, but she sidestepped him, her legs trembling so badly she was afraid she'd fall directly into his arms. "Please." Her arm extended out in front of her in an effort to ward him off.

Steve moved toward her and paused. "Tell me you don't love me and I'll leave."

Did she love him? The pain of his betrayal had been so sharp and intense she had assumed her love for him was as strong today as it was the day he married her sister. But was it?

He must have recognized the indecision on her face. Steve extended a hand to her, palm up imploring. "I love you." The admission came on a husky whisper. "I've loved you forever. I was wrong to ever let you go. I was wrong to have married MaryAnne."

Now it wasn't only her legs that were trembling but her whole body. "She's my sister!" Cathy shouted because it was the only way she knew to reason with him. "MaryAnne is going to have your baby."

Steve ran a weary hand over his face. "I should never have married her."

"But you did," she reminded him forcefully.

His gaze was riveted to her face. "You don't love Grady. Why are you doing this? Why are you marrying him when you love me?"

Cathy swallowed at the lump of painful hoarseness in her throat. "Why did you marry my sister when you didn't love her?" Her only defense was to keep reminding herself that it was MaryAnne, her pregnant sister, who was involved in this. The younger sister she'd loved and protected all her life.

"Come with me," Steve begged. "Now, before it's too late. We can fly out of here before anyone knows we're gone."

"What a touching scene."

Shock came crashing in on Cathy as she saw Grady poised in the open door. His mouth, his eyes, his jaw, every feature stamped with undisguised contempt.

Steve recovered first. "She doesn't love you." He

triumphantly hurled the words at Grady. "It's me she cares about."

Grady shrugged as if her feelings were of little significance to him. He walked into the room and closed the door. "You two are so in love with one another it doesn't matter whose life you ruin, is that it?"

"Cathy loves me and I love her." Steve came to stand protectively at her side. "No one can stop us now. Not even you, Jones. I'll kill you rather than let you take Cathy now."

Grady flicked a hair from the shoulder of his suit coat, again giving the impression of lazy indulgence. "I welcome the opportunity for you to try," he said in a low drawl. "But there's no need for us to fight when Cathy can make her own decision."

"Tell him you love me and are coming with me," Steve implored, his fingers biting into her shoulders.

Cathy stared blankly from one man to the other in shocked dismay. Her head was screaming one thing and her heart pleading another.

When she hesitated, Steve paled visibly. "Darling, I was wrong to marry MaryAnne. You'd only be worsening the situation to marry Grady. Don't ruin the rest of our lives."

"Well?" Grady questioned, his eyes as hard as stone.

Paralysis gripped her throat.

"Two wrongs don't make a right," Steve said, a desperate ring to his voice.

Then it came to her. This was her sister. The sister she'd spent her entire life loving and protecting. The memory of MaryAnne's expression as she placed a loving hand over her abdomen flashed through Cathy's mind. She looked to Grady.

He stood proud and tall. He wouldn't tell her he loved her, he wouldn't issue a single word of inducement. Not that he needed her, not that he wanted her. Not that he cared one way or the other. He said nothing.

The heart that had only begun to mend, broke in pieces again as she walked to Grady's side and placed her hand on his arm. Out of the corner of her eye she saw Steve slump to the bed in defeat and bury his face in his hands.

Everyone was waiting at the church when Grady and Cathy arrived. With time to compose herself, Cathy freshened her makeup and offered her sister and her best friend a feeble smile.

"You look as nervous as I did the day Steve and I were married," MaryAnne said with a laugh. "And speaking of Steve, he phoned the church a few minutes ago. He's feeling sick, I think it may be something he ate yesterday. You don't mind if I slip away shortly after the ceremony do you? I want to make sure he's okay."

"Of course," Cathy assured her.

Standing in the church foyer, Linda pinned the pink rosebud corsage onto Paula Thompson's dress before handing Cathy a small bouquet of the same color flowers.

"That Grady," Linda laughed, retying the sash to Angela's pink satin dress. "I told him he wasn't supposed to see the bride before the wedding, but he insisted he do the honors instead of Dan and me. I imagine you were shocked when you opened the hotel room and discovered your husband-to-be."

"Yes, I was." More than anyone would ever know.

Heaving a long sigh, Linda stepped back and inspected everyone. "Perfect." She smiled. "Just perfect."

Together the small party moved up to the altar and were joined by Pastor Wilkens. Cathy's only thought was how was she ever going to find the proper gift to thank Linda for everything she'd done to make this wedding run smoothly.

The next thing Cathy remembered was the pastor telling Grady he could kiss his bride. Instinctively she lowered her eyelids as Grady's mouth moved over hers. The contact was brief and could hardly be considered a kiss. Not that it mattered.

As she said, MaryAnne slipped out of the church to return to the hotel shortly after the ceremony. A room had been reserved in a restaurant for a wedding meal. A cake decorated with dainty pink rosebuds was waiting on a table surrounded by gifts.

With Grady's hand pressing into the small of her back, he led her through the remainder of the formalities. The meal tasted like cotton, but she managed to choke down a few bites. Somehow she was able to cut the cake and feed Grady a bite. Camera flashes seemed to come at her from every direction as Dan and Linda thought it important to record every detail of the day. Cathy couldn't understand it, but she submitted weakly to the ordeal, accepting it as just another irritation.

Finally they could escape. Ray tossed the suitcases into the back of the plane and helped Cathy climb aboard. She smiled when she noticed Ray had painted *Just Married* on the side of the plane below *Alaska Cargo*. If she had been in a decent mood she would have laughed at the sight of Ray standing on the runway on a bitter cold November afternoon dressed in his warmest gear and hurling rice at them.

Cathy hardly paid attention as they taxied onto the runway waiting for instructions from the air traffic controller. With a burst of power they took off. It wasn't until they were unable to see Fairbanks city lights that Cathy spoke.

"Where are we going?" Only now that they were in the air did it interest her.

"For our honeymoon."

Her sharply inhaled breath became a soundless gasp. "I…I thought you said we didn't have time for a honeymoon. The school is expecting me back Monday morning."

"You'll be there," he said shortly.

Grady seemed disinclined to talk as they flew through an ebony night. The drone of the engine lured Cathy to sleep.

She woke when Grady began his approach to another airfield. Rubbing a hand over her eyes, she looked at this man who was now her husband. His expression was tight, and unyielding.

"Where are we?" she asked in a quiet voice.

He didn't look at her. "Does it matter?"

"No." Sadly she shook her head. Absently she toyed with the wedding band so recently placed on her finger. Grady shot her an irritated look and she stopped, knotting her fingers.

They landed and taxied into a hangar, and Grady helped her step out of the plane.

Without a word he lifted their suitcases and with long purpose-filled strides walked away.

Stunned, Cathy watched him go. He hadn't spoken

an unnecessary word to her and grudgingly answered her questions. At the gate he paused and turned. "Are you coming or not?" he snapped.

For an instant Cathy was tempted to stamp her foot and scream "not." Instead she inhaled a slow breath, swung her purse strap over her shoulder, and followed him out of the hangar.

The air was warmer, the cold less brittle. The stars were out in a brilliant display of God's handiwork, like rare jewels laid upon rippling folds of black satin. Funny, she hadn't noticed how beautiful the night was when they were in the air.

Grady was several feet ahead of her, and she was forced to half-run, half-walk to keep up with him. Still she didn't know where they were. Grady paused in front of a sedan and placed the suitcases on the cement while he produced a key from the car's undercarriage.

Unlocking the driver's side, he climbed inside, leaned across, and unlocked her door. Cathy opened the passenger side herself.

The silence grew and grew until she was sure she'd scream if he didn't say something soon. Again her fingers unconsciously toyed with the wedding band.

"Will you stop," he demanded.

"Stop what?"

"Playing with that ring." His foot forcefully hit the car brakes. If it hadn't been for the restraining seat belt Cathy would have been jerked forward. His gaze flickered over her briefly before he focused his attention back on the road. "Get this and get it straight," he ground out through clenched teeth. "That ring is on your finger to stay."

"Yes," she returned in a tight whisper. "I understand."

By the time they arrived at the hotel, Cathy had guessed they were in Anchorage. She glanced around the expensively decorated lobby as Grady registered. Muted musical sounds drifted from the cocktail lounge.

"This way." Grady touched her shoulder to gain her attention, then just as quickly removed his hand.

She followed him into the elevator, watching the heavy metal doors glide closed. Her attention centered on the orange light indicating the floor number. The elevator made a swishing sound as it came to a halt on the ninth floor. Grady preceded her into the long narrow hallway, leaving her to follow.

Unlocking the door, he pushed it inward and placed the suitcases just inside the door. Unexpectedly he swung Cathy into his arms.

She gave a startled gasp, her arms looping automatically around his neck as he carried her over the threshold. His foot closed the door. His blue eyes seemed to burn into her gray ones, scorching her with the heat of his desire.

"This is going to be a real marriage, you understand that don't you?"

She had expected noting less. Slowly she nodded.

Her feet were lowered to the plush carpeting.

"Then you'd best get undressed," he said as a hand jerked the knot free from his tie before he unbuttoned the pale blue shirt.

Cathy watched him with a sense of disbelief. He couldn't be serious. She couldn't make love with him when he was this cold and calculating. She started to protest and then realized it would do no good.

Her hand shook as she unfastened the tiny buttons of the wool jacket. Hanging it in the closet, she slipped off her shoes, flexing her bare toes into the carpet. With her back to Grady she unzipped the skirt and hung it beside the jacket.

A hand at her shoulder turned her around. Her hand was at her throat prepared to unite the collar of the pink silk blouse. Grady removed her hand, untying the sash himself. Her arms fell lifelessly to her side.

She couldn't look at him as he slowly unfastened each button of her blouse. She couldn't bear to see the disappointment and anger in his eyes. Not now when she was about to become his wife in every way. The silk blouse slid off her shoulders and fell to the floor.

A hand at her back unhooked the lace bra and it too fell unheeded to the floor. Her heart was pounding so loud it was difficult to breathe. His mouth spread tiny kisses over her throat, and Cathy rotated her head to grant him easier access.

When he released her, she blinked in confusion as a shaft of cold air raced over her.

Again their eyes met as his hands slid over her ribs, pulling her close so that her front nestled against the black curly hairs of his chest.

"Why do you have to be so beautiful?" Grady questioned before his mouth captured hers.

Eight

The alarm buzzed and Cathy rolled over and blindly fumbled for the clock on the nightstand. She urgently groped for the button that would put an end to the irritating noise.

Success.

The bleeping stopped and she sighed unevenly. Five a.m. and it was pitch dark in their bedroom. With his back to her, Grady continued to sleep soundly.

Rousing her husband, Cathy slipped a hand over the lean, muscular ribs and gently shook him. "Grady, wake up."

Her words were followed by a low, protesting moan.

He rolled toward her, and instantly Cathy scooted to her side of the bed. No need to throw temptation his way. Although they'd been married three months, she still was amazed at how often he desired her. Always gentle and encouraging, he was a wonderful lover. She willingly submitted to him. She was, after all, his wife. She gave of herself what she could, knowing it wasn't enough to satisfy either of them.

Unexpectedly she was happy, as happy as she could

ever be without Steve. And content with her life. Grady had been right when he'd told her Angela needed a mother. The child had blossomed under Cathy's love and attention. Sometimes it was difficult to believe this bubbly, happy little girl was the same child she'd met last September.

Grady reached across the mattress and scooted her to his side. Instinctively she stiffened as his lips kissed the nape of her neck.

"Don't go all wintry on me," he whispered. "I just want to hold you a few minutes."

He did that some mornings, when he was reluctant to get out of a warm bed. Her head was cradled in the crook of his arm, and she could feel the even rise and fall of his chest beneath her palm. His breath stirred the hairs at the top of her head as his hand gently stroked the curve of her hip. The moment was serene and tranquil.

"Where are you flying today?" She whispered, not wanting the sound of her voice to shatter the quiet.

"Deadhorse."

Cathy released a ragged sigh. She didn't often ask him what time he would be home or if she should hold dinner for him. She remembered how her father had resented her mother's questions and how he'd snapped at her when Paula had innocently inquired.

Cathy didn't know why she'd asked this morning. A bush pilot from another company in Fairbanks had lost a man just the week before flying supplies into Nome for an oil company. The plane had engine trouble and was forced to make a crash landing. Grady had joined the search party. They found the plane and the man two days later. He'd survived the crash but had frozen to death before the crash site could be located.

In the days that followed, Cathy's stomach had tightened every morning when Grady left for the airfield. Not that she didn't respect his talent or his abilities, but the other man had been an excellent pilot too.

Her husband's hand brushed the hair from her temple, and he kissed her lightly before throwing back the blankets and climbing out of bed.

Instantly a chill ran over her, and she sat up and reached for her housecoat lying across the foot of the mattress. Peterkins had slept there from the time he was a puppy, but not anymore. The dog spent his nights with Angela now; Grady didn't want him in their bedroom. Cathy had struggled not to argue with him, but in the end she silently conceded it was probably for the best.

Snuggling her bare feet into thick, fuzzy slippers, she knotted the sash and started for the kitchen. The coffee was perking, and she poured Grady a cup when he joined her. His lunch was packed and his thermos filled when he gave her a kiss goodbye. Watching his headlights disappear down the deserted street from the living room window, Cathy felt like an ordinary, everyday wife. Only her heart reminded her she wasn't.

Scraping oatmeal-raisin cookies off the cookie sheet, Cathy nervously bit into her bottom lip. Eight-thirty and Grady wasn't home. In the past if he was going to be later than seven or so he phoned, or had Ray do it for him. The thoughtfulness had surprised her. But there had been no phone call tonight.

"Time for bed," she reminded Angela, who was watching television in the living room.

"Can I have a cookie?"

"Okay, but get your pajamas on first."

The little girl nodded eagerly, and raced into her bedroom. Peterkins followed in hot pursuit. Fifteen minutes later, Cathy prayed with the child, kissed her tenderly on the cheek, and tucked the blankets around her.

She had just closed the bedroom door when the phone rang. Her heart leapt to her throat as she hurried into the kitchen. *Dear God*, she prayed, *let Grady be all right.*

"Hello." Her voice sounded slightly breathless, as if she'd been running.

"Cathy?"

It was Linda Ericson, an excited, happy Linda Ericson.

"Is that you, Cathy?" her friend questioned.

Cathy tried to keep the disappointment out of her voice. "Yes, hello, Linda."

"Oh, Cathy, guess what, I'm going to be a mother."

"You're pregnant?" Cathy breathed in disbelief.

"Well, sort of," she laughed easily, her happiness bubbling over. "Dan and I just finished talking with the adoption agency, and we're getting a little girl about the same age as Angela. We're so excited. I really can't talk now, there are about thirty-five relatives I've got to phone, I'll explain everything in the morning. I've got so much to do. Dan and I are picking her up in two weeks."

They spoke for a few minutes longer, and Cathy offered her heartfelt enthusiasm. A smile trembled on her lips as she thought about having a baby, then sadly she shook her head. No, it was too soon yet, for both of them.

By nine-fifteen, Cathy was more than worried, she

was near frantic, pacing the floor. Certainly Ray would know what was happening.

Reaching for the phone she paused for an instant, unsure. Since their marriage, she'd never called Grady at work. Clenching her fist with indecision, she released a rough breath. Grady would hate it if he found out. She punched out his number anyway.

"Yes," the impatient, male voice answered.

A rush of pleasure raced over her, and weak with relief she lowered herself into a kitchen chair. Without a word she replaced the receiver. Grady need never know it was she who had phoned.

Less than a half-hour later he stormed in the back door. Cathy was reading in the living room, and she started at the violent sound of the kitchen door slamming. She laid the book aside and stood.

"Grady, what's wrong?"

His mouth was thinned into a tight line of anger. "That was you on the phone, wasn't it?"

The thought came to deny the whole thing, but the habit of being honest was deeply ingrained. "Yes," she answered without blinking, her shoulders squared.

"Why didn't you say something?" His voice was harsh, and impatient.

"I...I was worried. You've always phoned when you were going to be late."

"Why didn't you say something?" he demanded a second time.

"Because." She stamped her foot, angry with herself, angry with him. "I knew you'd be upset, and I was right."

Hands rested challengingly on his hips, his eyes narrowed. "Don't ever do that again. Understand?"

"Yes, your worshipfulness," she returned in mock servitude.

Grady ran a hand over his face. He looked tired, emotionally and physically weary. "Pam used to do that," he murmured in a tight voice.

This wasn't the first time Grady had compared her to his dead wife, and she didn't like it any better now than she did before. "Listen, Grady," she said forcefully, punctuating her words with an accusing finger. "I'm not Pam."

"Then don't act like her," he returned calmly.

Anger simmered just below the surface. "If you were so miserable with your first wife, then why didn't you divorce her? Why do you hurl accusations at me that have to do with her? You're being unfair, Grady Jones."

"I couldn't leave her," he said calmly. "She was sick." He pivoted sharply and left the room.

Cathy followed him into their bedroom. "Did you walk away every time Pam and you had an argument? No wonder she packed her bags. It was a desperate attempt to get some reaction out of you."

Grady swiveled. She had never seen a man look more unsettled. He didn't say another word for the rest of the evening.

If there had been a wintry feeling in their bed before, that night it was an Arctic blast. Ramrod stiff, Cathy laid on her back staring sightlessly at the dark ceiling. She couldn't sleep, not with this terrible tension hanging between them.

It's your own fault, she told herself. It was a childish prank to hang up the phone without speaking. *But it's his fault, too,* she continued to reason. He could have called to let you know he would be late. Why hadn't he contacted her when he had in the past? Not that it mattered who or what had caused the argument, Grady would never apologize.

"Grady," she asked quietly. "Are you asleep?" She knew he wasn't.

"No." Even his whisper sounded gruff and impatient, as if he didn't want to have anything to do with her.

She held her breath, reaching down inside herself. Apologizing wasn't going to be easy. This was the mistake she'd made before that had ruined her relationship with Steve. She refused to repeat it. "I don't want to fight with you," she began. "I'll never phone you like that again."

He was silent for so long Cathy wondered if he had heard her. "Grady?" she repeated his name.

"I heard." He scooted across the short distance and pulled her into his arms, holding her the same way he had that morning.

Her dark hair fanned out across his shoulder. She hoped one day her husband would find it within himself to admit when he was in the wrong. Pride, determination, arrogance were so much a part of this man that she wondered if anything or anyone was capable of bringing him to his knees. "Why didn't you let me know you were going to be late?" she questioned weakly.

"I thought Ray had," he whispered in a low voice. He paused before adding, "I shouldn't have compared you to Pam."

It was the closest she was going to get to an apology, as minute as it was, and Cathy couldn't help feeling encouraged.

"There's something you should know about Pam." Grady breathed in deeply, and the sound seemed to echo around the bedroom. "Pam was mentally ill. I did everything I could to help her, but she didn't want help. She hated me, she hated Angela. In the end she hated herself. Angela was less than two years old when Pam committed suicide."

Cathy was speechless. From all the bits and pieces of information Grady had given her, she should have guessed that the desperate ploys for attention Pam had used pointed to a deeper problem.

"I'm sorry," she whispered, her hand caressed his jaw and felt the muscles work convulsively beneath her fingers. Slowly she lowered her lashes, knowing what it had cost him to tell her about Angela's mother.

Fiercely his arms closed around her, holding her so close that for a moment she was afraid he might crush her. His breathing was labored, as if revealing this part of himself and his first marriage had physically drained him.

Her heart cried out to this man who was her husband. The guilt he must have endured, the helplessness, the frustration. Tenderly she weaved her fingers through his hair, holding his head to her breast. A longing rose within her to assure him, to console him, but Grady didn't need the words. He needed her.

He reached for her then in that familiar way, letting her know what he wanted. She came to him eagerly. When he shifted positions she raised her arms so he could remove her night gown. He slipped it over her head and his mouth rocked over hers as he gently laid her back against the mattress.

Her long fingernails dug into the muscled strength of his bare back as his mouth sought the places he knew would excite her beyond reason.

When she was weak with her need for him, Grady paused and lifted his face and muttered thickly, "Give yourself to me, Cathy, I need you."

How could she give him more than she was already? He wasn't referring to a physical struggle but the mental one. He wanted all of her, her heart as well as her soul. He asked for more than what she could offer him. Her arms curved around him, as a bitter sob erupted from her throat.

Grady paused and Cathy felt the regret run through his body. Gently he gathered her in his arms and kissed away a tear that had slipped through her lashes. His calloused hand caressed her cheek. "Don't cry," he whispered. "I understand."

In a crazy way, she was sure he did.

"I'll be back before eight," Cathy explained and leaned down to kiss Grady on the cheek. The gaily wrapped gift was clenched in one hand.

"Mite stingy, aren't you?" he said with a stern look before tossing the newspaper to the carpet. He grabbed her by the waist and pulled her into his lap.

Angela giggled with delight. "Are you going to kiss her, Daddy?"

"You bet your boots I am," he told his daughter and proceeded to do just that. The kiss was cajoling, a sensuous attack that spoke more of passion than farewell. Her senses reeling, Cathy made a weak effort to fight him off. He had been like this since the night of their first argument. The night he had told her about Pam.

They hadn't made love since, but he was more loving than she had dreamed possible. He made excuses to touch her, and brought her small gifts, almost as if he were courting her.

"Grady," she whispered, struggling to maintain an even breath. "I've got to go or I'll be late."

He chuckled and helped her up, escorting her to the door. "Drive carefully."

"I will." The shower was for Linda Ericson. The adoption had gone through, and Dan and Linda were going to pick up six-year-old Katy that weekend. Cathy, along with the other teachers from school had decided to throw a surprise shower for her.

"I want a kiss goodbye, too," Angela insisted, running into the room.

"Honestly." Cathy feigned her dismay. "You'd think I was going to be gone a year instead of a few hours. What about you, Peterkins, do you want me to kiss you goodbye too?"

The spaniel barked, and she stooped to rub his floppy, black ears.

When Cathy returned two hours later, she sensed almost immediately that something was wrong. Even before she walked in the back door a strange, eerie feeling came over her. She paused just inside the back porch as a chill raced down her spine.

Soft sobs could be heard coming from the living room. Grady was holding his daughter on his lap, gently rocking her, comforting her. He didn't seem to know Cathy was home.

Setting her purse on the table, she hurried into the room.

"What's wrong?"

Angela took one look at Cathy and burst into giant

sobs. "I'm so sorry," she pleaded, her young shoulders shaking pitifully.

Puzzled, Cathy knelt on the carpet in front of the pair. Even Grady looked unnaturally pale. "Sweetheart, there's nothing you could have done to make you cry like this. Now tell me what's made you so sad," she whispered reassuringly and gently soothed the hair from the child's forehead.

Angela buried her face in her father's shoulder.

Grady's eyes burned into hers. "Peterkins is dead," he said without preamble.

Shock rippled over her. Cathy felt as if the world had suddenly come to a screeching halt. Her eyes pleaded with Grady to tell her it wasn't true.

"What happened?" Somehow the words made it through the expanding lump of disbelief and pain that filled her throat. She knew she'd gone deathly pale.

"Peterkins wanted outside, and Angela let him out the back door. When he didn't immediately want back in she forgot about him for a minute or two. When she checked he was lying at the back door bleeding. He'd been attacked by an animal, he bled to death before I got to the vet. Dr. McFeeney said it was probably a wild dog. The artery in his leg was severed."

As Grady recounted the details, Cathy had the feeling that this wasn't happening. It was a dream, it couldn't be real. She nodded, not knowing how she could be so calm. "Angela," she whispered soothingly, "it's not your fault. Any one of us could have let him out."

Gentle cries racked the small shoulders as Angela climbed out of Grady's lap and placed her arms around Cathy's neck.

Tears blurred her eyes as Cathy wrapped the child in her embrace.

An hour passed before Angela had cried herself into a state of exhaustion. She fell asleep in Cathy's arms. Grady carried her into her bedroom and paused until Cathy pulled back the bed covers. She lingered in the room, stroking the hair from Angela's face until she was confident the little girl would sleep.

Grady was waiting for her in the living room and handed her a glass. "Drink this," he instructed.

Without question she did as he asked. The liquid burned all the way down her throat, but immediately a warmth begin to seep into her bones.

"I did everything I could." Apparently Grady felt the need to assure her he wouldn't have wished any harm on the dog.

"I know." Deliberately she took another sip from the glass. "Where is he?"

"Cathy." Grady's voice was gentle.

"I want to see him one last time, please, Grady."

He stood and came to kneel beside her, taking both her hands in his. "You can't, the vet has disposed of the body."

She nodded, lowering her lashes. It was too late; she would never see her little spaniel again.

Grady held her for a long time that night. He fell asleep with her pressed close to his side. For several hours Cathy lay listening to the rhythmic flow of his breathing while happy scenes with Peterkins continued to play in her mind. When the tears came they slipped from the corners of her eyes and onto the pillow. Not wishing to wake Grady she carefully scooted out of the bed, put on her housecoat and slippers, and wandered into the living room. The hurt flowed freely once she was alone.

With her knees drawn up beneath her chin, she gently rocked back and forth. Steve had given her Peterkins. Now there was nothing of him or their relationship left in her life. Everything was gone.

Peterkins was the only good thing Steve had ever given her. Everything he'd done had been a source of pain. Perhaps she should feel a sense of freedom. But she didn't, only an aching emptiness for the small dog she had loved and she would never see again. She felt nothing for Steve. It came to her that she'd felt nothing for him one way or another for a long time.

Cathy stopped the rocking motion, shocked at her thoughts. She felt nothing for Steve. She didn't love him, she realized that now. The day his letter had arrived she had known. It hadn't been the shock of him wanting her back or that running off with him would destroy her sister. Nor was it his letter. That day she realized she couldn't possibly love a man like Steve was now. Her reaction to Grady's proposal wasn't out of fear she would go to Steve. It was in response to the knowledge of exactly what kind of man she had once loved so deeply.

If that was so then what was the real reason she had married Grady? Had she loved him? As soon as she asked the question, Cathy recognized the truth. It had happened so gradually she'd been unaware of her changed heart.

Silvery moonlight filled the room as she silently wept for the dog she'd loved. Cathy heard Grady's movements behind her before she saw him. She yearned for the comfort of his embrace, she wanted to tell him the truth of what she'd discovered. But the words wouldn't come, not now in her grief.

As if he understood her need for gentleness, Grady sat on the sofa beside her. Tenderly he gathered her in his arms, brushing the damp curls off her cheek and kissing away the tears. Linking her hands behind his neck, she lifted her lips to Grady. With an eagerness she would have been unable to explain she willingly met each kiss with an abandon he had never known from her. She felt the surprise wash over him.

He paused, taking in a ragged breath, his eyes studying her. He stood, lifting her effortlessly. She looped her arms around his neck and released a long sigh as she rested her head upon his shoulder.

He laid her on the mattress of their bed and leaned forward to cover her parted lips with his mouth. Again and again his mouth sought hers until the world was reeling with her need. Her lips parted in protest when he broke the contact. He groaned his own dissatisfaction and caressed her face with his cheek. Brushing her ear with his lips he questioned, "Cathy, are you sure?"

She nodded eagerly, her mouth finding the thick column of his throat, as her fingers pressed him close.

Cathy woke before dawn. The room was filled with golden streaks from the shifting moon. A sadness seemed to be pressing against her heart, and she remembered the loss of her precious dog. She turned to Grady, gliding her hand over his chest and laying her head on his shoulder. Their lovemaking the night before had been gentle and sweet. The memory of his tenderness was enough to bring tears to her eyes. How blind she had been, how stupid, not to realize how deeply she loved this man. Pressed close, their legs entwined, Cathy fell back to sleep.

"Okay, Cathy, you can come look!" Excitedly Angela ran into the kitchen and grabbed Cathy's hand. All morning Grady and his daughter had been acting strange, sharing some deep, dark secret.

Wiping her hands on a terry cloth dish towel, Cathy allowed Angela to drag her into the living room. A large box with a bright red bow sat in the middle of the carpet.

"Go ahead," Angela urged. "Open it."

Cathy glanced to Grady, who looked at her with an amused expression. "Go ahead," he added his encouragement. His voice was gentle, almost caressing. He'd been that way with her from the time Peterkins had died two weeks before. There had never been a time in her life that she had felt closer to anyone than she had to Grady these past weeks. He was often home early now, spending high-quality time with Angela in the evenings, as if he suddenly realized what it meant to be a father. If this was the honeymoon, Cathy decided, she never wanted it to end.

A whimpering sound came from the box, and Cathy's eyes rounded. Perplexed, she lifted the lid to discover a small puppy huddled in the corner. Quickly she stifled a cry of dismay. She didn't want another dog. No one would ever replace Peterkins. She felt Grady's eyes upon her, narrowing with disappointment.

As if acting in slow motion, she reached inside the cardboard box and lifted out the tiny basset hound.

"Isn't he gorgeous?" Angela cried. "Daddy let me pick him out." Cathy looked at the big brown eyes, the white nose and black ears. She didn't think he was gorgeous. Without thought she handed the puppy to Angela, tears blurring her vision as she ran into the bedroom and closed the door.

Grady followed her. "What's wrong?" he demanded. The hard set of his jaw told her how angry he was.

Lifting her hand she pointed to the living room. "I don't want that dog. Why…why didn't you ask me?" Her voice shook treacherously. "A puppy isn't going to take Peterkins's place."

"I didn't expect he would." Grady jerked his fingers through his hair. When he lifted his head, she noted that much of the anger was gone. "This dog is more for Angela than you. No matter how much we assure her, she still carries some guilt over the loss of Peterkins. She loved him almost as much as you did, and now there's a void in her life. For her sake will you take the dog?"

Standing quietly beside the bed, Cathy nodded, not knowing of any way she could refuse.

Angela eyed them warily when they came out of the bedroom. "Did you have an argument?" she questioned softly. "Melissa Sue said her parents have arguments all the time. She said her mother goes to the bedroom and closes the door, and that's what you did, Cathy."

"No," Grady answered for her. "Cathy and I were discussing something, that's all."

"You don't like the puppy, do you?"

Cathy knew better than to disguise her feelings from the child. She sat and pulled Angela to her side. "Sometimes when you love someone so much, it takes a long time to heal the hurt of having them gone. Right now I miss Peterkins too much to think about another dog. But that doesn't mean I'll always feel that way. So for right now, can we make the puppy your special friend?"

Angela regarded her quizzically. "You mean you want me to feed him and take care of him and train him and do all those things?"

"Yes, for right now," Cathy confirmed.

The tiny face showed no qualms. "Does that mean I can name him too?"

"I think that would only be fair," Cathy said with a gentle smile. "What would you like to call him?"

"Arnie," Angela replied without hesitating. "There's a boy in my class named Arnie and he has a silly smile and when I saw the puppy I thought of Arnie and his smile."

"Then Arnie it is."

Grady was quiet most of the day. He spent part of the afternoon at the office, something he hadn't done on a weekend for a long while. Later, when musing over the events of the day, Cathy wondered if Grady thought she was referring to Steve when she was explaining to Angela about how it sometimes takes a long time to get over loving someone. She decided to make certain that night that there be no misunderstanding.

A roast was baking in the oven as Angela and Cathy peeled apples for a pie when Grady came in the house. Immediately Cathy set everything aside and slipped her hands over his shoulders and kissed him hard and long.

"What was that for?" he asked, his breathing irregular as his hands cupped her hips. Abruptly he dropped his arms and turned away.

"Can't a wife kiss her husband if she wants?" she asked saucily. Something sharp bit into her pant leg and jerked her foot back. "Ouch!"

Arnie's teeth were caught in the denim fabric of her

jeans, and he was tossing his head back and forth in a frenzied effort to gain release.

"Arnie," Angela snapped.

Cathy bent down to free herself, lifting the puppy from the floor and cradling him in her arms. "I don't know how anyone can call you gorgeous," she teased, referring to Angela's remark. "You're an ugly-looking mutt to me."

"Ugly Arnie," Angela repeated with a happy smile that revealed two newly formed front teeth. "That's a good name."

"It's a horrible name," Grady said. "In fact, the whole idea of another dog was a rotten one."

The smile disappeared from Angela's face as the hurt shivered over her. Moisture filled the six-year-old's eyes.

"That's not true," Cathy replied in confusion. "I…I thought we agreed—" She stopped midsentence as Grady walked out of the room.

Cathy watched him go, stunned and disbelieving. Something was wrong, something was very wrong. Grady hadn't spoken to her in this harsh tone since their wedding day. Just a few hours before his look had been filled with tenderness. Now the deep, smoky blue eyes were hard and unreadable.

"I'm sure your father didn't mean that," Cathy tried to assure Angela before following Grady into their bedroom. She stood in the doorway watching him open and close dresser drawers, carelessly dumping clothes in a duffel bag. "Are you going somewhere?" she questioned in a shaky, unsure voice.

"Isn't it obvious?" His jaw was clenched, all expression hidden from her.

"Where?"

He straightened and cast her an irritated glance. "Did you suddenly join the FBI?"

"No." She stepped inside the room and leaned against the door, shutting it. With her back pressed against the wood she watched his hurried movements. "What's wrong? You're angry about something, and I want to know what it is."

Grady's mouth compressed into a taut line. "Things aren't going well at the field, I've got to fly into Nome tonight on an emergency run. I probably won't be back until Sunday afternoon." He relayed the information reluctantly, as if he resented having to make explanations.

"Maybe Angela and I could fly up with you, it'd only take us a minute to pack our things."

"No." He didn't even pause to consider her suggestion.

"I'll miss you, Grady," she admitted, and her voice wavered slightly.

His sigh was heavy before he swung the bag over his shoulder. On the way out the door he paused to caress her cheek, his hand lowered to the nape of her neck, urging her mouth to his.

Cathy didn't need encouragement. She turned, slipping her arms around his waist and answering the hungry demand of his kisses. Cathy experienced a sense of triumph when she heard the duffel bag drop to the floor. His arms grasped her waist, lifting her from the floor. Eagerly she spread kisses over his face, teasing him with small, biting nips that promised but didn't deliver. Finally he groaned, moving his hand to the back of her head, forcing her mouth to his. Twisting, tasting, teasing, his open mouth sought hers with a greed she had become accustomed to from Grady. Her body flooded with a warm excitement, and when he lifted his head, his breathing was more ragged than her own.

The honeymoon wasn't over.

Nine

"Is Daddy home yet?" Angela asked, placing a hand over her mouth to hide a wide yawn.

"Not yet, sweetheart." Cathy pulled the pajama-clad child into her lap. "What woke you, a bad dream?"

Snuggling in Cathy's arms, Angela nodded. "I had a dream you went away like Louise and Mrs. Rafferty and Miss Bittle."

Carefully smoothing the hair away from the sleepy face, Cathy kissed the troubled brow. "I'm not going away. Don't you know how much I love you and your father? I could never leave you."

"Are you going to have babies?" Angela lifted her head so she could watch Cathy's expression, as if this information was important to her.

"Would you like a little brother or sister?" Cathy could well understand Angela's hesitancy. Her stepdaughter had been an only child for seven years. It wasn't until recently that Grady had given the little girl the attention and love she needed. It wouldn't be unreasonable for her to be jealous, or wish to remain the focus of their attention.

Eagerly the young head bobbed up and down. "Melissa Sue's mother is preg...going to have a baby. She's going to be a big sister, I want you to have a baby too."

Hugging her all the closer, Cathy gently swayed in the wooden rocker. "Then I think we'll discuss the subject with your dad very soon."

With the small head pressed gently against her breast, Cathy continued to rock until Angela's even breathing convinced her the little girl was asleep.

She sat in the rocker for a long time, staring at the clock over the fireplace. Midnight. Grady hadn't been home before eleven in almost a week, not since he returned from Nome. Ray telephoned regularly every evening to tell her Grady would be late once again. For the first couple of times she waited up for him, but he'd adamantly insisted he'd rather she didn't. From then on she'd been in bed pretending to be asleep. Grady knew that. She was sure of it. Although he played his own game of creeping around, undressing in the dark and crawling into bed, staying as far as possible on his side of the mattress.

At first Cathy assumed he was simply too tired to make love, but after a week she was beginning to wonder. Other than a fleeting caress or a perfunctory kiss, he hadn't touched her since flying to Nome. The sensation that something was wrong persisted. But what? And why wouldn't Grady say anything if there were? Unwilling to read something more into his actions she had remained perplexed. Things had been going along so beautifully the last few weeks. She wanted to confront him but with the long hours he put in at work, she didn't want to hassle him or start an argument.

But tonight she was awake and would remain so

until Grady was home. Whatever was wrong needed to be set right. Gradually she fell asleep in the rocking chair with Angela in her arms. Ugly Arnie's bark from the back porch roused her about one, and she heard Grady stop to pet the pooch and quietly enter the house through the kitchen.

He paused when he saw her, stopping just inside the living room. "I thought I told you not to wait up for me."

"Shh-shh," Cathy responded, placing a finger over her lips. Instead of words she extended her hand in silent entreaty.

His gaze holding hers, Grady walked into the room, stopping just in front of the rocking chair. "Is Angela sick?" Lines of concern knitted his brow.

Unable to break the spell of tenderness that suddenly seemed to exist between them, Cathy shook her head. "No, it was a bad dream," she whispered. "She thought I was going away."

Grady's mouth tightened into a grim line. "Are you?"

The question shocked her. "Of course not. How can you even think such a thing?" She spoke louder than she intended, and Angela stirred, sitting upright.

"Daddy," she said, rubbing her eyes. "You're home."

Grady lifted his daughter into his arms. "Well, sleepyhead, are you ready to go back to your bed?"

"You know what Cathy said?" More alert now, Angela looped her arms around her father's neck joining her fingers, and she leaned back so she could look at him. "Cathy said you and her might have babies. She said that I'd be a big sister someday just like Melissa Sue."

The room suddenly seemed to go still. Grady's gaze

flickered to Cathy before carrying Angela into her bedroom.

She heard him talking softly to the child but couldn't make out what he was saying. Sitting on the top of their bed, she waited until he had showered and changed.

Grady looked surprised that she was still up when he entered the bedroom.

"Can we talk a minute?" Her senses were clamoring, desperately wanting things to be right between them.

He sat on the edge of the mattress, his back facing her. "Not tonight," he pleaded. "I'm exhausted." Pulling back the covers, he climbed into the bed and leaned to turn off the bedside lamp.

The room was instantly dark, and not knowing what else she could do, Cathy followed, crawling beneath the covers and scooting to Grady's side, placing a hand over his ribs and cuddling close.

"You're not pregnant, are you?" The question was low, and full of concern.

"No," she replied, a sudden chill coming over her at the reluctance in his voice.

"Good." The one word was clipped.

No more than a minute later, Grady was asleep. Cathy listened to the even flow of his breathing for hours.

The pattern was repeated the next week. Grady worked long hours, and the time he spent at home became less and less. Cathy seldom waited up for him, and when she did he was overly tired and irritable. But every night in his sleep he would gather her in his arms and hold her so tight that she never doubted his need for her.

Determined to clear the air and talk to her husband, Cathy purposely laid awake. April had arrived and the days were growing longer. Spring was beginning to color the earth, and she would have survived her first winter. Even Ugly Arnie had claimed a spot in her heart, and the pain of losing Peterkins grew less and less every day.

The only problem that continued to tax her was Grady's behavior. Had he guessed how much she loved him? Perhaps that was what troubled him, her love. Maybe he never intended to lay claim to her heart. Grady had gone into this marriage openly admitting he didn't love her. Now that her feelings were in the open did he find it an embarrassment? Doubts and questions seemed to grope at her from every direction.

A sound filtered through the confusion, and Cathy realized he was home. Lying perfectly still she waited as he fussed in the kitchen. Usually she kept a dinner plate ready for him so he could eat when he got home. The movements were hushed as if he would do anything not to wake her.

A few minutes later the shower ran, and when Grady appeared, the drops of beaded moisture that clung to his hair were shining in the moonlight.

"Grady." She whispered his name.

He sat on the edge of the mattress, and leaned forward, bracing a hand on either side of her head. "Sh-hh," he mouthed soothingly, "go back to sleep. I'm sorry I woke you."

Seeing him there in the moonlight, his blue eyes so intense, his face barely inches above her own. "Grady," she said again, his name a husky caress on her lips. Of their own volition her arms circled his neck and urged his mouth to hers. The resistance was only momentary, and with a muted groan his mouth closed over hers, parting her lips. The kiss lingered and lingered as if he couldn't get enough of her. His arms closed around her so fiercely that she was half lifted from the bed.

Once again in the circle of his arms, she eagerly met each kiss until they were both breathless and reeling from the effects.

"Cathy."

Never had she heard her name sound so beautiful. Within one word she recognized his need, his longing, and sighed heavily knowing her needs, her longings were equal to his. His thumb traced her lips in a featherlight caress and was followed by hungry, almost desperate kisses. Her mouth was warm and trembling when he laid her back against the pillow and joined her in the bed.

The next afternoon, Cathy sat at the kitchen table helping Angela with her schoolwork. The girl had made giant strides over the past months. She no longer attended the tutor as Cathy had worked with her from the time she and Grady were married. Teasingly she claimed she was a bargain wife because of all the money she saved him. Grady had laughed and assured her she was worth far more to him than a tutor.

But that had been before.

Before he worked sixteen-hour days, before he accepted assignments that would keep him away from home as long as possible. Before he flew both night and day.

Unconsciously, Cathy expelled her breath in a lingering sigh. The night before everything had been so perfect, so beautiful. They hadn't spoken, not a word. Their lovemaking had been urgent, fierce. He held her close afterward and asked if he'd hurt her. When she assured him he hadn't, Grady kissed her gently and fell into a deep sleep.

The phone rang, startling her. Angela popped off the chair and raced across the kitchen.

"Hello, this is the Jones residence, Angela speaking." The words were polite and eager. "Oh, hi, Ray, yes, she's here." Angela handed the phone to Cathy.

"Yes," she said and breathed in irritation. Not tonight, not again. She knew even before Ray said anything that Grady would be late again.

"Grady wanted me to phone and let you know he'll be late tonight."

Disappointment shivered over her until she thought she could cry with it. "Thanks for calling," she replied unable to hide her disappointment and frustration.

Ray seemed reluctant to hang up. "Things okay with you, Missus Jones?" he questioned after a long minute.

Cathy wanted to scream no, something was terribly wrong but she didn't know what. "I'm fine, thank you, Ray, and you?"

"Working hard," he grumbled, "but not half as hard as that husband of yours. If Grady pushes himself much further he's going to end up sick, or worse."

Cathy shuddered at the thought and didn't doubt the truth of the statement. "Why is he staying again tonight, did he say?"

"Nope, Grady don't say much to anyone anymore."

"He's not flying, is he?"

"Not that I know of, but as I said, Grady doesn't confide much in me." The voice was husky and did little to disguise the concern in Ray's voice.

Cathy thought about the call for a long time afterward. Her mother's warning played back in her mind. *Don't make the same mistakes I did.* Cathy wondered if there was anything her mother could have done in the beginning of her marriage that would have changed the way her father had been?

"Daddy won't be home until late, will he?" Angela's sad eyes the identical color of Grady's filled with tears the child couldn't restrain. "It's just like it was before you and Daddy got married. He never used to have dinner at home then either."

"Tonight I think we're going to surprise your father." Cathy stood, scooting the kitchen chair to the table.

Wiping the tears from her cheeks, Angela was instantly at her side. "What are we going to do?"

"If Grady can't come home for dinner, we'll take dinner to him."

"A picnic?" The tiny voice was immediately filled with excitement. "Can Ugly Arnie come too?"

"I don't see why not. If Mohammed won't go to the mountain then—" Cathy stopped because Angela was giving her funny looks. Tugging a long braid, Cathy laughed. "Never mind."

Cathy made a big deal of packing the picnic basket. Somehow in one small wicker container they were able to squeeze chicken, potato salad, wine, cheese, bread, fruit, cookies, and a doggie biscuit. Singing a song Angela had learned at school they drove to the airfield, Ugly Arnie barking and howling from Angela's arms.

Ray met them, wiping his greasy hands on an equally greasy pink cloth as a smile lit up tired old eyes. His face was a huge network of wrinkles that extended from his forehead to his round chin, a smile creating giant grooves into the sides of his mouth.

Angela bounded from the front seat and ran to meet the older man. "Hello, Ray, we brought Daddy a surprise."

"Well if it isn't Miss Angela Jones herself," Ray said with a crooked grin. "Could hardly tell it was Grady's girl, you've grown so much. Pretty as a picture, too, just like Cathy."

Angela glowed with pleasure. "Do you still keep chocolate in your pocket? You used to when I was a little kid?"

Ray edged back his hat with the tip of his index finger. "Can't say that I do, guess I've have to check my toolbox." He tossed Cathy a wink. "You go ahead and see Grady, I'll take care of the young'un."

Cathy nodded, her eyes silently thanking him. As she headed toward the office she heard Ray ask Angela about Ugly Arnie, his question followed by a boisterous laugh.

The door to Grady's office was closed, and she knocked tentatively.

"It's open," came his harsh response.

She entered the room and watched as a look of shock came over his face.

"What's goin' on?" he demanded as he stood.

Setting the picnic basket on the floor, she offered him a feeble smile. "Angela and I decided we were tired of eating alone, so we brought dinner to you."

"How touching."

Blinking back the hurt, she didn't move. He didn't want her here, didn't want to have her connected in any way with his company. It was as if she were a separate part of his life that could be tucked away and brought out when it was convenient. She had been fooling herself with the belief she would ever come to mean more to him than Alaska Cargo. "I…I take it that it's…inconvenient for us to intrude on you." After their lovemaking from the night before she'd expected things to be different.

"I thought I made it clear a long time ago that I didn't want you calling here or coming here."

"You didn't mention anything about my coming to—"

"Honestly, Cathy," he interrupted, "you're being obtuse."

An aching loneliness swept over her, and she lowered her gaze, studying the intricate pattern of the floor. "I don't mind you working so hard or so late, but it's hurting Angela. I wish you'd make an effort to be home for her sake."

"Not yours?" The question was tossed at her jeeringly.

She swallowed and shook her head. "No," she lied, "not mine."

The silence hung like a stormy, gray cloud between them.

"Is that all?" Grady questioned.

"Yes," she nodded, her eyes avoiding his. "I won't trouble you again."

"Good."

With that she walked to the door, her hand on the knob. "After all I know exactly why you married me. As a live-in babysitter, my place isn't here or sharing your life."

Her accusations seemed to irritate him all the more. "My reasons or lack of reasons for marrying you have nothing to do with this."

"Then what does?"

A weary look stole over him, and he rubbed a hand over his face and eyes. "Nothing. I'll try and be home for dinner for Angela, but I won't promise anything."

"I suppose I should thank you for that, but somehow it's not in me."

To his credit Grady made a genuine effort to be home for dinner. Afterward he spent time with Angela, but when the little girl was in bed he often made an excuse to return to the office. Within a week he was back to the late nights, although he'd speak to Angela over the phone if he was going to miss dinner.

This whole craziness with Grady had been going on for almost a month and Cathy had yet to learn what was troubling him. He hardly spoke to her unless it was necessary. Only when he was asleep did he hold her close or display her any heed.

"Daddy's birthday is tomorrow," Angela announced at the breakfast table Monday morning.

Cathy continued to stir her coffee. The black liquid formed a whirlpool that swirled long after she removed her spoon.

"Can I bake him a cake all by myself?" Angela questioned between bites of hot cereal. "And Ugly Arnie and me could put up a sign and have a surprise party and make hats and decorate the table and—"

Laughing, Cathy waved her hand to stop the child. "I get the idea."

"Oh, Cathy, can I please, can I, all my myself for Daddy?" Her pretty blue eyes studied her imploringly.

"Sure." Cathy attempted a smile. "It'll be fun." Nothing was fun anymore. After a while even Linda had noted something was wrong. Cathy had been able to disguise most of her unhappiness because Linda was preoccupied with Katy. When she questioned her, Cathy had done her best to brush off Linda's concern, but her crushed spirit was impossible to hide, and when asked, Cathy had burst into tears. It was impossible to tell Linda what was wrong when she didn't know herself.

"I can bake the cake all by myself?" Angela questioned again. "And the frosting?"

"Only if you let me lick the beaters," Cathy teased.

Cathy rose with Grady the next morning, packing his lunch and filling the thermos with coffee.

"What time will you be home tonight?" Her back was to him. She didn't need to turn around to feel Grady's resentment. He hated accounting for his time to her or anyone. She wouldn't have asked him now except that Angela had worked so hard planning a surprise party.

"I'll be home when I get here," he said tightly. "Don't push me, Cathy."

She whirled around, her eyes flashing angry sparks. "Don't push you?" she hurled back. "Blast it, Grady Jones, either you be on time for dinner or…or…" She couldn't think of anything that would put a chink in the steel-hard wall he had erected blocking her out of his life.

"Or what?" he taunted, his voice grating as if he found her sudden display of temper amusing.

Defeated, she avoided his eyes. "Please, Grady, just be home."

He didn't answer. Instead he grabbed his lunch and stalked out the back door.

"Cathy, come look," Angela called from the living room. "Everything's ready." The decorated cake sat in the middle of the dining room table surrounded by several small gifts. Angela's banner hung across the doorway made of bold colored letters spelling out *Happie Birthday, Love Angela.* Beside the name she had drawn a paw print. From the time Angela walked in the door that afternoon she had spent every minute working on getting ready for the party. Proudly she had baked the cake and frosted it. Thirty-four candles were tilted on a lopsided surface.

For her party Cathy had baked Grady's favorite salmon casserole and tossed a fresh spinach salad, ignoring the exorbitant price of the spinach at the store.

"Perfect." She surveyed the room with a proud glint shining from her eyes. Silently she was pleading for Grady to be on time, just this once. Surely he must have known she had asked him for a reason.

Everything was prepared and waiting at six-thirty. The table was set with their best dishes. The chilled bottle of wine was ready to open. Angela changed into the pink satin dress she had worn for the wedding, and Cathy was amazed to note that the child had shot up a good inch in the five months since she'd married Grady.

"Wear something fancy too," Angela insisted and proceeded to go through Cathy's closet choosing a dress.

Cathy smiled weakly at the sleek evening gown Angela brought out. The dress was the only really fancy one she owned. She had worn it to a Christmas party two years ago with Steve. Even as she'd placed it in the suitcase when packing for Alaska she had asked herself why she was bringing it. The temptation had been so strong to hold on to any part of the relationship that she kept it. It had been childish, stupid. She realized that now. Her love for Grady had opened her eyes to several things she'd refused to recognize in the past.

"No." Cathy struggled to keep her voice even. "I don't think I should wear that dress, it's too fancy. Let's pick out something else."

With a disappointed sigh, Angela did as she asked. Finally Cathy agreed to wear the white wool suit she had worn on her wedding day.

Next Angela insisted they wait in the living room. The minute they heard Grady the plan was to hide, then scream surprise when he walked into the room. Eager and fidgeting Angela waited until almost seven-thirty.

"This is ridiculous," Cathy complained and stormed into the kitchen to telephone his office. The phone rang several times before there was an answer.

"Yeah."

Ray. Cathy swallowed and turned her back to Angela, who was anxiously watching her. "Ray, is Grady there?"

"No," the gruff voice returned. "He left about an hour ago. Anything wrong, Missus Jones?"

She wanted to scream that everything was wrong. Grady couldn't disappoint Angela this way, it would break the child's heart after she had worked so hard. "Do you happen to know where he went?" She hated to pry and pressed her mouth closed so tight that her teeth hurt.

Ray hesitated. "Can't say that I do, but as I explained not long ago, Grady don't say much to me anymore."

With shaking hands she switched the telephone from one ear to the other. "It's Grady's birthday and Angela had everything ready for a party and—"

"Don't tell him," Angela cried, tugging furiously

on Cathy's wool jacket. "It's suppose to be a surprise." Huge tears welled in the child's eyes.

"If you happen to see Grady..." She let the rest of what she was going to say fade. If Ray had heard Angela in the background there wasn't any need to continue.

"I'll see what I can do." The sound of his voice was stern and impatient. Cathy realized that for the first time in her acquaintance with Ray the older man was angry, really angry.

By the time she replaced the receiver, Angela was crying in earnest. Huge sobs shook her small frame, and Cathy cradled the child in her arms, fighting back her own disappointment.

Before nine Angela fell asleep on the sofa. Cathy left her where she was and covered her with a blanket. Nothing could convince the child to eat. Angela insisted she'd have dinner when her father came home.

After changing her clothes, Cathy took the casserole out of the oven and set it on top of the range. Having warmed for so many hours the casserole was overdone and crisp, pulled away from the edges of the dish. Her lower lip was quivering, and Cathy couldn't remember a time she was more upset or angry.

Grady had done this on purpose. He had stayed away because she had asked him to come home. If he was looking for a way to punish and hurt her he had succeeded. All her life Cathy had believed marriage was forever. Divorce was unheard of in her family. Five months was all it'd taken to destroy her marriage, and the craziest part was that she didn't even know the reason. Moisture brimmed in her eyes, and she furiously wiped the tears from her cheek.

With a burst of energy she brought out the sewing

machine. A few weeks ago she'd cut out a skirt pattern for Angela. Maybe if she kept busy she'd forget how much her heart ached.

She'd been sewing about an hour when she heard the back door open. Stiffening her back she concentrated on her task and ran the material through the machine at fifty miles an hour.

"What a domestic scene," Grady muttered as he strolled into the room. His arms were crossed in front of his chest as he stepped in front of the kitchen table.

Jabbing a pin into the cushion Cathy ignored him.

"I bet you wish that was me you were poking." Cathy ignored him completely, tucking the material together before carefully lowering the metal pressure foot and needle. She could feel Grady's gaze raking her.

"I understand you sent Ray out looking for me."

The taste of blood filled her mouth as she bit into her lip to keep from changing her expression. Again she chose to ignore him, knowing if she said anything she would regret it later. For now it was utterly important to sew.

Placing his palms on the tabletop he leaned forward. Cathy could smell beer on his breath and closed her eyes to the thought of him drinking in some tavern to avoid coming home simply because she'd asked it of him. More and more the evidence pointed to exactly that.

"All right, Cathy, what are you so mad about?"

His face was so close to hers that all she had to do was turn her head to look him in the eye. Without a word she continued sticking pins into the cotton material.

"Oh here it is, the silent treatment, I should have known I'd get it from you sooner or later." He exhaled slowly, his breath ragged and uneven. "You must have taken lessons from Pam. That was one of her tricks."

Remaining outwardly stoic, her nails cut into the palms of her hands. "I asked you before not to compare me with Pam," she said in an even, controlled voice that was barely above a whisper.

"If you don't want to be compared to her then maybe you shouldn't be as unreasonable as she was," he said.

"Unreasonable." She hurled the material onto the table and stood abruptly, knocking the kitchen chair to the floor. Jamming an index finger into his chest she stood to the full extent of her five feet eleven inches and punctuated her speech with several more vicious pokes. "I told you once before, Grady Jones, I'm not Pam. And what was between the two of you is separate from me. Is that understood?"

Grady looked taken aback for a moment but was quick to recover. His laugh was cruel. "All women are alike."

Cathy recoiled as if his words had physically struck her. Could this be the same man she'd married? The same man she had come to love? Struggling within herself she closed her eyes and heaved a sigh, swallowing back bitter words.

"I'll admit you're a much better bed partner." His voice did little to disguise his own hurt. "What do you do, pretend I'm Steve?"

Without thought or question she swung her open palm at him, intent on hurting him as much as he was hurting her.

Grady caught her wrist. Their eyes clashed, and Cathy could barely see the blurry figure that swam before her. Inhaling a sharp breath she jerked her arm free and hurried out of the kitchen. Somehow she made it to their bedroom and threw open the closet door. Dumping clothes over her arm, she carried them across the hall to the guest bedroom, making trip after trip until all her things had been transported to the spare room.

Grady stood outside the room in the narrow hallway watching her. "I expected some kind of reaction to that remark," he laughed, but the sound contained no amusement. "The truth always gets a reaction."

"The truth?" Wave after wave of hurt rippled over her. "You wouldn't know the truth if it hit you in the face."

A cold mask came over his expression.

"Daddy, Daddy."

The child's voice diverted his attention from her, and he turned as Angela hurled herself into his arms. "Happy birthday, Daddy. Did you find my surprise? Did you see the cake I baked for you? Cathy let me do it all by myself. We planned a party for you, but you were late. Come and open your gifts now, okay? Ugly Arnie got you one, too, but really it's from Cathy."

"Yes, Grady," Cathy whispered, her voice trembling, "happy birthday."

Ten

Tucking Angela into bed an hour later the little girl beamed Cathy a contended smile. "We really surprised Daddy, didn't we?"

"Yes, we did," Cathy confirmed.

"He liked all his presents, too, didn't he?" Angela whispered the question.

"I'm sure he did," Cathy said. The flesh at the back of her neck began to tingle, and she was aware that Grady had come into Angela's room. "Now it's way past your bedtime, so go to sleep, okay?"

"Okay," Angela agreed.

Tenderly Cathy kissed the child's brow and stood. She stepped around Grady as she left the room and walked into the kitchen. She was placing the cover on the sewing machine when Grady found her a few minutes later.

An electricity hung in the air like an invisible curtain between them.

"I'll do that." Grady took the portable sewing machine cover, snapped it in place, and returned it to the heated back porch, where she kept it stored. Ugly Arnie, seeing the golden opportunity to get into the house, shot between Grady's legs and scampered into the kitchen.

"Hey, fellow, you know better," Cathy admonished gently, scooping him into her arms. "You belong on the porch at night. Angela will let you in tomorrow morning."

"Here, I'll take him," Grady offered, extending his arms. His eyes just avoided meeting Cathy's.

Before handing Grady the pup, she gave the dog an affectionate squeeze and kissed the top of his head. Ugly Arnie would never claim the part of her affection that belonged to Peterkins. But more and more she recognized the wisdom Grady had shown by getting her another dog.

"You like the puppy now, don't you?" Grady questioned softly, giving her a sideways glance as he lowered Ugly Arnie to the floor and cautiously closed the back door.

"Yes, I'm grateful that we have him. You were right, there would have been a void in all our lives with Peterkins gone." She drew in a deep breath and turned toward the stove. "Did you eat?"

"No."

Cathy reached into the cupboard to take down a plate.

"Don't fix me anything. I'm not hungry."

"You can't live on coffee." Grady was losing weight, she noticed not for the first time. His clothes were beginning to hang on him. But then so had she. Try as she might she couldn't understand why were they doing this to one another.

"Don't forget the beer. I expect you to throw that at me any minute."

Clenching her fingers together, her nails dug into her

palms, cutting the skin. "Don't put words in my mouth, Grady. If you drink or work twenty-four hours a day it has nothing to do with me. You've made my position in your life clear."

"Oh, and how's that?" He leaned against the kitchen counter, crossing his arms as he regarded her steadily.

She shook her head and averted her gaze. What good would it do to accuse one another? Not tonight, not when she was hurt and angry. "Grady, I'm tired." She made the excuse. "I don't want to talk about it now. All I want is a good night's sleep. Maybe you can get by on three and four hours' rest, but I can't."

"I suppose you're waiting for a humble apology—"

"No," she interrupted him abruptly. "I've come to the point that I don't expect anything from you."

A faint shadow of regret and uncertainty was revealed in his expression as he followed her out of the kitchen.

She paused in the hallway outside their bedroom. Her things had been haphazardly thrown across the mattress in the guest bedroom. In the room she shared with Grady the dresser drawers were left open and dangling, a testimony to their argument a short while before. Now she had to decide where she would sleep. Should she make a pretense of going into the other room and wait for Grady to stop her? Would he? Should she cling to the last vestige of her pride and march into the other guest bedroom?

As if he understood her dilemma, Grady stopped a few feet behind her and said, "Maybe it would be better for all concerned if you slept in the other room."

Cathy swallowed hard and nodded. He'd made the decision for her.

"That was what you wanted, wasn't it?" The question came at her harshly. "You're the one who wanted out."

Pride directed her actions. "Yes, I did," she murmured sadly and entered the room, softly closing the door. She stood there for several moments, fighting the urge to throw away her pride; rush to Grady and demand to know what had happened—what had gone wrong with them. Instead she strode to the bed and began making neat piles of clothes on the floor so she would have a place to sleep.

Sleep, her lip curled up in a self-derisive movement. What chance was there with Grady across the hall? He may well have been on the other side of the world for all the good it did her. She rolled over, hoping to find a more comfortable position on the lumpy mattress. If she lay still she could hear Grady's movements from the room opposite hers. All she could do was hope that he was even half as miserable as she. All she could do was pray that he longed for her the way she yearned for the comfort of his arms. More and more it was clear that he didn't care about their marriage. And frankly, she didn't know how much longer they could continue with this terrible tension between them? Questions seemed to come at her from all sides. But Cathy found no answers.

"You look awful."

Linda's observation flustered Cathy as she poured herself a cup of coffee in the teachers' lounge early the next morning.

"I'm okay." She brushed off her friend's concern and added a teaspoon of sugar to the coffee, hoping something sweet would give her the fortitude to make it through the first class.

"Things aren't right with you and Grady, are they?"

Linda never had been one to skirt around a subject. If she had something on her mind, she said it.

"No, they're not," Cathy replied truthfully and set her mug on the circular table.

"Why?"

Cathy rested her hand over the top of her mug, the steam-generated heat burned her palm. "I don't know." Tears just beneath the surface welled in the dark depth of her gray eyes. "I just don't know." She hung her head, unwilling for Linda to see the emotion that seemed to bleed out of her.

"Then find out." Linda made everything sound so simple, so basic.

"Don't you think I've tried?" The sound of Cathy's voice fluctuated drastically. "I'd give anything to know what's wrong between us. Grady's pulling away from me more and more every day. I hardly see him anymore and...and we aren't even sleeping together. The crazy thing is—" she stopped and took in a quivering breath "—I haven't the foggiest idea why."

"Talk to him, for heaven's sake," Linda suggested as if it was the most logical thing to do. "You can't go on like this, Cath. You're so pale now, your face is ashen, and you've lost weight."

"It isn't that easy," Cathy snapped, then immediately regretted the small display of temper. Linda was only trying to help. There had never been a time in Cathy's life when she felt she needed a friend more.

"I'm sure it isn't," Linda agreed in a sober voice. "But nothing worthwhile ever is. What you need is some time together alone."

"But there's Angela." Several times in the past weeks

the opportunity had come to confront Grady, but Angela had always been present. Although she dearly loved the child, Cathy didn't feel she should air their differences in front of her.

"I'll take Angela for the night," Linda offered.

Cathy looked up, surprised.

"No, I mean it. I've been wanting Katy and Angela to see more of one another. I'd like for the girls to become friends. I'll pick her up after school, and that way when Grady gets home you two will be alone and can talk this thing out without an audience."

"Oh, Linda, would you?"

"What are friends for?" she asked with a warm smile.

Cathy's spirits lifted immediately. This was what she and Grady needed. Whatever had happened, whatever she'd done, the air would finally be cleared.

Not until that afternoon when Cathy was sitting at her desk contemplating the confrontation with Grady did she consider that the change in his personality might not be because of their relationship. Maybe something was wrong with Alaska Cargo. Certainly something as traumatic as his business would account for the personality switch. More than that, Grady was unlikely to confide in her if he was experiencing troubles with his company.

Linda picked up Angela at the house a few minutes before five, and Cathy stood in the driveway waving as the car pulled onto the street. Two brown heads bobbed up and down from the backseat, and Cathy smiled at her friend's eagerness to be indoctrinated into the delights of motherhood.

Releasing a sigh, Cathy looked around her. The sun was shining and the sky was that fantastic blue she had marveled at when first moving to Alaska. The day held promise, more promise than she had felt in a long time.

Ugly Arnie tangled with her feet as she came in the door, and she stooped to pet his short fur. "How is it a handsome fellow like you got stuck with a name like Ugly Arnie?" She giggled and stopped midstep aghast at the sound. She had laughed! Cathy couldn't remember how long ago it had been since she had found something amusing.

Glancing at her watch she noted that it could be long hours before Grady arrived home. He was flying into Anchorage for supplies. She'd overheard him telling Angela as much that morning. If there was something wrong with the business, there was only one person she knew who would tell her. Ray.

Without questioning the wisdom of her actions, she drove to the field. Ray walked out of the hangar, a look of surprise furrowing his brow as he met her.

"Howdy, Ray." Her voice was carried with the wind. It whipped at her hair, tossing the long tendrils across her face. She pulled the strands free from her cheek with an index finger. "Grady's not around is he?"

Ray shook his head, wiping his hands on the ever present rag that hung from his back hip pocket. "Nope, he's in the air."

"Good." She laughed at Ray's expression. "It's you I want to talk to."

"Me?" The older man looked ever more astonished.

"Don't suppose you have any of that stuff you call coffee around?"

"Put a fresh pot on only yesterday," he teased with a roguish grin. "Let's go in the office, we're not as likely to be disturbed there."

Cathy followed him, and Ray stepped aside in a gentlemanly gesture, allowing her to precede him into the office. Glancing around her, a smile touched the edges of her mouth. The room never seemed to change. The same newspapers littered the worn chairs, the ashtray was just as full and the counter just as crowded.

"Here." Ray handed her a white styrofoam cup filled with steaming coffee.

Cathy blew into the liquid before taking a tentative sip, then grimaced at the bitter taste. Grady claimed all the hair on his chest was due to Ray's coffee. One sip and she didn't doubt it.

Ray pulled out a chair for her to sit down as he leaned against the counter, his hand cupping the mug.

"I want to talk to you about Grady," Cathy said, her eyes nervously avoiding his.

"To be truthful," Ray replied, "I'd like to ask you a few things, too."

"You would?" Her head shot up.

"Grady ain't been himself lately."

"I know," Cathy said with a sigh. "Ray, I'm worried. I thought it might be something at the office."

The mechanic's mouth twisted in a wry smile. "I assumed it was something at home."

"You mean you don't know what's wrong either?" Her voice was filled with disappointment.

The thin shoulders lifted with a shrug. "After you were first married Grady seemed more content than I can remember him being in a long time. He even hired a couple extra men to take on some of the flying he used to do so that he could spend more time at home. Several days he'd come into work whistling, happy as

I've ever seen him. Then suddenly—" he paused and snapped his fingers "—everything changed."

"But what?" she cried out softly.

Sadly, Ray shook his head. "I don't know. I just don't know. But I don't mind telling you, I'm plenty concerned. He's going to kill himself if he doesn't let up soon."

A feeling of utter helplessness washed over her.

"You love him, don't you?" The question was more a statement of fact.

"Oh, yes," she said and breathed, "very much."

Satisfied, Ray nodded. "Then things will work out, don't you fret."

Later as Cathy pulled into the driveway she felt reassured by Ray's attitude. Ugly Arnie scampered to the front door and jumped against her pants legs in greeting. "Come on, boy," she instructed, not bothering to remove her coat. She strode into the spare room and immediately returned her things to the master bedroom where they belonged. It took far longer to cart her things back than it had to remove them the night before.

Hands resting on her hips, she surveyed the room once everything had been transported. With a satisfied smile she released a small breath.

The phone rang, and she hurried into the kitchen.

"Hello."

"Hi." It was Linda. "I hope I'm not interrupting anything."

"No, Grady's not home yet. Is something wrong?"

"Not really, but Angela forgot her suitcase and she was wondering if you would bring it over. I've assured her several times that she can wear Katy's pajamas tonight, but apparently the suitcase contains some irreplaceable treasures."

Cathy smiled. "I'll bring it right away." They spoke for a few minutes longer before Cathy replaced the receiver.

The suitcase was on top of Angela's bed, and Cathy couldn't contain her amusement. It looked as if Angela had packed everything she owned. Opening the clasp she viewed enough clothes for a three-week vacation, plus several stuffed animals and the child's favorite books.

Hauling the suitcase into the living room, Cathy turned at the unexpected sound. Grady stood poised in the kitchen doorway.

Her gray eyes blinked at the tall dejected figure. He looked more defeated than she had ever seen him, his shoulders hunched as if he was carrying the heaviest of burdens.

Held motionless by the sadness in his eyes, Cathy inhaled sharply, watching the color drain out of his face. Clearly something was drastically wrong. She followed his gaze, which rested on the suitcase in her hand, then stared back into his bloodless features. *He thinks I'm leaving him,* she thought miserably.

He thinks I'm running away. An eternity passed and still she couldn't pull her eyes from him. Tears clouded her vision, and for the first time Cathy realized how useless the situation was between them. Things had gone too far, and there was nothing she could do to save this marriage.

Every step was slow, calculated as she turned around and walked away.

He wouldn't stop her. She remembered a conversation they'd had shortly after they first met. Pam would pace her bags and threaten to leave him and he refused to stop her. She'd been shocked that he could be so heartless, but his pride wouldn't let him stop her. He wouldn't her stop her either. Squaring her shoulders, she headed toward the door.

Grady inhaled sharply and cried out. "Don't go."

Cathy stopped, her face incredulous. "What did you say?" she asked in a hushed whisper.

Eleven

Grady continued to stare at her, his eyes dark and haunted. He ran a weary hand over his face and looked away. "Don't leave me."

Just as she assumed, he believed she was playing games with him the way Pam had done, packing her things, threatening to leave.

"Why?" The question was bitter.

"I need you." He sounded gruff, almost defensive. "I know how much you love Steve but—"

"Steve!" she cried, dropping the suitcase. "How can you think I want Steve when I'm in love with you?"

The dark, tortured eyes deepened, followed by a short, bitter laugh. "Cathy, don't lie to me," he murmured.

"Lie?" The muscles of her throat were so tight she could barely swallow. "I love you so much that if you push me out of your life any further I think I'll die."

Disbelief drove creases into his brow. "But I love you." The words were issued in an aching whisper as he advanced into the room.

Cathy didn't need any encouragement to meet him

halfway. She walked into his arms, knowing how much the words had cost him. Grady's arms closed around her so hard and strong she couldn't breathe. Not that it mattered when he told her of his love.

His breathing was ragged and uneven as he buried his face in her hair, and she felt him shudder against her. For a long breathless moment he did nothing more than hold her. Never had Cathy felt such peace, such contentment.

His kiss was filled with so much need that the single meeting of their lips was enough to erase all the pain and uncertainty of the past month.

"I need you," he breathed into her hair. "I didn't mean to fall in love with you. I thought we could marry and I'd remain detached from any emotional commitment."

Her hands reached to his face, gently caressing the proud line of his jaw. "I love you so much, how could you have doubted?"

Grady broke the embrace and took several short steps before pivoting back to her. "We'd only seen one another a couple of times before I guessed that you'd been deeply hurt by another man. It didn't take much longer to realize you were still in love with him." He paused and ran his fingers through the curly hair at the side of his head. "I think I almost preferred it that way. You had a relationship you were trying to forget and so did I."

"But the past is over," she whispered. "I confess I thought I was in love with Steve when we married. But I wasn't. Not until the night Peterkins died did I realize that I couldn't love Steve when I was in love with you."

She saw the look of surprise come over him. She moved to his side, lifting her lips to his lean jaw.

He cupped her face with his hands, his thumb tracing her lips, his mouth following.

With her arm wrapped around his waist, Cathy laid her head upon his chest and heard the rapid, staccato beat of his heart.

"That was the first night you initiated our lovemaking," he whispered against her hair.

"There'll be more times," she promised with a contented smile. "You were so tender, so gentle that night, almost as if my pain were your own."

"It was." His breath stirred the hairs at the crown of her head. "I knew how much you cared about Peterkins. I also knew that Steve had given you the dog. Getting a puppy so soon afterward wasn't a brilliant idea, but when I saw the way you looked at Arnie."

"Ugly Arnie," she corrected.

"Ugly Arnie," he repeated, a smile evident in his voice. "I realized then that you would probably never get over loving Steve."

"But you're wrong," she said desperately. "Peterkins was separate from Steve. I was so afraid you would misconstrue that. You left for the office that day, and I knew my reaction to Ugly Arnie had hurt you. I was angry with myself when later I realized it was at that point that you drew away from me."

"That wasn't it." His hold on her relaxed, and she heard the deep, uneven breath he expelled. "When I got to the office that day a letter from Steve was waiting for me."

Shock jerked her head back as she stared at Grady. "A letter from Steve? Why?"

Gently he kissed her forehead. "He reminded me that you were in love with him. It seemed so logical, especially after the scene that afternoon with the puppy and you telling Angela that when a person loves someone it takes a long time to forget that person."

"But, Grady," she said in a determined tone, "I was referring to the dog, not Steve."

Tight-lipped, he nodded. "But at the time I didn't doubt the truth of his statement. Steve said that if I had any deep feelings for you then I would see the truth and would set you free."

"No," she gasped and tightened her arms around his middle.

"Steve told me what had happened and how he'd gotten caught in a chain of events that led to the wedding with your sister. He explained how things got so involved and tangled to the point that he couldn't back out of the marriage. He said it was the same thing that had happened with us."

"But, Grady, that's not true. You know it," she whispered emphatically. "You were there at the hotel room, you gave me the choice."

"But I knew when you came to me you loved Steve. The letter made sense. The man admitted what a terrible mistake he made in marrying MaryAnne. But he realized what he'd done and loved and needed you. He begged me, Cathy, he begged me to set you free. A man doesn't do that kind of thing lightly. He loves you."

"No, he doesn't," she contradicted forcefully. "If Steve had actually cared for me he would never have married my sister."

Grady's look was hard, resolute. "I didn't expect to love you. After the letter arrived I knew I should probably do the noble thing and send you to Steve. I guess these past weeks I was attempting to drive you away.

Then today one look at you with that suitcase and I knew if you left a part of me would die. I love you more than I thought it was possible to love another human being. You've brought happiness and joy into my life and Angela's."

"But, Grady." Both hands cupped his jaw, and she turned his face so she could look into the intense blue eyes. "I wasn't leaving."

A disbelieving look came over him. "But the suitcase."

"Is for Angela, she's spending the night with Linda, Dan, and Katy." She laughed softly, her heart overflowing with an unrestrained happiness. "Angela's staying with them so you and I could talk. I couldn't bear to have things as they were between us. I had to find out what was bothering you."

Grady's look was tender and searching. "For a month I've lived with a terrible guilt, knowing I should set you free and holding on to you. For a time I tried to convince myself that I couldn't let you go for Angela's sake. But I was only trying to fool myself. I love you, Cathy Thompson Jones. You are my wife and will remain so all our lives." He spoke in a tone that was almost reverent.

"And you, Grady Jones, are my husband, the man I want to share my life, to father my children. You must promise me never, ever to hide anything like that from me again. Promise never to doubt me again or my love for you and Angela."

"I promise." The words were emitted on a husky breath just before his lips sealed the vow.

Contentedly Cathy lay in her husband's arms. Slowly her eyelids lowered as she suppressed a yawn. Grady's arm curved around her possessively, and she nestled into the crook of his arm.

"Are you happy?" he questioned and brushed his lips over her temple.

"Blessedly so." One long fingernail drew tantalizing circles over his bare chest, tangling the curly hairs that grew in abundance there.

Grady lackadaisically ran his fingers through the long silken strands of her hair and gradually down the fragile hollow of her throat. His lips were pressed against her hair as if he couldn't yet believe she was here with him in their bed.

"Don't ever send me to the guest bedroom again," she said with a sigh, turning her face so her tongue could provocatively explore his neck and throat. She paused in her examination. "The mattress is lumpy."

Grady laughed quietly. "Never again."

"Did you notice I moved my things back in here this afternoon?"

"No." He raised himself up on one elbow, his gaze doing a sweeping inspection of the room.

"I wasn't about to give up on 'us,' Grady. Not when I love you so much."

"I don't think I've ever noticed how talkative you are," he murmured, smoothing the hair away from the sides of her face. A moan of anticipation came deep from within him as he lowered his mouth to hers, covered her body with his.

Immediately Cathy was aware of his need and answered with her own, wrapping her arms around him. A long time passed before either of them spoke again.

"Grady," she whispered, loving the feel of his hands as they caressed her. "I'm going to have a baby."

The room became instantly silent, even Grady's breathing seemed to have stopped.

"A baby," he repeated incredulously.

The silence grew and grew.

"How?"

"How?" She laughed and pressed her lips to the pulse hammering wildly at the base of his neck. "Would you like me to show you…how?"

"You know what I mean."

"I do?" she teased.

"A baby," he murmured huskily. "Why didn't you say something earlier? You should never had kept this from me." He took in a huge, wondrous breath. "I guessed as much when Angela said something about being a big sister not long ago. I even asked you. But you denied it."

"Grady," Cathy attempted to explain, but his arms closed around her fiercely, and she asked, "Are you pleased?"

"Oh, yes, very pleased. When are you due?"

Laughter bubbled from her throat. "In about nine months, give or take a week."

"Nine months?" he shot back with a chuckle. "Should we start now?"

The sharp trill of the phone broke into the conversation. Instantly Cathy sat up in the bed, pulling the sheet over her naked breasts. "Angela," she said in alarm. "I didn't take her the suitcase."

A half hour later Grady and Cathy had dressed and were on their way out the back door. Grady carried the large suitcase in one hand and slipped the other arm around his wife's waist, pulling her close to his side.

"I've been thinking I'd like you to teach me to fly," she said, a tremulous smile lighting up her face.

Grady's look was tender as his gaze rested on her. "Want to learn to soar to unknown heights, is that it?"

Cathy laughed, leaning against the quiet strength of this man she loved. "When I'm with you, Grady Jones, who needs a plane?"

* * * * *

BORROWED DREAMS

One

"Don't worry about a thing," George Hamlyn stated casually on his way out the door.

"Yes...but—" Carly Grieves interrupted. This was her first day on the job in Anchorage, Alaska, and she was hoping for a bit more instruction. "But...what would you like me to do?"

"Take any phone messages and straighten the place up a bit. That should keep you busy for the day." He removed his faded cap and wiped his forearm across his wide brow as he paused just inside the open doorway.

All day! Carly mused irritably. "What time should I expect you back?"

"Not until afternoon at the earliest. I'm late now." His voice was tinged with impatience. "A couple of drivers will be checking in soon. They have their instructions."

Fleetingly, Carly wondered if their orders were as vague as her own.

"See you later." George tossed her a half smile and was out the door before she could form another protest.

Carly dropped both hands lifelessly to her sides in frustrated displeasure. How could George possibly expect her to manage the entire office on her own? But, apparently, he did just that. On her first day, no less. With only a minimum of instruction, she was to take over the management of Alaska Freight Forwarding in her employer's absence.

"Didn't Diana warn you this would happen?" She spoke out loud, standing in the middle of the room, feeling hopelessly inadequate. Good heavens, what had she gotten herself into with this job?

Hands on hips, Carly surveyed the room's messy interior. George had explained, apologetically, that his last traffic supervisor had left three months ago. One look at the office confirmed his statement. She couldn't help wondering how anyone could run a profitable business in such chaos. The long counter was covered with order forms and a variety of correspondence, some stained with dried coffee; the ashtray that sat at one end was filled to overflowing. Cardboard boxes littered the floor, some stacked as high as the ceiling. The two desks were a disaster; a second full ashtray rested in the center of hers, on top of stacked papers, and empty coffee mugs dotted its once polished wood surface. The air was heavy with the smell of stale tobacco.

Forcefully expelling an uneven sigh, Carly paused and wound a strand of rich brown hair around her ear.

Straighten the place up a bit! her mind mimicked George's words. She hadn't come all the way from Seattle to clean offices. Her title was traffic supervisor, not janitor!

Annoyed with herself for letting George walk all over her, Carly got her desk in reasonable order and straightened the papers on the counter. She grimaced as she examined the inside of the coffeepot. It looked like someone had dumped chocolate syrup in it. She guessed it had never been washed.

When the phone rang, she answered in a brisk, professional tone. “Alaska Freight Forwarding.”

A short hesitation followed. “Who’s this?”

Squaring her shoulders, she replied crisply. “Carly Grieves. May I ask who’s calling?”

The man at the other end of the line ignored the question. “Let me talk to George.”

It seemed no one in Alaska had manners. “George is out for the day. May I ask who’s calling?”

Whoever was on the line let out a curse. “I beg your pardon?”

“When do you expect him back?”

“Well, Mr. Blanky Blank, I can’t rightly say.”

“I’ll be there in ten minutes.” With that, he abruptly severed their connection.

Sighing, Carly replaced the receiver. Apparently Mr. Blanky Blank thought she could tell him something more in person.

A few minutes later, the door burst open and a man as lean and serious as an arctic wolf strode briskly inside and stopped just short of the counter. Dark flecks sparked with interest in eyes that were wide and deeply set. He was dressed in a faded jean jacket and worn jeans, and his Western-style, checkered shirt was open at the throat to reveal a broad chest with a sprinkling of curly, dark hair.

“Carly Grieves?” he questioned as his mouth quirked into a coaxing smile.

“Mr. Blanky Blank?” she returned, and smiled. His lean face was tanned from exposure to the elements. The dark, wind-tossed hair was indifferent to any style.

This man was earthy and perhaps a little wild—the kind of wild that immediately gave women the desire to tame. Carly was no exception.

"Brand St. Clair," he murmured, his friendly eyes not leaving hers as he extended his hand.

Her own much smaller hand was enveloped in his callused, roughened one. "I'm taking a truck," he announced without preamble.

"You're what?" Carly blinked.

"I haven't got time to explain. Tell George I was by—he'll understand."

"I can't let you do that…I don't think…" Carly stammered, not knowing what to do. Brand St. Clair wasn't on the clipboard that listed Alaska Freight Forwarding employees. What if one of the men from the warehouse needed a truck later? She didn't know this man. True, he was strikingly attractive, but he'd undoubtedly used that to his advantage more than once. "I can't let you do that," she decided firmly, her voice gaining strength.

Brand smiled, but the amusement didn't touch his dusky, dark eyes. Despite the casual way he was leaning against the counter, Carly recognized that he was tense and alert. The thought came that this man was deceptive. For all his good looks and charming smile, it could be unwise to cross him.

"I apologize if this is inconvenient," she began, and clasped her hands together with determination. "But I've only just started this job. I don't know you. I don't know if George Hamlyn is in the habit of lending out his trucks, and furthermore…"

"I'll accept full responsibility." He took his wallet from his back hip pocket and withdrew a business card, handing it to her.

Carly read the small print. Brand was a pilot who free-lanced his services to freight operators.

"A hiker in Denali Park has been injured," he explained shortly. "I'm meeting the park rangers and airlifting him to British Columbia." The impatient way he spoke told Carly he wasn't accustomed to making explanations.

"I…I…" Carly paused, uncertain.

"Do I get the truck or not?"

She unclenched and clenched her fist again. "All right," she finally conceded, and handed over the set of keys.

He gave her a brief salute and was out the door.

She stood at the wide front window that faced the street and watched as Brand backed the pickup truck onto the road, changed gears and sped out of sight. Shrugging one shoulder, she arched two delicate brows expressively. Life in the north could certainly be unnerving.

"A pilot," she murmured. Flying was something that had intrigued her from childhood. The idea of soaring thousands of feet above the earth with only a humming engine keeping her aloft produced a thrill of adventure. Carly wondered fleetingly if she'd get the opportunity to learn to fly while in Alaska.

She paused, continuing to stand at the window. Her attraction to the rugged stranger surprised her. She preferred her men tame and uncomplicated, but Brand St. Clair had aroused her curiosity. She couldn't put her finger on exactly why, but it felt as real and intense as anything she'd ever experienced. He exuded an animal magnetism. She'd been exposed to those male qualities a hundred times and had walked away yawning. Whatever it was about him, Carly was intrigued. She found she was affected by their short encounter. She stood looking out the office window, watching the road long after the truck was out of sight.

Once the formica counter was cleaned, the orders piled in neat stacks, and the boxes pushed to one side of the office, Carly took a short break. The phone rang several times and Carly wrote down the messages dutifully, placing them on George's desk. A warehouse man came in and introduced himself before lunch, but was gone before Carly could question him about the truck Brand St. Clair had taken.

With time on her hands the afternoon dragged, and Carly busied herself by sorting through the filing cabinets. If the office was in disarray, it was nothing compared to the haphazard methods George Hamyln employed for filing.

When George sauntered in around five he stopped in the doorway and glanced around before giving Carly an approving nod.

"I'd like to talk to you a minute," she said stiffly. She wasn't above admitting she'd made a mistake by moving to Alaska. She could cut her losses and headed back to Seattle. If he needed someone to clean house, she wasn't it.

"Sure." He shrugged and sat down at his desk. Although George possessed a full head of white hair, he didn't look more than fifty. Guessing his age was difficult. George's eyes sparklied with life and vitality. "What can I do for you?" he asked as he rolled back his chair and casually rested an ankle on top of his knee.

Carly remained standing. "First off, I'm a freight

traffic supervisor. I didn't cart everything I own a thousand miles to clean your coffeepot or anything else."

"That's fine." George's smile was absent as he shuffled through the phone messages. "Contact a janitorial service. I've been meaning to do that myself."

His assurance took some of the steam from her anger. "And another thing. Brand St. Clair was in and took... *borrowed* a truck. He said it was an emergency and I wasn't sure if I should've stopped him."

"No problem." George glanced up, looking mildly surprised. His thoughts seemed to have drifted a thousand miles from her indignation. "One of these days that boy will come to his senses and give it up."

"'Give it up'?" Carly repeated, amused that she'd verbalized the thought.

George nodded, then set the mail aside. "I've been after Brand to join up with us. He's a good pilot." His eyes moved to Carly and he lifted one shoulder in an indifferent shrug. "Not likely, though, with all those medical bills he's paying off. He can earn twice the money free-lancing."

"Medical bills?" Carly asked, curious to find out what she could about the man.

George appeared not to have heard her question. "Any other problems?"

"Not really."

He shook his head, his eyes drifting to the stack of mail. "I'll see you in the morning then."

There was no mistaking the dismissal in his tone. Already he had turned his attention to the desk.

Carly left the office shortly afterward, wondering how much longer George would be staying. The man was apparently married to his job. There was little evidence in the office that he had a wife and family. And the hours he seemed to keep would prohibit any kind of life outside the company.

The apartment Carly had rented on Weimer Drive was a plain one-bedroom place that was barely large enough to hold all her furniture. Some of her things were being shipped from Seattle and wouldn't arrive for another month. Diana—dear, sweet, Diana—couldn't believe that Carly would give up a good job in comfortable surroundings on the basis of a few phone conversations with George Hamlyn from the parent company. Her friend was convinced Carly was running. But she wasn't. Alaska offered adventure, and she'd been ready for a change.

Hugging her legs, her chin resting on a bent knee, Carly sat on the modern, overstuffed sofa in her new living room. She hadn't expected to find Alaska so beautiful. The subtle elegance, the immensity had enthralled her. Barren and dingy was what she'd been told to expect. Instead, she found the air crisp and clean. The skies were as blue as the Caribbean Sea. This state was so vast it was like a mother with her arms opened wide to lovingly bring the lost into her wide embrace.

"A mother…" Carly smiled absently. The perfect Freudian slip.

The nightmare returned that night. For years she'd been free of the terror that gripped her in the dark void of sleep, but that night she woke in a cold sweat, sitting up in bed and trembling. Perspiration dotted her face and she took several deep, calming breaths. The dream was so vivid. So real. What had brought back the childhood nightmare? Why now, after all these years?

As she laid her head against the pillow and closed her eyes, Carly attempted to form a mental image of her mother. Nothing came but a stilted picture of the tall, dark-haired stranger in the photo Carly had carried with her from foster home to foster home.

She woke the following morning feeling as if she hadn't slept all night. After the nightmare her sleep had been fitful, intermittent. Dark images played on the edges of her consciousness, shadows leaping out at her, wanting to engulf her in their dusk. Half of her yearned to surrender to the black void that beckoned, while the other half feared what she would discover if she ventured inside.

Brand St. Clair was sitting on the corner of her desk, one foot dangling over the edge, when Carly walked into the office later that morning.

"Morning." His greeting was casual.

"Hi." Carly's response was equally carefree. "Come to borrow another truck?"

"No. I thought I'd bring you coffee and a Danish as a peace offering."

Her gaze went to the white sack in the center of the desk. "That wasn't necessary."

He opened the sack and took out a foam cup, removing the plastic lid before handing it to her.

"Thanks."

Brand removed a second cup for himself. "I don't suppose you do any bookkeeping on the side?"

The question took her by surprise. "My dear Mr. St. Clair, I am a traffic supervisor, not an accountant." A thin thread of humorous sarcasm ran through her voice. "I haven't studied bookkeeping since high school."

Amusement flashed across his handsome features. “I’d be willing to pay you to take a look at my books. The whole accounting system is beyond me.”

“You’re serious, aren’t you?”

He smiled. Carly studied him and speculated that the crow’s-feet weren’t from smiling.

“I couldn’t mean it more.”

Carly took the chair and crossed her long legs, hoping he’d notice her designer nylons with their tiny blue stars. “Unfortunately, I’ve only had a few courses in bookkeeping. I’d only make matters worse.” *Dear heavens,* Carly mused, stifling a laugh. She was flirting. Blatantly flirting! She hadn’t done anything so outrageous in years. Her first impression of Brand yesterday was accurate. He was a wolf, all right, and more sensual than just about any man she knew. She guessed there was more to him than met the eye—and her response to him proved there was more to *her* than she’d realized.

Whistling, George sauntered into the office, carrying a steaming mug in one hand.

“Good morning,” he greeted in a cheery singsong voice. He seemed surprised to see Brand. “Good to see you, St. Clair. How did everything go yesterday?”

The glance Brand threw to Carly was decidedly uncomfortable. “Fine.” The lone word was clipped and impatient.

“I talked to Jones this morning,” George continued. “He explained the situation. I would have hated your losing that commission for lack of a truck.”

“Commission?” Carly’s dark eyes sparked with anger. “Was that before or after you rescued the poor injured hiker off Denali?”

"Hiker?" George's gaze floated from one to the other.

"You wouldn't have given me the truck otherwise," Brand inserted, ignoring George.

"You're right, I wouldn't have."

"I got a message that you wanted to see me." Brand directed his attention to George.

"As a matter of fact, I did." George adopted a businesslike attitude. "Come into the warehouse. I want to talk to you about something." He turned toward Carly and grinned sheepishly. "I don't suppose you'd mind putting on a pot of coffee? We're both going to need it before this morning's over."

Carly opened and closed her mouth. Coffee making hadn't been listed in her job description, but she complied willingly, rather than argue.

The two men were deep in conversation as they headed toward the door. Brand stopped and turned to Carly. "Think about what I said," he murmured, and smiled. It was one of those bone-melting, earth-shattering smiles meant to disarm the most sophisticated of women. But the amazing part of it all was that he didn't seem to recognize the effect he had on her. The gesture should have disarmed her; instead, it only served to confuse her further.

She was busy at her desk when Brand returned alone a half hour later.

"I meant what I said about paying you for some bookkeeping."

"I'm sorry," she returned on a falsely cheerful note, "but I'm busy. There's an important rescue I'm performing in Denali Park this weekend."

Brand didn't look pleased.

To hide her smile, Carly pretended an inordinate interest in her work, making a show of shuffling papers around. "Was there anything else?"

Slowly, his gaze traveled over her. When he didn't answer right away, Carly looked up. She'd been angry at his deception, disliking the way he'd gone about borrowing the truck. But one look and she had to fight her way out of the whirlpool effect he had on her senses.

"Think about it," he said in a slightly husky voice.

"There isn't anything to think about," she returned smoothly, her tone belying the erratic pounding of her heart. When he walked out the door Carly was shocked to discover that her fingers were trembling. "Get a hold on yourself, old girl," she chastised herself in a breathy murmur, half surprised, half angry at her reaction to this man. Brand St. Clair had an uncanny knack for forcing her to recognize her own sensuality. And Carly found that highly disturbing.

As the week progressed, Carly couldn't decide if she was pleased or disconcerted when she didn't see Brand again. Her job was settling into a routine aside from a few minor clashes with George. He gladly surrendered the paperwork to her, preferring that she handle the collection and claims while he took care of the routing.

On Friday afternoon Brand strolled through the office door and beamed her a bright smile. "Hello again."

"Hello." Carly forced an answering smile. "George is out for the day."

"I know. It's you I wanted to see."

"Oh." She swallowed uncomfortably, disliking the way her heart reacted to seeing him again.

"I just stopped by to see if you'd be interested in going flying with me tomorrow."

Carly stared at him blankly, confronted with the choice of owning up to what she was feeling or ignoring this growing awareness. In all honesty, she'd prefer it if he walked out the door and left her alone.

"Why me?" She didn't mean to sound so sharp, but she wanted to know what had prompted him to seek her out. Had she been flashing him subliminal messages?

His eyes narrowed fractionally. "I want your company. Is that a crime? Come fly with me."

Carly hesitated. His challenge was open enough, and she found that the answer came just as easily. She wanted his company too. True, Brand possessed a dangerous quality that captivated as well as alarmed her. One flight with him could prove to be devastating. But she'd love to fly. "How long will we be gone?" Not that it mattered; she hadn't planned to do anything more than unpack boxes.

"Most of the day. We'll leave in the morning and be back in time for me to take you to dinner." His faint drawl enticed her.

"What time do you want me to meet you?" she asked. Red lights were flashing all around her, but Carly chose to ignore their warning. Brand St. Clair was a challenge—and she'd never been able to resist that. In some ways it was a fault, and in others it was her greatest strength.

The next morning, as Carly dressed in jeans and a thick jacket, she wondered at the wisdom of her actions. Only when she was strapped into the seat of the Cessna 150, her adrenaline pumping at the roar of the engine, did she realize how excited she was. She started to ask Brand about the panel full of gages when she was interrupted by the voice of the air traffic controller, who gave them clearance for takeoff.

Brand turned and gifted her with another of his earth-shattering smiles before taxiing onto the runway and pulling back on the throttle. Then, with an unbelievable burst of power, they were airborne. Her stomach lurched as the wheels left the safety of the ground—but with exhilaration, not alarm.

Looking out the window, Carly watched as the ground below took on an unreal quality. She had flown several times, but sitting in a commercial airliner was a different experience compared to floating in the sky in a small private plane.

"This is fantastic." She shouted to be heard above the roar of the engines. The skies were blue with only a few powder-puff clouds, the view below unobstructed. "Will we see Mount McKinley?"

"Not this trip. We're headed in the opposite direction."

Carly responded with a short nod. She was anxious to view North America's largest mountain. Mount Rainier, outside Seattle, and the Cascade range featured distinctive peaks, but from what she'd read about McKinley, the mountain was more blunt, less angular than anything she'd seen.

"It's so green," she shouted, and pointed to the dense forest below. When Carly had made up her mind to take this job, her first thought had been that she would be leaving the abundant beauty of Washington behind. "I'm really impressed," she said with a warm smile.

Brand's gaze slid to her. "What would it take for *me* to impress you?"

Carly threw back her head and laughed, refusing

to play his game. There wasn't much he could do that would impress her more than he had already.

Brand took her hand and squeezed it. "What did your family think about you moving north?"

Carly was reluctant to admit she didn't have a family. "They didn't say anything. I'm over twenty-one." The lie was a minor one. She'd never known her father, and only God knew the whereabouts of her mother. The longest Carly had ever stayed in one foster home was four years. With only herself to rely upon, she'd become strong in ways that others were weak. Carly didn't need anyone but herself.

"How long have you been flying?" She discovered that the best way to defuse questions was to ask one of her own.

"I've flown since I was a kid. My dad owned an appliance business and traveled all over Oregon. I took my first flying lessons at sixteen, but by that time I had been in the air a thousand times."

"Are you from Portland?"

He answered with an abrupt nod.

"What made you come to Alaska?"

He didn't hesitate. "The money."

Carly remembered George saying something about heavy expenses. "Medical bills, right?"

Brand turned to study her. Carly met his gaze. "Yes," he answered without elaborating. Carly didn't question him further.

His attention returned to the sky and Carly watched as a proud mask came over him, letting her know that this was a subject off limits. The transformation in him confused her. She was unsure of Brand, but he didn't intimidate her. In some ways she sensed that they were alike. Each had buried hurts that were best not shared so early in a relationship. Sighing, she glanced away. His attitude shouldn't bother her.

They were both quiet for a long time. "What do you think of Alaska?" Brand asked her unexpectedly, as if he were attempting to lighten the mood that had settled over them.

"I love it," Carly responded freely. "Of course, I haven't survived an Alaskan winter yet, so I might answer your question differently a year from now."

"A lot of people see Alaska as big and lonely. Its appeal isn't for everyone." His smile was wry.

"Alaska is isolated, that much I'll grant you. But not lonely. I've sat in a crowded room and been more alone than at any time in my life. Alaska demands and challenges, but not everyone is meant to face that."

Abruptly, Carly broke off and bit her lip. This was the very thing that had attracted her to this frozen land of America's last frontier.

Brand studied her, his expression revealing surprise at her answer. "George purposely hired someone in early spring," he told her. "Only a fool would move to Anchorage in winter."

"That bad?" She, too, hoped to lighten the mood.

"You have to live through one to believe it." The edges of his mouth deepened to reveal a smile.

"I'll make it," Carly returned confidently. She wasn't completely ignorant. Diana had taken delight in relaying the fact that temperatures of twenty degrees below zero weren't uncommon during the winter months in Anchorage. Carly had known what to expect when she'd accepted the job.

"I don't doubt that you will." His dark gaze skimmed

her face. "I like you, Carly Grieves," he admitted, his voice low and gravelly, as if he hadn't meant to tell her as much.

"And I trust you about as far as I can throw you." she teased. "But then, I'm stronger than I look."

Once they returned, they ate in a restaurant not far from the Anchorage airport. A companionable silence hung between them. The men Carly had dated in the past were talkers; she preferred it that way. The experience of sharing a meal with a man she had seen only a handful of times and feeling this kind of communication was beyond her experience and that excited her.

They rode back to the airport, where Carly had left her car. "Come into my office and I'll show you around," Brand invited. "I'll put some coffee on."

"I'd like that."

He opened her car door for her, and she followed him into the small building that served as his office.

A flicker of uncertainty passed over Carly's features as she entered the one-room office. The area was too private, too isolated. Once inside the darkened room, Brand didn't make any pretense of getting coffee. Instead, he turned her into his arms, a hand on each shoulder burned through her thick jacket. He seared her with a bold look as his eyes ran over her.

"I'm not interested in coffee," he muttered thickly.

"I knew that," she answered in a whisper.

His hand cupped the underside of her face as his thumb tested the fullness of her mouth. Then his hand fell away and Carly involuntarily moistened her lips.

She watched, fascinated, as a veiled question came into his eyes. He looked as if he were making up his mind whether to kiss her or not. His fingers slid into her hair, weaving through the dark strands and tilting her head back. Although her heart was pounding wildly, she continued to study him with an unwavering look. His eyes were narrow and unreadable.

With a small groan, he fit his mouth to hers. Carly opened her lips in welcome. The kiss was the most unusual she had ever experienced: gentle, tender, soft… almost tentative. Gradually, he deepened the contact, his arms pulling her closer until she was molded tight against him. His hands roamed her back, arching her body as close as possible as his mouth courted hers, exploring one side of her lips and working his way to the other in a sensuous attack that melted any resistance.

He broke away, his mouth mere inches above hers. His warm breath fanned her face as his fingers worked the buttons of her coat. Again his mouth covered hers in long, drugging kisses as he slipped the coat from her shoulders and let it fall unheeded to the floor.

Carly fought for control of her senses. This was too much, too soon, but she couldn't tear herself away. The throbbing ache his mouth, his hands, his body were creating within her was slowly consuming her will.

She moaned softly as he buried his face in the curve of her throat. Her eyes closed as she tangled her fingers in the hair that grew at the nape of his neck.

"Brand." Breathlessly, she whispered his name, not sure why she had.

Instantly he went still, as if the sound of her voice had brought him to his senses. His hand closed over her wrists and pulled them free. "What's wrong?" she pleaded.

He took a step in retreat. His eyes no longer met

hers, but were cast down at the floor as he took in deep breaths. When he looked up and ran a hand along the back of his neck, Carly saw something flicker in his eyes that could be read either as regret, or guilt or perhaps shock?

The world came to a stop as she realized what must have happened. How could she have been so blind not to see what was right in front of her. All the clues were there. She'd been so stupid. A coldness settled over her as a hoarseness filled her throat.

"You're married, aren't you?"

Two

"No." Brand issued the single word with a vengeance.

"I'm not entirely stupid." Carly's voice became a whisper.

"I'm a widower," Brand interrupted harshly, wiping a hand across his face.

It doesn't matter, Carly's mind screamed as she retrieved her coat. If she hadn't been so blinded by her pure physical attraction to him, she would have recognized those blatant red lights for what they were. His wife might be dead, but it didn't make any difference.

"Carly, listen."

She ignored him, irritated with herself for her own stupidity. "I had a great time today," she murmured.

"Carly, I want to explain."

She could hear the frustrated anger in his voice. The anger wasn't directed at her, but inward. Every dictate of her will demanded she turn around and run from the building. Both hands were tucked deep within her pockets as she took a step backward. "Thank you for dinner. We'll have to do it again sometime." Not waiting for his response, she hurried from the office. By the time she reached her car, Carly's knees felt as though they could no longer support her.

When she arrived back at her apartment she had an upset stomach. *Brand had been married.* Forcing herself to breath evenly, she deliberately walked around the living room, running her hand over the back of the sofa. Everything she owned had been purchased new. She wouldn't take second best in anything. Not clothes, not cars, not jobs. After a life filled with secondhand goods and a hand-me-down childhood, she wasn't about to start now—especially with a man. All right, she was being unreasonable, she knew that; Diana had taken delight in telling her so a hundred times. But Carly didn't see any reason to change. She liked herself the way she was—unreasonable or not.

Three days later, she was still unable to shake the confusion and disappointment that Brand's announcement had produced. She'd made up her mind not to see him again. Yet her mind entertained thoughts of him at the oddest times. She forced his image from her brain, determined to blot him from her life completely.

Thursday evening, when the phone rang, Carly stared at it in surprise. The telephone company had installed it at the beginning of the week and, although she'd made several calls out, she had yet to receive one.

"Hello."

"Carly?" The voice reverberated, sounding as if it came from the moon.

"Diana?" The soft echo of her words returned over the line.

"I couldn't stand it another minute. I had to find out how everything's going. I miss you like crazy," Diana said softly. Then, as if she'd admitted more than she'd wanted, she quickly changed the subject. "How's Alaska? Have you seen any moose yet?"

"No moose and I love Alaska," Carly responded enthusiastically, knowing that her friend was uncomfortable sharing emotions. "It's vast, untouched, beautiful."

"That's not the way I heard it," Diana said and released a frustrated sigh. "How's the job and the mysterious George Hamlyn?"

"We've had a few minor clashes, but all in all everything's working out great."

"After all I did to convince you to stay in Seattle you wouldn't admit anything else," Diana chided. "How's the apartment?"

"Adequate. I'm looking into buying a condo."

"I knew it." Diana didn't bother to disguise her friendly censure. "I wondered how long you'd last in a *used* apartment."

"It's not that old," Carly responded with a dry smile. Her friend knew her too well.

"When are you going to get over this quirk of yours?"

"Quirk?" Carly feigned ignorance, not wanting to argue.

"No, it's become more than that." The teasing quality left Diana's voice. "It's an obsession."

"Just because I happen to prefer new things doesn't make me obsessive. I can afford the condominium." But barely. The payments would eat a huge hole into her monthly paycheck.

"How's Barney?" Carly quickly changed the subject. "Have you got a ring through his nose yet?"

Diana's laugh sounded forced. "So-so. If I'm going to marry again, you can bet that this time I'm going to be sure."

"I've heard love is better the third time around."

"Love maybe, marriage never. Besides, that's supposed to be the *second* time around."

"In your case I had to improvise."

Diana gave a weak snort. "I don't know why I put up with you."

"I do," Carly supplied with the confidence of many years of friendship. "I'm the little girl you've always wanted to mother. Problem is, I'm only six years younger than you."

"I'm feeling every minute of thirty-one. Why'd you bring that up?"

"Good friend, I guess."

"Too good. Listen, sweetie, I'm worried about you. Don't let your pride stand in the way if you want out of that godforsaken igloo."

"Honestly." Carly released an exasperated breath. "I'm perfectly capable of taking care of myself. So straighten up, crack the whip over Barney's head and quit being such a worrier. I'm doing fine on my own."

"True. You don't need me to louse up your life, especially since I've done such a bang-up job of screwing up my own. You'll keep in touch, won't you?"

"A letter's already in the mail," Carly assured her.

"I suppose I should go."

"It's good to hear your voice, my friend."

Diana sighed softly. "You're the best friend I've ever had. Take care of yourself and let me know when you've come to your senses and want to head home."

"I will," Carly promised. But she wouldn't be moving back to Seattle. In fact, she doubted that she ever would. Alaska felt *right.* In a few short weeks it seemed more like she thought a home should than anything she'd known as a child.

Late Friday afternoon, as Carly was working on a claim, George sauntered into the office, an oily pink rag dangling from his back pocket. He'd been working with a mechanic. It hadn't taken Carly long to discover that George was a man of many talents.

"Get Brand St. Clair on the line for me," he said on his way to the coffeepot.

Carly's fingers tightened around the pencil she held. As much as she'd fought against it, Brand had remained on her mind all week.

Flipping through the pages of the telephone directory, Carly located Brand's number and punched the buttons of the phone with the tip of her eraser. She would be polite but distant, she decided. He hadn't made any attempt to contact her this week, so apparently he was aware of her feelings towards him.

With the receiver cradled against her shoulder, Carly continued working on the claim.

"No answer," she told her employer, hoping that relief in her voice was well disguised.

"Leave a voice mail and try again in five minutes," George returned irritably. "That boy wears too many hats. He's working himself to death."

Carly had punched out Brand's number so many times by the end of the afternoon that she could have done it in her sleep. At five-thirty she straightened the top of her desk and removed her purse from the bottom drawer. George was talking to a mechanic when she stepped outside to tell him she hadn't been able to reach Brand.

"I never did get hold of St. Clair." The brisk wind whipped her shoulder-length hair about her face until it stung her cheeks.

George glanced at Carly with a smile of chagrin. "Since it isn't out of your way, would you mind stopping off at his office and leaving a message on the door?"

Carly swallowed tightly. "Sure."

"Tell him I've got a couple of jobs for him next week and ask him to give me a call."

"Consider it done." She turned before he could see her reaction. She didn't object to doing George a favor. What she wanted was to avoid Brand. If someone were to see her and tell him she'd been by, he could misinterpret her coming.

The portion of the airfield that housed Brand's office was only a mile or so from Alaska Freight Forwarding. As Carly eased her vehicle into the space nearest his office, she noticed him walking toward her from the air field. He'd obviously returned from a flight and had just finished securing his aircraft. Carly groaned inwardly and climbed out of her car.

Six days had passed since she'd last seen him, but time had done little to wipe out the pure physical impact of seeing him again. His glance was dry, emotionless, as he moved closer, his face lean and weathered from the sun. Mature.

"Hello." He stopped in front of her, revealing none of his feelings. The least he could do was look pleased to see her!

"George sent me over with a message." It was important that he understand she hadn't come of her own accord.

His nod was curt.

"He wanted me to tell you he has work for you next week if you're interested." She prayed the slight breathlessness in her voice would go undetected.

"I'm interested."

A shiver skipped over her skin at the lazy, sensual way he studied her. Carly had the crazy sensation that his interest wasn't in the flying job.

"You're on your way home?" he asked her unexpectedly.

Her eyes refused to meet his. "Yes. It's been a long week." Goodness, she shouldn't have said that. He might think she'd been waiting for his call.

"Have you got time to stop someplace for a drink?"

"No." The word slipped out with the rising swell of panic that threatened to engulf her.

"Why not?" he demanded.

"Let's just say that I consider married men off limits. Even widowers. Especially widowers who have eyes that say, 'I loved my wife.'"

"I can't argue with you about that," Brand agreed easily. "I did love Sandra."

"That's the way it's suppose to be." Carly was sincere. She couldn't imagine Brand not having loved… Sandra. Her mind had difficulty forming the name. It was easier to think of Brand's wife as a nonentity. "Well, it was nice seeing you again." She fumbled in her purse for her keys.

"Do you have anything against friendship?" Brand's features suggested a wealth of pride and strength. In the shadows of early afternoon, they appeared more pronounced.

"Everyone needs somebody." Reluctantly, she turned

back. She was thinking about Diana, the only true friend she'd ever had.

"Are we capable of that, Carly?" He refused to release her gaze.

Unable to find the words to answer him, she shrugged.

"Surely a drink between friends wouldn't be so bad."

She remained unsure. "I won't date you, Brand." Making that much clear was important.

"Not to worry." He beamed her a dazzling smile. "This isn't a date. Friends?" He extended his hand to her.

Her mind was yelling at her, telling her this wouldn't work. But it didn't seem to matter as she held out her hand to him for a curt shake.

Mentally chastising herself every block of the way, she followed him to a lounge, parking her car in the space beside his. Together they stepped into the dimly lit room.

Brand cupped her elbow, but when Carly involuntarily stiffened, he dropped his hand. "Sorry, I forgot we're just friends," he said as they walked across the room.

No sooner were they seated when a waitress appeared. Carly was undecided about what she wanted to drink, and while she was making up her mind, Brand took charge and ordered for her.

"I prefer to order for myself," she said after the waitress had gone, disliking the way he had taken control. She wasn't his date. He went still, then shrugged. "Sorry, I keep forgetting."

He was strangely quiet then, Carly thought, considering the way he'd pressed the invitation on her. After a few minutes of small talk he settled back in his chair, seemingly content to listen to the music.

"I don't know what to make of you," Carly said, uncomfortable with the finely strung tension between them.

"Little wonder," he said with a wry grin, and took a sip of his Scotch. "You've been on my mind all week."

Carly sat upright and leaned forward. "I don't think friends are necessarily on one another's minds."

He discounted her words with an ardent shake of his head. "Some friends are. Trust me here."

"The last man who asked me to trust him trapped me thirty thousand feet in the air and demanded that we make love."

"What did you do?" He straightened slightly, the line of his jaw tightening.

Carly smiled, taking a sip of her wine before she spoke. "Simple. I jumped. He was my sky-diving instructor."

"Did everything turn out all right?"

"Depends on how you look at it. I wrenched my ankle and landed a mile off target. But on the other hand, it felt good to outsmart that creep."

"My goodness, you live an adventuresome life."

"That's nothing compared to what happened to me the weekend I climbed Mount Rainier."

"I don't think I want to hear this," he murmured, nursing his drink. "Have you always had this penchant for danger?"

"It never starts out that way, but I seem to walk blindly into it." She leaned against the back of the chair, a hand circling her wineglass.

"Have dinner with me?" Then he quickly added, "As friends, of course."

Carly knew she should decline, but something within her wouldn't let her refuse. "All right, but I have the feeling I was safer on Mount Rainier."

He smiled as he rose and led the way into the restaurant that was connected to the lounge.

Once they were seated at the red, upholstered booth, a middle-aged waitress in a black skirt and peasant blouse handed them each a menu.

Quickly, Carly surveyed the items listed, mainly a variety of seafood and steak dishes. "If you don't mind, I'll order for myself this time," she teased, keeping her gaze centered on the oblong menu.

"Red wine was Sandra's favorite drink." Brand's words seemed to come out of nowhere.

"Oh, ," Carly shut her eyes tightly and set the menu aside. "I wish you hadn't told me that."

"I was just as shocked as you when it slipped out."

Carly half slid from the booth. "I think I'd better leave."

"Don't go. Please."

Carly had the impression he didn't often ask something of anyone. She stopped, her heart beating at double time.

"Did I ever tell you about the time I came face-to-face with a Kodiak?" he asked.

"A bear?"

His gaze was intent as he studied his water glass. "Crazy as it sounds, I'm more frightened now here with you."

Carly exhaled, releasing her breath in a rush. "Good grief, we're a fine couple."

He smiled. "We're only…"

"Friends." They said it together and laughed.

"All right," Brand said, and breathed in a wobbly breath. "I'll admit it. This is the first time I've been out with a woman since Sandra died. She's been gone almost two years now. But the past is meant to be a guidepost, not a hitching post. I need a…friend."

Carly was unsure this friendship would work from the moment he first suggested it. He seemed to confirm her suspicions every minute she was with him. "Brand, I don't know."

"You're not even trying. At least hear me out. It's been a while since I was into the dating scene. I realize you don't want to date me. I don't understand why, but apparently it's an issue with you. But I was thinking that maybe I could practice with you. We could go out a couple of times until I see what kind of action there is." His tone was suddenly light, casual.

"Not on dates." Her fingers surrounded her wineglass and a chill moved up her arm and stopped at her heart.

"No, these wouldn't be *real* dates."

"Just practice, until you find someone who interests you?" Something deep inside her said she was going to regret this. Diana should be the one he was talking to. Diana was the rescuer. Not her.

Brand lifted his gaze until their eyes met, granting Carly the opportunity to study his face. His mood had shifted again, and now she realized that the look she had recognized earlier wasn't maturity, but pain. Without him saying a word she realized he'd been through hell. His wife's death had brought him to his knees and nearly broken him. Carly's first response was a desire to ease that pain. Such intense feelings were foreign to her.

"I can't see how it would hurt, as long as we both understand one another," she said cautiously.

The waitress came and took their order.

"How'd we get so serious?" Brand's smile was forced, but the effort relaxed the planes of his face and again Carly found herself responding involuntarily.

"I don't know."

"Let's talk about something else. As I recall, women like to talk about themselves."

"Not this woman. I'd bore you to death," Carly returned with a weak laugh. "I was born, grew up, graduated, found a job..." She hesitated, her eyes smiling into his. "Shall I continue?"

"Seattle?"

"Mostly." The tip of her index finger circled the rim of her wineglass. "What about you?"

He answered her question with another of his own. "What about men?"

"What about them?" Carly shot back.

"You've never married?"

"No." Her laugh was light. "Not even close."

"Sandra and I were barely out of college..."

Carly sighed with relief when the waitress returned, delivering their meals. She didn't want to hear about Brand's wife. Yet in another way it was good that she did, because it reminded her that it would be a colossal mistake to fall in love with Brand.

Carly's salad was piled high with crab. Lemon wedges dipped in paprika decorated the edges and thin slices of hard-boiled eggs defined the bowl. "This looks wonderful." Picking up her fork, she dipped into the crisp lettuce leaves. Brand followed suit, and they ate in silence. Several times during the meal Carly felt Brand watching her, his gaze disconcerting, making her uncomfortable.

"Did I commit some faux pas?" she asked, setting aside her fork as she met his eyes.

"No. Why?" Brand glanced up curiously.

"The looks you've been giving me make me think I've got Thousand Island dressing all over my chin."

"No, you haven't." Brand's chuckle was low and sensuous.

To avoid his look, Carly glanced into the lounge. Couples with arms wrapped around each other were dancing on the small polished floor to the slow music. Dancing had never been her forte, but the thought of Brand holding her produced a willful fascination. She shook her head to dispel the image.

"Do you dance?" she asked but frankly she hoped his response would be negative.

His fork paused midway to his mouth as he gave her a startled glance.

Carly looked away. "Don't look so shocked. My interest was purely academic. It wouldn't be a good idea for us to dance."

"Why not?"

"Because—" She swallowed. He was enjoying her discomfort. "Well, because of the close body contact…I just don't think it would be a good idea…for us seeing that we're only friends."

"But I'll need to practice a few times, don't you think?"

"No," she said, wishing now she'd never introduced the subject. "Dancing is like riding a bicycle. It all comes back to you even if you haven't gone riding in a long time." She pushed her plate aside, indicating that she was finished with her meal.

Brand mumbled something under his breath. Carly didn't catch all of it, but what she did hear caused hot color to warm her cheeks. He'd said something about hoping that the same was true when it came to love-making.

While Brand paid for their dinner, Carly wandered outside. With hands thrust deep into her jacket pockets, she stared at the dark sky. The stars looked like rare jewels laid out on folds of black satin. The moonlight cleared a path through the still night. With her face turned toward the heavens, Carly walked past their parked cars and down the narrow sidewalk. Alaska was supposed to be cold and ruthless. Yet she felt warm and content, as if she belonged here and would never want to leave. Brand had reminded her that she hadn't suffered through an Alaskan winter. But the thought didn't frighten her. She was ready for that challenge.

Brand joined her. "I want to tell you about Sandra."

Carly didn't want to hear about the wife he'd loved and lost, but she recognized that Brand needed to tell her. If he talked things out with her, a virtual stranger, maybe then he could bury the past.

"We met in college. I guess I told you that, didn't I?"

Carly's hands formed fists deep inside her pockets. "Yes...yes, you did."

"She was probably one of the most beautiful women I've ever seen. Blonde and petite. And so full of life. You couldn't walk in a room full of people and not find Sandra. Funny thing, though—she was the quiet sort.

She didn't like a lot of attention." His face sharpened. "We were married almost eight years."

Carly's heart was pounding frantically. Each pain-filled word seemed to come at her like an assault. He didn't need to say how difficult it was for him to speak of his wife. It was evident in his voice, in the way he looked straight ahead, in the way he walked.

"She had myelocytic leukemia. The most difficult type to treat and cure. We knew in the beginning her chances of beating it were only one in five. Watching her die was agony." He paused, waiting several moments before he continued speaking. "But death was her victory. She was at peace. She had every right to be bitter and angry, but that wasn't her way. I struggled to hold on to her but in the end she asked me to let her go and I did. She closed her eyes and within the hour she was gone"

Carly felt tears form which she quickly blinked away, embarrassed that he would see the emotion his story caused in her.

They continued walking for a long time, neither speaking. Carly didn't know what to say. Any words of comfort wouldn't have made it past the huge lump in her throat.

"I loved her," he said in a low, tortured voice. "A part of me will go to the grave grieving for Sandra."

Carly's heart swelled with emotion as she searched desperately for some way to communicate her regret. But no words would come. She wanted to tell him she understood how hard it must have been to release the one he loved. But she couldn't pretend to know how much it had cost him to watch his wife die. Gently, she laid her hand on his forearm, wanting to let him know her feelings.

Brand's fingers gripped hers as he paused and turned toward her. Tenderly, he brushed the hair from her face and kissed her forehead. "Thank you," he said simply.

"I didn't do anything." Her voice sounded weak and wobbly.

"Just by listening you've done more than you know," he whispered and took her hand in his. Silently, their hands linked, they strolled down the moonlit sidewalk.

Carly had a difficult time sleeping that night. Brand hadn't attempted to hold or kiss her, and for that she was grateful. She didn't know if she had the strength to refuse him anything. The thought was scary. Everything about Brand confused her. If she had a rational head on her shoulders she wouldn't have anything more to do with him. But he was a rare kind of man, more rare than the gold that had prompted so many into Alaska's fertile land a hundred years before.

For a long while she lay awake watching shadows dancing on the walls, taunting her. She shouldn't see him again, she told herself. Yet she could hardly wait for tomorrow afternoon, when they had planned to meet again.

Carly awoke the next morning with renewed determination. Brand needed her…for now. She didn't walk away from anything. Her independence, her ability to meet challenges had become her trademark. Friends didn't desert one another in times of need. And this was a crucial time in Brand's life. A time of transition. She would help him through that, be his friend. Perhaps she would even have the opportunity to introduce him to a few women.

Falling back against her pillow, Carly released a long, tortured sigh. Who did she think she was kidding? Introduce Brand to another woman? She nearly laughed out loud.

The phone rang just as she stepped into the shower. Wrapping a towel around herself, she hobbled into the living room, leaving a trail of water behind her.

"Yes," she breathed irritably into the receiver.

"Carly?" It was Brand. "You sound angry. What's wrong?"

"Some idiot phoned and got me out of the shower."

"Don't tell me you're standing there naked." His voice became low and slightly husky.

"I am standing in a puddle of water, catching a chill."

His warm chuckle quickened her heartbeat. "I won't keep you. I just wanted you to make sure you hadn't changed your mind about this afternoon."

"I probably should. But no, I'll be ready when you get here."

Carly dressed in designer jeans, cowboy boots and a Western-style plaid shirt. She was putting the finishing touches on her makeup when the doorbell rang. A hurried glance in the mirror assured her that she looked fine.

"Good afternoon," she said, and smiled a greeting. Her heart warmed at the sight Brand presented in gray slacks and a loose-fitting blue V-necked sweater. The long sleeves were pushed up past his elbows.

"I'm not dressed too casually, am I?" They were attending an art show. Diana thought Carly's generally informal dress outrageous. But Carly was herself and wore what she wanted, where she wanted. Cowboy boots and jeans sounded fine for an art show to her.

"Not at all." He smiled, holding her gaze for several seconds. He wrinkled his nose appreciatively and sniffed the air. "What smells so good?"

"Probably my perfume," she said, and playfully exposed her neck to him.

"It smells like clams."

Carly released a heavy sigh. "I hope you realize that you're going to have to learn to be a little more romantic than that. I had a bowl of clam chowder for lunch."

"I'll try thinking romantic thoughts then. That's good advice." He helped her into her three-quarter-length leather jacket.

"Tell me about the art show. I'm not much into the abstract stuff, but I like the Impressionists."

His hand snaked out across her shoulder. "You'll like this show," He promised. "I don't want to tell you too much. I want your opinion to be unbiased."

"I know what I like."

"Spoken like a true expert."

The Anchorage Civic Center was crowded when they arrived, and they were forced to park several blocks down the street. Inside, people were clustered around a variety of paintings and sculptures.

With Brand at her side, Carly wandered from one exhibit to another. Not until she was halfway through the show did she see the painting of the child. Abruptly, she stopped, causing Brand to bump against her. He murmured something, but she didn't hear him as she walked to the lifelike oil painting.

The child was no more than five. Vulnerable, lost,

hurting. Her pale pink dress was torn, the hem unraveled. Her scuffed shoes had holes, and one foot was dejectedly turned inward. The tousled hair needed to be combed. But it was the eyes that captured Carly's attention. Round, blue and proud. So proud they defied her circumstances.

Carly stared at the painting for a long time before she noted that, in the far corner of one of the child's eyes, a tear had formed. Emotion rose within her. This was Carly as a child; this was the little girl in the nightmare.

Three

The dream was always the same. It ran through her mind like flickering scenes from a silent movie. She was small, not more than five, and hungry. So hungry that her stomach was empty and hurting. It was morning and she couldn't wake her mother. Several times she'd gone into the other bedroom and pulled at her mother's arm, but to no avail. At first Carly crawled back into her bed and cried, whimpering until she fell asleep. When she woke a second time, her stomach rumbled and gnawed at her. Sitting up, she decided she would cook her own breakfast.

The refrigerator was almost empty, but she found an egg. Mother always cooked those, and Carly thought she knew how. Filling the pan with water, she placed it on the stove and turned the knob. Then, afraid of a spanking, she ran into her mother's room and tried to shake her awake. But the dark-haired woman growled angrily at Carly and said to leave her alone.

Standing on a kitchen chair, Carly watched the egg tumble in the angry, boiling water. She didn't know how long Mama cooked things. Her mistake came when she pulled the pan from the stove. The bubbling water sloshed over the side and burned her small fingers. When she cried out and jerked her hand away, the pan of boiling water slid to the edge of the stove and toppled down her front.

This was the point where Carly always woke, usually in a cold sweat, her body rigid with terror. The dream had always been vivid, so very real. She didn't know if she had been burned as a child. No scars marred her body. There was only the dream that returned to haunt her at the oddest times.

"Carly." Brand's large hand rested on her shoulder. "Are you all right? You've gone pale."

"I want to buy this picture."

"Buy it?" Brand repeated. "It could run in the thousands of dollars."

Carly shook her head and shrugged his hand from her shoulder. She didn't want him near. Not now. She raised her fingertips to her forehead and ran them down the side of her face as she continued to study the portrait.

Of course, the child wasn't really her; she recognized that. The eyes were the wrong color, the hair too straight and dark. But the pain that showed so clearly through those intense eyes was as close to Carly's own as she had ever seen.

"The program states that this painting isn't for sale," Brand said from behind her.

Frustration washed through Carly. "I'll talk to the artist and change his mind."

"Her," Brand corrected softly. "Carly?" His voice contained an uncharacteristic appeal. "Look at your program."

Forcefully, she moved her gaze from the painting

that had mesmerized her and glanced down at the sheet she'd been handed as she walked in to the center door. For a moment her gaze refused to focus on the printed description. The painting was titled simply "Girl. A Self-Portrait" by Jutta Hoverson.

"Is she here?" Carly was surprised at how weak her voice was. "I'd like to meet her."

Brand placed his hand on her shoulder, as if to protect her from any unpleasantness, a gesture Carly found almost amusing. "I think you should read the front of your program," he said gently.

He was so insistent that Carly turned it over to examine what it was Brand found so important. The instant she read the heading she sighed and sadly shook her head. The art show was a collection of works done by prisoners: murderers, thieves, rapists, and only God knew what else.

Carly lifted her gaze from the program to the oil painting. "I wonder what crime she committed."

"I thought you knew."

"It doesn't matter. I still want this picture," she murmured, noting the way Brand was studying her. She didn't want to explain why this was so important to her. She couldn't.

"You feel more than just art appreciation," he said as his gaze skimmed her face thoroughly.

"Yes, I do." Levelly, she met his look, which seemed to pierce her protective shield. She opened her mouth to explain, but nothing came out. "I…I was poor as a child." She couldn't say it. Something deep and dark was restraining the words. Being raised in foster homes wasn't a terrible tragedy. She'd been properly cared for without the stigma that often accompanied girls in her circumstances. Having never known her mother might have been the best thing. The woman was a stranger, an alcoholic. For reasons of her own, her mother had never put Carly up for adoption. Carly resented that; the right to a normal family life had been denied her because her mother had refused to sign the relinquishment papers. As an adult, Carly thought that it wasn't love that had prompted her mother to hold on to her rights, but guilt.

"You might write"—Brand hesitated as he turned the program over, seeking the artist's name—"Jutta Hoverson and ask her to change her mind. It says here that she's at the Women's Correctional Center in Purdy, Washington. If I remember correctly, that's somewhere near Tacoma."

"I will," Carly confirmed. Jutta Hoverson might be a stranger, but already Carly felt a certain kinship with her. She continued to stare at the painting, having trouble taking her eyes from something that so clearly represented a part of her past. "There, but for the grace of God, go I." She hadn't meant to speak the words aloud.

"What makes you say that?" Brand questioned.

Carly's momentary glance of surprise gave way to a dry smile. "Several things." She didn't elaborate.

Although they spent another hour at the show, Carly's gaze continued to drift back to the painting of the child. Each time she examined it she saw more of herself: it was all there, in the dejected stance, the way one small foot was turned inward…in the hurt so clearly revealed in the eyes, the solitary tear that spoke of so much pain. So often in her life Carly had resisted crying, holding herself back until her stomach ached with the need to vent her emotion. Tears were considered sign of weakness, and she wouldn't grant herself permission for such a display of helplessness.

The apartment looked bleak and dingy when they returned. Carly paused just inside the door, unable to decide if it was the apartment itself or her mood. Brand had followed her inside, although she hadn't issued an invitation.

"Carly." Just the way Brand said her name caused a warmth to spread through her. One large hand rested on each of her shoulders from behind. "Won't you tell me what's troubling you? You've been pensive and brooding all afternoon. Ever since you saw the painting."

"It's nothing," she said as she unzipped the leather jacket, forcing his hands from her shoulders as she slipped it from her arms and hung it in the closet. She couldn't very well ask him to leave without being rude, but she wanted to be alone for now.

"I'm sorry the show brought back memories you'd rather forget. But I think this is just the kind of thing friends are for. I spilled my guts last night. Now it's your turn." He lowered his long frame onto her sofa and leaned forward, his elbows resting on his knees, lacing his fingers together. "Talk. I'll try and be as good a listener as you were last night."

"I…" Carly's arms folded around her middle. "I… can't." She bit her lip. Brand's frustration was in his eyes for her to read. Her own feelings were ambivalent. She wanted to be alone, yet in an inexplicable way she wanted him there. The intense longing she felt for him to hold her was almost frightening. "What I need is time. Alone, if you don't mind."

"No problem." He jerked himself to his feet and was gone before she could say another word.

"Damn." She was being stupid and she knew it. But that didn't change the intensity of her feelings. Nor did it alter her black mood.

That night, Carly sat in the kitchen as she wrote a letter to Jutta Hoverson. Page after page of discarded attempts littered the table. There were so many things she wanted to say and no way she knew of putting them into words. After midnight, she settled on a few short sentences that simply asked Jutta if she would be willing to reconsider and sell the portrait.

Even after the letter was completed, Carly couldn't sleep. She hadn't meant to offend Brand, but she clearly had. He had revealed a deep and painful part of his own past, and she had shunned him this afternoon when it would have been natural to tell him why the painting had made such an impression on her.

She'd hesitated to open herself to him. The words had danced in her mind, but she'd been unable to say them. True, she didn't make a point of telling people her circumstances, but she didn't hide them either. Something about the afternoon—and Brand—had made her reluctant to reveal her past.

No more sure of the answers when she awoke the next morning, Carly dressed and put on a pot of coffee. On impulse, she decided to phone Diana. Sometimes her friend could understand Carly better than she did herself. After ten long rings, she replaced the receiver. Diana had probably spent the night with Barney. She wished those two would marry. As far as Carly could tell, they were perfect for one another. Barney was the first man Diana had ever loved who didn't need to be rescued from himself. Invariably, Diana fell for the world's losers; she apparently felt her undying love would redeem them. After two disastrous marriages, Diana was in no hurry to rush to the altar a third time. But Barney was different. Surely Diana could see that. He loved Diana. Barney might not be Burt Reynolds, but he was wonderful to Diana, and Carly's friend deserved the best.

Carly spent the morning writing Diana a long letter, telling her about the painting and Jutta Hoverson. Almost as an afterthought, she decided to add a few lines about Brand and their...*friendship.* She'd only meant to say a few things, but writing about her reactions to him helped her to understand what was happening. A couple of lines quickly became two long pages.

Both letters went in Monday's mail.

By Wednesday, Carly still hadn't heard from Brand. Apparently, he'd come into the office one afternoon while she was out, but had spoken with George and hadn't left a message for her. That evening, Carly decided she couldn't bear another night of television. Shopping was sure to cure even the heaviest of moods.

Before Carly knew where she was headed, she found herself on the sidewalk outside of Brand's apartment house. After punching out his phone number so many times that past Friday, Brand's address had become embedded in her memory. His late-model car was parked against the curb. She didn't know which apartment was his, but all she'd need to do was look at the mailboxes.

Her first knock was tentative. Coming to see him was a *friendly* gesture, she assured herself. And she did feel bad about the way she'd behaved Saturday.

"Yes?" The door was jerked open impatiently. Brand stopped abruptly as surprise worked its way across his handsome features. "Carly." He whispered her name.

"Hi." Cheerfully, she waved her hand. "I was in the neighborhood and thought I'd stop in and see how you were doing. But if this is a bad time, I can come back later."

"No, of course not. It's a great time. Come on in." He stepped aside and ran his hand along the back of his neck.

Carly had to smile at the stunned look on his face. As she stepped inside, she noted that the interior of the apartment was stark. Carpet, furniture, drapes—nothing held the stamp of Brand's personality or made this home distinctly his. Strangely, Carly understood this. Since Sandra's death Brand's life had been in limbo. He carried on because time had pushed him forcefully into doing so. She imagined that he didn't even realize how stark his home and his existence had become.

"Actually, your timing couldn't be better," he said as he led the way into the kitchen. The apartment wasn't as spacious as her own. The living room blended into the kitchen and the round table was covered with a variety of slips and paper. "I was trying to make heads or tails out of this bookkeeping nonsense. It might as well be Greek to me."

"I don't suppose you'd like some help?" Carly volunteered, and laughed at the relief that flooded his face.

"Are you crazy? Does a starving man reject food?" Turning one scratched oak chair around, Brand straddled it, looking somewhat chagrined. "I insist on paying you."

Mockingly, Carly pushed a ledger aside. "No way. Isn't helping each other out what friends are for?" His eyes smiled into hers, and she noted the lines that fanned from their corners in deep grooves. The realization that those lines weren't from laughter was reinforced as she caught sight of a framed picture on the television. *Sandra.* Carly's heart leaped into her throat.

Brand's gaze followed hers. "I told you she was beautiful."

Beautiful. The word exploded in her mind. Sandra had been far more than that. She was exquisite. Perfect. Carly scooted out of her chair and walked across the room, lifting the picture to examine it more closely. Blonde and petite, just as Brand had described. But vibrant. Her blue eyes sparkled with laughter and love. This woman had been cherished and adored, and it was evident in everything about her that she'd returned that love in full measure.

"She was an only child," Brand explained. "Her father died of a heart attack shortly after we learned that Sandra had leukemia. Her mother went a year after Sandra. I think grief killed her. She simply lost the will to live."

Carly couldn't do anything more than nod. She was gripping the picture frame so hard that her finger ached. She forced herself to relax, replacing the photograph on top of the television.

"There's another in the bedroom with Shawn and Sara, if you'd like to see that one."

Carly shook her head emphatically. The way she had reacted to that one picture was enough. Shawn and Sara? Did Brand have children? Certainly he would have explained if the two were his children. He would have mentioned them long before now. No, they were probably a nephew and niece. They had to be. Knowing that Brand had been married had been enough of a blow. Adding children to that would be her undoing.

Carly gave herself a vigorous mental shake. Brand could have ten children and it shouldn't bother her. She was his friend. They weren't dating. Saturday had been just another of their "this-is-not-a-date" outings. Even her coming to his place today hadn't been anything more than a friendly gesture.

Coming to stand beside her, Brand lifted the photo from the television. Carly heard him inhale deeply. "I think the time has come to put this away."

"No." The word came out sounding as if she'd attempted to swallow and speak at the same time. Carly wanted him to keep the picture out to serve as a reminder that she couldn't allow her feelings for him to shift beyond the friendship stage.

He ignored her protest, staring at the photo as if he were saying good-bye. A deep frown marred his brow. "I can't very well bring a woman to my apartment and have a picture of my wife sitting out," he explained reasonably.

Carly had difficulty swallowing. "I guess you're right."

He carried the picture into another room and returned a moment later. Carly was at the table, looking over the accounting books, pretending she knew what she was doing. Her bookkeeping classes had been years ago.

"Is what happened last weekend still bothering you?"

Carly shrugged her shoulders. "I suppose you've guessed that I had a troubled childhood." Her fingers rotated the pencil in nervous reaction, and she didn't meet his eyes; instead, she focused her gaze on the light green sheets of the ledger. "The state took me away from my mother when I was five. I don't remember much about her. I got a letter from her once when I was ten. She was drying out in an alcoholic treatment center and wrote to say that she'd be coming for me soon and that we'd be a real family again. She sent her picture. She wasn't very pretty." Carly paused, thinking that the family resemblance between them was strong. Carly wasn't pretty either. Not like Sandra.

"What happened?" Brand prompted.

Carly set the pencil on the table and interlaced her fingers. "Nothing. She never came."

"You must have been devastated." Brand resumed his position in the chair beside her, his voice gentle, almost tender.

"I suppose I was, but to be truthful, I don't remember. At age twelve I was sent to the Ruth School for Girls for a time, until another foster home could be found. That was where I met my friend, Diana. Since then we've been family to one another—the only family either of us needs." Her voice was slightly defensive.

"But who raised you?"

"A variety of people. Mostly good folks. With all the horror stories I've heard in recent years, I realize how fortunate I was in that respect."

"The art show upset you because you saw yourself in that portrait." His observation was half question, half statement.

"That picture was me at five. Seeing it was like looking at myself and reliving all that unhappiness."

Brand reached out and tenderly cupped the underside of her face. Carly's hands covered his as she closed her eyes and surrendered to the surging tide of emotion.

Brand didn't say a word. He didn't need to. His comfort was there in his healing touch as he caressed the delicate slope of her neck. His fingertips paused at the hammering pulse at the hollow of her throat before lightly tracing the proud lift of her chin.

"You're a rare woman, Carly Grieves," he whispered huskily.

Their eyes met and held. They were two rare souls. The wounded arctic wolf and the emotionally crippled little girl.

Slowly, ever so slowly, his hands roamed from the curve of her neck to her shoulders, cupping them and deliberately, tantalizingly, drawing her mouth to his.

Her lips trembled at the feather-light pressure as his mouth softly caressed hers. This wasn't a kiss of passion, but one of compassion.

Confused emotions assaulted her. She knew what he was trying to convey, but she didn't need or want his sympathy. Her hand curved around the side of his face, her fingers curling into the thick hair at his nape. "Brand," she whispered urgently, the moist tip of her tongue outlining his mouth.

He moaned as he hungrily increased the pressure, his arms half lifting her from the chair as he claimed her lips with a fierceness that stole her breath—and melted her resistance.

Simultaneously, they stood, their bodies straining against one another as their mouths clung. His tongue probed the hollow of her mouth, meeting hers in dancing movements that sent wave after wave of rapture cascading through her. His hands found her hips and buttocks as he molded her against his unyielding strength. Her senses exploded at the tantalizing scent of tobacco and musk and the taste of his tongue.

The profound need building within Carly was quickly

becoming a physical ache. Her hard-won control vanished under the onslaught of his touch. Her cool, calm head—the one that before this had reacted appropriately to every situation—deserted her. Raw desire quivered through her, warming her heart and exposing her soul.

Breaking the contact, Brand's eyes locked with hers. He seemed to be searching for some answer. Carly could give him none, not understanding the question. Together, their breaths came ragged and sharp as they struggled to regain their composure. Carly fought desperately for her equilibrium and pressed her forehead against the broad expanse of his chest.

"Are friends supposed to kiss like that?" Her voice was barely above a whisper.

Brand's arms went around her as he rested his chin against the crown of her head. "Some friends do." He didn't sound any more in control of himself than she did.

"I'm...I'm not sure I'm ready for you to be this type of friend." A rush of cool air caressed her heated flesh, bringing her gradually back to reality. Gently, but firmly, she pulled free from his embrace. Suddenly she felt naked and confused. Kissing Brand was like striking the head of a match; their desire for one another overpowered common sense. They'd only known each other a short time and yet she was weak and without will after only a few kisses. Diana wouldn't believe she was capable of such overwhelming emotion. Carly had trouble believing it herself.

"I've frightened you, haven't I?"

Her arms were folded across her stomach. "Brand, I'm twenty-five years old. I know what to expect when a man kisses me." Carly knew she sounded angry, but that anger was directed more at herself than him.

His low laugh surprised her. "I'm glad *you* know about these things because I feel as shaky as I did the first time I kissed a woman. It's been over two years since I've made love."

Carly's hands flew to her ears. She didn't want to hear this. Not any of it. With brisk strides, she walked to the other side of the room. Coming here today had been a colossal mistake. One she wouldn't repeat—ever.

"Gee, look at the time." She glanced at her gold wristwatch and slapped her hands against her sides. "Time passes quickly when you're having fun, or so they say."

"Carly?" he ground out impatiently.

She took a couple of steps in retreat until she found herself backed against the front door. She turned, her hands locking around the doorknob in a death grip.

"I'll talk to you later in the week," Brand murmured, and just the way he said it told her that their next meeting wouldn't end with her running out of the door like a frightened rabbit.

The phone was ringing when Carly stepped through the door of her apartment. Thinking it might be Brand, she stared at it several long seconds while she shrugged off her jacket. No, he wouldn't phone. Not so soon.

"Hello," she answered, a guarded note in her voice.

"Carly, it's Diana."

"Diana!" Carly burst out happily. Rarely had there been a time she'd needed her friend more. "You can't afford these calls, but thank God you phoned."

"What's up? You sound terrible and it's not this crummy long-distance echo, either."

"It's a long story." It wasn't necessary to explain everything to Diana; just hearing her voice had a soothing effect. "Tell me what prompted this sudden urge to hear my voice."

"I couldn't stand it another minute." Diana laughed lightly. "Your letter arrived and I didn't want to have to write and wait for your reply. Tell me about him."

Carly's heart sank. "Do you mean Brand?"

"Is there someone else I don't know about?"

Stepping over the arm of her sofa, Carly walked across the couch, dragging the telephone line with her as she went. "There's nothing to tell. We're only friends."

"When you show this much enthusiasm for any male, I get excited. Now what's this bull about the two of you just being friends? Who are you kidding?"

"Diana..." She exhaled a trembling breath as she sat down. "I don't know what to think. Brand's been married."

"So? If you remember correctly, I've left two husbands in my wake."

"But this is different. She died of leukemia and it nearly killed him, he loved her so much."

"Well, sweetie, I hate to say it, but this guy sounds perfect for you. You're two of a kind. Both of you are walking through life wounded. Has he gotten you into bed yet?"

"Diana!" Carly was outraged. Hot color seeped slowly up her neck.

"I swear, you must be the only twenty-five-year-old virgin left in America."

"If you don't stop talking like that, I'm going to hang up," Carly threatened.

"All right, all right."

Carly could hear Diana's restrained laughter. The

woman loved to say the most outrageous things just to get a rise out of Carly.

"Take my advice." Diana's tone was more serious now. "You can hunt all your life for the perfect male and never find him. He doesn't exist. And even if by some fluke of nature you find someone who suits you, he's liable to expect the perfect female. And neither one of us is going to fill those shoes."

Crossing her legs Indian-style beneath her, Carly managed a weak sigh. "I suppose you're right."

"I'm always right, you know that," Diana responded with a small laugh. "Now, listen, because I've got some serious-type news."

"What?" Carly straightened at the unusually deep intonation in Diana's voice.

"Against my better judgment and two miserable failures, Barney has convinced me that we should get married."

"Diana, that's wonderful. *You* two are the ones who belong together. This is fantastic."

"To be honest, I'm rather pleased about it myself. I'm not getting any younger, you know, and I'm ready to face the mommy scene. Barney and I've decided to have a family right away. Can you picture me pinning diapers and the whole bit?"

"Yes," Carly returned emphatically. "Yes, I can. You'll make a wonderful mother."

"Time will tell," Diana chuckled. "At least I know what *not* to do."

"We both do," Carly agreed. "Have you set the date?"

"Next month, on the fifteenth."

"But that's only a little over three weeks away." Mentally, Carly was chastising Diana and Barney for not getting their act together sooner. This was one wedding she didn't want to miss. But she could hardly ask for time off now.

"Believe me, I know. But the wedding won't be anything fancy. It'd be ridiculous for me to march down the aisle at this point. Barney and I want you here. It's important to both of us."

Disappointment made Carly's hand tighten around the receiver. "I can't, Diana," she said with an exaggerated sigh. "Why couldn't you have made up your mind before I left Seattle?"

"Barney insists on paying your airfare. Now, before you say a word, I know about that pride of yours. But let me tell you from experience, it's better not to argue with Barney and all his money. So plan right now on being here."

Carly would have enjoyed nothing more. "But I can't ask for time off from work. Hamlyn would have my head."

"Threaten to quit," Diana returned smoothly. "If Hamlyn gives you any guff, tell him where to get off. By this time he's bound to recognize what a jewel you are."

"Diana, I don't know."

Some of the teasing quality left Diana's voice. "You're the closest thing I've got to family, Carly. I've been married twice and both times I've stood before a justice of the peace and mumbled a few words that were as meaningless as the marriage. I want this time to be right—all the way."

Carly understood what Diana was saying. She hadn't been present at either of her friend's other weddings. "I don't care what it takes," Carly replied staunchly, "wild horses couldn't keep me away."

"Great. I'll let you know the details later. We're seeing a minister tonight. Imagine me in a church!" She laughed. "That should set a few tongues wagging!"

"I'll phone sometime next week," Carly promised as she replaced the receiver. A smile softened the tense line of her mouth. Diana a mother! The mental picture of her friend burping a baby was comical enough to lighten anyone's mood. But she'd be a good one. Of that Carly had no doubt.

The days flew past. Carly dreaded seeing Brand, but she didn't doubt that he'd be true to his word. The next time they were together could prove to be uncomfortable for them both. He wouldn't avoid a confrontation, that she recognized.

Friday afternoon, George casually mentioned that Brand was on a flying assignment and wouldn't be back until the following day. Carly breathed easier at the short reprieve. At least she would have more time to think about what she wanted to say to him. One thing was sure: it would be better if they didn't continue to see one another. Even for *non*-dates. She didn't know what unseen forces were at work within her, but Brandon St. Clair was far too appealing for her to remain emotionally untouched. He needed a woman. But not her. She'd make that clear when she saw him. Once it was stated, she could go back to living a normal, peaceful life. She might even investigate learning to knit. By the time Diana was pregnant, Carly might have the skill down pat enough to knit booties, or whatever it was babies wore.

Carly was sorting through her mail late Friday afternoon, still thinking about motherhood and how pleased she was for her friend. As she shuffled through several pieces of junk mail, a handwritten envelope took her by surprise. Glancing at the return address, she noted it was from the Women's Correctional Center in Purdy. The name on the left-hand corner was Jutta Hoverson.

Four

Memories of the proud child in the oil painting ruled Carly's thoughts as she clutched Jutta Hoverson's reply. Disappointment washed through her. The letter had been direct and curt. Jutta Hoverson hadn't bothered with a salutation. I TOLD THE PEOPLE TO SAY THAT THE PAINTING IS NOT FOR SALE. I DON'T WANT TO SELL THIS ONE. Her large signature was scrawled across the bottom of the lined paper. And then, as if in afterthought, Jutta had added: I HAVE OTHER PAINTINGS. She'd provided no information. No prices. Not that it mattered; Carly only wanted the one.

She must have read Jutta's brusque words a dozen times, seeking a hidden meaning, desperately wanting to find some clue that the woman was willing to sell the self-portrait. There hadn't been many things in her life that Carly had wanted more than that painting. A week after the art show, the small child remained vivid in her memory; she could still envision the proud tilt of her chin and the hidden tear in the corner of one eye. So many times in her life Carly had joked about her past. If someone had questioned her about being raised as she was, Carly's flippant reply was always the same: Superman had foster parents. Even in the bleakest moments of her life, Carly had forced herself to be optimistic. Her childhood had made her emotionally strong and fortified her fearless personality. But tonight, with the letter from Jutta in her hand, Carly didn't feel like playing a Pollyanna game. She felt like eating twenty-seven chocolates, soaking in the bathtub, reading a book and downing an aspirin…all at the same time. Diana would get a kick out of that.

As it turned out, Carly didn't do any of those things. She went to a theater and paid to see a movie she couldn't remember. She sat in the back row and slouched so far down that she had trouble seeing the screen. After devouring a bag of popcorn, she returned home and downed half a jar of green olives and considered the popcorn and olives her dinner.

Carly woke the next morning depressed and slightly sick to her stomach. Her mood swings weren't usually this extreme. She liked to think of herself as an even-keeled sort of person, although Diana claimed she was eccentric. Admittedly, she didn't know anyone else who slept with knit socks on her feet or kept earmuffs on her nightstand in case of a storm so she wouldn't hear the thunder.

What an ironic sort of person she was. Unafraid of change or danger, Carly often leaped into madcap schemes without thought.

She knew Diana had worried herself sick the weekend Carly had climbed Mount Rainier. The only mountain climbing she'd ever done had been that one weekend on Washington State's highest peak. And yet, Carly was frightened of a tempest.

A long walk that morning released some of the coiled tension. Her fingers pressed deep within the side pockets of her jeans, she kicked at rocks and pieces of broken glass along the side of the road. Something green flittered up at her. The reflection of the lazy rays of the sun flashed on a discarded and broken wine bottle. Carly stooped to pick it up. It was a broken piece of glass, with its edges worn smooth by time. Feeling a little like a lost child, Carly tucked the fragment into her pocket. A rush of emotion raced through her. *She* was like that glass. Discarded and forgotten by her mother, scoured by time.

Carly had followed her feet with no clear destination in mind, and soon found herself in a park. The happy sound of children's laughter drifted toward her. She stood on the outskirts of the playground, watching. That was the problem with her life, she mused seriously. She was always on the outside looking in.

Well, not anymore, her mind cried. *Not anymore.* With a determination born of self-pity, she ran to the slowly whirling merry-go-round.

"Hi." A boy of about seven jumped off a swing and climbed onto the moving merry-go-round. "Are you going to push?"

"I might." Carly started to trot around. The boy looked at her as if she were a wizard who had magically appeared for his entertainment.

"Didn't your mother ever tell you not to talk to strangers?" Carly asked him as she ran, quickly losing her wind. She climbed onto the ride and took several deep breaths.

"You got kids?" the boy countered. "I think it would be all right if you had kids."

"Nope. There's only me." But Carly wasn't trying to discourage his company. She had no desire to be alone.

The boy's brows knit in concentration, before he gave Carly a friendly grin. "You're not a real stranger. I've seen you in the grocery store before."

Carly laughed and jumped off the merry-go-round to head toward the swing set.

"I saw you buy Captain Crunch cereal." He said it as if that put her in the same class as Santa Claus and the Tooth Fairy. He ambled to the swing set and took the the swing next to hers, pumping his legs and aiming his toes for the distant sky until he swung dangerously high. Carly tried to match him, but couldn't.

"I saw you pick up something on the path. What was it?"

"An old piece of glass," Carly answered, still slightly out of breath.

"Then why'd you take it?" He was beginning to slow down.

"I'm not sure."

"Can I see it?"

"Sure." Using the heels of her shoes to stop the swing, she came to a halt and stood to dig the piece of glass from her pocket.

The young boy's eyes rounded eagerly as she placed it in the palm of his hand. "Wow. It's neat."

It was only a broken, worn piece of a discarded wine bottle to Carly. Tossed aside and forgotten, just as she had been by a mother she couldn't remember.

"See how the sun comes through?" He held it up to the sky, pinching one eye closed as he examined it in the sunlight. "It's as green as an emerald."

"Feel how smooth it is," Carly said, playing his game.

The boy rubbed it with the closed palms of his hands and nodded. "Warm like fire," he declared. "And mysterious, too." He handed it back to her. "Look at it in the light. There's all kinds of funny little lines hidden in it, like a treasure map."

Following his example, Carly took the green glass and held it up to the sun. Indeed, it was just as the young boy had said.

The muffled voice came from the other side of the park.

"I gotta go," the boy said regretfully. "Thanks for letting me see your glass." Taking giant steps backward, he paused to glance apprehensively over his shoulder.

"Would you like to keep it?" Carly held it out for him to take.

His eyes grew round with instant approval, and just as quickly they darkened. "I can't. My mom will get mad if I bring home any more treasures."

"I understand," Carly said seriously. "Now, get going before you worry your mother." She waved to him as he turned and kicked up his short legs in a burst of energy.

Carly's hand closed around the time-scoured glass. It wasn't as worthless as she thought, but a magical, special piece. What else was there that was as green as an emerald, as warm as a fire and as intriguing as a treasure map? Tucking it back in her pocket, she strolled toward her apartment, content once again.

Stopping off at the supermarket, Carly returned home with a bag full of assorted groceries. The flick of a switch brought the radio to life. The strains of a classic Carole King song filled the small room with "You've Got a Friend." Carly hummed as she unloaded the sack. Unbidden, the image of Brand fluttered into her mind. She straightened, her hand resting on her hip. Brand was her friend. The only real friend she'd made in Anchorage.

The soft beat of the music continued, causing Carly to stop and ponder. The song said all she had to do was call his name and he'd be there, because he was her friend.

But Brand was flying today. At least, George had said he wouldn't be back until late afternoon.

Maybe she should phone him just to prove how wrong that premise was. Carly reached for her cell and punched out Brand's number. Her body swayed to the gentle rhythm of the song and she closed her eyes, lost in the melody.

"Hello," Brand answered gruffly.

The song faded abruptly. "Brand? I didn't think you'd be back." Her heart did a nonsensical flip-flop. "I…ah…how was your trip?" She brushed the bangs from her forehead, holding them back with her hand as she leaned her hip against the counter.

"Tiring. How are you?"

"Fine," she answered lightly, disliking the way her pulse reacted to the mere sound of his voice. As much as she hated to admit it, Carly had missed Brand's company. Then, to fill an awkward pause: "The radio's playing 'You've Got A Friend.'"

"I can hear it in the background."

Carly could visualize Brand's faint smile.

"I heard from Jutta Hoverson." Her fingers tightened around the receiver.

"Jutta…oh, the artist. What did she say?"

Carly exhaled a pain-filled sigh. "She's not interested in selling."

"Carly, I'm sorry." Brand's voice had softened. "I know how much you wanted that painting."

She appreciated his sympathy but didn't want to dwell on the loss of the artwork. "I'll bet you're hungry," she surprised herself by saying. "Why don't you come over and I'll fix you something? Friends do that, you know."

He didn't hesitate. "I'll be there in ten minutes."

Brand sounded as surprised by the invitation as she was at making it. But it *was* understandable, Carly mused; she wanted to be around people. If she'd been in Seattle, she'd have wandered around the waterfront or Seattle Center. Setting up a tray of deli meats and a jar of olives, Carly realized that her mood required more than casual contact with the outside world. She wanted Brand. The comfort his presence offered would help her deal with Jutta's refusal to sell the painting. Wanting Brand with her was a chilling sensation, one that caused Carly to bite her bottom lip. She didn't want Brand to become a habit, and she feared being with him could easily become addictive.

The doorbell chimed. She glared at the offending portal, angry with herself for allowing Brand to become a weakness in her well-ordered life.

"Hi." She let him in, welcoming him with a faint smile.

"Here—I thought these might brighten your day." Brand handed her a small bouquet of pink and white carnations and sprigs of tiny white flowers. The bouquet wasn't the expensive florist variety, but the cheaper type from the supermarket.

Without a word, Carly accepted the carnations, her fingers closing over the light green paper that held them together. Brand's gesture made her uneasy. Flowers were what he might bring a *date.* And George had mentioned something about the heavy medical bills Brand was paying off. His *wife's* bills. She didn't want him spending his hard earned dollars on her. She frowned as she took the bouquet from him.

"What's the matter?" Brand asked and she was reminded anew how easily he read her.

Carly lowered her chin, not wanting to explain. "Nothing."

"Are we back to that?" Irritation marked his words. "Have we regressed so far in such a short time?"

"What do you mean?" She raised her head, barely managing to keep her voice even and smooth. Moistening her lips was an involuntary action that drew Brand's attention. He wanted to take her in his arms and hold her; it was written in his eyes. He knotted his hands, and Carly recognized the strength of the attraction that pulsed between them. The knowledge should have given her a feeling of power, but instead it upset her. As much as possible she hoped to ignore the attraction between them.

"We went to the art show and it was obvious something was troubling you," Brand said, studying her closely. "I wanted you to tell me what troubled you, but you made me ask. I don't remember your exact words, but the message was clear. There was nothing wrong." His voice became heavy with sarcasm. "Well, Carly, that was a lie. There *was* something wrong then, just as there's something the matter now. I have a right to know."

Carly pressed her lips firmly together. She tried to hide her feelings but found it impossible. In the past she'd gone out of her way to anger him whenever he got too close. Brand inhaled a steadying breath as his hands settled to either side of her neck and he pulled her toward him. "I won't let you do it, Carly. I'm not going to fight with you. Not when you've wiggled your way into my every waking thought for the past week."

Pride demanded that she turn away but Brand's hold tightened, his fingers bringing her so close she could feel his warm breath against her face. A battle warred in her thoughts. She cursed herself for craving the comfort of his arms, and in the same breath, she reached for him. Not smiling. Not speaking.

Needing was something new to her, and Carly didn't like to admit to any weakness.

Brand's arms slipped around her waist as he drew her into his embrace. The only sound in the room was the radio, playing a low and seductive melody from the far corner.

He didn't try to kiss her, although she was sure that had been his original intention. Apparently he realized she needed emotional comfort at that moment. While he might want to kiss her, he restrained himself. Carly was grateful. Her defenses were low. His hand cupped the side of her face, pinning her ear against his heart. She could hear the uneven thud of his pulse. It felt so incredibly good to be in his arms and comforted. She felt secure and at peace. Good to be with him…bad for her emotionally for fear she might come to depend on him…

Confused, Carly didn't know what to think anymore. All she knew was that she was too weak to break away.

"I thought you offered to feed me," Brand said after a long, drawn-out moment, his voice husky.

"Are sandwiches all right?" She turned and brought out the tray of deli meats and the bottle of green olives, setting them on the counter. A loaf of bread followed, along with a jar of mayonnaise and another of mustard.

"Fine. I could eat a..." He paused as he surveyed the contents of the plate. "...pastrami, turkey, beef and green olive sandwich any day."

"There are store bought cupcakes for dessert."

"Fine by me," Brand replied absently as he built a sandwich so thick Carly doubted that it would fit into his mouth.

After constructing her own, she joined Brand at the kitchen table. "I guess I should have warned you that my cooking skills are somewhat limited." She popped an olive into her mouth.

"Don't apologize."

"I'm not. I'm just explaining that you'll have to take me as I am. Fixing a meal that requires a fork is almost beyond my capabilities."

Chuckling, he lifted his napkin and dabbed a spot of mustard from the corner of his mouth. "Do you think there's any chance that Jutta will change her mind and sell the painting?"

The letter was on the table and Brand couldn't help but notice it. Carly took it out of the envelope and handed it to him to read. "I don't think she'll sell, but I don't blame her. She'd like me to ask her about some of her other work."

"What do you plan to do?" Brand pushed his empty plate aside and reached over and took an olive from hers.

She slapped the back of his hand lightly and twisted

to reach for the jar on the counter. "Take your own, bub," she rebuked him with a teasing grin.

Brand emptied several more onto his plate and replaced the one he'd taken of hers. "Well?" He raised questioning eyes to hers.

"I think I'll write her again. Even if she won't sell the portrait, I'd like to get to know her. Whoever Jutta Hoverson is or whatever she's done doesn't bother me. It's obvious the two of us have a lot in common."

Brand didn't respond directly; instead, his gaze slid to the bouquet of carnations she'd flippantly tossed on the countertop. His expression was gentle, almost tender. "You'd better put those in water."

Carly's gaze rested on the pink and white carnations and she released her breath. "You should take the flowers home with you."

"Why?" He regarded her closely, his expression grim.

"I thought you were paying off Sandra's medical bills."

"What's that got to do with anything?"

"We're friends, remember?" Her voice was low. "Flowers are something you'd bring to impress a date. You don't need to impress me, St. Clair. I'm a friend. I don't ever plan to be anything more."

Brand sat still and quiet, and although he didn't speak, Carly could feel his irritation. "I wasn't trying to impress you." His voice was deep. "My intention was more to cheer you up, but I can see that I failed." Silence filled the room as Brand stood, carried his empty plate to the sink and, without a word, opened the cupboard beneath her sink and tossed the flowers into the garbage. His expression was weary as he turned back to face her.

"Brand," Carly tried. She hadn't expected him to react so disgruntled.

He ignored her as he headed toward the front door. "Thanks for the sandwich," he said before the door closed behind him. The sound vibrated off the walls and wrapped its way around Carly's throat.

An hour later, Carly had written a reply to Jutta Hoverson. The second letter was easier to write than the first. Again she mentioned how much she'd enjoyed Jutta's work, and recounted the time she'd visited the Seattle Art Museum in Volunteer Park. She told Jutta that she didn't appreciate the abstract creations, but a friend told her that they supposedly had a lot more meaning than met the eye. Rereading that part of the letter caused Carly to smile. Of course, the friend had been Diana, and the comment was typical of Diana's sense of humor.

Carly closed the letter by asking Jutta to send more information about her other paintings. As she took a stamp from the kitchen drawer, she caught sight of a single carnation that had remained on top of the counter next to the sink. She paused with the stamp raised halfway to her tongue. The carnation looked forlorn and dejected. Feeling bad about the way she'd treated Brand, she opened the cupboard beneath the sink and pulled the bouquet from the can. She gently brushed the coffee grounds from their pink and white petals. Having no vase, Carly placed them in the center of the table in the empty olive jar, which served admirably as a holder.

She regretted what she'd said to him. There were better ways of expressing her feelings. But hindsight was twenty-twenty. That was another of Diana's favorite witticisms. Dear heaven she dearly missed her friend.

After a restless evening in which her mind refused to concentrate on any project, Carly realized that she wouldn't feel right about anything until she'd apologized. Humble pie had never been her specialty, but as she recalled, though the initial bite was bitter, the aftertaste was generally sweet. At least she'd be able to go on with the rest of her day. And the sooner the apology was made, the better. To take the easy way out and phone him tempted her, but Carly resisted. Instead, she donned a thick cable-knit sweater and drove the distance to Brand's apartment.

Her knock on his door was loud and hard. She waited long enough to wonder if he was home. His truck was outside, but that didn't mean much. She finally heard movement inside the apartment and placed a pink carnation between her teeth before the door was opened. "Peace?" she offered.

"Carly." He frowned as if she was the last person he expected to see. His expression clouded before he said, "Come in."

Carly removed the flower and attempted to spit out the taste of the stem and leaves as she moved inside. "Well?" she questioned.

Brand moved a hand over his face, as if he thought she might be an apparition. "Well, what?"

"Am I forgiven for my cavalier attitude?"

He looked at her blankly, as if he still didn't understand what she was asking. "You mean about the flowers?"

Carly tipped her head to one side. Brand had obviously been asleep and she'd woken him. Things were quickly going from bad to worse. "I'm sorry, I…I didn't know you were in bed."

"Care to join me?" Brand teased softly and pulled her into his arms. He inhaled, as if to take in the fresh scent of her. "It's been a long time since I had someone warm to cuddle."

Carly tried to remain stiff, but the instant she was in his arms, she melted against him. He smiled down on her and his finger traced the smooth line of her jaw. His touch had the power to weaken her resolve. This was bad and it was getting worse. To complicate matters even more, Brand could see exactly how she felt.

He chuckled softly, his breath tingled the side of her neck as he leaned forward to nuzzle the curve between her neck and shoulder. "Why don't you put on some coffee while I grab a shirt and shoes?" He reluctantly moved away.

Carly released a sigh of relief when he left her. Not knowing what to do with herself, she wandered into his kitchen.

Her back was to him when Brand entered the room a few moments later. "My coming today was a gesture of friendship," she began, and smiled tightly as she turned to face him. "I felt badly about what happened at my place. My attitude was all wrong. You were being kind and I…"

"Friendship." Brand repeated the word as if he found it distasteful. "I think it's time you woke up to the fact that what I feel for you goes far beyond being pals."

"But you agreed…" Carly was having difficulty finding her tongue. "We aren't even dating."

The coffee was perking furiously behind her and Brand brought down two mugs and filled them before carrying both to the table. "We aren't going to argue about it. If you want to ignore the plain and simple truth, that's up to you."

The arrogance of the man was too much. "You think I'm going to fall in love with you?" she asked incredulously.

Brand blew into the side of the ceramic cup before taking a tentative sip. "If you're honest with yourself, you'll admit you're halfway there already."

Carly slapped one thigh and snickered softly. "I don't think you're fully awake. You're living in a dream world, fellow."

Brand shrugged. "If you say so."

"I know so." Carly sat across from him and cupped the cup with both hands, letting the warmth chase the chill from her blood. "In fact, if that's your attitude, maybe it'd be better if we didn't see one another again. Not at all."

Brand shrugged, giving the impression that either way was fine with him. "Maybe."

Carly laid the palms of both hands on top of the table and half raised herself out of her chair. "Would you please stop it?"

Brand tossed her a look of innocence. "I told you I wasn't going to argue with you, Carly. That's exactly what you want, and I refuse to play that game. Anytime you feel someone getting too close you do whatever to takes to push them away. It took me a while to realize it, but now that I do, I'm not going to let you do it with me."

"You're so wrong," she insisted.

"Am I?" he challenged.

"Okay, whatever. I don't want to fight." She could see it would be a losing battle and she was a poor loser.

"But fighting is what you do best, isn't it?" he asked.

Closing her eyes, Carly clenched her teeth and groaned. "You know, I'm beginning to think that the rocks in my head would fill the holes in yours."

Brand laughed and reached across the table to take her hand and raised it to his lips, but Carly pulled it free.

Undeterred, Brand continued, "Why don't you come over here and put your arms around my neck and kiss me the way you've wanted to do from the moment you walked in the door?"

Stunned, Carly nearly dropped her mug. It thumped against the table, and hot coffee sloshed over the sides. She jumped up to get a rag to catch the liquid before it flowed onto the floor. The color drained from her face as she sopped up the mess. She *had* wanted to kiss him. In the back of her mind, she had formed a picture of her apology being followed by Brand kissing her senseless. Carly closed her eyes and exhaled sharply.

The sound of Brand pushing back his chair filled her with panic. She nearly panicked with the need to escape.

"Oh, no, you don't." He spoke softly as his hand caught her shoulder and turned her into his arms.

. "Brand, I don't think this is a good idea," she pleaded, and then swallowed to control the husky tremor in her voice. "I have to go…there's something…"

She wasn't allowed to finish as his mouth swooped down on hers. Her lips parted, whether to protest or welcome him she couldn't tell. Her response had an immediate effect on him and all gentleness left him and his hold tightened as he hungrily devoured her mouth. His hand at the back of her neck increased its pressure, lifting Carly onto the tips of her toes.

If she'd been confused before, it was nothing compared to the deluge of sensations that rocked her now. Her knees went weak. Nothing made sense as she surrendered to her swirling desire. Her tongue outlined Brand's mouth and he groaned. He broke off the kiss long enough to move with her to the chair and pull her into a sitting position on his lap.

Their eyes locked, and words became unnecessary as he wrapped his hands in her dark hair, directing her mouth back to his. She felt his hunger as his mouth reclaimed hers. Together they strained to satisfy each other. When she felt she could endure no more she broke away and buried her face in the curve of his shoulder.

Brand's hands explored her back beneath the sweater. "Don't fight me so hard," he murmured.

Carly sighed thoughtfully. "The way I see it, I'm not fighting near hard enough." She could feel his smile against her temple. "The things you make me feel frighten me," she whispered after a long moment.

"I know."

"I don't want to fall in love with you," she whispered.

"I know that too."

Carly's eyes rested on the clean top of the television. "What did you do with Sandra's picture?" He'd put it away, she knew, but she needed to know where.

"It's in a drawer."

Somehow she'd expected him to wince when she mentioned the wife he'd lost, but he didn't. "Top or bottom?"

A hand on each shoulder turned her so that she could look him in the eye. "Bottom."

She lowered her gaze, embarrassed at revealing the depth of her insecurity.

"Now," he said, and a hint of firmness stole into his voice. "When are you going to stop running from me?"

"I don't—"

Narrowed, disbelieving eyes forbade her from finishing. "Carly, look at me. I'm through with this 'we're-not-dating' business. We are *seriously* dating and I won't take no for an answer. Understand?"

She nodded numbly. All the old insecurities bobbed to the surface of her mind, but when Brand put his arms around her those doubts seemed inconsequential. Only when she was alone did they grow ominous and forbidding.

Brand patted the lump of discarded glass in her jeans pocket. "Either you've got a serious problem with your bones or you're sprouting something in your pocket."

Carly smiled and arched her back so she could withdraw the glass. "Here." She gave it to Brand. "I found a treasure."

"Treasure?" He eyed her warily.

"It's as green as an emerald."

"Yes," Brand agreed.

She took it back, rubbed it between the palms of her hands and held it to his face. "And warm as fire."

"Not quite that hot."

"We're imagining here," she chastised playfully. "Now hold it up to the light."

Brand did as she requested. "Yes?"

"See the cracks and lines?"

"So?"

"It's as intriguing as a map. A treasure map," she added, repeating the youngster's assessment. "And I bet you thought this was just a plain old piece of broken glass that time had smoothed."

Brand closed his fingers over the green glass and a sadness suddenly stole over him. "That's the kind of wonder Shawn would discover in this."

"Shawn?" A chill settled over her even before Brand could explain.

"My son."

"You have children?" The question came out breathlessly, her voice low and wobbly.

"Yes. Shawn and Sara."

Suddenly Carly knew what it must feel like to die.

Five

Several hours later the knot in her stomach still hadn't relaxed. Even now her breath came in short, painful wisps. Brand had children. Beautiful children. He'd taken a family photo from his wallet and Carly had been forced to stare at two blond youngsters. Both Shawn and Sara had been gifted with Sandra's beautiful eyes and Sandra's hair color.

For every second that Carly had studied the picture she'd died a little more. Brand had explained that his children were living with his mother in Oregon, but they'd be joining him in a couple of months once school was out for the summer.

"How old are they?" Somehow Carly managed to ask the question.

Brand's eyes were proud. That he loved and missed his family was obvious. "Shawn's seven and Sara's five."

Carly nodded and returned the photo.

"You'll like them, Carly."

Brand had sounded so confident, unaware of the turmoil that attacked her.

A few minutes after that, Brand walked her to his front door. "I'll see you tomorrow," he said and gently kissed her brow. "We can talk more about us."

Carly wanted to scream that there wasn't anything to discuss, but she held her tongue, realizing an argument would solve nothing.

On the way out the door, Carly's shoe caught on the rug and she stumbled forward. She would have fallen if Brand hadn't caught her.

"Are you okay?"

"Fine," she mumbled. "I'm fine."

Brand knelt at her side and retrieved her shoe. "The heel's broken. I can probably fix it, if you like."

"No, no, it's fine. Don't worry."

The instant Carly was back in her apartment, she took off the shoes and threw them both in the garbage. For the first time in recent memory she was pleased that Diana wasn't around to witness this latest attack of wastefulness. Yes, the shoes could be repaired. But not for her. All too often in her life she'd been forced to wear repaired shoes. But not any more.

Diana saw her attitude as ridiculous, but Carly considered the cost of new shoes a small price to pay.

Moon shadows danced across the walls as Carly lay in bed, unable to sleep. It was hours later. Already she was dreading seeing Brand again and what she had to tell him. Every condition she'd set for their relationship had been broken. He had come right out and told her he wanted more from her than friendship.

The most disturbing thing had been that Brand had known how badly she'd wanted to kiss him. He had been able to see it when she hadn't even admitted it to herself. If she was that easy to read, Carly doubted that she could disguise any of her feelings. And she was dangerously close to falling in love with Brandon St. Clair. Placing Sandra, Shawn and Sara out of the picture, Brand could make her feel more of a woman than she had at any other time in her life. The attraction between them was so strong she didn't know if she could fight against the swift current that seemed to be drawing them together.

In the morning, Carly dressed for work. Standing in the kitchen, she was buttering a piece of toast when the discarded loafers caught her eye. Throwing them out was a wasteful, childish action. Having them repaired would be such a little thing. This quirk, this penchant for perfection, was ruining her life. Carly turned her back and ignored the shoes. They were old, worn, and she'd have thrown them out in a few weeks anyway. *But they were comfortable,* her mind returned quickly.

At the front door on her way out, Carly suddenly turned around and went back into the kitchen. She lifted the shoes out of the garbage and set them on the floor. Time. All she needed was time to think things over.

"Morning, George." Carly set her purse on top of her desk and walked across the room to pour herself a cup of coffee.

George had a clipboard in his hand. A deep scowl darkened his face. "Do you remember the Longmeir shipment to Palmer?"

Leaning her hip against her desk, Carly cupped the coffee mug with both hands. "Sure, we trucked that out last week."

George set the clipboard aside. "It didn't arrive."

"What?" Carly straightened. Two days after arriving at Alaska Freight Forwarding, she'd learned that Longmeir was their best and most demanding customer. The mining company had bases throughout the state and depended on Alaska Freight to ship the needed supplies to each site in the most expeditious, most dependable and most economic way. Carly had been the one to decide to truck this latest shipment rather than use rail cars. George had concurred with her suggestion, but the decision had been hers.

"Needless to say, that freight's got to be found. And fast."

Brushing the hair from her forehead, Carly pulled out a desk chair. "I'll get on it right away."

"Do that," George ordered crisply.

By late afternoon Carly had gone through fifteen cups of coffee. Near closing time she tracked down the lost shipment. The truck driver had delivered it to the wrong camp, but that site had no record of accepting the shipment. There had been foul-ups at both ends—and Charles Longmeir wasn't a man to accept excuses. Carly stayed until everyone else had left for home. She had an idea that once the handler at the other camp inventoried his supplies, they'd be able to verify the location and make the necessary adjustments. However, that couldn't be done until morning. Rotating her neck to ease the tense muscles, Carly couldn't recall a worse Monday.

Letting herself into her apartment, she felt mentally and physically exhausted. George had voiced his displeasure all day. If they lost the Longmeir account, she might as well kiss her job goodbye. George hadn't actually said as much, but the implication was there. To complicate matters, she was due to investigate a large claim on another order that had arrived damaged. Her stomach felt acidy and she could feel the beginnings of a headache prickling at her temple. Little wonder. She hadn't eaten anything since her toast that morning.

The phone rang at seven-thirty, and Carly didn't answer it, certain Brand was at the other end of the line. She didn't feel up to seeing him that night. All she wanted was a tall glass of milk, a hot bath and bed. In that order.

She hadn't finished the milk when someone knocked on her door. Carly didn't need to be told it was Brand.

"Hi." He greeted her with a light brush of his mouth against hers.

Carly was astonished that such a little thing as this brief kiss could affect her, but it did. "Brand, I've had a rotten day. I'm not in the mood for company."

"I know. George told me about the Longmeir shipment." He ignored her lack of welcome and walked past her into the kitchen, carrying a grocery bag. "I'll only stay a few minutes," he promised. "Now, sit down, put your feet up and relax."

"Brand," Carly moaned, half pleading, half amused. She was still holding the front door open, but he was in her kitchen humming merrily. "Just what do you think you're doing?" she challenged.

"Taking care of you."

Carly closed the door and marched into the kitchen. "I don't need anyone."

Brand was at her stove, a dish towel draped over his arm as he cracked fresh eggs against the side of a bowl. "I know that." Again he pretended not to notice her lack of welcome. "You've been on your own for a long time. But I'm here now."

"Brand, please..."

He turned and planted his hand on both of her shoulders, his eyes holding hers with such warmth that she couldn't resist when he lowered his mouth to hers. His kiss brought her into quick submission.

He smiled down on her. "Now, go relax. I'll call you when dinner is ready."

Carly complied, wondering why she allowed him this amount of control over her. Leaning her head against the back of the love seat, her eyes drooped closed. The sound of Brand's humming as he worked lulled her into a light, pleasant sleep. Eyes shut, Carly's mind followed Brand's movements about her apartment. She heard him whipping the eggs and chopping something on the cutting board; she heard the sizzle of the butter when he added it to the hot skillet. That sound was followed by another she couldn't identify, then finally she heard the eggs being stirred in the pan and bread being lowered in the toaster. Delicious smells drifted toward her, and Carly realized how hungry she was.

"Dinner's ready," Brand called and he stood behind her chair, waiting to pull it out as she approached.

Her eyes widened at the sight of the appealing omelet. Melted cheese and pieces of onion and green pepper oozed from the sides of his tantalizing masterpiece. "Wow," she said as she sat down. "You never told me you could cook like this."

"There wasn't any reason to mention it before now. I've been on my own long enough to learn the fundamentals."

Carly took the first bite and shook her head in wonder. "This is fantastic."

"I didn't think you'd want dinner out."

"After a day like today, all I want is a hot bath and bed."

A mischievous grin curved the edges of Brand's mouth. "If that's an invitation, I accept."

The sexual banter between them seemed to grow more pointed with every meeting. Carly shook her head forcefully. "No, it wasn't," she announced primly.

She finished her meal and carried the plate to the sink. "How did you know I hadn't eaten?" Carly asked, not turning around. Most people would have had their dinner before now. A glance at her wristwatch told her it was nearly nine.

His eyes grew warm. "Because I'm beginning to know you, Carly Grieves. You don't eat when you're upset."

"I drink coffee."

"Yes, you drink a ton of coffee. It's a wonder you haven't gotten an ulcer."

Making busywork at the sink, Carly was torn between needing him to stay and wishing he'd leave her alone. The feelings she'd battled over the weekend returned a hundred fold. "Aren't you going to thank me for dinner?" he asked softly, coming to her side. He slipped his arms around her waist from behind and kissed the gentle slope of her neck.

Carly went still as she breathed in the clean male scent of him. "Thank you, Brand." Her voice was barely above a whisper.

"I was hoping you'd have other ways of expressing

your appreciation," he whispered and gently nibbled on the lobe of her ear.

"I don't." She prayed he couldn't detect the thread of breathlessness in her voice.

His hand stole beneath her sweater and slid across her ribs as his mouth sought and found the sensitive areas on her neck. Carly tilted her head to one side, loving the delicious sensations he brought to life within her. A trembling weakness shook her and she melted against him, her softness reveling in the touch of his hard length. Brand turned her into his arms and she linked her hands at the base of his neck.

"Kiss me, Carly," he ordered huskily.

She defied him with her eyes, not wanting to give in to him. Not so easily. Her pride—and so much more—was at stake. She couldn't allow herself to become involved with this man.

Their gazes locked in a silent battle of wills. His dark eyes were narrowed with demand. Unable to meet his look, Carly's gaze slid to his mouth. His lips were slightly parted, eager. And Carly couldn't deny him… couldn't deny herself.

Finally she obliged, her mouth slanting over his, kissing him with a thoroughness that left them both weak and breathless. He clung to her as if he was afraid to let her go.

"Are you happy now?" she asked, rubbing her cheek along the side of his jaw in a feline caress. The abrasive feel of his unshaven beard against her skin's smoothness was strangely welcome.

"No." He kissed the corner of her mouth, seeking more, but Carly successfully forestalled him. "Brand, I want you to teach me to fly."

"What?" He stiffened and pulled his head back to study her.

"You heard me."

"But why?"

"Why not?" she quizzed.

"I can think of a hundred reasons."

"I thought you said you wanted me to look at your accounting books."

"You know I do." He broke away from her and strode to the other side of the kitchen, his face tight and troubled. The mute suggestion that he couldn't think with her in his arms pleased her. He paused and folded his arms over his chest.

"I suggest we trade labor," Carly continued.

Brand didn't look pleased, although he appeared to be mulling the suggestion over. "You'll have to read several books."

"I'm not illiterate," Carly challenged with a light laugh. "I'll have you know I read books all the time."

Brand's glance was wry and he returned evenly, "Yes, I imagine you do."

"Well?" The idea made perfect sense to her.

Brand shrugged and walked into the living room to pick up the remote. "I suppose," he said and turned on the television.

Carly wasn't fooled. Brand didn't like her idea, but she'd show him how much sense it made. The afternoon they'd spent in the air had only whetted her appetite for more. Soaring through the air, viewing the world from the clouds would be a magical experience. And having Brand teach her would be the most feasible way.

"Come and watch this movie with me," Brand said.

A trace of amusement sparkled from his eyes, and invitation.

"What's so funny?"

"Nothing." He returned his attention to the television. His hand moved to cup her shoulder when she sat down beside him.

The movie was one Carly had seen, but she didn't say anything. It felt warm and pleasant to be held by Brand. His touch was gentle, yet almost impersonal.

He didn't leave until after the eleven o'clock news, kissing her lightly at the front door. "Are you sure you don't want to thank me for dinner again?" he whispered against the soft wisps of hair that grew at her temple. "I could easily be persuaded to accept your gratitude."

His voice was only half teasing, and Carly knew it. "Next time I'll throw you out the door," she declared with mock severity.

"I'll see you tomorrow night—it's your turn to cook," he said with a self-assured chuckle.

"My turn..." She had no intention of seeing him the following day.

"Yes. I'll bring the ledgers over after work."

"Brand, I told you before I'm not much of a cook. I eat a lot of green olives and chocolate." Carly crossed her arms to chase away a sudden chill.

"Don't worry about it. Until tomorrow," he said, and gave her a lingering kiss to seal the promise.

Carly's spirits lifted the next morning when she got a call confirming that the lost shipment was indeed at the wrong warehouse, as she'd pinpointed. The handler promised to have the equipment en route to the proper camp that afternoon, by company truck.

George looked as relieved as Carly felt. "None of this trouble was your doing," he said by way of apologizing. "And, listen, I've been thinking about that wedding you said you wanted to attend."

Carly's hand tightened around her pencil. When she'd approached George about Diana's wedding, he'd been less than enthusiastic about giving her the three days off. He hadn't answered her, but had mumbled something under his breath about no vacation time being due her until next summer. His expression had been so forbidding that she'd let the matter drop.

"Yes," she said, holding her breath.

"Go ahead. Just be sure your assignments are complete and all the claims have been taken care of."

"I will," Carly responded evenly, then grinned up at the white-haired man. Over the weeks she'd come to overlook his gruff exterior. "Thanks, George."

"Just make sure your friends understand that I won't have you gallivanting to Seattle every time one of them decides to get married."

"I wouldn't dream of asking." Lowering her head, Carly tried unsuccessfully to disguise a smile.

"When will you be leaving?" George flipped open the appointment book on the top of his desk.

"I'd like to leave a week from Thursday." She waited for a flurry of complaints, but none came.

"Fine. When can I expect you back?"

"The following Tuesday—Wednesday at the latest."

George didn't blink. Carly could hardly believe it. She would phone Diana the minute she got home… oh, darn, Brand was coming over for dinner. And she couldn't cook. He *knew* that. Well, a couple of frozen dinners would discourage him. Brand seemed to be under the impression that just because they were trading skills, they would be seeing one another every night. She hadn't made this proposition as an excuse to see more of him—but he'd learn that soon enough.

During the drive from work to her apartment, Carly felt the faint stirrings of guilt. After a hard day, Brand would need something more than a frozen dinner, and she wasn't capable of putting together anything more than soup and a sandwich. Frustrated with herself because she cared, she took a short side trip to the local fried chicken outlet.

Brand was at the door only minutes after she arrived home. His arms were loaded with books. "Whatever you're cooking smells good."

"I didn't cook anything," she announced coolly as she set two plates out on the table.

"You don't sound very relaxed. Did you find the freight?"

"I located it. And it was exactly where I'd assumed it had to be," she answered absently, neatly folding two paper napkins and placing them beside the plastic forks.

"Are you going to kiss me hello or will I be forced to take you in my arms and—"

Carly leaned over and brushed her lips against his cheek in a sisterly manner. "Go ahead and put that stuff on the coffee table."

For a second it looked as if Brand was going to argue with her. He hadn't appreciated her miserly kiss and his look said as much.

"Go on," she urged, struggling to hide her satisfied smile. "Everything here's ready." She surveyed the table. Fried chicken, mashed potatoes, giblet gravy, coleslaw and fresh biscuits. She hadn't eaten a meal like this since Diana and Barney had taken her out for a going-away celebration.

"I'll be back in a minute." Brand set the books aside and returned a moment later with a large box.

"Good grief, what's that?"

He glanced sheepishly at the department-store box under his arm. "Receipts, canceled checks and the like."

"A whole box?"

Brand nodded, slightly abashed. "I'll help if you want."

She'd been party to his kind of assistance in the past. "No, thanks." She raised one hand in defense. "You'd only mess up my system." *And my mind,* she added silently.

They talked as they ate. Brand explained that he would be around town most of that week, but he had some distance flying coming up in the early part of the next. Carly listened, thinking that he was talking to her as he would a wife. The idea terrorized her. She'd hoped to pull away from Brand, but her life became more entwined with his every day. The crazy thing was that it was her own doing. She was the one who'd suggested they trade skills.

"Speaking of traveling," she said, wiping her fingers clean on a yellow napkin. "I'm going to be doing some of my own. I'll be leaving next week for Seattle."

"Any special reason?" His smile seemed an effort.

"Diana's getting married." Her eyes brightened with an inner glow of happiness for her friend. "I'm booking my flight for a week from Thursday morning." The wedding was scheduled for Friday night, but Carly wanted to be there early enough to soothe any attacks of nerves Diana might have.

"And you'll be back..."

"The following Tuesday. Brand..." She took a deep breath. "What do you think of the idea of me stopping in Purdy and meeting Jutta Hoverson? It wouldn't be out of my way. Diana would let me use her car. I'd really like to meet her."

"Why?"

She glanced away, not wanting him to see how much the idea excited her. "Several reasons."

"Are you hoping that she'll sell you the painting?"

The question unaccountably provoked her. "No, of course not. That's not it at all. I...I just want to see what she looks like, that's all. I'm sorry I mentioned it." Carly frowned. "Not everyone has ulterior motives, you know."

Brand laughed. "Now, don't get all shook up. I was only curious."

Carly removed a piece of lint from her wool skirt. "I think you should remember something, St. Clair." Her words were clipped and impatient. "I have more in common with Jutta Hoverson than I'll ever have with you."

His frown darkened. "You're doing it again. I'm getting too close and you'd rather fight and I won't do it."

"Is this what you did every time Sandra had a complaint? Did you refuse to fight with her, too?"

"Leave Sandra out of this."

"No," she snapped.

Silence hung between them like a dark, gray thundercloud. Electricity filled the room, ready to arc at the slightest provocation.

Rising, Brand rammed his hands deep within his jeans pockets. "Sandra and I fought just like every couple does, but I won't fight with you, Carly."

"Why?" She felt like shouting at him, but when she spoke her voice was low and filled with frustration.

"Because it's exactly the excuse you're looking for to shove me out of your life. I've been chipping away for too long at the wall you've built around yourself to blow it over a stupid argument." He paused and rubbed his eyes. "I was in Oregon last week."

Brand had been gone almost the entire week and she'd assumed it was on business. He didn't need to tell her what had drawn him to his home. His children were there.

"For the first time since Sandra died, I found I could look at my son and daughter and not feel the gut-wrenching pain of having lost their mother. You've done that for me, Carly."

"No," she mumbled and shook her head from side to side.

"Yes. Now, listen to me. If you weren't running so hard from me you'd see what's right in front of your nose."

Coming to her feet, Carly took Brand's plate from the table and carried it to the sink. She didn't want to look at him, she didn't want to hear him. Filling the sink with water, she hoped to drown out his words.

"I took Shawn and Sara to Cannon Beach with me. Sandra loved the beach," he continued, ignoring Carly's frenzied movements. "I hadn't been there since she died."

Carly's fingers gripped the edge of the sink as she closed her eyes, silently screaming for him to stop. She wasn't a part of his life. He had no reason to tell her these things. She shouldn't be that important to him.

"I'd always thought, whenever I went back, that I

wouldn't be able to stand looking at the ocean again. Sandra had loved it so much. But nothing had changed… even though I guess maybe I thought it would. But the wind blew and the sea rumbled and the shorebirds soared as they always have."

"Please," Carly pleaded. "I don't want to hear this."

"But you're going to, even if it means I have to force you to listen."

Without turning around, Carly knew that Brand's mouth had tightened into a grim line. Arguing would be useless.

Brand began again. "One afternoon, while Shawn and Sara were playing in the sand, I stood with the wind blowing against me and closed my eyes. A picture of Sandra filled my mind. But not in the ordinary sense of remembering. She was there smiling, happy as she'd always been at the beach, smelling of wildflowers and sunshine. As long as I kept my eyes closed she was there with me and the children. The only sounds were those of the children, and the whisper of the wind. But when I strained I thought for an instant I could hear the faint call of Sandra's laughter."

Tears filled Carly's eyes and she blinked in a desperate effort to forestall their flow. "Don't," she murmured, "please don't do this to me." Her mind was filled with the image of this proud man standing on the beach with the wind buffeting against him, communicating with his dead wife.

"You don't understand," Brand said softly. "For the first time since she died, I felt her presence instead of her absence. For two years my memories of her have been tied up with the agony of her death. I looked out at the ocean and felt a sense of life again. That desolate darkness I'd wrapped myself in was gone. The time had come to go back. Back to the world. Back to people. Back to my children. But mostly back to you."

Carly wiped the tears from her face with both hands.

"It was you who brought back to life feelings I had assumed were long dead. You, Carly." He moved so that he was standing directly behind her. "I'm falling in love with you. From the moment I walked into your office I knew there was something special about you. You've hidden from me, dodged me, fought me. But the time's come, my sweet Carly, for you to look out over the ocean and choose life."

Her lips went dry and she moistened them. Fresh tears burned for release, but she held them back as she'd always done, her throat aching with the effort. Turning, she slipped her arms around his waist and buried her face against his broad chest. Brand wrapped his arms around her so tightly that for a moment she couldn't breathe. He needed her; Carly could feel it. His breathing was slow and ragged, as though it was an effort for him to hold back the emotion.

"I guess this means we're dating," she said after a long moment.

Her words were followed by the low rumble of Brand's laughter. "Yes, I guess you could say that."

"Brand..." She hesitated. "All this frightens me."

"I know. I was afraid too."

"But you're not anymore?"

"No." His hand traced the outline of her face, tilting her chin so that he could meet her troubled gaze. "Not anymore."

"Why..." She swallowed at the painful knot blocking her larynx. "Why didn't you tell me about your children?"

"I had trouble even talking about them. They were part of the life I'd left behind."

"But you said they're coming to Alaska soon."

"As soon as school's out. I told them about you."

Carly stiffened. "What did you say?"

He kissed the tip of her nose. "I told them I had a special friend that I was beginning to love just as I loved their mother."

"Oh, Brand, I wish you hadn't," she whispered, her voice trembling.

He ignored her, but his grip tightened, as if he was afraid she'd bolt and run as she'd done so many times in the past. "A funny little friend who climbed mountains and jumped out of airplanes and liked to eat green olives and chocolate."

"And…and what did they say?"

Brand laughed and mussed the top of her head with his chin. "Shawn wanted to know if you'd take him with you the next time you decide to climb Mount Rainier. And Sara was more concerned about whether or not you liked video games."

Carly's smile was shaky.

Sandra's children would be joining him soon. A sense of unrest attacked her. True, she could climb mountains and jump out of airplanes, but the thought of meeting these two children filled her with indescribable terror.

Six

Brand came into Carly's office yawning on Thursday afternoon. " I'm bushed," he declared as he sat down on George's desk chair. "I don't know, Carly. Someone's changed the rules in the last ten years."

Rising, she poured him a cup of steaming coffee. "What do you mean?"

"I'm too old for these late nights. I used to be able to get by on four or five hours sleep. But no longer. I'm too old for this."

They'd been together every day. They talked, watched television, went for long walks and discussed flying. Not once had Brand left Carly's apartment before midnight.

Responding to his tiredness, she put her hand over her own mouth and yawned loudly.

"I'll be late tonight," Brand said after taking the first sip from the coffee cup.

"Good," Carly returned with a lazy smile. "That'll give me a chance to go over those flying theory books you brought me."

Brand lowered his gaze, but not before Carly saw his

frown. Although he hadn't said anything to discourage her, it was obvious he didn't want her to learn to fly. He'd know soon enough, Carly mused now, that she was her own woman. Diana had often reacted with the same show of reluctance at Carly's adventurous inclinations. Carly could almost hear her friend protesting her sudden interest in gaining a private pilot license.

"Do you want me to have dinner ready for you?" The offer was more selfish than generous; Carly realized how much she looked forward to their time together in the evenings. Not that they did a lot of social things. Brand's finances wouldn't allow for much of that. Maybe once a week, they could dine out or take in a movie, but certainly not every night.

Brand wanted to take her to dinner Friday night and Carly had agreed although she felt less nervous when the captain of the football team had asked her for a date in high school!

"I may not be back until after ten," Brand warned.

"No problem. And you know better than to expect a three-course meal."

Setting his empty mug aside, Brand stood and kissed her on the cheek. "I'll see you later," he promised, his voice low and husky.

George returned to the office just as Brand was leaving. Carly stood at the window until Brand had climbed into his car and was gone.

"You two have been seeing a lot of one another, haven't you?"

Carly's answer was a nod. Her private life had nothing to do with the office and she wasn't going to elaborate on her relationship with Brand to satisfy George's curiosity.

"He's a rare man, Brand St. Clair."

She could feel George studying her. Carly's boss had seen the look on her face—and knew the cause. "Yes, he is," Carly agreed, and turned back to her desk.

"He's driven himself hard. But he looks more relaxed now than I can ever remember," George continued.

Carly said nothing, not wanting to encourage him.

"I don't suppose you could say anything to him about becoming a full-time pilot for Alaska Freight Forwarding, could you?"

Mercifully, the phone rang, so Carly didn't have to answer George. By the time she'd replaced the receiver, her employer had left the office.

When Carly returned to the empty apartment that evening, she felt restless. Usually Brand arrived shortly after she did. Now, for the first time in days, the evening stretched out ahead of her devoid and lonely. The thought shocked Carly. A couple of times she found herself glancing at her watch and mentally calculating how long it would be until Brand arrived. This was exactly what she hadn't wanted.

Bit by bit, Brand had wiggled his way into her life. She did his bookkeeping, and in return he was teaching her how to fly an airplane. That had been their original plan. Instead their evenings had been spent simply enjoying each other's company. Sometimes Brand dropped by the office unexpectedly, for no more reason than to have a cup of coffee and chat for a few minutes. Now, a day without spending time with Brand seemed unnatural. She had tried to tell Diana about these fears concerning her relationship with Brand, but never quite did. What she was feeling about him came from the heart, and not from the mind. These emotions were foreign to her, and she wasn't sure she could explain what was happening to her dearest friend when she wasn't entirely sure herself. And although she loved her friend, there were certain things even Diana couldn't be expected to understand.

There was so much Carly didn't know about Brand, and yet she felt she knew everything she would ever need to know. Nothing in his life had ever been done halfheartedly. Only a man who loved with such intensity could grieve the way he had for Sandra. Only a man with as much insight and understanding of her personality could be as patient as Brand had been with her.

For all that she was, she loved him. The realization came to her gently, warm and secure, kindling a fire that glowed. She did love Brand. What she didn't know was whether or not her love for him was strong enough to overcome the fears and anxieties ingrained on her conscience since childhood.

The FCC flight manual was balanced on her bent knee and the television was on with the volume turned down when Brand knocked lightly against her door.

"Hi." She greeted him with a hug. "Are you hungry?"

"Starved," he groaned, and pulled her into his arms. "But before you go into the kitchen I expect a proper greeting. None of those miserly kisses you seem to be so fond of giving me."

Smiling seductively, Carly slid her hands up his chest and allowed them to rest on the curve of his shoulders. "Remember," she whispered huskily as she fit her body intimately to his, "you asked for this." She kissed one corner of his mouth and then the other. Then, she outlined the contour of his lips with her tongue, darting it in and out of his mouth with a teasing action that affected her as much as it did Brand.

His hands began to caress her back in an unhurried exploration as his mouth opened to hers, taking the role of aggressor. His lips parted hers. Carly clung to him, drained of strength.

They broke apart, each gasping for air.

"A few more of those and I won't be responsible for what happens," he murmured breathlessly.

All the blood flowed from her face. The point in their relationship was fast approaching when kissing would satisfy neither of them. Carly knew that Brand yearned to make love to her, and frankly she wanted him too, but this was a serious step in their relationship and she wasn't sure either of them were ready.

"Let me get your dinner," Carly said as she turned away. She could feel Brand's smile hit her straight between the shoulder blades. He was assuming she was running again, and he was right.

Happy—perhaps happier than she'd ever been at any time in her life—Carly worked in her small kitchen as Brand leafed through the newspaper. She built him a three-tiered sandwich, piling each piece of bread high with meat from the local deli, adding sliced tomatoes and cut pickles. She topped her creation with a giant green olive that was speared with a toothpick. Then she adorned the plate with potato chips and proudly carried her masterpiece in—only to discover that Brand was asleep on her sofa.

Carly toyed with the idea of waking him, but he looked relaxed and so peaceful that she couldn't make herself do it.

Returning to the kitchen, Carly bit into a crunchy potato chip and covered the sandwich with plastic wrap. He could eat it tomorrow. Leaning against the counter, Carly yawned.

She tucked an extra pillow under Brand's head and covered him with a spare blanket. The temptation was strong to linger at his side, to make an excuse to touch him. Her fingers flexed with the desire to brush the thick, dark hair from his forehead. But such an action might wake him, and she didn't want to risk that.

An hour later the flight manual could no longer hold her wandering attention. Time and again her gaze slid from the fine print on the page to the sleeping figure across from her. If Brand hoped to bore her with dull reading, he was succeeding, but she wouldn't let him know that. A lot of what she'd gone over tonight might as well have been in a foreign language. What she needed was a *pre*-preflight instruction manual. But she wouldn't give up. Now she was more determined than ever to get her pilot license.

She hesitated in the lighted doorway of her room, watching the moon shadows surround Brand. Realizing that she loved Brand was one thing; what she was going to do about it was something else entirely. So many questions remained unanswered. Most important were the ones neither of them had voiced.

When Carly woke the next morning, Brand was gone. A note was propped on the table apologizing for his lack of manners. He assured her that his falling asleep didn't have anything to do with her company, but only the fact that thirty-three years were taking their toll. He reminded her of their dinner date that evening and asked her to wear her best dress because they were going to do the town. His hurried postscript mentioned that the sandwich had been fantastic.

Carly sat with a glass of orange juice and a plate of toast as she reread every word of his note. The happiness she'd felt finding it washed over her. It was as if Brand had written her a poetic love letter. Perhaps she was suffering a second adolescence. Good grief, she hoped not. The first one had been difficult enough.

That afternoon, at the stroke of five, Carly was out the office door. She wanted to luxuriate in a scented bath and be as beautiful and alluring as possible for when Brand arrived.

The phone was ringing when she walked through the apartment door.

"Hello." Her voice was singsongy with happiness.

"Carly, I'm going to be late."

"Brand, where are you?" The line sounded as if it were long distance.

"Lake Iliamna."

"Where?" He might as well have said Timbuktu.

"The largest lake in Alaska. There's a lodge here."

"Oh." That didn't mean anything to her. "I take it you're using the float plane."

Brand's low chuckle warmed her blood. "The woman's a genius."

"When should I expect you?"

"Honey, I don't know. It could be hours yet."

The endearment rolled off his tongue seemingly without thought, and Carly wondered if that was a name he'd called Sandra. She pushed the thought from her mind forcefully. She couldn't, she *wouldn't* allow

Brand's first wife to haunt their relationship. Not any more than she already did.

"Carly, you're terribly quiet all of a sudden. Are you angry?"

She jerked herself from her musings. "Of course not. Listen, Brand, would you rather cancel the whole thing? I don't mind. We can go out to dinner another time."

"No," he returned. "I want to see you. I *need* to see you. That is, if you don't mind waiting."

"No," she whispered softly. "I don't mind."

By eleven, Carly was yawning and rubbing her eyes to keep from going to sleep. An old rerun of Law and Order was the only thing that kept her from drifting into a welcome slumber.

Brand arrived at midnight. "Carly, I'm sorry," he said the moment she opened the door. "I came right from the airport. Give me another half hour to go home and change. I'll be back as soon as I can."

"We can't go out now." Carly could only guess what it had taken for him to offer. One look at the fatigue in his eyes was all she needed to see that he was exhausted. "Nothing's open at this time of night," she reasoned in a soft voice.

"We'll find something," he assured her, but not too strenuously.

"Nonsense. I'll let you do your magic with eggs and we can eat here."

His arms brought her into his embrace even with his eyes closed. "I can't argue with you there. It's been a long day."

"What time did you leave my apartment?" He'd spent at least part of the night on her sofa.

"Three. Which was a good thing, since I was due to take off from the airport at four."

"Good heavens, Brand," she lamented, "you've been up nearly twenty-four hours."

His smile faltered. "Don't remind me. Tell me about your day."

"There's not much to tell. I got a letter from Jutta Hoverson. She wrote me the day my letter arrived, which makes me feel good."

"What did she have to say?"

"Not much. She's doing some charcoal sketches. The painting of the child was her first oil work. Unbelievable, isn't it?"

Brand sat down in the kitchen while she finished taking leftovers from the refrigerator. "And I phoned Diana to tell her what time my flight would be landing in Seattle. She's too calm about this wedding business. It won't surprise me if she tries to cancel the whole thing at the last minute."

Carly set a tall glass of milk in front of Brand. "Drink," she ordered. "I'll whip up something in a jiffy."

It surprised her that Brand didn't fall asleep in her kitchen chair. After he'd eaten, she led him to the front door. His good-night kiss was as gentle as it was sweet. "I'll phone you tomorrow," he promised. He was making several short flights on Saturday, but couldn't invite her along because he was scheduled to fly crew into camps and there wouldn't be any space in the plane for her.

Carly spent Saturday morning shopping for a dress for Diana's wedding. Although she spent several hours browsing, she couldn't find what she wanted. Problem was, she wasn't sure what she was looking for. But she knew she'd recognize it when she saw it. Shopping had never been her forte and she decided to leave it until she arrived in Seattle. Diana would know exactly where to go.

The rest of the afternoon was spent answering Jutta's short letter. The woman hadn't said much. Few personal details were given in the note. Carly had no idea of her age or background. In her reply, she explained that there was a possibility that she would be able to visit Jutta the following week. She mentioned that she'd like to look at the charcoals then.

With the letter finished, Carly glanced at her watch, surprised to see that it was dinnertime. Not having heard from Brand, Carly assumed that it would be another late night for him.

He showed up around nine, declined her offer for dinner, and promptly fell asleep on her sofa. This time Carly decided to wake him. Enough was enough. .

"Brand." Her hand on his shoulder shook him lightly awake.

He bolted upright and blinked. "What happened? Did I fall asleep again?"

Arms crossed, Carly paced the floor in front of the sofa, unsure how to express her frustration.

"What's wrong?" He was awake enough to recognize that she was upset.

"Plenty, and—and don't tell me that you don't want to argue, because this time you're listening to me. Understand?"

Brand wiped a hand across his eyes and nodded. A wary look condensed his brow as his eyes followed her quick, pacing steps.

Without preamble, Carly began. "I won't be a pit stop in your life, Brand. Maybe some women can live like that, but I'm not one of them. I want to talk to you when you're not so tired that you're rummy. And when I leave the room I want to come back and find you awake."

"A pit stop?" Brand repeated blankly. "Carly, it's not that. Seeing you, being with you is more important to me than anything."

"Then why am I stuck with the leftovers of your life?" The hurt was impossible to hide.

He rose with the intention of taking her in his arms, but Carly wasn't in any mood to be kissed. She sidestepped him easily. "Go home, Brand. Get a decent night's sleep, and maybe we can talk later."

Sitting back down on the couch, Brand rested his elbows on his knees. He folded his hands together with his index fingers forming a small triangle. "I don't want to leave. We need to talk this out." His eyes showed the strain of the past week.

"As far as I can see, there's nothing more to say. I understand why you work the hours you do." She took the chair opposite him. "You can't start a new life with me or anyone else while Sandra's medical expenses are hanging over your head…"

"I paid those off six months ago," he announced in a tight whisper.

"Then why are you pushing yourself like this?"

He didn't answer; instead, he stood and walked to the far side of the room. He paused with his back to her and smoothed the hair along the side of his head. "You're right, Carly. You deserve more than what I've been giving you." His look was sober as he turned, his eyes searching hers. "I love you, Carly. I thought those feelings within me had died with Sandra. But I was wrong." His voice was a hoarse whisper. "I love you my sweet Carly."

Brand didn't need to tell her that he'd only said those words to one other woman in his life. Carly's fingers were trembling so badly that she clenched them into fists at her sides. Everything that she wanted and everything that she feared was staring her in the face.

"Well?" Brand was waiting for some kind of reaction.

"Thank you," she whispered, her voice so tight it was hardly recognizable. "I'll always treasure that."

"You don't know how you feel about me?" Brand asked.

"I…know what I feel." Swallowing was difficult.

"And?"

"You're waiting for me to declare my love. That's what you want, isn't it?" She was speaking loudly and being obtuse because she was afraid.

"Only if that's what you feel." Everything about Brand softened, as if he recognized the turmoil taking place within her.

"All right, I love you! Are you happy?" she cried out on a sob. Her whole body was shaking.

"I'm not, if it makes you so miserable."

"It's not that." Oh no, she was going to cry. Her throat ached with the effort to suppress the tears.

"Carly, I want to marry you."

"No." The denial was torn from her in shocked dismay. This was the one thing she'd feared the most. Tears slid down her face and scalded her cheeks. A hand covered her mouth as she shook her head violently from side to side. "I can't, Brand. I won't marry you."

"Why not?"

There wasn't any explanation that made sense, even to herself. How could she possibly hope to make him understand? "You…you had Sandra. You have children." Her voice wobbled and she tried desperately to control its quivering, but failed.

"What's that got to do with anything?"

Carly moved into the kitchen and picked up the low-heeled loafer from beside the garbage pail. "I'm throwing these away because…because there was never enough money for me as a child and everything had to be fixed and repaired until it was beyond rescuing. I don't want that anymore."

"Carly, you're not making any sense."

"I don't expect you to understand. But I am what I am. You've been married and you've loved." She swallowed down the hurt. "I want to be a man's first love. I want a man to feel for me what you did for Sandra."

"Carly, I do."

"But I want to be your first love," Carly cried. "Don't you understand? All my life I've been forced to take someone else's leftovers. I've always been second and I won't be again, not with a husband. Not with a man." Brand looked as if he might come closer to her and she held out a hand to warn him to stay away. "You have beautiful children, Brand. A boy and a girl. Don't you see? I can't give you anything you don't already have. You've had a wife. You have children."

The grimness of pain returned to his eyes. "Then what do you suggest we do?"

"Must we do anything?"

"Yes," he said, and then repeated softly, "yes. When two people love as strongly as we do, they must."

Carly lowered her eyes under the intensity of his. "I don't know what to do, Brand," she said, her voice low and throbbing. "Maybe we could be..." The word stuck in her throat. "Lovers."

A sad, wry smile slanted Brand's mouth as he shook his head. "Maybe that kind of relationship would satisfy some men. But not me. I've never done anything halfway in my life." His pause demanded that she meet his gaze. "There's so much more that I want from you than a few stolen hours in bed. What I feel goes beyond the physical satisfaction your body will give mine. I want you by my side to build a new life here in Alaska."

"Please," Carly pleaded, struggling to speak, "don't say any more."

Brand ignored her. "Together we can give Shawn and Sara the family life they crave. And, God willing, we'll have more children."

Her pain was real and felt like a knife blade slicing through her. "No. I'm sorry...so sorry. I can't."

He took a step toward her and Carly backed up against the kitchen counter, unable to retreat further.

"You're reacting with your emotions."

She glared at him, wanting him to give her some insight she didn't already have. "None of this makes sense to you. I realize that. I'm not sure I can even fully understand it myself. All I know is what I feel. I won't be a secondhand wife and a secondhand mother."

"Carly..."

"No." She shook her head forcefully. "We've said everything that's important. Rehashing the same arguments won't solve a thing."

He clenched and unclenched his hands with frustration and anger.

"Please," she whispered in soft entreaty. "We're both tired."

Wordlessly, Brand turned, grabbed his jacket from the back of the sofa and left. When the door closed behind him, Carly began to shake with reaction. If it wasn't so tragic, she'd laugh. Brand was so far ahead of her in this relationship. He wanted to marry her—and she had gone only as far as admitting they were dating.

It was nearly two a.m. before Carly went to bed. She knew she wouldn't sleep, and she lay waiting until exhaustion overtook her troubled thoughts. Tomorrow was soon enough. Maybe tomorrow some clear solution would present itself. Tomorrow…

But the morning produced more doubts than reassurances. Loving someone didn't automatically make everything right. And, yes, she loved Brand. But Diana was right, as her friend almost always was when it came to understanding Carly. Brand and Carly were two wounded people who had found one another. The immediate attraction that had sparked between them wasn't physical, but spiritual.

When Carly hadn't heard from Brand by Monday afternoon, she realized that he was giving her the room she needed to think things through. His actions proved more than words the depth of his love. Arguing with her would do nothing but frustrate them both.

At any rate, on Thursday morning she would be leaving for Seattle and Diana's wedding. With all the stress Diana was under, Carly couldn't unload her problems on her friend, but at least she would have some time away, close to the only people she had ever considered real family. And Carly needed that.

Tuesday morning, at about ten, Carly heard the familiar sound of Brand's car pulling up outside the office building. Her hand clenched the pencil she was holding tightly, but a smile was frozen on her face when he walked through the door.

"Hello, Carly." He was treating her politely, like a stranger.

"Hi." Her lips felt so stiff she could barely speak.

"You're leaving this week, aren't you?"

He knew exactly when she was going, but Carly played his game. "Thursday morning."

He sauntered over to the coffeepot, and poured himself a cup. Without looking at her, seemingly intent on his task, he spoke. "Will you go out to dinner with me Wednesday night?"

"Yes." There was no question of refusing. The breathing space he'd given her hadn't resolved her dilemma. If anything, she felt more troubled than before. "I'd enjoy that."

He nodded, and for the first time since entering her office, smiled. "I've missed you."

"I've missed you too," she whispered.

Brand took a sip of his coffee. "Where's George?" he asked, suddenly all business.

"In the warehouse." She cocked her head to one side, indicating the area to her right.

"I'll pick you up at seven," he announced, his hand on the doorknob.

"Okay." He was gone and Carly relaxed.

* * *

Wednesday evening, with her suitcases packed and ready for the morning flight, Carly dabbed perfume at the pulse points behind her ears and at her wrists. The dress she wore was the most feminine one she owned, a frothy pink thing that wasn't really her. Diana had insisted she buy it, and in a moment of whimsy Carly had done just that. She wasn't sure why she'd chosen to wear it for her dinner date with Brand tonight. But she'd given up analyzing her actions.

Promptly at seven, Brand was at her door. He looked uncomfortable in the dark suit he wore. His hair was cut shorter than she could remember seeing it, and he smelled faintly of musk and spice.

They took one look at each other and broke into wide smiles that hovered on the edge of outright laughter.

"Are we going to act like polite strangers or are we going to be ourselves?" Brand arched one dark brow with his query.

Carly toyed with her answer. If they remained in the roles for which they'd dressed, there was a certain safety. "I don't know," she answered honestly. "If I return to 'Carly, the Confused Woman in Love,' then the evening could be a disaster."

"I, for one, have always courted disaster." He ran his finger down her cheek and cupped the underside of her face before kissing her lightly. "And so have you," he added.

Warm, swirling sensations came at her from all sides and Carly had to restrain herself from wrapping her arms around his neck and kissing Brand the way they both wanted.

He took her to the most expensive restaurant in town and ordered a bottle of vintage Chablis.

"Brand," Carly giggled, leaning across the table. "You can't afford this."

His mouth tightened, but Carly could see that he was amused and hadn't taken offense. What was the problem, then? She put her niggling worry aside as Brand spoke. "Don't tell me what I can and can't afford."

"I do your books, remember?"

"Sometimes I forget how much you know. Now, sit back and relax, will you?"

"Why are you doing this?"

"Can't a man treat the woman he loves to something special without her getting suspicious?"

"Yes, but—"

"Then enjoy!" His humor was infectious.

They toasted her trip and Carly talked about Diana and Barney, recalling some anecdotes from her friends' courtship.

Midway through dinner, Carly knew what was troubling Brand. It came to her in a flash of unexpected insight. She set her fork aside and lazily watched Brand for several moments.

"What's the matter?" He stopped eating. "Is something wrong with your steak?"

Carly shook her head. "No, everything's fine."

"Then why are you looking at me like that?" Brand watched her curiously as she stretched her hand across the table and took his.

"Running has been a problem ever since I met you, hasn't it?" she asked softly. "But, Brand, this time I'm coming back."

Brand nodded, still showing only a facade of unconcern. "I know that."

"But you were worried?" She released his hand.

He concentrated on slicing his rare steak, revealing little of his thoughts. "Perhaps a little."

"You don't need to worry. If I ever walk away, you'll know when and the reason why."

He answered her with a brief shake of his head, but Carly noticed that he was more relaxed now. "Do you want to go dancing after dinner?" he surprised her by asking.

"Dancing?" She eyed him suspiciously. He'd told her he didn't dance the first time they'd gone out for a meal. "I thought you said you didn't."

"That was before."

"Before what? Have you secretly been taking lessons?" she teased.

The humor drained from his eyes, and he sought and found her gaze. "No, that was before I ever thought I'd find anyone who'd make me want to dance again."

Seven

Carly eased the strap of her carry-on bag over her shoulder as she made the trek through the long jetway from the airplane into the main terminal at Sea-Tac Airport.

Her eyes scanned the crowd at baggage claim, until she caught a a glimpse of Diana, who was nervously pacing the area. Her friend hadn't changed. Not that Carly had expected her to. Somehow she never got used to the fact that Diana was only five foot four inches. Their hair color was the same ordinary shade of dark brown. But there the resemblance stopped. Carly was a natural sort of person who didn't bother much with fashionable hairstyles or trendy clothes. She was too proud of her individuality to be swayed by the choices of others. But it was not so with Diana, who often dressed in the most outrageous styles and clothes. *Flamboyant* was an apt one-word description of her best friend.

"Diana."

Carly watched as her friend whirled around and quickly made her way through the crowd.

"Darling, you're gorgeous." Diana threw her arms

around Carly. Such an open display of affection was typical of Diana, who acted as though she hadn't seen Carly in years instead of only a few weeks. "But too thin. You're not eating enough. I knew this would happen. I've read an article that said how hard it is to get supplies into Alaska. You're starving and too proud to admit I was right. I hope to high heaven you're ready to move back where you belong."

Carly laughed. "If you think getting supplies is difficult, you should try heating an igloo."

They teased and joked as they waited for Carly's suitcase to come around the turnstile in baggage claim.

"Where's Barney?"

"Working. He sends his love, by the way." Each carrying a suitcase, they crossed the sky bridge to the parking garage. "Wait until you see his wedding gift to me."

"Diamonds? Furs?"

"No." Diana shook her head solemnly. "I told him not to bother. Neither one of my other husbands did."

When Diana paused in front of a red convertible, Carly's mouth dropped open. "The car. Barney got you a red convertible?" This was the kind of car Diana had always dreamed of owning.

Diana shook her head in feigned dismay. "That's only half of it."

"You mean he got you two cars?"

One delicately outlined brow arched. "Better."

"Better?" Carly gasped playfully.

A few minutes later Carly understood. Diana exited off the freeway and took a long, winding road that led to an exclusive row of homes built along the shores of Lake Washington.

"Barney bought you a house!"

"He said I'd need some place to park the car," Diana explained excitedly as she pulled into the driveway and turned off the ignition. "I still get a lump in my throat every time I see it." She bit her bottom lip. "I remember not long after we met, Barney was telling me that someday he was going to build a house. I told him about the one I had pictured in my mind from the time I was a little girl. A house full of love."

"And Barney built you that house." Carly shook her head in wonder. "Tell me again where you found this man!" she begged.

"The crazy part of it is how much Barney loves me!" Diana sounded shocked that anyone could care for her with such fervor. "And it isn't like I'm a vestal virgin who's coming to him spotless. With my track record, any sane man wouldn't touch me with a ten-foot pole." Tears filled the dark brown eyes. "You know, Carly, for the first time in my life I'm doing something right."

Carly's hand squeezed her friend's as tears of shared happiness clouded her own vision. "Look at us," she said, half laughing, half sobbing. "You'd think we were going to a funeral. Now, are we going to sit out here all day or are you going to show me the castle?"

With a burst of energy, Diana led Carly from room to room, pointing out details that a casual inspector might have overlooked. Every aspect of the house was impressive, with high ceilings and the liberal use of polished oak.

"It's beautiful," Carly said with a sense of awe. "I counted four bedrooms."

"Two boys and a girl," Diana announced thoughtfully. "As quickly as we can have them."

Shaking her head, Carly eyed her friend suspiciously. "And you used to tell me diaper rash was catching."

Laughing, Diana led the way into the kitchen and opened the refrigerator. "Barney and I can hardly wait for me to get pregnant." She handed Carly a cold soda. "Here, let me show you what I got him for a wedding gift." She led Carly into the family room off the kitchen and pointed to the leather recliner. "They delivered it a couple of days ago. For a while I was afraid it wouldn't arrive before the wedding."

"I'll bet Barney loves it."

"He hasn't seen it yet," Diana explained. "He won't be moving in until after the wedding."

"Oh." The surprise must have shown in Carly's eyes. The couple had been sleeping together for months.

"I suppose it sounds hypocritical at this point, but Barney and I haven't lived together since we talked to the pastor."

"Diana," Carly said softly. "I'm the last person in the world to judge you. Whatever you and Barney do is your business."

"I know. It's just that things are different now. We're different. We even started attending church. Every Sunday. Can you believe it? At first I thought the congregation would snicker to see someone like me in church. But they didn't. Everyone was so warm and welcoming. In fact, a few ladies from the women's group volunteered to have a small reception for us after the wedding."

"That's wonderful."

"Barney and I thought so, too." Diana's eyes lit up with a glow of happiness. "For a long time I expected something to happen that would ruin all of this. It's been like a dream, and for a time I felt I didn't deserve Barney or you or the people from the church."

"But, Diana—"

Diana interrupted by putting her hand over Carly's. "My thinking was all wrong. Pastor Wright pointed that out to me. And he's right, no pun intended. We did a lot of talking about my background, and now I see how everything in my life has led to this point."

Carly wondered if she'd ever find this kind of serenity or that special glow of inner happiness Diana had.

"I hope you're hungry," Diana said. "We're supposed to meet Barney in a half hour for lunch."

"I'm starved." Carly sighed dramatically. "As you've guessed, I haven't eaten a decent meal in weeks. Food's so hard to come by in the Alaskan wilderness. And I just haven't acquired a taste for moose and mountain goat."

Dressed in her pajamas, Carly sat cross-legged on top of Diana's huge king-size bed. "One thing I've got to do tomorrow is buy a dress. I couldn't find anything I liked in Anchorage, but then, I wasn't in much of a mood to shop."

"I already beat you to it. Knowing you'd put it off to the last minute, I scheduled time for us to go shopping tomorrow." Diana sat at the vanity, applying a thick layer of white moisturizing cream to her face. "Are you going to tell me about him or do I have to pry every detail out of you with the Chinese water torture?"

Carly dodged her request. "It may take months for you to get pregnant if Barney sees you smear that gook on your face every night."

"Quit trying to avoid the subject." Some of the teasing humor left Diana's eyes.

"All right, all right. I'm in love with Brand." The burst of happy surprise Carly had expected didn't follow.

"I already knew that. I've known from the moment you started telling me about him. Obviously, he's in love with you, too."

Carly answered with a curt nod. "He asked me to marry him before I left for Seattle."

"And?"

"I told him no," Carly said sadly. "I can't, Diana. He's everything I want and everything I fear all rolled into one."

"Is it because of his wife and the two kids?"

"Aren't you nervous about the wedding?" Carly asked hastily, wanting to change the subject.

"This is my third wedding. I'm over the jitters. Now, let's get back to you and Brand."

"I don't want to talk about me," Carly said stubbornly. "Brand and I have gone over every detail until we're blue in the face. I can't change the way I feel."

"Sweetie." Diana only called her that when she was either very sad or very serious. "It's time you grew up."

Somehow she'd hoped that Diana, of all people, would understand. "All right, I admit that there will probably never be anyone I'll feel this strongly about again."

"But you're afraid?" Diana prompted.

"Out of my wits."

Diana's soft laugh filled the bedroom. "I never thought you'd admit it."

"This is the exception." Carly fiddled with the nylon strings of her pajama top. "In a lot of ways you and I are alike. For one thing, I have trouble believing Brand could honestly love me. I'm terribly insecure, often irrational, and a card-carrying emotional cripple."

"Do you remember how long it took Barney to convince me to marry him? Months."

"Brand's not as patient as Barney. He thinks that because we're in love everything will work itself out."

"He *sounds* like Barney," Diana murmured more to herself than for Carly's benefit.

"His children are coming to Alaska the middle of next month." Carly's voice was unsteady. Shawn and Sara were the focus of her anxieties.

"Sandra's children." Diana had a way of hitting the nail on the head.

Carly winced and nodded.

"And nothing's ever frightened you more."

"Nothing." Her whisper was raw with fear.

"All our lives I thought you were the fearless one," Diana whispered, "but deep down you've been as anxious as I have. Be happy, Carly." She wiped the moisturizer from her face with tissues as she spoke. "As much as I'd like to, I can't tell you what to do. But I urge you to stop being so afraid of finding contentment. Believe that Brand loves you. Count yourself blessed that he does."

Carly laughed, but the soft sound came out more like a sob. "For not wanting to tell me what to do, you sound like you're doing just that."

Diana's eyes locked with Carly's in the vanity mirror. "Go for it, kid."

Carly couldn't remember a more beautiful wedding. Tall white baskets filled with huge floral arrangements adorned the sanctuary. A white satin ribbon ran the length of the railing in front of the altar.

Barney, the short jeweler Diana had met at a Seahawk's football game, stood proudly with his bride at his side. His dark hair had thinned to a bald spot at the top of his head, and his nose was too thin for his round face. Barney definitely wasn't the type of man to stop female hearts. Carly recalled the first time she'd met him, and her surprise that Diana would be dating such a nondescript man. But her attitude had soon changed. From the first date, Barney had treated Diana like the most precious woman in the world. Carly loved him for that. Barney's love and acceptance had changed Diana until she glowed and blossomed under it.

Diana had never looked happier or more beautiful. She stood beside Barney, their hands entwined, linking them for life. As the maid of honor, Carly held the small bouquet Diana had carried to the altar.

Both Diana's and Barney's voices rang strong and true as they repeated their vows. A tear of joy slipped from the corner of Carly's eye as Barney turned and slipped the diamond wedding band onto Diana's slim finger.

Diana followed, slipping a simple gold band onto Barney's thick finger, her eyes shining into his as she did so. This time Diana was confident she was marrying the right man. And Carly was convinced Diana was the right woman for him.

"I now pronounce you husband and wife." The pastor's strong voice echoed through the church.

Diana looked at Barney with eyes so full of love that Carly felt a lump in her throat. Whatever the future held, these two were determined to nurture their love and faith in one another. The commitment was on their faces and in their eyes for everyone to read. And it didn't go unnoticed.

The reception was held in the fellowship hall connected to the church. The wedding party was small. Diana had invited only a few friends, while Barney had asked his two brothers and their families. Three or four other couples who had met Diana and Barney through the church also attended.

Carly stood to the side of the reception hall and sipped her punch. Her eyes followed the newly married couple. Suddenly an intense longing she couldn't name filled her.

She wanted Brand with her. She wanted to turn and smile at him the same way that Diana was smiling at Barney. And more than that, she needed to see again the love that had shone from his eyes as he had waved goodbye to her at the airport. Her chance for happiness was waiting for her in Anchorage; the question was whether or not she had enough courage to look past the fact that Brand had known this kind of love and happiness before meeting her.

Carly paused and took another sip of the sweet punch. With all her hang-ups, she wondered what kind of mother she would be to Shawn and Sara. Only a minute ago she'd begun to feel a little confident; now she was filled with as many insecurities as ever. As much as she wanted to find parallels in her relationship with Brand from what had happened between Diana and Barney's, she couldn't. The two couples faced entirely different circumstances.

Following the reception, Diana, Barney, Barney's relatives and Carly went to dinner at Canlis', a plush downtown Seattle restaurant. From the restaurant, the newlyweds were leaving for a two-week honeymoon in Hawaii Sunday evening. Diana insisted that Carly stay at the house, and also gave her the keys to the car so that she could drive it home.

It was some time later when, yawning, Carly walked into the guest bedroom and kicked off her tight heels. The thick carpet was like a soft cushion under her bare feet. The day had been full and she was tired, but the thought of bed was dominated by her need to hear Brand's voice.

He answered on the first ring, and even a distance echo couldn't disguise how glad he was to hear from her.

"How was the wedding?"

"Wonderful. Oh, Brand, I can't even describe how beautiful everything was."

"Well, I certainly hope it had the desired effect. There's only one wedding I want to attend, and that's *ours*." The teasing inflection in his voice didn't mask his sincerity.

"Oh, Brand, please don't go there. I couldn't bear to argue."

"Arguing is the last thing I have on my mind." His voice became low and sensual. "In fact, if you knew what I was thinking, you'd probably blush."

"I do not blush." She might be a virgin, but she wasn't a shrinking violet.

Brand chuckled. "This time you would."

"I take it you miss me."

He laughed. "You have no idea."

"But I've only been gone a day."

"Almost two days. Not that I've noticed."

"I can tell."

"Well, come on. Say it," Brand prompted.

"Say what?"

"How much you've missed me. I'm especially interested about what went on in that beautiful mind of yours when you heard your friend repeat her vows. Did you think of me and wish that I was at your side so we could say them to one another?"

"Obviously you crept into my thoughts or I wouldn't have phoned." Carly would admit to nothing. She wrapped a strand of hair around her ear. Sometimes Brand knew her as well as she knew herself.

"But you won't admit to thinking about me during the wedding ceremony."

"You're right," Carly said in a low, sensual tone. "I won't admit to anything until I see you."

She heard Brand's swift intake of oxygen. "You'd better not have changed your mind about flying home Monday."

"No, I'll be there. But don't say anything to George—he thinks I'm arriving later in the week."

"Don't worry. My lips are sealed."

"Darn. I have a thing about sealed lips."

"What's that?"

"I never kiss them," she announced and the sound of Brand's laughter mingled with the sound of her own.

They talked for almost an hour, and could have gone on for another. Even after she hung up, Carly itched to phone him back and say all the things she hadn't had the courage to mention the first time. Only the knowledge that she would be back home Monday evening deterred her.

After talking to Brand, Carly took a hot bath, soaking up the warmth of the water. A chill had found its way into her blood. Tomorrow she would be driving to Purdy and the State Correctional Center for Women. Jutta Hoverson hadn't replied to Carly's latest correspondence, but one thing was certain. It wasn't the charcoal sketches Carly was interested in seeing. It was Jutta Hoverson.

Visiting hours were scheduled for the afternoon, so Carly had a late breakfast and lingered over the morning paper. She dressed carefully, wanting to appear neither too casual nor too formal. Finally, she chose a three-piece slacks suit that was just right. Fleetingly, she wondered if Jutta had any apprehensions about the meeting. Probably not.

Once at the Center, Carly signed in at the desk and was asked to place her valuables in a rented locker. Carly had seen identical ones at airports and bus depots. She placed her purse inside, inserted the quarter and stuck the key into her jacket pocket.

The waiting area was soon filled to capacity. An uncomfortable sensation came over Carly as she studied the others in the room. Not in the habit of making snap judgments about people, she was amazed at her immediate distrust of the few men who regarded her steadily. Carly admitted that she did stick out like a little green Martian. Compared to the others, she was decidedly overdressed. Her uneasy feeling intensified as the waiting area emptied. The visitors were led away in small groups to another room, where they walked through a metal detector and were briefly questioned. From there, each group was directed into a large room with several chairs against the walls.

There Carly took a seat close to the window and tried to ignore the iron bars that obstructed the view. The stark silence of the room was interrupted by a crying child who was pitifully asking to see his mommy.

An iron door slid open and the women prisoners filed into the room one by one. Carly had filled out a card when she entered the building, requesting to see Jutta Hoverson, but she had no way of identifying her.

The little boy broke loose and ran into the arms of one woman, who swooped him into her embrace. The scene was a touching one and Carly wondered what the young woman had done in her life to be thus separated from her child.

"Are you Carly?"

Carly's attention skidded from the youngster to the tall, thin woman standing before her. "Yes." She rose. "Are you Jutta?" Never would Carly have envisioned Jutta this way. Her hair was long and hung in straight braids the same shade of brownish-red, except that it was mostly gray now. The glasses she wore slipped down the bridge of her nose and Carly doubted that they had ever fit her properly. Her clothes were regular street clothes, but drab and unstylish. Jutta looked as nervous as Carly felt.

"It's good to meet you," Carly began stiffly.

"They wouldn't let me bring out the sketches without some kind of approval beforehand."

"That's all right." The stilted, uncomfortable feeling intensified. "Can we sit down and visit for a while?"

Jutta shrugged one shoulder and sat. "I don't suppose you've got a cigarette?"

"Sorry, no…"

"I forgot, they don't let you bring anything in here do they?

"I suppose you're curious to know what I did to end up here," Jutta challenged, clearly on the defensive.

The one thing Carly didn't want to do was make the woman uncomfortable. "Not unless you want to tell me."

"I don't see why not. It's a matter of public record. I forged checks, and it wasn't the first time, either."

"How long is your sentence?"

"Long enough. I've been in Purdy two years now and I don't expect to get approval from the parole board for another two."

"Did you start painting in…here?"

"Yes."

"I thought the painting of the child was excellent."

"I won't sell that one."

"Yes, I realize that," Carly assured her quickly. "Since it obviously means so much to you, I don't think you should."

"What I can't understand is why someone like you would want it." Jutta's deep blue eyes narrowed as they studied Carly. "You're a regular uptown girl."

That was probably the closest thing to a compliment that Jutta would give. "The picture reminded me of myself when I was five."

"You were poor?"

Carly answered by nodding her head.

"You seem to be doing all right now."

"Yes. I'm fine."

"You haven't mentioned a man. Are you married?"

"No." Carly shook her head automatically. "But… I've been thinking about getting married," she said stiffly.

"It seems to me if you have to think about it, then you probably..."

"No," Carly interrupted. "It isn't that. I love him very much. But...well, he's got children."

"I'd have thought you'd be the type to like children."

"I do." Carly was uncomfortable with this line of conversation and sought a means of changing it. "Do... do you have children?"

"I've got a kid, but I never married," Jutta stated defensively. "He's grown now. I haven't seen him in ten, maybe fifteen years. Last I heard he was in prison. Like mother, like son, I guess. Don't keep in contact with him much."

Carly hadn't expected Jutta to be so honest. If anything, she'd thought the artist would rather not answer personal questions. "I don't remember my mother," Carly admitted softly, her gaze falling to her hands. "The state took me away from her and put me in a foster home when I was young."

"Have you seen her since?"

"No. I did try to find her when I was twenty. But I didn't have any luck. To be honest, I think her drugs and alcohol must have killed her."

"A lot of women get hooked on that stuff. And worse."

"I don't feel any bitterness or anything. I can hardly remember her."

"She beat you?" Jutta asked.

"No. At least I don't think so."

"Then you were lucky."

"Yes," Carly agreed. "I was lucky."

Carly thought about their conversation as she drove back toward Seattle over the Narrows Bridge. Jutta wasn't at all what she'd expected. The woman was forthright and sincere. She was brusque and a little abrasive, but her life had been hard, her experiences bitter. In some ways Carly saw the mother she had never known in Jutta. And in other ways she saw reflections of the proud child of the painting.

Their conversation had been stilted in the beginning, but by the end of the hour they were slightly more comfortable in one another's company. Jutta had explained far more about herself than Carly expected. She said that there was a letter waiting for Carly in Anchorage and admitted, almost shyly, that she enjoyed getting mail.

Diana and Barney returned home early Sunday afternoon, from their one night honeymoon before their flight to Hawaii. They were both radiant.

"Welcome home," Carly said and embraced Diana warmly. "I didn't expect you back so soon."

"Barney's got a business meeting this afternoon. And I wanted to get back early enough to pack and get ready for our trip."

"I've already called for a taxi." Carly glanced at her watch. "My flight leaves in another two hours."

"But I thought we'd have time to visit."

"Are you nuts?" Carly said and kissed her friend on the cheek. "I'm leaving so you and Barney can begin your life together in peace."

"We're going to be so happy," Diana said with confidence.

"I know you are. And I can't think of anyone who deserves it more than the two of you."

"I can." Diana's happy gaze clouded with concern. "I want you to know this kind of happiness, Carly. You're the closest thing I have to family. If you walk away from Brand, it's something you'll regret all your life."

Unable to break the tension in the air Carly hugged her friend again. "I'm not going to lose Brand," she whispered the promise.

The taxi arrived ten minutes later. Amid protests from both bride and groom, Carly left. Diana and Barney, arms entwined, stood on the sidewalk waving as the driver pulled away. From her position in the backseat, Carly turned and blew them both a kiss. Leaning the back of her head against the seat, Carly closed her eyes for the remainder of the ride to the airport.

Although he hadn't mentioned it, Carly was certain Brand would meet her plane. And when she saw him she'd know that look would be in his eyes again—the look that demanded an answer to his wedding proposal. She wanted to marry him, but pushing all her doubts and insecurities aside wouldn't banish them.

Jutta had assumed that Carly couldn't love Brand if she hesitated before marrying him. Yet, just the opposite was true; every minute she was away she discovered she loved him more. Little by little, bit by bit, he had worked his way into her life, until she realized now how lost she would be without him.

Diana had said the time had come for her to grow up, to set aside the hurts of her childhood and deal with the realities that faced her. How simple it sounded. But she was dealing with emotions now. Not reason. So many times in the last few days Carly had caught herself wondering about Brand and Sandra. Such thinking was dangerous. And unreasonable. Sandra was gone. *She* was here now, and crazy in love with the leftovers of Sandra's life.

With the approach of summer the days were growing longer now. It would be dark in Seattle now but when the plane touched down at the Anchorage airport the sun was still shining.

As she'd hoped and as she'd feared, Brand was there. She paused midstride when she saw him standing to the side, waiting for her. He seemed tired, and his eyes were sad. She hadn't seen him like that since the night he'd first told her about Sandra.

When he smiled the look vanished, and her heart melted with the potency of it. Quickening her pace, she walked to his side. "Hi," she whispered, her eyes not leaving his.

"How was the flight?"

"Uneventful."

He took the carry-on bag from her grasp, his eyes not quite meeting hers. "All day I had the fear you'd stay in Seattle."

"I told you I was coming back."

He nodded as if he didn't quite believe her. "I don't know, Carly." He ran a hand through his thick hair in an agitated action. "I've told myself a thousand times I was making a fool of myself. It's not a comfortable feeling to think the woman you love is going to walk out on you without a minute's hesitation."

"Brand," she argued, "I'm not going to do anything of the sort."

Long strides took him to the area where they were to wait for her luggage. "I don't like what I'm becoming..."

A chill came over her at the fear in his voice. Carly's hand gripped his forearm. "Do I get a chance to say something or do I have to listen to your tirade first?"

"Go ahead," he answered, without looking at her.

She swallowed. "I guess the simplest way of saying it is yes."

"Yes what?"

"Yes, I want to be your wife."

Eight

Brand blinked twice and then straightened. Carly watched as his face mirrored his confusion. "What did you say?"

"You did ask me to marry you, didn't you?" For a fearful instant, she feared she'd been wrong. "And, by heavens, you'd better not have changed your mind. Not after all the soul-searching I went through to reach a decision."

"I haven't changed my mind." An intense look darkened his eyes and a muscle worked along the side of his jaw as his stared at her as though seeing her for the first time. He looked as if he couldn't quite believe her. "Let's get out of here." He jerked her suitcase from the carousel at the baggage claim area and ushered her out of the airport terminal.

Brand didn't say another word until they were inside her apartment. "Now, would you care to repeat yourself?"

"I said I'd marry you?"

An incredulous light brightened his eyes as the beginnings of a smile spread across his mouth. "You mean it?"

"Of course I do." Carly smiled softly as she reached out and traced the outline of his lips with the tip of her index finger.

Brand pulled her into his arms. Crushed against him, Carly opened her mouth to his probing kiss, reveling in the passion she felt in him. Again and again his lips ravaged hers as if he couldn't get enough of her.

"I won't let you change your mind," he whispered against her temple. "Not now. Not ever."

Weak with longing Carly pressed light kisses on his eyelids, his cheek and his jaw. "I'm not going to back out. I only pray that we're doing the right thing."

"We are." His arms tightened around her waist. "I know it in my heart."

He kissed her again with a gentleness that stirred her. She *was* doing the right thing. Yes, she was afraid, and there were many fears yet to face, but Diana was right. If Carly walked away from Brand and his children she would be turning away from the best thing that had ever happened to her. The choice was clear—either marry Brand or lose him forever.

Brand inhaled deeply and took a step back. His hands settled on either side of her face as his eyes met hers. "We'll get the blood test tomorrow."

Carly nodded. "And be married by Friday."

Her lashes fluttered down. Everything was happening so fast. Clearly, Brand feared she'd have second thoughts. "Okay," she agreed, but her voice wobbled.

His warm breath fanned her face an instant before he covered her mouth with his. Carly dug her fingers into his shoulders, unaccustomed to the sensations that he was arousing within her. Her lovemaking experience was limited, but Brand wasn't aware of that. He would learn of her inexperience soon enough.

She wound her arms around his neck and buried her face in his throat, kissing him with a compulsion she couldn't define. All she knew was that she wanted to be closer to him.

"Carly," he groaned.

He kissed her with driving urgency, setting her down on the sofa and pressing her back so that she was lying flat.

"Carly…dear God." He brushed the hair from her face, his eyes finding hers. His fingers were shaking as he framed her face with his hands. "If we don't stop now, we'll end up making love right here."

Something in his eyes gave him away. "Are you afraid?" she whispered. He'd told her once that he hadn't made love to a woman since Sandra.

He released her and the silence stretched until Carly raised herself up on one elbow to study him. He regarded her steadily and nodded. "It's been a long time."

His honesty had been painful for him, but Carly offered him a trembling smile and lovingly kissed his brow. "We've waited this long. We can wait until after we're married."

His mouth teased the corner of hers as their breaths mingled. "I don't deserve you," he murmured, holding her close. "I'm no bargain."

Her soft laugh followed. "For that matter, neither am I."

Later, as Carly dressed for bed, she examined herself in the mirror and was shocked at how pale and waxen her features were. She prayed she was doing the right thing in agreeing to marry Brand. She was afraid, too, far more than he realized. His honesty had been a measure of his love. He wouldn't lie to her, and Carly admired him all the more for that.

The following morning, Brand picked her up and they went together for their blood tests.

"I'd like to have a minister marry us," Carly announced after they'd climbed into the car once more. They hadn't discussed who would perform the ceremony. From the way Brand was rushing things, Carly had the impression that he wanted a justice of the peace to do the honors.

Brand's fingers captured hers as he smiled faintly. "I'd prefer that, too."

An inner glow of happiness touched her eyes. "Where to next?" she asked cheerfully.

Brand reached for the folded newspaper on the seat between them. "I thought we'd look for a house to rent."

The mention of a house was a forceful reminder that Shawn and Sara would be joining them in less than a month.

"Yes," she said and swallowed back the surge of panic that filled her. "We should do that."

Brand handed her the newspaper. "We'll need at least three bedrooms."

Carly nodded stiffly and read off a couple of the listings. "Do you want to check them out now?"

His eyes sought hers. "Sure. We have all day."

They found a rental through a real estate broker that sounded perfect. The picture showed a modern home with three bedrooms and a large yard. Another room off the kitchen could be used as an office for Brand.

"It's perfect, I know it. We don't even have to go see it." Carly watched Brand's eyes agree as he read over the details.

"There's a problem." The broker went on to explain that the house was badly in need of a thorough cleaning and paint job.

"It'll work out fine," Carly assured Brand later when they were back in the car. "We can do the painting at night after work. If we work hard enough, everything will be ready by the time Shawn and Sara arrive."

"Carly." One corner of his mouth lifted. "The first weeks after we're married, we're going to have enough to do without fixing up a house."

She snuggled closer to his side and playfully nibbled at his earlobe. "I thought soon-to-be-husbands were supposed to humor their soon-to-be-wives."

"I have a lot more in mind than humoring." His voice was husky with longing as he turned her into his arms.

Carly surrendered to his kiss, wondering if she would always feel this rush of excitement at Brand's touch. She couldn't imagine it ever being any different.

After lunch they stopped in and talked to George, who pumped Brand's hand in congratulation and frowned when he heard Carly would need Friday off, in addition to a few extra days later on when they moved.

Later, when Brand dropped her off at her apartment and left to do errands, Carly had to pinch herself. She could scarcely believe that in a matter of days she was going to be both a wife and a mother.

A hot cup of coffee helped soothe her nerves. She

was taking on a lot in a short amount of time. As of ye
she had yet to meet Brand's children. The responsibilit
of taking over the role as their mother overwhelmed her
But she'd do it. She'd be the best stepmother she coul
be and love them in a way that honored their mother
"Do you want to call Diana and Barney?" Brand aske
later that night.

"No. Not until after we're married. Otherwise Dian
will insist on leaving Hawaii and flying here to chec
you out before the wedding." She was only half-teasing

"I want to meet this friend of yours," Brand said.

"And you shall but all in due course," she promised

He frowned a bit. "Don't you want Diana here fo
our wedding?" Her husband seemed to forget Dian
and Barney were on their honeymoon. "Brand, Diana'
barely been married a week. I'd love to have her at ou
wedding and she'd be here too but not if we're marrie
this Friday. Do you want to wait?"

He looked at her as if she were joking. "No way."

"That's what I thought." The truth was, Carly didn'
want to wait either. "There will be plenty of time fo
you to meet Diana and Barney. I'll keep our wedding
secret until after the ceremony, and then tell her." Carl
couldn't see interrupting her friend's honeymoon.

"Will she be surprised?"

Carly knew Diana's reaction would be closer t
shock. "Yes." She laid her head on Brand's shoulde
"But there are advantages to being married only a wee
after my best friend," she said lightly. "We'll be able t
celebrate our anniversaries together."

Brand's arm came up around her shoulders. "We'
have lots of those, Carly." His warm breath musse

her hair. "You've given me so much. Now it's time for me to return some of that. We'll be happy, won't we?"

She closed her eyes at the tenderness in his voice and responded with a gentle shake of her head because her throat felt thick with emotion.

No week had ever passed so quickly. Friday evening, with only a handful of people present, Carly Grieves became Brandon St. Clair's wife. A simple gold band adorned her ring finger. With so many expenses coming their way in the near future, Carly had decided against diamonds. Brand wore a gold band identical to hers.

Following the ceremony, Brand's eyes smiled into hers. His arm wrapped around her waist and held her close to his side. "Hello, Mrs. St. Clair."

"Hello, Mr. St. Clair."

George, looking uncomfortable in a suit and tie, shook Brand's hand and slipped him an envelope. "Just to give you two a start on a few things you're going to need," he said gruffly.

"Aren't you going to kiss the bride?" Carly asked her boss with familiar affection.

George cleared his throat and looked to Brand for permission.

"Go ahead," Brand urged and squeezed Carly's waist.

Standing on the tips of her toes, she lightly brushed her lips against George's cheek.

The older man flushed with pleasure. "I suppose this means you're going to be wanting extra time off every week."

"No. Things should settle back to normal once we return from Oregon," Carly said, lowering her gaze.

They would be making a trip to Portland next week. She didn't mention that Brand's children would be coming in less than a month. The changes that would mean in her schedule hadn't been discussed.

"Are you ready to leave?" Brand asked.

"For our prehoneymoon?" Carly questioned eagerly. Brand had been busy all week on what he termed "their surprise weekend plans." Carly suspected they wouldn't be leaving Anchorage, since they both were due back at work on Monday morning. Brand was scheduled to fly into Dutch Harbor on the Aleutian Islands in the first week of the month; he wanted Carly to fly with him, and on the return trip they'd stay at the lodge at Lake Iliamna. That was to be their official honeymoon. But this first weekend was a surprise Brand had planned especially for her.

His late-model Chevy was waiting for them in front of the church. Brand helped her inside and ran around to the front of the vehicle. "Are you ready for this?" he asked as he inserted the key in the ignition.

Carly tucked her arm in his and leaned her head quietly against his shoulder. "I've been ready for this all my life, Brandon St. Clair."

"Do you want to guess where we're going?"

"I haven't the foggiest idea. But it must be special, after all the time you've dedicated to it this week." She had only seen him one night that week after work.

Brand pulled up to the curb and parked the car. "Recognize this?"

"The rental house?" Wide brown eyes turned to Brand. "We got it?" Brand hadn't mentioned the house since that first day.

"Come and see." He jumped out of the car and walked around to the passenger side, lifting her into his arms. He closed the car door with his foot.

One step inside the house and Carly saw that the real estate agent hadn't underestimated the extent of the repairs that it required. The walls were badly in need of paint and the entire place required a thorough cleaning.

"Close your eyes," Brand instructed. "All this is to be blocked from your mind." He carried her through the living room and down a long hallway.

"Brand, for heaven's sake, let me down," Carly objected. "You'll hurt your back."

"Don't tell me you're going to be one of those wives who complains all the time."

Carly laughed, her mood happy. "All right, I won't tell you." Playfully, she nibbled on the lobe of his ear.

Brand's hold tightened as he leaned forward and opened the door that led to the master bedroom.

The teasing laughter faded as Carly looked at the room for the first time. The walls were freshly painted in a light shade of blue. The navy blue bedspread and drapes were made from identical floral patterns.

"Oh, Brand," Carly breathed with a sense of awe. No wonder she hadn't seen him all week. He'd obviously been working here every night.

"The bedroom set is my wedding gift to you," Brand said tenderly as he lowered her feet to the plush carpet.

Running her hand along the polished surface of the oak dresser, Carly felt a surge of love that ran so deep it stole her breath. Finding the words to say what was in her heart would be impossible. Letting the spark of appreciation in her eyes speak for her, Carly looped her hands around Brand's neck and kissed him. "Thank you," she whispered. "You must have worked every night."

Brand arched her closer by pressing his hands into the small of her back. She could feel his smile against the crown of her head. "At least I was able to keep my hands off you. Maybe it's old-fashioned, but I wanted you to be my wife before we made love."

A sigh escaped her and Carly laid her head on his chest, closing her eyes. She'd thought a lot about their wedding night and her feelings were mixed. She was eager and excited, but at the same time apprehensive. In some ways she wished their lovemaking had been spontaneous and in others she was pleased that they'd waited until after the ceremony.

A finger under her chin raised her mouth to Brand's. When he kissed her, all of her pent-up longings for him exploded in a series of deep, hungry explorations. His hand manipulated the zipper at the back of her dress and artfully slipped the garment down her arms until it fell at her feet. Carly stood before her husband wearing only her creamy silk camisole and nylons. His hands at her breasts were tantalizingly intimate through the flimsy material and her nipples became pebble hard, straining against his palm.

"Brand," she murmured breathlessly. "My suitcase is in the car. My silky nightgown's in there." She became lost again in one of his kisses.

"I want to get these things off you," Brand groaned, "not add another set."

"But I bought it especially for tonight."

Immediately, his mouth hardened in possession,

claiming the trembling softness of hers. "Does it mean that much to you?"

Her hands crept upward, fingers sliding into the thick hair that grew at the base of his neck. "No. All I need is you."

The silk camisole had ridden up, and she could feel the roughness of his suit against her bare midriff. The buttons of his shirt left an imprint on her soft skin.

Brand's mouth worked sensuously over hers as Carly moved away just far enough to unfasten his buttons and slide his suit jacket and shirt from him. He helped as much as he could, his warm breath igniting her desire. Once free of the restricting clothing, Brand lifted the camisole over her outstretched arms so that her bare breasts nuzzled his chest. Wave after wave of pleasure lapped against her as her fingers sought his face, marveling at the strength of his face, his features sharpened now in his excitement.

"Carly." He ground out her name as he shifted his attention to the creamy curve of her neck and shoulder. Wordlessly he took a step in retreat and, jerking aside his belt, removed the remainder of his clothes. Carly slipped out of her things and walked into his loving embrace. Brand lifted her into his arms and carried her to the bed.

"I love you, Carly," he whispered.

"And I love you," she returned. Her eyes misted with the intensity of her feelings. "I'll make you a good wife, Brand," she vowed. "And I'll be a good mother."

Tenderly, he laid her on top of the bed and placed a hand on either side of her face, his eyes boring into hers. "I already know that," he said and pressed the full weight of his lean body onto hers. Carly's pulse raced hot and wild and she knew he was just as aroused as she. His skin was fiery to the touch as she ran her hands down his back and hips. The heat fused them together.

"Carly?" Brand's voice was filled with wonder and surprise after their lovemaking. "Did I hurt you?"

"No," she said with a heartfelt sigh. "It was wonderful."

He smoothed the hair from her face. "It gets better," he promised each time. He held her tightly, kissing her cheek and eyes until his breathing had returned to normal. "Why didn't you tell me you were a virgin?"

"I didn't know how," she whispered, relaxing in the crook of his arm. "It was beautiful. I had no idea it would be this good."

"You're not disappointed?"

Carly raised herself up on one elbow and kissed the corner of his mouth. "You're joking."

Chuckling, he brought her back into his arms, his hand pressing her head to his chest. "It was wonderful for me, too, Carly."

"Can we do it again?"

"Again?" he asked. "You shameless hussy, I've barely recovered from the first time. Give me five minutes."

"That long?" Her mouth made a languorous foray over his chest and up past his shoulder until she located his mouth, teasing him with short, biting kisses. She centered her attention on one side of his mouth and worked across to the other.

Brand's fingers tightened as he rolled with her in his arms so that their positions were reversed. He kissed her deeply, urgently. They made love quickly; the explosive chemistry between them demanded as much.

Carly clung to him afterward, not wanting ever to let him go.

"Satisfied now?" he whispered against her ear.

She shook her head. "I don't think I'll ever be satisfied."

"Me either," he said, holding her tightly at his side.

The next thing Carly knew, Brand was kissing her awake. "Are you hungry?"

"No, sleepy," she said with a yawn. "What time is it?"

"Ten. We haven't eaten dinner yet and I'm starved."

Carly sat up and pulled the sheet over her bare breasts. She'd hardly eaten all day and recognized the ache in the pit of her stomach as hunger pangs.

Brand slipped out of bed and reached for his pants. "I packed us a picnic basket. Wait here and I'll get it."

A couple of minutes later, Brand returned, carrying Carly's suitcase and a basket with a bottle of champagne and two glasses resting on the top.

Carly slipped her white lace and silk gown over her head while Brand opened the champagne and poured them each a glass.

"To many years of happiness," Brand said as he touched his glass to hers.

"To us," Carly added, and she took a sip of the sparkling liquid. The champagne tickled her throat. Laughing, she held her glass out for more. "What's there to eat?"

After refilling her glass, Brand opened the basket

and brought out a large jar of green olives, a thick bar of chocolate and some fried chicken.

Carly was so pleased she wanted to cry. “Oh, Brand, you’re marvelous.”

“I know what you like.”

“You do?” she asked him seductively, locking her arms around his neck. “You may have to revise your list.”

He pulled her into his embrace and nuzzled her neck. “Gladly,” he whispered just before his mouth claimed hers.

The only time they left the bedroom over the next two days was to make a quick run to Carly’s apartment for more food.

Sunday morning Carly phoned Diana and Barney.

Diana answered her cell. “Carly!” she exclaimed. “This is a surprise. How’s everything?”

“Great. But I thought you should know that I took your advice.”

“My advice?”

“Yup. Would you like to talk to my husband?”

“Carly, you did it? You actually married Brand. My goodness, you’re right, he is a fast worker! Why didn’t you let me know? Yes, yes, let me talk to Brand.”

Carly handed the phone to Brand and let him introduce himself to her friend. Wrapping her arms around his waist, she laid her head on his chest and was able to listen in on their conversation.

“No fair giving away all my childhood secrets.” Carly’s voice was playfully indignant when she took back the receiver.

"I wasn't," Diana denied with a telltale laugh. "Well, not *everything*."

"I like being married," Carly admitted with a catch in her voice. "Why didn't you tell me how great it is?"

"That's the problem," Diana said quickly. "You've got to be married to the right man."

Carly couldn't imagine sharing her life with anyone but Brand. "I've found him."

"So have I," Diana murmured. "Be happy, Carly."

Diana sounded as though she was close to tears. "I will. You too."

When she replaced the receiver, Brand took her in his arms. "Shall we name our first daughter Diana?"

"Diana?" Carly feigned shock, and teased him lovingly. "I was thinking more along the lines of Brandy—after her father."

Groaning, Brand shook his head. "I think I'll pray for sons."

"Brand." She took his hand and batted her long lashes. "You want to try it in the shower here?"

"Are you crazy? You nearly drowned me the last time."

"Yes, but it was fun, wasn't it?"

"Carly." Brand brushed the hair from his forehead and sighed, attempting to hide a smile. "I'm too old for those kinds of tricks. I prefer a nice, soft mattress."

"But I'm sure we must have done something wrong. Everyone makes love in the shower. At least they always do in the books I read."

Brand rolled his eyes mockingly. "All right, if you insist." He pulled her into his embrace and kissed her until she was breathless and clinging. "This is my punishment for marrying a younger woman," he complained.

"No..." She giggled. "This is your punishment for marrying a virgin."

Monday arrived all too quickly. Brand dropped her off at the apartment so she could drive her car to work.

"Do you want to meet back here this evening or at the house?"

Brand appeared to mull the question over. "The house. I'll pick up something for dinner and we can start painting after we eat."

Carly dreaded the job. Every room in the house needed a fresh coat. She wanted to do Shawn's and Sara's bedrooms herself. It seemed like a little thing, but it would help her to assimilate the fact that she was going to be a mother to those two. Having come into a similar situation, Carly was determined to make them feel loved and welcome from the beginning.

Brand met her at the house with hamburgers and two thick vanilla malts.

They sat at their hastily purchased kitchen table and Carly handed her malt back to Brand.

"I thought you liked vanilla."

"I do, but I'm watching my weight."

He arched one brow questioningly. "You're almost too thin as it is."

"That's because you nearly starved me to death this weekend," she tossed back.

He stood and came around to her side of the table. "Is that a fact?" he asked as he took her in his arms.

Her hands slid over his chest as their eyes met and

held. The look in his eyes trapped the oxygen in her lungs.

"Ever read anything in those novels you mentioned about making love on the top of a table?" he asked her in a low, husky tone, his eyes sparkling with mischief.

"Mr. St. Clair, you shock me."

Brand straightened and began undoing the buttons of his shirt.

Surprised, Carly watched him with her mouth hanging open. "I thought you were teasing."

"Nope." He unbuckled his belt.

"What about dinner?"

"It can wait." He reached over and unfastened the buttons of her blouse.

Holding her breath, Carly reached around and unzipped her skirt. "I thought you wanted to paint."

"What I want should be evident."

The skirt fell to the floor, leaving her standing in her teddy and stockings.

Brand was devouring her with his eyes. She undid his pants and dropped them to the floor.

Slowly, his hands shaking slightly, Brand removed the remainder of her clothes until they were both naked. Then he scooped her up and carried her down the hall.

Their lovemaking was urgent, explosive, and they clung to one another afterward.

"I thought you wanted to do it on top of the table."

"The bedroom wasn't that far away."

She smiled and kissed the side of his neck. "Almost too far, as I recall."

"I don't think you fully understand yet what you do to me," he whispered.

Carly rolled onto her stomach and hooked one bare leg over his. "If we keep this up we won't be finished painting the house till Christmas."

Brand wrapped his arms around her and breathed in deeply. "The thought of hiring painters is growing more appealing by the minute."

Nine

The clock radio clicked and immediately soft music floated into the sunlit bedroom.

"Morning." Brand pulled Carly close to his side and leisurely kissed her temple.

"Already?" she groaned. Her eyes refused to open as she snuggled deeper within Brand's embrace. He was warm and gentle and she felt too comfortable to move.

"Do you want me to make coffee this morning?"

Dark brown eyes flew open and she struggled to a sitting position. "No, I'll do it." Pausing at the side of the bed, Carly raised her hands high above her head, stretched and yawned.

"Aren't you ever going to let me get up first?" Brand teased with loving eyes.

"Nope." She leaned over and lightly brushed her mouth over his.

Brand's arms snaked around her waist and he deepened the contact with hungry demand. "What time is it?" he growled in her ear.

"Late," she teased and kissed him back spiritedly. "Much too late for what you have in mind." Giggling, she escaped from his embrace and grabbed her light cotton housecoat from the end of the bed before heading for the kitchen. Mornings were her favorite part of the day. Waking up with Brand was the culmination of every dream she'd ever hoped would come to pass.

When the coffee had finished perking, she carried a cup in to Brand. He generally left for work an hour earlier than she needed to be at Alaska Freight, but they woke together and Carly dutifully cooked his breakfast and got him out the door. Then she turned her efforts to preparing for her own day.

Brand strolled into the kitchen as she was laying strips of bacon into a hot skillet. The fat sizzled and filled the room with the aroma of cooking meat. Nuzzling the side of her neck, Brand wrapped his arms around her from behind. "You smell good."

"That's not me, silly. That's the bacon."

His hand slid from her waist to press against her smooth, flat abdomen. "We haven't talked about this much, but I'd like it if you got pregnant soon." He was so pensive and serious, a mood neither of them had had time for during these past few days.

Carly set down her fork and turned in his arms. "There's no rush, is there? I'd like to adjust to one family before starting another."

Brand pulled out a kitchen chair and sat down. His hands hugged the coffee mug. "There won't be two families, Carly, only one."

Sighing, she came up behind him and slipped her arms around his neck. "That's not what I meant. Even if I was to get pregnant tomorrow, there'd still be six years between the baby and Sara. It would be almost like raising two families."

Brand nodded and placed his hand on hers. "I know. It's just that I've been separated from Shawn and Sara for so long that I don't want to put any more distance between us. I want us all to be one family, no matter how many children you and I may have."

"We will be a family," she promised and returned to the stove. This weekend was the time they'd arranged to fly to Portland so Carly could meet the children and Brand's mother.

The two eggs were overcooked when she set the plate in front of Brand. He didn't say anything, but she knew he preferred his eggs sunny-side up. "Sorry about that," she said.

"Don't worry, the eggs are fine."

Carly took a long swallow of her orange juice.

"Are you worried about this weekend?" Brand wanted to know.

She was terrified, but didn't want Brand to guess. "I'm looking forward to meeting your family...*our* family," she corrected.

Brand kissed her tenderly before heading out the door. "Have a good day, honey."

The endearment rolled easily off his tongue, and again Carly had the feeling it was the same affectionate term he'd used with Sandra. She cringed. The pain was quick and sharp. She bit the inside her cheek as she pulled open a kitchen drawer and brought out a cookbook. For the sixth time in as many days, she read the recipe for chicken and dumplings. The meal was to be a surprise for Brand. This would be her first home-cooked dinner for her husband.

Before very long, cooking would be a part of her everyday life, and the sooner she mastered the skill, the better. Shawn and Sara wouldn't be satisfied with green olives and chocolate. At least not after the first week.

The chicken was simmering on the stove as Carly dressed for work. The aroma of the bacon had made her feel weak with hunger. The small glass of orange juice had constituted her entire breakfast, and dumplings were out. To be on the safe side, she stepped on the scale. Two pounds. She'd been starving herself for ten miserable days and was only down two pounds. *Some* women were naturally svelte and others had to work at it. There wasn't any justice left in the world anymore, she grumbled on her way out the front door.

On her lunch break, Carly savored an apple, cutting it into thirty pieces in an effort to take her mind off how hungry she was. As part of her lunch break, Carly drove into town and bought Sara a doll, and Shawn a book on Mount McKinley. She knew so little about these two who were destined to be a major part of her life. Her nerves were crying out with vague apprehension at the coming meeting. Fleetingly, she wondered how they felt about meeting *her.*

Before returning to the office, Carly stopped off at the apartment and checked on the dinner. She reread the cookbook instructions, confident that she had done everything properly.

On the way out she stopped at the mailbox and collected the mail. Another letter from Jutta had arrived, and she ripped it open eagerly. Jutta sent her congratulations and claimed to be working on another oil painting that she thought Carly would like. She said she'd sell this one cheap.

Carly smiled, folded the letter and placed it back inside the envelope. Jutta seemed to think the only interest Carly had in her was because of her artwork. As their friendship grew, she was certain that Jutta would feel differently.

Because she wanted Brand to be pleasantly surprised with her dinner, Carly left the office early. George was being a dear about everything, including the extra days off she needed. Carly felt like giving him a peck on the cheek as she rushed out the door, but hesitated, knowing he wouldn't know how to react to her display of affection.

Brand got home a half hour after she did. "I'm home," he called cheerfully.

"Hi." She stepped from the kitchen. The corners of her mouth trembled with the effort to hold back her tears.

He stopped in the middle of the living room and sniffed the air. "Something smells bad."

"I know." She swallowed tightly. "I tried to cook you a special dinner. It…it didn't work out." She gestured with one hand in angry bewilderment. "I…I don't know what I did wrong."

"Let me see," Brand offered as he headed for the kitchen.

"No!" she cried theatrically. "Don't go in there!"

"Carly." He gave her a look she felt he must reserve for misbehaving children.

Bristling, she cradled her stomach with her arms and shouted at him, "Go ahead then, have a good laugh."

Brand's eyes softened. "I'm not going to laugh at you."

"Why not? It's hilarious. How many husbands do you know who come home to be greeted with the news that their dinner's on the ceiling?"

Brand did a poor job of disguising his amusement.

Anger swelled like a flood tide in Carly until she wanted to scream. "I'm sorry I can't be as perfect as Sandra. I tried." Sobs took control of her voice. "I really tried."

"Carly. ." He went pale and reached for her.

She broke from his grasp and gave way to huge hiccuping sobs, warding him off with her arm. "Don't you dare touch me." Each word was enunciated clearly.

Brand looked as if she'd struck him physically. He moved to the sofa and sat down. "I wondered." His voice was husky and raw. "But I didn't want to believe what was right in front of me."

The tears welled up and spilled down her face as she held her breath in an effort to stop crying.

"You did all this because of Sandra?" Brand asked flatly.

Carly nodded. "And this insane dieting is because of her as well." Again it was a hard statement of fact and not a question.

"She was svelte."

"She was *gaunt.* Cancer does that to people." He rubbed his hand over his face. He was upset and didn't bother to conceal it. His mouth was pinched, and his eyes narrow. "What do I have to do to make you understand that I don't want another Sandra?"

"I thought…"

"I know what you thought." He paced the floor. "For two years I grieved for Sandra. The ache inside me was so bad I ran from my children and separated myself from the world."

She kept her face averted, burying her chin in her shoulder. A dark curtain of hair fell forward.

"I love you, Carly. Your love has given me back my children and a reason to go on with my life. I don't want to bury myself in the past again. With you at my side, I want to look ahead at the good life we can share." He turned and walked over to her. "I want you. None other." Holding her, he wove his fingers in her hair and forced her to look up at him. She couldn't bear it and closed her eyes. Fresh tears squeezed through her lashes. Every breath was a sob.

"What I feel for you is entirely different from my love for Sandra," he continued. "She was an only child, pampered and loved all her life. Even as a little girl she was sickly. Her family protected her, and when we married I took over that role."

Carly made an effort to strain away from his hands, but her attempt did little good. She didn't want to hear any more about Brand's first wife. Every word was like a knife wound.

"With Sandra, I felt protective and gentle," he said in a low, soothing voice. "But with you I'm challenged and inspired. My love for you is deeper than anything I'd ever hoped to find on this earth. Don't compete with a dead woman, Carly."

She groaned with the knowledge that he was right. There was no winning if she set herself up as a replacement for Sandra. Trying desperately to stop crying, she put her arms around his neck. "I'm sorry," she wept. "So sorry."

"I am too, love," he breathed against her hair. "I should have recognized what was happening."

"I wanted to be perfect for you and the children."

"You are," he whispered tenderly. "Now, let's see what can be salvaged from your dinner."

"Not much, I'm afraid." She inhaled a steadying breath. "It may be far worse than you realize," she said, avoiding his eyes. "I think my dumplings may have dented the ceiling and we'll be out the damage deposit."

He started laughing then, uncontrollably and soon she was laughing with him, free and content with the knowledge that she was loved for herself.

Ten

Carly's fingers tightened around Brand's arm. "Are you sure I look okay?"

"You're beautiful." He squeezed her hand. "You're perfect. They're going to love you."

Carly wished she had the same unfailing optimism. Shawn and Sara would be meeting them at the Portland Airport and the FASTEN YOUR SEAT BELT sign was already flashing in preparation for landing.

A thin film of nervous perspiration broke out across her upper lip and forehead and she wiped it away with her free hand. A thousand nagging apprehensions crowded their way into her mind. The tightening sensation that attacked the pit of her stomach was identical to the one she'd experienced as a child whenever she'd been transferred into a new foster home. If she couldn't fit in with this new family, her life would be a constant battle. The identical situation was facing her with Shawn and Sara. So much of her happiness with Brand depended on what happened this weekend.

"Carly." Brand squeezed her hand again. "Relax. You're as stiff as new cardboard."

"I can't help it." Even her whisper was tortured. "What will we do if Shawn and Sara don't like me?"

"But they're going to love you," Brand argued.

"How can you be so sure?" She knew she sounded like a frightened little girl. How could anyone who'd leaped headlong into as many adventures as she had be so terrified of two small children?

Brand tightened his hold on her fingers and raised them to his mouth to tenderly kiss the inside of her palm. "They're going to love you because I do."

A flood of emotion clouded her eyes. "I want to make this work, Brand," she said, and she lowered her eyes so he couldn't see how overemotional she was becoming. "I really do."

"I know, love."

Carly's heart fell to her ankles when the plane touched down. A few minutes later, they were walking down the jetway that led to the cavernous terminal and the baggage claim area.

"Daddy, Daddy." The high, squeaky voice of a young girl came at them the moment they cleared the secure area.

Brand fell to one knee as blond-haired Sara threw herself into his arms. Shawn followed, and squeezed his father's neck so tightly Carly was amazed that Brand was still breathing. With a child on each hip, Brand stood.

"Shawn and Sara, this is Carly."

"Hi, Carly." They spoke together and lowered their eyes shyly.

"Hello."

"Daddy told us all about you," Sara said eagerly.

"Did you really climb a whole mountain?" Shawn queried with a hint of disbelief.

"It was the hardest thing I ever did in my life," Carly confirmed. "By the time I made it down, my nose was redder than Rudolf the Red-Nosed Reindeer's and my lips had blisters all over them."

"Wow." Shawn's big blue eyes were filled with awe. "I'd like to climb a mountain, too."

"Someday, son," Brand promised.

"Welcome home, Brand." A crisp, clear voice spoke from behind them.

Carly's attention was diverted to the older woman who stood apart from the small group. Her hair was completely gray, but her eyes were like Brand's—only faded and with a tired, faraway look.

Brand lowered the children to the floor. "Mom, this is my wife, Carly."

"Hello, Mrs. St. Clair." Carly stepped forward and extended her hand.

Brand's mother shook it politely and offered her an uncertain smile. "Please, call me Kay. With two Mrs. St. Clairs around, there's bound to be some confusion."

Carly's spirits plummeted. Brand's mother didn't bother to disguise her lack of welcome. "Thank you," she said stiffly.

The older woman's eyes centered on the children, and softened. "Say hello to your new mother, children."

"Hello," they cried in unison, with eager smiles.

"I imagine you're tired," Kay St. Clair said conversationally on the way to pick up their luggage. "How was the flight?"

"Fine." Her mind searched frantically for something

to say. "The weather certainly is nice." Bright, sunny skies had welcomed them to Oregon.

"But then, this must be paradise compared to Alaska," Kay returned in the same bland tone she'd used earlier.

The sky had been just as blue and beautiful in Anchorage, but Carly let the subject drop. There wasn't any reason to start off this relationship with a disagreement by comparing the two states. Indeed, Oregon was beautiful, but Alaska was equally so, only in a different way. But Carly doubted that she could explain that to Brand's mother.

Lunch was waiting for them back at a stylish, two-story brick house with a meticulously kept yard and spotless interior. The entire house was so clean that Carly thought it had probably been sterilized. Framed pictures lined the fireplace mantel in the living room. There were photographs of Brand's two younger brothers and their families—and a picture of Brand with Sandra on their wedding day. Carly's gaze was riveted to the picture and the color washed from her face. Abruptly, she turned away, unable to bear the sight. By keeping the photo on the mantel, Brand's mother had made her statement regarding Carly.

If Brand noticed how little she ate, he said nothing. Shawn and Sara carried the conversation beautifully. Their joy at seeing their father again was unabashedly enthusiastic. Carly discovered that it would be easy to love those two, and she silently prayed that they could come to love and accept her.

Kay St. Clair cleared her throat before addressing Carly. "Tell me, what did your family think of this rushed marriage?"

"My family?" Carly knew just by looking at Kay St. Clair that she was a woman who put a lot of stock in one's background. "I'm afraid I don't have any, Mrs. St. Clair…Kay," she amended.

"Don't be silly, child, of course you do. Everyone has family."

"Carly was raised in foster homes, Mother," Brand explained for her.

"You were orphaned?" Kay St. Clair disregarded her son and centered her full attention on Carly.

"Not exactly. I…I was taken from my mother by the state when I was Sara's age."

"What about your father?" Shock had whitened the aging face. Lines of disapproval wrinkled her brow as Kay St. Clair set her fork aside.

"I never knew my father."

A soft snicker followed. "Are you sure your parents were married?"

"Mother," Brand barked. "You're insulting my wife."

Carly placed a hand on his forearm and shook her head. She didn't want to cause any discord between Brand and his mother. "As a matter of fact, I'm not completely sure that they were."

Shawn and Sara had lowered their heads at the sound of raised voices. They sat across from Carly looking so small and frightened that her heart ached with the need to reassure them.

"I hope you like surprises." Carly directed the comment to the children. "Because I brought you each one."

"You did?" Shawn's face brightened with excitement. "Can I see it?"

"Can I see mine, too?" Sara's eyes found her grandmother's and some of her eagerness faded. "Please," she added politely.

"After we finish lunch," Carly promised and winked.

"Both Shawn and Sara have to brush their teeth first," Kay St. Clair inserted with a heavy note of censure.

"We never brush our teeth after lunch. Why do we have to do it today?" Shawn asked, a puzzled look in his eyes.

Their grandmother bristled noticeably. "Because we were too busy this morning. And until you move in with your father and...Carly, you must do as I say."

"Yes, Grandma," Shawn and Sara returned like finely trained puppets.

Carly watched as a frown worked its way across Brand's face. His mother's reaction to Carly seemed to be as much of a surprise to him as it was to her. Brand hadn't told her a lot about his mother, and she'd pictured her as the round, grandmotherly sort. Kay St. Clair certainly wasn't that. She obviously cared for Shawn and Sara, and they returned that love, but she wasn't the warm, open person Carly had expected. But then, *she* wasn't the bride Kay St. Clair had anticipated, either.

"You have a lovely home, Kay." Carly tried again, knowing how difficult this meeting was for the older woman.

"Thank you. I do my best." The words were polite.

Carly swallowed tightly and looked at Brand. He was pensive, sad. He must have felt her gaze because he gave her a reassuring smile. But it didn't fool Carly. She knew what he was thinking.

"Are there parks in Anchorage?" Shawn wanted to know.

"Lots of them," Brand confirmed.

"Are there any close to where we're going to live?"

"Not real close," Carly answered. "Farther than walking distance. But there's a big backyard in the house we're renting and I think we can probably persuade your dad to put up a swing set."

"Really?" Sara's blue eyes became round as saucers. "Grandma doesn't like us to play on her lawn."

"Children ruin the grass," Kay announced in starched tones. "So I take Shawn and Sara to the park."

"Almost every day," Sara added.

"How nice of your grandma to do that for you." Brand's mother had obviously tried hard to give the children a good home.

"I'll be sending a list of instructions with Shawn and Sara," Kay said, her eyes avoiding Carly's. "It's quite extensive, but I feel the transition from Oregon to Alaska will be much smoother for them if you follow my advice."

"Mother, I don't think—"

"That was thoughtful of you," Carly said, interrupting her husband. "I'll be pleased to read them over. Mothering is new to me, and I'll admit I have lots to learn."

"I'm finished now, Grandma," Shawn said eagerly. "Can I go brush my teeth?"

"Say it properly," Kay St. Clair ordered.

"May I be excused, please?"

A small smile of pride cracked the tight lines of the older woman's face. "Yes, you may be excused. Very good, Shawn."

"May I be expused, too?" Sara requested.

"Excused," Kay corrected. "Say it again."

"Excu…excused." Sara beamed proudly at having managed the difficult word.

"Yes. Both of you brush your teeth and then you can see what your father brought you."

"Carly brought the gifts." Brand corrected the intended slight.

Her meal was practically untouched when Carly set her fork aside. "If you'll excuse me, I'll get the gifts from my suitcase." She didn't wait for Kay's permission, although she had the suspicion that it was expected of her.

The edge of the mattress sank with her weight as Carly covered her face with her hands. This meeting with Kay St. Clair was so much worse than she'd anticipated.

"We brushed our teeth." Shawn and Sara stood in the open doorway, startling her.

Carly forced herself to smile. "Then I bet you're ready for your presents."

They both nodded with wide-eyed eagerness.

Carly took out the two decoratively wrapped packages from inside her suitcase and handed them to Shawn and Sara.

They sank to the floor and ripped off the ribbon and paper with a speed that was amazing.

"A doll," Sara cried, her young voice filled with happy delight. "I've always, always wanted one just like this." Two young arms circled Carly's neck and hugged her close.

Carly squeezed her fondly in return. "I'm glad you like it."

"Wow." Shawn's eyes were wide as he leafed through

the picture book about the Alaskan mountains. "Thank you."

"Can we show Grandma?" Sara wanted to know.

"Of course." Carly followed them into the living room and noted again the censure in Kay St. Clair's eyes as she examined the gifts.

"I never did approve of those dolls." She spoke to her son, but the slight was meant for Carly.

Indecision flared in Brand's eyes. He was as confused and unsure as Carly.

"Daddy said you were going to be our new mother. Can I call you Mom?" Sara asked, tugging at Carly's pants leg.

"If you like."

Kay St. Clair's mouth narrowed into a tight line.

"Maybe you should call me Carly," she added hurriedly.

Brand brought Sara onto his knee. "You do what's the most comfortable for you."

"But I thought we already had a mom."

"You did," Kay St. Clair inserted coolly. "But she died."

"I think I'll call you Carly," Shawn stated thoughtfully after a long pause.

"If that's what makes you most comfortable." Carly responded as best she could under the circumstances. In one foster home where she'd lived, the parents had insisted she call them Mother and Father. Half the time the words had stuck in her throat. She wouldn't be offended if Shawn chose to call her by her first name.

"I think I'll call you Mom," Sara said from her father's knee. "I don't remember my other mommy."

"Sure you do, Sara," Kay St. Clair said sharply.

"All I can remember is that she smelled funny and she didn't have any hair."

A pained look flickered in Brand's eyes, one so fleeting that for a moment Carly thought she'd imagined it. But when he spoke, the pain in his voice confirmed the sadness in his eyes.

"That was the smell of the hospital and all her medicine," Brand explained carefully. "She lost her hair because the doctors were doing everything they could to make her well again. One of those treatments was called chemotherapy."

"And it made all her hair come out?" Two pairs of serious blue eyes studied Brand.

He nodded. "But your mother had real pretty hair. Just like yours, Sara."

The small face wrinkled in deep thought. "I wish I could remember her better."

"I do too, sweetheart," Brand murmured tenderly, holding his daughter in his arms.

Standing outside the circle of this poignant family group, Carly felt a brooding sense of distance, of separation. These three—four, if she included Brand's mother—were a family in themselves. The breath caught in her lungs as she watched them. All the emotional insecurities of her childhood reared up, haunting her, confronting her with the unpleasant realities of this marriage.

Again, just as she had been as a child, she was on the outside looking in. She belonged, and yet she didn't. She wasn't part of the family, but separate. Any love and attention she'd received when growing up had always been what was left over from that given to the family's real children. She wasn't Brand's first wife, but his second. And clearly a poor second, judging from his mother's reaction after meeting her.

"If you'll excuse me, I'd like to lie down." Her voice was barely above a whisper. She avoided Brand's eyes as she turned toward the bedroom.

Her heart was pounding so hard and fast that by the time she reached the bed she all but fell onto the soft mattress. Everything she'd dreaded and feared was happening. And the worst part of it was she could do nothing to change what was going on around her.

When she heard Brand's footsteps, Carly closed her eyes and pretended to be asleep. He hesitated in the doorway—before turning away.

Carly didn't know how long she stared at the ceiling. The muted sounds coming from the bedroom next to hers distracted her troubled thoughts. As much as she wanted to hide, Carly knew she couldn't stay in the bedroom for the entire weekend.

After combing her hair, she added blush to her cheeks. If she didn't, Brand was sure to comment on how pale she looked.

As she walked past Sara's room, Carly paused and glanced inside. The little girl was sitting on top of her mattress. A jewelry box was open in front of her and whatever was inside commanded her attention.

"Hi."

"Hi…Mom." Sara looked up and spoke with a shy smile.

"What are you looking at?"

"Pictures of my other mommy."

Carly's heart plummeted. She was a fool to believe that Sandra wouldn't haunt her. Borrowed dreams were all the future held. Another woman's husband. Another woman's children.

"Would you like to see?"

Some perverse curiosity demanded that Carly look. Sitting on the bed beside the sweet, blond-haired child, she examined each color print.

"My hair is like hers, isn't it?"

"Yes." The strangled sound that came from Carly's throat made Sara turn and stare at her.

"She was real pretty, too," Shawn said from the hallway. "Sometimes she sprayed on perfume and smelled good." Shawn seemed to want to correct his sister's memory.

"Did she read to us?" Sara inquired softly. "Like Grandma does sometimes?"

"Yup. Don't you remember, Sara? Don't you remember anything?"

Carly couldn't stand much more of this. She was certain the children didn't often talk about their mother. Brand's presence had resurrected these curious memories. The pain it caused her to listen to them speak about Sandra was beyond description. She couldn't take their mother away from them, but she wasn't sure that she could live in the shadow of Sandra's memory.

"I think I'll go find your father," Carly said, hiding behind a cheerful facade.

"He's talking to Grandma on the patio," Shawn provided. "We're supposed to be resting." He added that second fact with a hint of indignation. "Second-graders shouldn't have to take naps," he mumbled under his breath just loud enough for Carly to hear. "When we come and live with you and Dad, I won't have to, will I?"

Carly ruffled the top of his blond head. "No," she whispered. "But don't say anything to your grandmother."

Shawn's wide eyes sparkled and they shared a conspiratorial smile.

"When are we moving to Anchor…Alaska?" Sara asked, tucking the pictures back inside the jewelry box.

"Three weeks." Hardly any time at all, Carly realized. Certainly not enough to settle the horrible doubts she was facing.

"Will you read to us and tell us stories?"

Carly stared blankly at the pair. "If you like."

"Goody." Sara clapped her hands gleefully.

"Shh," Shawn warned. "Grandma will hear."

Raised voices on the patio outside stopped Carly halfway through the kitchen. Brand and his mother were in the middle a heated exchange. Their voices struggled to remain calm and composed. Carly doubted that Brand's mother ever shouted.

"But you hardly know her," Kay returned with an uncharacteristic quiver that revealed how upset she was.

"I know everything that's necessary. Carly's given me back a life I thought I'd lost when Sandra died." There was an exasperated appeal in the way Brand spoke.

"There was no need to remarry so soon. Certainly you could have found someone more suitable," Kay St. Clair said as she examined the rose bushes that grew in abundance around the patio.

Carly stood next to the sliding glass door, but neither was aware of her presence.

"I wish you'd give her a chance, Mother. Carly's the

best thing that's ever happened to me. Don't I deserve a little happiness? Shawn and Sara..."

"That brings up another matter," his mother interrupted crisply. "How can you possibly think Carly is a proper replacement for the care I've given Shawn and Sara? When I told you I wanted to relax and travel for a time, I assumed you'd hire a housekeeper. I had no idea you'd marry the first woman to turn you on."

Brand's jaw went white and he seemed to struggle with his anger. The lines that were etched out from his eyes relayed the effort it took. There was a silent, dangerous glare in his eyes. "Carly is everything I've ever hoped to find in a woman."

Slowly, deliberately, Brand's mother shook her head with disapproval. "Can't you see that she's trying to bribe the children? Bringing them presents, telling them about a swing set. Really, Brand. And her family..."

"What does that have to do with anything?" Brand's tight expression grew grim.

"Honestly, son, sometimes you can be so blind." Kay cut a delicate rosebud from the flowering bush. "I don't mean to sound crass when I say that Carly is hardly the type of woman that men marry."

Shock waves tumbled through Carly. Her hand reached for the kitchen counter to steady herself. Her knees felt so weak that she thought for a moment that she might collapse. In all her life no one had ever said anything that could hurt her more. With an attitude that bordered on the fanatical, she'd tried desperately not to be anything like her mother. Anger and outrage seared her mind.

Brand looked as if he was about to explode.

Stepping onto the patio, Carly tilted her head at a

proud angle. "You will apologize for that comment, Mrs. St. Clair."

Carly didn't know who was more shocked: Brand or his mother.

Kay was obviously flustered, but to her credit, recovered quickly and cleared her throat. "It's often been said that people who listen in on conversations don't hear good things about themselves."

Brand moved to Carly's side and slipped an arm around her waist, bringing her close to him. "You owe us both an apology, Mother."

Carly didn't want him to touch her but hadn't the strength to escape him. She felt stiff and brittle. Her heart was pounding so loud, she was convinced the whole city could hear it.

Kay St. Clair conceded. "Perhaps. Only time will prove what I say. Until then, I can only offer my regrets for any thoughtlessness on my part." Without a hint of remorse, she returned her attention to the rose bush.

Brand took Carly's hand and pulled her into the kitchen. "Let's get out of here," he insisted. "I won't have you subjected to this."

"No." Her throat worked convulsively. "We can't."

"Oh yes we can." He raked a hand through his hair, his voice tight with impatience. "You don't have to take this from anyone. Least of all my mother."

Gently, Carly shook her head. "She loves you, and she loves Shawn and Sara. I'm a stranger who's invaded her world. And I'm not carrying the proper credentials."

"Carly." Brand frowned, unsure.

"I understand her better than you think," Carly whispered. "If we leave now, the situation will be unbearable for Shawn and Sara."

"We could take them with us," Brand argued.

"And cause an even greater rift between you and your mother? Taking the children now would be heartless. She loves them, Brand."

"But she's hurt you and I won't stand for that." His eyes roved over her face.

"Your mother's doubts and mistrusts are natural."

Brand's fingers bit into her upper arms. "Don't make excuses for her."

Carly closed her eyes and slowly shook her head. "The family I moved in with when I was fourteen had a natural daughter the same age. She hated me. It wasn't that I'd done anything. But I was there. I took away from the attention and love she felt was *her* due—not mine. I was a stranger with a murky past."

Brand brought her into his arms. "You're not a teenager anymore, Carly. You can't compare that to what's happening with my mother now."

Her smile was sad. She wouldn't argue with him, but in her heart, she knew. The situation was no different—and in many ways it was worse.

That night Carly lay awake. She could tell by the way Brand was breathing that he wasn't asleep either. The space between them seemed greater than just a few inches. In some ways whole universes stretched between them.

"You awake?" he whispered.

"Yes." She turned to cuddle him, nestling her head against his shoulder. The need to feel his arms around her was strong. "I'm cold."

Immediately, Brand's arms brought her more fully into his embrace. "Tell me what happened in that foster home you were talking about earlier."

"Why?"

"I need to know," he returned in a slow, uneven murmur.

"Her name was Joyce," Carly murmured softly. "She never did learn to like me. I was a threat to her. Not with just her family, but at school as well. When we were allowed to date, it didn't matter who asked me out, Joyce had to prove that she could take that boy away from me."

"Did she?"

Carly shrugged. "Sometimes. But it didn't matter." The only man Carly had ever really loved was Brand.

"Did you compete with her?"

"I tried hard not to," she admitted and smiled wryly. "But she was intimidated, simply by my being there."

"Her parents couldn't see what was happening?"

"I'm sure they could, but their hands were tied. If they'd intervened, then Joyce would have had all the more reason to hate me."

"So you were left to sink or swim," he said dryly.

As he spoke, Carly's fingers playfully tugged at the hairs on his chest.

"If you don't stop doing that, I won't be responsible for what happens," Brand ground out near her ear.

Carly giggled, releasing the tension that had stretched between them only seconds before. "That sounds promising."

"I can offer you a lot more than promises," Brand mumbled and stopped her fingers, capturing one arm. Twisting, he repositioned himself so that he was holding her hands down at either side of her head. "Do you surrender?"

"Never," Carly said and laughed softly. "I'd be crazy to give up when I'm winning."

"Winning?" he asked incredulously.

"You bet." She lifted her head just enough to press her mouth lightly to his. In a short, teasing action her tongue moistened his mouth. Brand released a short sigh and melted against her. His hands no longer pinned her to the bed as they sought softer, more feminine areas. Carly wasn't given the opportunity to move as his mouth ravaged hers. Pressing her into the mattress, he buried his face in the hollow of her throat, teasing her with his tongue.

"See?" she whispered happily. "What did I tell you? I'm winning."

"You're mighty brave in my mother's house." Brand knew how uncomfortable she'd be making love with only a thin wall separating them from Kay.

"Wait until you see how bold I can get!" Carly said with a soft, subdued laugh.

"Daddy?"

The sound of the soft voice startled Carly. Brand rolled aside and Carly sat upright.

"I can't sleep." Sara stood in the doorway, tightly clutching her new doll under her arm.

"Did we wake you up?" Carly wanted to know, tossing Brand an accusing glare.

"No. I had to go potty and then I heard you giggle and I wanted to giggle, too."

Carly motioned with one finger for Sara to come to her. The little girl scooted eagerly across the floor to Carly's side of the bed. Leaning over, she whispered in Sara's ear and the child broke out in delighted laughter.

"What'd you say about me?" Brand demanded mockingly.

"How'd you know I said anything that had to do with you?"

"You had that look in your eye."

Carly threw back the sheets and Sara crawled under the covers with her. "You can't blame me if women often react to you with laughter. Isn't that right, Sara?"

The little girl agreed with an eager nod.

"What's all the noise about?" Shawn stood in the doorway, rubbing his eyes.

"Did your father wake you up, too?" Carly asked.

"No, Sara did. She was giggling."

"That was Carly," Brand corrected.

Shawn hesitated. "How come Sara gets to sleep with you?"

"That wasn't my idea," Brand said, and lifted the covers. "Might as well get the whole family in here."

Shawn climbed in beside his father. "I'm sleepy. Good night," he whispered.

Brand looked at Carly, with Sara snuggled close in her arms, and the tenderness in his eyes was enough to make her want to cry.

"Good night, family," Brand issued softly and reached for Carly's hand.

Eleven

The float plane veered to the left after taking off from Dutch Harbor. The small settlement was in the long tail of the Aleutian Islands, which stretched like a graceful arc of stepping-stones between two continents. The Aleutians extended for hundreds of miles to the farthest western extension of North America. Carly gazed out of the window at Unalaska Island, which was wedged between the frigid North Pacific and the storm-tossed Bering Sea.

June had arrived, and Alaska had shed its cold winter coat, stretching and waking to explode in flowers and sunshine. To Carly, with Brand at her side, it was paradise.

She had only flown with him a handful of times, and usually on short trips that were accomplished in less than a day. Now, high above the dark waters, she was amazed by the harshness of the terrain below. The islands had few trees, all of stunted growth. Grass grew in abundance and covered the ground. The contrast with the magnificent cliffs and the forests thick with life on the Alaska mainland was striking.

Looking around her now, she was struck again by the serene mountains. Capped with snow, they stretched for miles in a land called "America's Siberia." Brand had explained that the Aleutian Islands contained the longest range of active volcanoes in the United States. Forty-six was the number he'd quoted her.

Brand turned his attention from the controls. "You're very quiet," he said above the roar of the engine. Reaching for Carly's hand, he kissed her fingertips.

She offered him a dry smile.

"Are you tired?"

"Not at all. I'm overwhelmed by Alaska's diversity." What she was really thinking was how much she wanted Brand to teach her to fly. His reluctance was more obvious every time she brought up the subject. Carly didn't kid herself. She knew why.

"Dutch Harbor's got quite a history," Brand remarked. "During World War II, when Japan was preparing for the battle of Midway, they bombed Dutch Harbor."

"Did their bombers fly off course?" Carly teased. "Midway's in the *South* Pacific."

"No, they'd hoped to draw the Pacific fleet north. The United States spent fourteen months and hundreds of lives in liberating the islands. Most of those men never saw the enemy. They died from the weather and disease."

Carly's mind filled with images of young men bloody, shaking and freezing. She recalled having read something about the war in the Aleutians.

"How long before we arrive at Lake Iliamna?" She wanted to direct her thoughts from the unpleasant paths her mind was exploring.

"Not long. Are you anxious for our honeymoon?"

"What I want to know is what you had to promise George for me to get all this time off. I thought he'd explode because I wanted to attend Diana's wedding. Now he's given me time off two weeks running."

"What makes you think I promised him anything?"

"I know George." In some ways she knew him better than she did Brand.

His gaze roamed possessively over her face. "Don't ask so many questions."

Carly had faced a lot of unanswered questions this past week. Brand's children were beautiful, delightful. But she couldn't look at them without seeing Sandra. Brand knew that, and had tried in some illogical way to make it up to her all week. His mother had reminded Carly forcefully that she would never fit into Kay's image of a wife and mother. For a time Carly might be able to fool herself, but it wouldn't last long. She was an intruder in their lives, just as she had infringed on other lives as a child. There were no dreams for her. Only the borrowed ones of others.

Brand had sensed her qualms. All week he'd been watching, waiting. For what, Carly wasn't sure. He might have thought she was going to leave him, but she wasn't. At night, he'd reach for her. "I love you, Carly," was all he'd say. Their lovemaking was volcanic. With his arms wrapped securely around her, he fell asleep afterward. Carly wasn't so fortunate. She'd slept fitfully all week, waking in the darkest part of the night that precedes dawn. Often she was up and dressed when Brand awoke. They were both praying with a desperation born of silent torment that this time alone, this honeymoon, would set things right.

Lake Iliamna was as beautiful as Brand had described. The male proprietor of the log-cabin lodge welcomed them like family. He'd known Brand since childhood—which meant he'd known Sandra, as well.

Carly tried not to think about that as they climbed the polished stairs that led to their suite. The honeymoon suite.

The moment the door closed, Brand reached for her and kissed her hungrily. His mouth lingered to tease the curve of her lips.

"Carly," he whispered as he lifted the thick Indian sweater over her head. "I need you." His fingers hurried with the buttons of her blouse, pushing it from her shoulders.

Carly's fingers were just as eagerly working at his clothing, and when they fell into the bed, she kissed him and whispered, "I do love you, Brand." Her voice was small and filled with emotion.

"I know." The desperate ring of his response spoke of his own fears. As if afraid he had admitted something he shouldn't have, Brand kissed her. The hard pressure of his mouth covered hers as he pushed her deep into the comfort of the mattress. It wasn't long before Carly lost herself in the golden sensations of his lovemaking.

Carly stood in her silk robe, gazing out of the window onto the serene, blue lake in the distance. Brand continued to sleep peacefully, undisturbed by her absence. She turned and studied him for an instant as she tried to swallow back the doubts that reared up to face her like a charging enemy. After they'd made love, Carly had lain in his arms and thought how much simpler life would be if she had become his lover instead of his wife. Shawn and Sara were due to arrive in Anchorage in less than two weeks and she wasn't ready. Not emotionally. Not in any way that mattered. These two wonderful children expected a mother…a family—not some emotionally insecure little girl who was struggling to reconcile her past. Shawn, Sara and Brand deserved much more than what she could give them. At least, what she was capable of giving them now.

"Morning." Brand joined her at the window, slipping his hands around her slim waist. His mouth came down to lightly claim her lips and nibble on their softness.

"Why didn't you wake me?" His warm breath mingled with hers.

Carly wrapped her arms around his neck and tried to respond, but her body refused to relax.

"Honey, what's wrong?" His hands rubbed her back in a soothing, coaxing motion as his eyes lovingly caressed hers.

Whenever Brand called her by that affectionate term, she bristled and wanted to scream at him. "Don't call me that," she returned stiffly, hating herself for being so petty.

"'Honey'? Why not?"

Carly inhaled sharply. "Because that's what you used to call Sandra."

The morning light accentuated the frustrated, tired look in Brand's dark eyes. He released her and walked to the other side of the room. Jerking his hand through his hair, Brand expelled a hard breath. "Yes, sometimes I did. But that was then. You're now. Sandra has no part in our lives."

"But ultimately she affects us."

"Carly, please" he said, his fists clenched as he struggled to control his anger. "Sandra is *gone.* How long are you going to compete with a dead woman?"

Her arms cradled her stomach as she turned from him and stared sightlessly out the window. Arguing the matter was useless. Her heart was breaking. She couldn't let them continue as they had this week—stepping around one another, avoiding confrontations, pretending nothing was wrong. "I should never have married you, Brand. We would've been wonderful lovers." Her voice became a low, aching whisper. "But what we have now isn't going to work."

"I don't accept that. You're my wife and I won't let you go."

"You'll have to," she said gently, hating the emotion that moistened her eyes. "It isn't in me to let Shawn and Sara arrive feeling the way I do."

"They're coming and there's nothing that can be done about it now." Frustration thinned his mouth. Her heart cried in anguish, but for a moment no sound came from the tight muscles of her throat.

"Do you think I enjoy feeling like this?" she cried . "I'd give anything to be different. Shawn and Sara are beautiful, warm children. But they're *Sandra's* children."

"They're our children," he returned.

"Then why do I see Sandra every time I look at them?"

"Because that's all your self-pity allows you to see. If you'd look past your own insecurities, you'd recognize how much they want and need you. All three of us do, Carly." The desperate edge to his voice was painful to listen to. "Sandra has nothing to do with us," he said in a pleading voice.

"Then you can't recognize what's right in front of your eyes," she whispered, fighting back the emotion. "What makes you so uncomfortable about me learning to fly?"

Dark eyes narrowed harshly. "It's dangerous and any one of a hundred things could happen...."

"And I could be killed," she finished for him. "Sandra died and you're afraid I will, too."

"All right," he shouted. "But what's wrong with being cautious? If I lost you, it'd kill me. If you blame Sandra for that, you're right."

"But where does it stop? Will you be afraid to let me climb or hike or anything else?" She didn't wait for him to respond. "I'm my own person and there will be lots of things I'm going to try."

"I just don't want you to do anything dangerous."

Carly fought to remain outwardly calm and controlled, but the battle was a losing one. "Because of Sandra," she repeated.

"Okay, you're right. I've already lost one wife."

"Brand," she murmured softly, "I can't take that kind of protective suffocation."

He began pacing the floor, clenching and unclenching his fists. Irritation and bewilderment produced a deep frown in him, but when he spoke his voice displayed no emotion. "I think I knew this was coming," he murmured, his voice thick with resignation. "You haven't been the same since we got back from Portland."

"Your mother is a very perceptive woman. She knew instantly that I wasn't the right kind of wife for you. And certainly not the kind of mother Shawn and Sara need."

"My mother knows nothing." Brand hurled the words at her. He turned and stormed across the room, dressing quickly. His hand was already on the doorknob when he paused and turned to Carly. "And you know nothing. Go ahead and run. See how far you get. I won't let go of you, Carly. You're my wife and I intend to stay married to you the rest of my life." He left then, leaving Carly standing at the window feeling more wretched and miserable than she could ever remember.

The remainder of their honeymoon was a nightmare for Carly. They barely spoke to one another, and when they did, it was in stilted, abrupt sentences.

On the flight back to Anchorage, neither of them said a word. The lush green beauty of the world below was overshadowed by the heaviness in their hearts.

Brand carried their suitcases to and paused inside the door. Silently, he lugged Carly's luggage into the bedroom while she shuffled through the mail and noted that there was a long letter from Jutta. They corresponded often now. Carly felt she had gained a valued friend in the older woman. From that first stilted meeting at the correctional center, their relationship had flowered through the mail. Carly was often surprised at how articulate Jutta could be. She was often insightful and wise.

Brand hadn't said a word as they'd arrived home. She tried to remain unaffected by his attitude, but she was having trouble succeeding. He'd been cold and distant since that first morning. Not that she blamed him.

Brand sat on the sofa, and when Carly chanced a glance at him, she noted the deeply grooved sadness in his eyes. Part of her yearned to go to him and erase the tension. She'd give anything to be different. Then he raised his gaze to hers and their dark eyes clashed. His narrowed and hardened, as if anticipating a battle. Rising, he moved to his luggage. "I'm going to the house. Until you've settled things within yourself, I'll be there."

"Maybe…maybe that would be for the best," she said evenly. "What about the children? They'll be arriving soon."

A thick brow quirked with mockery. "Why should you care?"

"Because it's only natural that I do. It wouldn't be fair for them—"

"Can't you accept them for who they are?" Brand demanded suddenly, cutting her off.

Carly went white. "Don't you realize how miserable I am over this whole situation?" she cried. "This horrible guilt is eating me alive." Somehow she realized that no amount of arguing would adequately explain her feelings. Nothing she could say would help him understand.

Brand bent down and picked up his suitcase. His face darkened. "I have two beautiful children. I'm tired of making excuses for them. And yes," he said, inhaling sharply, "they look exactly like Sandra."

Shock froze her for an instant at the deliberate pain he was inflicting. "You don't need to make excuses for Shawn and Sara," she said, "you just don't understand what—"

"You're right," he interrupted. "I *don't* understand." He turned, and a moment later the front door slammed shut.

Stunned, Carly stood as she was for what seemed an eternity. The hand she ran over her face was shaking uncontrollably. Brand was right, so very right. He should never apologize for children like Shawn and Sara. She moved into the kitchen and put hot water on to boil for coffee. Standing at the counter, her fingers gripped the edge until she felt one long nail give way under the punishing pressure.

"Carly, what's wrong? You never phone this late unless it's important."

"Nothing," Carly lied on a falsely cheerful note. "I'm just calling to see if you're pregnant yet."

Diana laughed with the free-flowing happiness that had echoed in her voice from the moment she'd announced that she was going to marry Barney. "Not yet. But not from lack of trying. What about you and Brand?"

"No." The strangled sound was barely recognizable.

A short silence followed. "Are you going to tell me what's wrong?"

Carly choked on a sob. "It's not going to work with Brand and me."

"What do you mean it's not going to work?" Diana sounded incredulous.

"We aren't living together anymore. Brand moved into the house this weekend. I'm still here at my apartment." Holding the phone to her ear with her shoulder, Carly wiped the tears from her face with both hands. Tilting her head back, she stared blankly at the ceiling light. "I've gone over it a thousand times in my mind. I should never have married him. I can't be the right kind of mother for his children."

"Sweetie, hold on," Diana said softly in the motherly tone Carly alternately loved and hated. But she needed it now more than she ever had in her life. "You haven't been married a month. Even my first two marriages lasted longer than that. If you love him and Brand loves you, then things will work themselves out. Trust me."

Attempting a laugh that failed miserably, Carly sniffled. "I wish it was that easy."

"Listen, sweetie, it's plain to me that we aren't going to be able to settle this over the phone. I've been looking for an excuse to visit you..."

"Diana—no. You can't do that," Carly said urgently, and sniffled again.

"Wild moose won't keep me away. I'll let you know later when my plane's scheduled to arrive."

Carly tried to argue Diana out of a wasted trip. But her friend wasn't going to be able to do or say anything to change her determination. But in the end Carly resigned herself to the fact that, once Diana had made up her mind about something, it would take more than a few words to change it.

A half hour after talking to Diana, Carly parked her car in the driveway behind Brand's. Her fingers clenched unmercifully around the steering wheel as she gathered her resolve.

The first knock against the door was tentative.

"Come in."

Brand was painting the living room. Newspapers littered the carpet as he spread the antique-white latex color along the neglected walls. Carly recalled choosing this shade for its brightening effect. His roller hardly paused as Carly walked through the door.

"What do you want?"

She died a little at the unfriendly tone of his voice. "I thought I should help. It's...it's only right." Every day brought them closer to the time when Shawn and Sara would be arriving.

"What's right is having you live in this house with me as my wife," Brand returned. "If you want to do anything to help, then do that."

"I…I can't."

Brand didn't even hesitate. "Then go."

Shocked, Carly stood frozen, unable to move.

"Go," he repeated.

Hanging her head, Carly closed her eyes. "I know how irrational I seem," she said in a voice that was barely above a whisper. "And I realize you must be having a hard time believing this, but I love you."

Brand's grunt was filled with amusement. "Sure you do. If telling yourself that helps soothe your conscience, you keep right on believing it."

"Can't we talk without fighting anymore?" she asked in a tired voice.

Brand tipped his head to one side and arched his thick brows mockingly. "I don't know—can we?"

Carly bristled. She wouldn't be provoked into an argument, and that was clearly what Brand wanted. "Are you going to answer every one of my questions with ones of your own?"

"Why not?" Brand was unhesitating. "I've been facing lots of questions lately."

The blood drained from her face so fast Carly thought she might faint. Every foster home, every family she'd ever known had been the same. Just when it seemed that she had finally found a place where she belonged—where she could fit in with a family—it would happen. Something would come about and she'd be sent away. Then everything she had worked to build up would be washed out from under her and she'd be forced to start again. She didn't want it to happen this time. She desperately wanted things to work out. But already Brand was willing to send her out of his life.

With her hands folded primly in front of her, Carly watched him silently as he worked. Even strokes spread the paint across the flat surface. Finally, she gathered enough courage to begin again.

"Diana's coming."

Brand paused in the middle of a downward sweep of the roller and turned around. "Are you running back to Seattle?"

"No." The thought of leaving Brand and the children was intolerable. "She's coming because she wants to talk some sense into me."

Brand turned back to the wall. "I wish her luck. Heaven knows, I've tried."

"Don't you think I know how unreasonable I sound?" Carly shot back angrily. "But it's not reason I *feel.* It's emotion. Is it so wrong to want to be a man's first wife? If that makes me sound selfish and childish, then I agree—that's exactly what I am. All my life I've accepted someone else's leftovers. It's the one thing—the only thing—I didn't want in a husband."

If she expected a reaction from Brand, he gave her none. With his back to her, he continued painting. Carly stood the grating silence as long as she could, then moved to the bedroom that was to be Sara's. Brand had already finished painting it a lovely shade of pink, but the windows were bare, as were those in the freshly painted blue bedroom across the hall. Everything was ready for Shawn and Sara. Everything except Carly.

Diana arrived two days later. Carly met her at the airport and hugged her tightly, holding back the tears.

"Good grief you look terrible."

"That's what you said the last time you saw me," Carly admonished. Heaven knew she couldn't look any worse than she felt. "I don't suppose Barney was thrilled to have you come."

"Barney sends his love. Don't worry about him." Diana put her arm around Carly's waist. "Now, let's get out of here before you burst into tears in the airport."

Carly felt she was ready to do exactly that. She hadn't seen Brand in two days. If *she* wasn't running, he was. Twice she'd gone over to the house, and both times he was nowhere to be seen. No doubt he was in the air, working twice as many hours as any other pilot.

She doubted that he even knew or cared that she'd been to the house. On her first visit, she'd put up priscilla curtains in Sara's room and made up her new bed with percale sheets printed with cartoon characters. The choice for Shawn's room hadn't been as easy, but she'd chosen drapes with *Star Wars* figures, and a matching bedspread.

In her wanderings around the house Carly had avoided the bedroom she'd once shared with Brand, but had ventured into the kitchen. Neatly washed dishes were stacked on the counter to dry. Brand's efficiency reminded her that he didn't need her to keep his home. He would be fine without her.

"It really is lovely in this part of the world," Diana was saying as Carly's thoughts turned from Brand.

"I told you it was." Her words sounded weak and emotionless even to her own ears.

When they arrived at the apartment Carly put on water for coffee. Her shoulders drooped as she closed her eyes and pressed her lips together.

"Are you sure you're not pregnant?" Diana asked softly. "I can't remember you ever being so pale."

A cold feeling washed over her. For one crazy second she was completely torn. One part of her felt a rush of excitement, while another experienced a deep sense of dread. Adding a child to this situation would only complicate their problems.

"Carly?" Diana prompted her gently.

"No," she said and swallowed. "There's no possibility of that." She brought down two ceramic mugs from the cupboard and added the dark coffee crystals. When the teapot whistled, she poured the liquid into the mugs. All of her movements were automatic.

As she delivered the steaming coffee to the kitchen table, Diana's eyes studied her carefully. "I've known you from the time you were an adolescent, Carly. I've witnessed these inner struggles of yours for years." Her hand reached across the table and patted Carly's. "Sweetie, isn't it time to bury the hurts of the past and move on?" Her wide-eyed gaze sought Carly's colorless face.

With her head bowed, Carly stared into the dark liquid. "He loved her so much." Her voice was trembling.

"But now Brand loves you."

"He still loves her, and she's standing between us like a steel wedge."

"Only because you see it that way. Won't you give Brand the right to have loved Sandra? He shared lots of years with her, and lots of memories. Are you trying to take that away from him, too?"

"Too?"

"He thinks that what you want is for him to give

up his children," Diana declared with a faint note of censure.

"How could he think that? I'd never, never," she repeated forcefully, "ask Brand to do anything of the sort—"

"But he doesn't know that."

Suspicions mounted within Carly. Diana seemed to know far too much about Brand's thoughts to be guessing. "How do you know all this? This has got to be more than speculation on your part."

Diana's gaze didn't flicker. "I talked to him a while ago."

"When?" Carly demanded in a shocked tone.

"Right after I talked to you. He phoned me, Carly. You've got him so twisted up inside he doesn't know what to do. He loves you, but he loves his children, too. Brand seems to think that if he were to have one of his brothers raise Shawn and Sara, then you'd be satisfied."

Carly's widened gaze sought Diana's face as an icy chill attacked her heart. "That's not it."

"I tried to assure him it wasn't."

The palms of her hands cradled the hot mug until her flesh felt hot and uncomfortable. "What's wrong with me, Diana? Why am I like this?" Tears clouded her vision. "Why can't I thank God that someone as wonderful as Brand loves me?"

"I don't know, sweetie. I don't know." Carly's sadness was echoed in Diana's low voice.

Carly paced her bedroom floor that night, unable to sleep. She couldn't remember the last time she'd eaten a decent meal. Diana had been adamant. She seemed to think that a ready-made family was just the thing Carly needed. Carly had almost laughed. A family, *this* family terrified her. She couldn't take Sandra away from the children, and she couldn't separate the children from Brand. There was no solution.

Diana was up before Carly the next morning. "How'd you sleep?" she asked.

"Fine," Carly lied. Exhaustion reduced her voice to a breathless whisper.

"Little liar," Diana murmured.

Carly went into the bathroom, avoiding her friend as she dressed for work. The sound of frying bacon filled the small apartment and Carly had no sooner vacated the bathroom when Diana came rushing in, looking pale and sickly.

Surprised, Carly watched as her friend lost her breakfast. When Diana was finished, Carly handed her a wet washcloth. "You okay?" she asked with a worried expression.

Diana took a couple of deep breaths. "I'm wonderful."

"You are pregnant!"

"I guess so. I had my suspicions, but I wasn't sure." She laughed lightly. "But I am now."

"Congratulations." Carly's voice was softly disturbed. "You should be home with Barney, not in Alaska."

"It won't be any big surprise. Barney guessed last week."

"But you should see a doctor, or purchase one of those test kits."

"I will." Diana's soft laugh was filled with happiness. "As soon as I get back to Seattle."

"Which will be today, if I have anything to say about it. The last thing I need is a pregnant woman on my hands." Carly was teasing her friend. Diana's life was so perfect. Barney's love had made her friend complete. No one would recognize the Diana of only a year ago in the softly radiant woman she was now. Love had done that for her.

But in Carly's instance, love had created dark shadows under her eyes. It had left her restless and sleepless until exhaustion claimed her in the wee hours of the morning.

Carly held back the tears when she dropped Diana off at the airport later that day.

"I don't think I've done anything to help you, but this is something you've got to settle within yourself," Diana said as she embraced her before boarding her flight.

"I know." Carly swallowed back the emotion building in her throat.

"Be happy," Diana murmured with tears glistening in her eyes. "Don't let the past rob you of the best thing to come along in your entire life."

Carly couldn't answer with anything but an abrupt shake of her head.

"Keep in contact now, you hear?"

Again Carly nodded. She waited until the plane had made its ascent into the welcoming blue sky before she wiped the moisture from her ashen cheek and headed back to the office.

When she pulled up in front of Alaska Freight Forwarding, the first thing Carly noted was that Brand's car was parked outside. Her heart raced with a thousand apprehensions. Starved for the sight of him, Carly hurried inside, afraid she'd miss him if she didn't move quickly enough.

"Brand." She couldn't disguise the breathless quality in her voice.

He turned, and the intensity in his eyes stopped her.

"Carly." George stepped around from his desk. "Welcome the newest employee to our firm. You didn't think I'd give you all those days off without striking a deal with Brand, did you?"

Twelve

"You're working here?" The question managed to make it past the lump of shock that tightened Carly's throat. From the time she'd first started at Alaska Freight Forwarding, George had been trying to get Brand to become a full-time pilot for the company. But the money he made freelancing his services to the various businesses around town was far and above what he would make flying with one company. That Brand would agree to such an arrangement jolted Carly. And he'd done it so they could visit Portland and Lake Iliamna. She had no doubt that he now considered both those trips wasted in light of what had followed.

"Carly." Brand's greeting was polite and stiff.

"Hello." She didn't trust her voice beyond the simplest welcome.

A perplexed expression skirted its way across George's wrinkled face. "Yes, well, it seems you two have things to discuss." He glanced uneasily from Brand to Carly. "I'll be in the garage."

She waited until the door clicked shut. "Why didn't you tell me?" she asked.

Brand gave an aloof shrug, glancing at the clipboard that contained the flight schedule for the week. "It didn't seem important at the time."

She turned to him. "Diana and I had a long talk—"

"Obviously it didn't make a lot of difference," he cut in sharply. "Otherwise your things would be at the house where they belong."

Carly ignored the censure in his voice. The lines about his mouth were tight and grim. She remembered that the grooves had relaxed when he'd held her in his arms and they'd made love. She closed her eyes against an unexpected surge of guilt. Unwilling for Brand to see her pain, Carly lowered her eyes and pretended an interest in the correspondence on her desk.

"Diana said you phoned her." She spoke after a few moments.

His dark eyes blazed for just an instant, and Carly realized she'd said the wrong thing. He hadn't wanted her to know that he'd contacted her friend.

"I'm glad you did, because I want to clear away a few misunderstandings."

"Such as?" He set the clipboard aside and poured himself a cup of coffee. Lifting the glass pot up to her, he inquired if she wanted a cup.

Carly shook her head. The only thing she wanted was for them to come to some understanding about their marriage and the children.

Brand took a sip of hot coffee. "You said something about misunderstandings," he prompted.

"Yes." Carly swallowed and moistened her dry lips. "It's about Shawn and Sara."

Brand's dark features were unreadable as he leaned against the side of George's wooden desk. "The kids are my problem." Heavy emphasis was placed on the fact that he now considered the children his, when once he'd insisted that they were theirs. And really how could she blame him? His attitude was the result of her insecurities and unreasonableness"But...I'm your wife and..."

Brand snickered. "My *wife?* Are you, Carly? Really?" he taunted, and turned abruptly toward the door. The knob clicked as he turned it. "My impression of husbands and wives was that they lived together. But then, I've been known to be wrong."

Carly bit into her lip. Brand was lashing out at her in his anger, because he was hurting. Not knowing what else to do, Carly stood at the window to watch him leave. He was heading for the airport. A glance at the clipboard confirmed that he'd be flying to Fairbanks. If there was any consolation to Brand being on the payroll, it was that at least now she'd know where he was and when to expect him back. But the solace that offered was little.

Carly purposely stayed late that night, waiting until Brand had checked in with George. She wasn't looking for another confrontation, just the assurance that he'd returned safely. Immediately, it became apparent that having Brand work for the same company had as many drawbacks as advantages. In some ways she'd rather not know his schedule. Ignorance was bliss when she didn't realize he was overdue. Now it would be there for her to face every minute of every day.

The thought of returning to a lonely apartment held no appeal, so Carly decided to take a short drive. Almost without realizing it, she found herself turning the corner that led to the house. Her heart leaped to her throat when she noticed that Brand had installed a swing set in the side yard.

A chill raced up her spine as she parked alongside the curb and examined the polished metal toy. The swings were painted in a rainbow design, with racing stripes wrapped around the poles. Without much imagination Carly could picture two pairs of blue eyes sparkling with happy surprise.

When her gaze slid away from the swing set, she saw that Brand was standing in front of the wrought-iron gate, studying her.

"Was there something you wanted?" he asked coolly.

A sad smile touched her mouth. "I see that you've risked bribing their affection with a swing set." She was reminding him of his mother's comment.

Their eyes met, and for a flickering moment amusement showed in his glance. "I saw the drapes. When did you bring those over?"

Looking away, Carly said, "A few days ago."

"Would you like to see what else I've done?"

Her nod was eager. If they talked, maybe Brand would come to understand her doubts. Maybe together they could find a solution.

If there was one.

He walked around the car and held open her door. When she climbed out, his hand cupped her elbow. The gesture of affection was an unconscious one; Carly was sure of that. But whatever his reason, or lack of it, she couldn't remain unaffected by his touch. A warmth spread its way up her arm. Brand had initiated her to the physical delights of married life, and after only a few days without him, she discovered that she missed his touch. She hungered for the need in his eyes when he reached for her and pulled her into his embrace. At night the bed seemed cold and lonely. She found that she tossed around in her sleep in an unconscious search for her husband.

Brand held open the screen door, allowing Carly to enter ahead of him. A small gasp of surprise escaped before she could control it. New furniture graced the family-size living room. A davenport and matching love seat was the pair they'd talked about purchasing from a local furniture store. Carly had liked the set immensely, but they'd decided to wait until they bought a house before purchasing furniture.

"You decided to go ahead and get the set," she stated unnecessarily. Another armchair was angled toward the fireplace. Carly had teased Brand about buying a chair that made up into a single bed. In discussing the purchase, she'd suggested that they try it out first by making love on it some night in front of a flickering fire.

The look in Brand's eyes confirmed that he remembered her idea. His hands moved to rest on either side of her neck. Carly closed her eyes at the pressure of his thumbs on her collarbones as he massaged her tender skin.

"Isn't the carpeting new, too?" She fought to keep her voice level and so not betray what the gentle caress of his fingers was doing to her.

"Yes," he muttered, dropping his hands.

Carly relaxed and released an unconscious sigh. She couldn't understand why Brand was making so many expensive changes in a rental house. He must have read the question in her eyes.

He turned away from her and ran a hand through his hair, mussing the smooth surface. "When you liked the house so much, I made inquiries about buying it."

Carly nearly choked on a sob. He had done this for her. The irony of the situation produced a painful throb in the area of her heart. Brand was offering her the first home she'd ever known, and she was walking away from him. "You're buying the house? Why?"

He didn't answer her for several long moments. "Anchorage is my home now. Everything I want in life is here. Or soon will be," he amended. "I'm no longer running from the past."

The implication that she still was coated his voice. She wanted to beg him to give her more time to reconcile herself to the fact that she couldn't be his first love. That the children she'd be raising were those of another woman. And again…again, as she had all her life, she would be living on borrowed dreams. Her eyes begged him not to tell her how unreasonable she was being. She already knew. She couldn't hate herself any more than she did at that moment.

"The carpet's beautiful," she murmured. Her gaze drifted past Brand into the cheery kitchen. The room had been repainted a brilliant yellow. He didn't need to tell her that he'd done that for her, too. Once, a few weeks ago, she'd explained that she felt a kitchen should reflect sunshine. Brand had teased her at the time, commenting that they had enough painting to do. Maybe in a couple of months they'd get around to that. As it was, they'd barely have enough time to prepare the house before Shawn and Sara arrived.

A sob jammed her throat, making speech impossible. Tears blurred her vision. Brand must have seen her reaction to the house and all he'd done. When he reached for her, she went willingly into his arms. His broad chest muffled her sudden tears. Everything she'd ever wanted was here with Brand, but she couldn't accept it.

Home. Family. Love.

The ache in her heart was so profound that she felt like a wounded animal caught in a crippling trap. Only in her case, the trap was of her own making. She couldn't stay. She couldn't go.

"Carly," Brand whispered, and a disturbing tremor entered his voice. He paused to brush the wet strands of hair from her cheek. "Don't cry like that."

Her shoulders shook so hard that catching her breath was nearly impossible. She gasped and released long, shuddering sobs as she struggled to regain her composure. "Hold me," she pleaded in a throbbing voice. "Please, hold me."

His arms came around her so tightly that her ribs ached. Carly didn't mind. For the first time in weeks, she felt secure again. His chin rested on the top of her head until her tears abated. Not until her breathing became controlled and even did she realize that, all the while she'd been weeping, Brand had been talking to her in soothing tones, reassuring her of his love.

"Are you okay?" he asked quietly.

"I'm sorry, so sorry," she murmured over and over.

Her sorrow wasn't because of the tears, but because of what she was doing to them both.

In the momentary stillness that followed, Brand allowed a small space to come between them. Her gaze met his penetrating one as he reached out and wiped the moisture from her pale cheek with his index finger. Her lips trembled, anticipating his kiss, and he didn't disappoint her. His mouth captured hers. Warmth seeped into her cold blood at the urgent way in which his mouth rocked over hers.

"Brand." She said his name in a tortured whisper, asking for his love. She needed him. Just for tonight she hungered for the feel of his arms around her, and she longed to wake with him at her side in the morning. Just for tonight, tomorrow, with all its problems, could be pushed aside.

Hugging her more tightly, Brand lifted her into his arms and carried her down the hall and into their bedroom. The springs of the bed made a squeaking sound as he lowered her onto the mattress.

Carly's arms encircled his neck, directing his mouth to hers. She tasted his restraint the moment his mouth brushed past her lips.

"Brand," she whispered, hurt and confused. "What's wrong?"

He sat on the edge of the bed and leaned forward. The shadow of a dejected figure played against the opposite wall. He looked broken, tired and intolerably sad. Carly propped herself up on one elbow and ran her hand along the curve of his spine. "Brand." She repeated her plea, not knowing what had prompted his actions. She was sure he desired her as much as she did him. Yet he'd called everything to an abrupt halt.

"Before we were married you suggested that we become lovers," Brand began. "I told you then that I wanted more out of our relationship than a few stolen hours in bed." His tone was heavy and tight. "I married you because I love you and need you emotionally, physically...every way that there is to need another person." He hesitated and straightened slightly. Wiping a hand over his tired eyes, he turned so he could watch her as he spoke. "My home is here—*our* home, our bedroom. I'm asking you to share that with me as your lover, your friend, your confidante, your husband. Someday I want to feel our child growing inside you. I won't accept just a small part of your life. I want it all. Maybe that's selfish of me, but I don't care anymore. All I know is that I can't continue living like this, praying every day you'll see all the love that's waiting for you right here. And worse, witnessing the battle going on inside you and knowing I'm losing. And when I lose, you lose. And Shawn and Sara lose."

Carly fell back against the mattress and stared at the ceiling. "Brand, please," she pleaded in a soft, pain-filled voice. He couldn't believe that she *wanted* to be like this. She'd give anything to change and be different.

"I'll be your husband, Carly," he said flatly, "when you can be my wife."

Her heart cried out, but only a strangled sound came from her throat. Her emotions had been bared and he'd known how desperately she'd needed him. There hadn't been any pretense in her coming to him tonight. She'd wanted his love and he was sending her away.

By some miracle, Carly managed to stumble out of the bedroom and the house. She didn't stop until she arrived back at the apartment. There were no more tears in her to cry as she paced the floor like a caged wild animal confined to the smallest of spaces. Mindless exhaustion claimed her in the early-morning hours, but even then she slept on the sofa rather than face the bedroom alone.

The following morning, Carly was able to avoid seeing Brand. Intuition told her that he was evading her as well.

At the end of what seemed like the longest day of her life, Carly drove to her apartment, parked the car and, without going inside, decided to go for a walk. If she was able to exert herself physically, maybe she'd be tired enough to sleep tonight. With no set course in mind, she strode for what seemed miles. Her hands were buried deep in her pockets, her strides urgent. At every street she watched in amazement as long parades of boys and girls captured her attention. Never had she seen more children. It was the first week of June and the evenings were light. Young boys were riding their bikes. For a time a small band of bikers followed her, dashing in and out of the sidewalk along her chosen route. Ignoring them, Carly focused her attention directly ahead until her eyes found a group of young girls playing with cabbage-faced dolls in the front yard of a two-story white house.

Quickening her pace, she discovered that she was near the library. A good book would help her escape her problems. But once inside, Carly learned that the evening was one designated for the appearance of a prominent storyteller. The building was full of children Shawn's and Sara's age. One glance inside and Carly hurried out. Her breath came in frantic gasps as she ran away.

For one insane moment Carly wanted to accuse Brand of planning the whole thing. She didn't need to be told her thoughts were outrageous, but the realization didn't help.

The remainder of the week passed in a blur. If she was staying away from Brand, then he had changed his strategy and was making every excuse to be near her.

"I don't mind telling you," George commented early Monday morning, "I've been worried about you and Brand. The air between you has seemed a mite thick lately."

Carly ignored him, centering her attention on the Pacific Alaska Maritime docking schedule. "We should get the Wilkens account to Nome by Thursday."

"I was worried," George continued, undaunted, "but the way Brand watches you, I know what brought you two together is still alive and well." He chuckled and rubbed the side of his unshaven cheek. "On his part, anyway."

Carly's fingers tightened around her pencil. "Have you looked over Primetime Gold's claim for the last shipment? Apparently, the dredging parts were damaged."

If George made one more comment on the way Brand was looking at her, Carly was sure the pencil would snap. Brand came into the office daily when he knew she'd be there. Often he poured himself coffee, looking for an excuse to linger and talk to her. He wasn't exactly subtle with what he had to say.

"Three more days" had been his comment this morning. He didn't need to elaborate. Shawn and Sara would be arriving on Thursday.

"I need longer than that," Carly had pleaded for the hundredth time. "I'm not ready for them. I want to be sure."

The pain in Brand's eyes mirrored her own. "Will you ever know? That's the question. Carly, how can you turn away from us when we love and need you?"

"I can't rush what I feel," she murmured miserably.

"If you're waiting for me to give up Shawn and Sara, set your mind straight right now. I won't."

"Oh, Brand," Carly cried softly, then lowered her head so that her chin was tucked against her shoulder. "I would never ask that of you."

"Then just what do you want? Three days, Carly," he repeated with grim impatience. "They're arriving in three days, and they expect a home and a mother."

"I won't be there. I can't," she cried on a soft sob.

The pain etched in Brand's eyes as he left the office haunted Carly for the remainder of the day.

George had already left for the afternoon when Brand checked in after a short flight. He filled out the information sheet and attached it to the clipboard for George's signature.

Although Carly attempted to ignore the suppressed anger in his movements, it was impossible. Silently, her eyes appealed to him. His gaze met hers boldly, and darkened.

"If you're through, I'd like to close up," she said,

struggling to control the breathless quality in her voice. The office keys were clenched tightly in her hand. She'd seen that look on Brand's face before. Frustration hardened his eyes to a brilliant shade of brown, wary anger that all but flashed at her.

"Why should your likes concern me? Obviously my needs don't trouble you," he taunted softly. "Carly, I'm tired of playing the waiting game. I want a wife." With every word, he advanced toward her. An unfamiliar harshness stole into his features as he reached for her. His mouth sought hers.

Carly tried to resist him but she was weak and panting with need when, he began kissing her. At first he was gentle, his mouth caressing and teasing hers until she responded, wrapping her arms around his neck and arching against him so that her body was intimately thrust against his.

"I should make love to you here and now," he whispered.

"Brand, no…not here," she pleaded. "Still he kissed her again and again until she cried out, certain she heard someone approach. Whoever it was went into the hanger and thankfully not the office.

Brand must have heard the noise too because he broke away. Stepping back he looked at her with wide, shock-filled eyes, as if he'd just woken from a trance and hadn't known what he'd been doing.

He released her.

If Carly was pale, Brand was more so. He looked for a moment as if he was going to be ill. He hesitated only long enough to jam his shirttails inside his pants. Without giving her another look, he turned toward the door.

"There was no excuse for that," he said, looking away from her. "It won't happen again."

"Brand…"

Half way out the door, he stopped and glanced over his shoulder, but he made no attempt to come to her. His eyes met hers in quiet challenge. There were so many things she wanted to say, but no thought seemed clear in her mind.

"I…I understand," she murmured.

Thirteen

On Tuesday afternoon, another long letter from Jutta Hoverson was waiting for Carly. She held off opening the envelope until she had a cup of coffee. Carrying the mug to the kitchen table, she sat down and propped her bare feet on the opposite chair.

Of all the people in the world, Carly expected that Jutta would understand the hesitancy she felt toward Brand and the children. Diana, whom she loved and respected, hadn't come close to comprehending the heart-wrenching decision Carly faced. More than once during Diana's short visit, Carly felt that Diana had wanted to give her a hard shake. For once, Carly needed someone to identify with her needs, her insecurities. Jutta could do that.

Slipping the letter from the long envelope, she read:

Dear Carly,

My friend. Your letter arrived today and I've read it many times. You speak of your love for this man you have married. But you say that you are no longer living with him. I don't understand. In your last letter you wrote about his children and I sensed your discontent. You love, yet you fear. You battle against the things in life that are most natural. Reading your letter reminded me of the time when I was a young girl who dreamed of being a great runner. I worked very hard to accomplish this skill. My uncle coached me. And in his wisdom he explained that running demands complete coordination. He said that to be a good runner, I must let everything I'd learned, and everything I knew deep inside, come together and work for me. But I lost every race. Even when I knew I was the best, I couldn't win. Again and again, he said to me that once I quit trying so hard to win, I would. Of course, I didn't understand him at the time. I struggled, driving myself harder and harder. Then, one day at race time, my uncle threw up his hands at me. He said I would never win, and he walked away. And so I decided I wouldn't even try. When the race began, I ran, but every step still felt heavy, every breath an effort. Then something happened that I don't understand even now. Maybe because I wasn't trying, because I no longer cared to win, everything my uncle had tried to explain came together. My feet no longer dragged and every step seemed only to skim the surface. I no longer ran. I flew. I made no effort. I felt no strain. My rhythm was perfect and I experienced a pure exhilaration and a joy I have never known since. I won the race and for the only time in my life, maybe, I made my family proud.

My friend, in many ways we are alike.
Jutta

Carly reread the letter three times. The message should have been clear, but it wasn't. Jutta had listened to the advice of an uncle and won a race. Carly couldn't see how that could relate to Brand and the children. The letter was a riddle Jutta expected Carly to understand. But Carly had never done well with word puzzles.

Not until Carly was in bed did she think again of Jutta's strange letter. The picture her mind conjured was of a young, dark-hair girl struggling against high odds to excel. In some ways, Carly saw herself. With her personality quirks, her chances for happiness had to be slim. Her thoughts drifted to the first few days of lightheartedness after she and Brand were married. Content in their love, they had lived in euphoric harmony.

Suddenly, Carly understood. Abruptly, she struggled to a sitting position and turned on the small lamp at the side of her bed. This kind of underlying accord was what Jutta had tried to explain in her letter. There was harmony in Jutta's steps as she ran because she no longer struggled. When something is right, really right, there is no strain, no effort. The harmony of body and soul supersedes the complications of life. There were rhythms and patterns to every aspect of human existence, and all Carly had to do was accept their flow and move with the even swell of their tides. Problems erupted only when she struggled against this harmony. Once she reconciled herself to this flow, she could overcome the trap of always fearing borrowed dreams.

Carly didn't know how she could explain any of this to Brand, but she knew she had to try. The physical strain that had marked her face over the last weeks relaxed as she reached for her phone. He'd think she was crazy to be calling him this late at night, particularly when she didn't know what she was going to say. Probably the best thing to do was blurt out the fact that she loved him and that together they'd work out something. The love they shared was the harmony in her life because it was right. A lot of uncertainties remained; she hadn't reconciled everything. But at least now she could see a light at the end of the tunnel.

The phone rang ten times and Brand didn't answer. Perplexed, Carly cut the call. A look at her wristwatch confirmed that it was after midnight. Brand worked hard, and he slept hard. It was possible he'd sleep through the interruption, but not likely.

A quick mental review of the week's flight schedule reminded her that Brand had been flying some Seattle personnel to one of the Aleutian Islands that day. The flight was as regular as clockwork. Brand had taken the same route a thousand times. He hadn't checked in before she'd left work, she remembered. But then, she'd left a little early. She really didn't have anything to worry about. If something had gone awry with Brand's flight, George would have contacted her.

A long, body-stretching yawn convinced Carly to go back to bed. In the morning she'd make a point of seeking Brand out. Shawn and Sara were due to arrive the day after next, and she was hoping they could talk about that meeting.

* * *

Brand's Chevy was parked by the warehouse when Carly arrived at work the following morning. A smile lit up her face at the reassuring sight. Everything was fine.

"Where's Brand?" she asked her boss as she breezed in the door. "I'd like to talk to him before he takes off."

George looked up from the report he was scanning. "He hasn't arrived yet."

Carly shook her head and gave George a bemused grin. Sometimes her boss could be the most forgetful person. "Of course he's here. His car's parked out back."

George glanced up and released an exaggerated sigh. "I tell you, he hasn't come in this morning." Glancing at the thick black watch on his wrist, George's brows rose suspiciously. Brand wasn't in the habit of arriving late.

"What time did he check in last night?" Carly questioned.

With deliberate care, George set the paper he was reading aside. "You tell me. I left early."

Carly discovered that her legs would no longer support her, and she sank into the swivel chair at her desk. "I thought he was checking in with you. I assumed…"

"You mean Brand didn't come back to the office yesterday?"

Carly felt her heart sink so low it seemed to land at her ankles. "You mean…" She couldn't voice the thought.

"His car's still here. He didn't come back." George finished for her. He stood and grabbed the clipboard that held the flight schedules down from the wall. "Don't panic—everything's going to be fine. There's no cause for alarm." The rising uneasiness in his own voice wasn't reassuring. "I'll contact the airport and confirm his flight plan." George was out the door faster than she had seen him move in three months of working at Alaska.

Numbly, Carly sat. She couldn't have moved to save the world. Constant recriminations pounded at her from all sides until she wanted to bury her head in her hands. This was her fault. If Brand was hurt, no one would ever be able to convince her otherwise. Again and again George had told her that Brand was an excellent pilot. The best. Alaska Freight Forwarding was fortunate to have him on their team. Hiring Brand had been a coup for George.

But even excellent pilots made mistakes. Anyone was more prone toward error when his mind was preoccupied—and heaven knew that Brand had lots on his mind. He was working hard, and if he was anything like Carly, he hadn't been sleeping well. The combination of hard work and lack of sleep was enough to bring down the best pilots in the business.

When George returned forty-five minutes later, Carly knew her face was waxen. Her eyes searched his eagerly for information.

George cleared his throat, as if reluctant to speak. "There've been screwups everywhere, including the airport. They figure Brand has been missing close to fourteen hours."

"No…no." Carly felt as if someone had physically slammed a fist into her stomach. She didn't say anything. The thoughts that flittered through her mind made no sense. She recalled that she had to go pick up some dry cleaning on her way home from work. Then she remembered that Diana had expected something horrible to happen once she'd decided to marry Barney. Happiness wasn't meant for people like her. Nor was it meant for someone like Carly.

"Carly, are you okay?" George was giving her a funny look, and she wondered how long he'd been trying to gain her attention.

"Search and rescue teams are in the air. They'll find him."

Carly was confident they would, sooner or later. The question neither of them was voicing was in what condition Brand would be found: dead or alive.

The entire day was like a nightmare. Only Carly discovered that, no matter what she did, she couldn't wake up. The amount of manpower and man-hours that went into finding a missing or downed pilot was staggering. Reports were coming in to the office from the command center at Anchorage Airport continually. If that was encouraging, the news wasn't. Brand hadn't been sighted, and a thick fog was hampering the search.

At ten that night, George put his hand over Carly's. "You might as well try to get a good night's sleep. I'll let you know the minute I hear anything."

Carly's answer was an abrupt shake of her head. "No. I won't leave. Not until I know."

George didn't try to persuade her further. But she noticed that he didn't leave. Both were determined to see this through, no matter what the outcome.

At some point during the long night, Carly fell asleep. With her head leaning against the wall, she'd meant to rest her eyes for only a few minutes, but the next thing she knew, it was light outside and the sun was over the horizon. Immediately, she straightened and sought out George, who shook his head grimly.

Two hours later, with her nerves stretched taut, Carly forced herself to eat something for the first time since breakfast the day before. She ran a comb through her dark hair and brushed her teeth.

George was staring into the empty coffee cup he was holding when she approached him.

"I don't know when I'll be back."

He looked at her blankly. "Where are you going?"

"To the main terminal. Shawn and Sara are arriving in a half hour. I don't want them to know Brand's missing. If you hear anything, I'll be at the house." She let out a tired breath. "I'll phone as often as I can."

Squeezing her numb fingers, George offered Carly a smile and nodded.

It didn't seem possible that a day could be so full of sunshine and happiness—and that Carly's whole world could be dark with an unimaginable gloom.

As the Alaska Airlines flight with Shawn and Sara aboard touched down against the concrete runway, Carly felt an unreasonable surge of anger. Maybe Brand had planned this so she would be forced to deal with his children. If he'd wanted to find a way to punish her, he'd been highly successful.

As the flight attendant ushered Shawn and Sara out from the jetway, Carly straightened her shoulders and forced a smile. Her composure was eggshell fragile. She hadn't yet figured out what she was going to say to the children.

"Mom." A brilliant smile lit Sara's sky-blue eyes.

She broke free from the young attendant and hurried toward Carly.

Scooting down, Carly was the wary recipient of a fierce hug from the little girl. Shawn was more restrained, but there was a happy light in his eyes she hadn't noticed during her visit to Oregon.

"Where's Dad?" Shawn was the first to notice that his father was missing.

Not quite meeting his inquisitive eyes, Carly managed a smile. "He told me to tell you how sorry he is that he couldn't meet the two of you today. But he's hoping you like the surprise he has waiting for you at the house."

"Can we go there now?" Sara asked. Her blond hair had been plaited into long pigtails that danced with the action of her head. The doll Carly had given her was clutched under her arm.

"I'll take you there now. Are you hungry?"

Both children bobbed their heads enthusiastically. Rather than find something to cook, Carly located a McDonald's. Shawn and Sara were delighted with the fact that their first meal in Alaska was to be a hamburger and milk shake.

When they reached the house, Shawn helped Carly unload the suitcases from the back of the car. "Grandma sent you a long letter. She said it was instructions."

"Then I should read it right away."

"Don't," Shawn returned soberly. "You can, if you want," he added after a momentary lapse in conviction. "But you don't have to do everything she says."

"At least not the nap part. Right?" She gave him a conspiratorial wink.

"Right," Shawn confirmed with a nod.

"Mom, Mom." Sara rushed from her bedroom. "I've got a loose tooth. Look." She started pushing one of her front teeth back and forth. "Does the Tooth Fairy live in Alaska, too?"

"You bet," Carly answered, wiggling the tooth to satisfy Sara.

While Shawn and Sara investigated their new swing set, Carly unpacked their clothes. A quickly placed call to George confirmed that there hadn't been any word. A glance out of the window revealed that both Shawn and Sara had discovered neighborhood children their age.

"This is Lisa." Sara had brought her newfound friend into the house. "Can I show her my bedroom?"

"Go ahead."

Sara looked surprised, as though she'd expected Carly to refuse. "We won't make a mess."

"Good," Carly said with a short laugh. "I'd hate to think of you spending your first day in Alaska cleaning your room."

"Sara's never messy," Shawn said with a soft snicker. "At least, that's what Grandma says."

With a superior air, Sara led her friend down the hall to her bedroom. Lisa gave an appropriate sigh of appreciation at the beauty of the room, which immediately endeared her to Carly.

After the children had settled in, and Sara had taken a short nap, Carly drove them over to the apartment. Every night after work, she'd dreaded coming home. Now she understood the reason. She didn't belong here.

While she packed her things, Carly thought through the sober facts that faced her. Reality said that Brand could be dead. Her heart throbbed painfully at the thought, but it was a fact she couldn't ignore. If so, the question she had to deal with was what would happen to Shawn and Sara. Brand's mother was traveling. Her long vacation was well deserved. Kay St. Clair had done her best for these children, but she'd more than earned a life of her own. The state could remand Shawn and Sara as they had Carly. She'd been five when she'd gone to her first foster home. Sara's tender age.

Carly's fist tightened at the ferocity of her emotion. No matter what it took, she wouldn't allow that to happen. Not to Shawn and Sara. They would be hers, just as if she'd given them life. Nothing would separate the three of them. The path of her thoughts brought another realization. All these weeks that she'd battled within herself, she'd been fighting the even flow of her life's rhythm.

It wasn't that she couldn't give Brand something he didn't already have. It was what Brand, Shawn and Sara could give her. Borrowed dreams were irrelevant. What they shared was new and vital. Brand had tried to tell her that in so many ways, and she hadn't understood.

"Mom." Sara stood in the open doorway, giving Carly a puzzled look. "I was talking to you."

Holding out her arms, Carly gave the small child a loving squeeze. "I'm sorry. I was thinking."

"Does thinking make you cry?"

Carly's fingers investigated her own face, unaware that tears had formed. She wiped the moisture from her cheeks and tried to laugh, but the sound couldn't be described as one of mirth. "Sometimes," she said with a sniffle. "Hey, you know what I really need? A big hug." Sweet Sara was eager to comply.

Both children wanted to listen to their favorite story once they returned to the house. Carly promised them a special dinner to go with the book. Somehow, she'd find a way to cook "green eggs and ham." Luckily, neither child seemed to find it out of the ordinary to see Carly move her clothes from one house to another. At least, they didn't mention it. But Carly wouldn't be moving again. Her place was here.

The book was Shawn's favorite Dr. Seuss. The boy sat beside her while Sara occupied Carly's lap. The thought slid through her mind as she opened the book that, although Shawn and Sara resembled their mother, they were amazingly like their father. The curious tilt of Shawn's head was all Brand.

Carly was only a few pages into the book when a movement caught her attention. The front door was open and George stood just outside the closed screen.

A myriad of sensations assaulted Carly. Their eyes met and Carly's clouded with emotion, begging him to tell her everything was all right. Tears blurred his expression. But in her heart she knew the news wasn't good. If Brand had been found alive, George would have phoned.

"You weren't here when I phoned," George said. "But what I have has to be seen."

Carly's arms tightened around the children, drawing them protectively close to her. Again she confirmed the thought that nothing would separate Shawn and Sara from her.

The screen door opened and Carly braced herself.

"Dad." Shawn flew off the love seat.

Carly jerked her head up to find Brand framed in the doorway. He scooped Shawn into his arms and reached down for Sara. Carly remained frozen.

"Mom said she didn't know what time you'd be home."

"Is that right?" Brand said, hugging his children close. "We'll have to make sure Mom knows from now on, won't we?" His eyes sought Carly's, bright with promise. "Isn't that right, Mom?"

"Yes." Carly nodded eagerly and walked into Brand's embrace. "Oh, Brand, tell me, tell me what happened? I was worried sick.... I thought I'd lost you forever." She wept into his shoulder, knowing he probably couldn't understand anything she was saying. It didn't matter now that he was here. Not when he was holding her as if his very life depended on it. Later, when the children were in bed, he could fill in the details.

"Mom unpacked all the suitcases," Sara said happily. "Even hers."

Brand relaxed his hold so that he could lift Carly's chin and brush the wet strands of hair from her face. "Are you staying?" The husky question was so low Carly could barely hear him.

"Hey, kids," George said, clearing his throat. "Why don't you two show me your bedrooms? And wasn't that a swing set I saw outside?"

A grateful smile touched Carly's lips as George led the children from the living room.

"I'm never leaving. Oh, Brand, I know it all sounds crazy, but I realize I belong with you. Shawn and Sara are *our* children." She couldn't hide the breathlessness in her voice. "Everything's clear now.... I'm not borrowing anyone else's dreams, but living my own."

Sara skipped excitedly back into the room and squeezed her small body between Brand and Carly. Brand reached down and lifted her up. Two small arms shot out. One went around Carly and the other around Brand. "I'm so glad you're here."

"I'm home now," Brand murmured in a raw, husky voice and his eyes found Carly's. "We're all home."

* * * * *

#1 *New York Times* bestselling author

ROBYN CARR

shares the joys, heartbreaks and triumphs of the people who inhabit the small Oregon town of Thunder Point.

With its breathtaking vistas and down-to-earth people, Thunder Point is the perfect place for FBI agent Laine Carrington to recuperate from a gunshot wound and contemplate her future. She may even learn to open her heart to others, something an undercover agent has little time to indulge.

Eric Gentry is also new to Thunder Point. Although he's a man with a dark past, he's determined to put down roots and get to know the daughter he only recently discovered. When Laine and Eric meet, their attraction is obvious to everyone. But while the law enforcement agent and the reformed criminal want to make things work, their differences may run too deep…unless they're willing to take a chance on each other.

Available now, wherever books are sold.

Be sure to connect with us at:

Harlequin.com/Newsletters

Facebook.com/HarlequinBooks

Twitter.com/HarlequinBooks

MRC1599

Life In Icicle Falls

SHEILA ROBERTS

Can a book change your life?

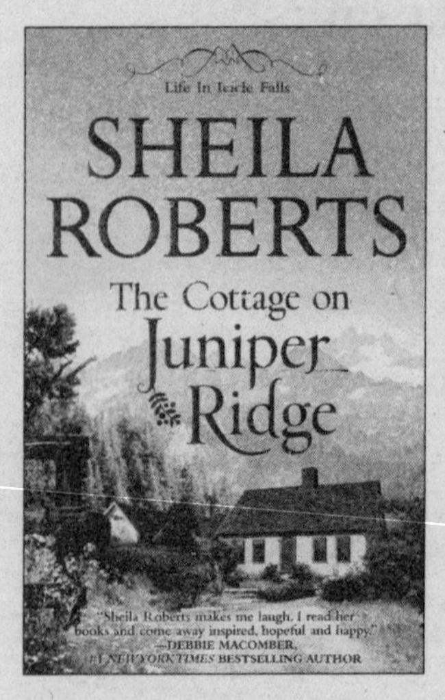

Yes! When it's *Simplicity,* a guide to plain living. In fact, it inspires Jen Heath to leave her stressful life in Seattle and move to Icicle Falls, where she rents a lovely little cottage on Juniper Ridge. There, Jen enjoys simple pleasures—like joining the local book club—and *complicated* ones, like falling in love with her sexy landlord....

Her sister Toni is ready for a change, too. She has a teenage daughter who's constantly texting, a husband who's more involved with his computer than he is with her, and a son who's consumed by video games. Toni wants her family to grow closer—to return to a simpler way of life.

But sometimes life simply happens. It doesn't always happen simply!

Available now, wherever books are sold!

Be sure to connect with us at:

Harlequin.com/Newsletters

Facebook.com/HarlequinBooks

Twitter.com/HarlequinBooks

MSR1454R